HUMAN TOUCH

M. A. CHAMBERS

As the promise of utopia gave way to reality, people looked to their government for answers. And we looked back at them, wondering when they'd realise we had none.

ELIZABETH MARSH, 'WHAT WE'VE LOST'

CONTENTS

ONE
A LOST ART

June 2043.
The City of London.

MIKE WAS TENSE, because he didn't have very much work to do today. And these days, that meant assuming you'd soon lose your job.

"You'll be there tonight, right?" It was made worse by his colleague's incessant, inane questions. "It's two for one tacos tonight."

"Of course, as always."

Jason nodded, then kept looking as if expecting more. Mike's eyes gestured back to his computer screen.

"See you there?"

"Right, right, back to it yeah? I've not had much since lunchtime today. Feels like they give me less and less this month. You too?" Mike's eyes went wide. "Ah okay, yeah I'll see you tonight."

His workload had, in fact, dropped quite significantly since lunch. It had most days in the past few weeks. It was welcome at first — who doesn't like a bit of downtime on the company dime — but that had since shifted to a listlessness and finally to a welling panic. It wouldn't be lost on the company that so much of Mike's, and apparently Jason's, time was being spent on so many things other than graphic design. "If it's a lost art, we've found it" he muttered to himself, parroting one of the company's many go-to lines when closing a deal. "People can always tell something was made by a machine," he'd had to hear his manager say dozens of times. He straightened up the various bits on his desk and looked back at the clock, thinking about half price tacos.

The walk out of the office usually lifted him out of these funks. The chipper nods to his colleagues, the line of people already headed for the lifts, the literal "hall of fame" where their many past triumphs hung. While HumanTouch was technically a recent addition to the graphic design landscape, they claimed a pedigree going back hundreds of years, to a once-legendary, now-forgotten advertising agency. The owners felt this lent an extra oomph to their pitches, and thus lined the walls with prints of some of their more famous work. Of course, literally no one at the company had worked on any of these, but British firms loved making dubious claims to lineage, so it wasn't met with much scepticism and was seen as expected or even charming.

Being in the middle of London they had a lot of after-work options, and being creatures of habit, they always chose the same one. A shabby-chic bar just a few minutes' walk had essentially become their private pub every Thursday for the past couple years. They'd sort-of inherited it when the last group of corporate regulars were advised by their management that they weren't allowed to hang out there anymore.

"Too big a risk they said. Imagine, drinking here being a

risk?" The bartender was happy to tell this story as often as you liked. "Too many reporters. Too many protesters. I didn't make 'em all wear their work badges when they'd come in. They did that to brag, I think. Anyway, their company built 'em a bar right in the office."

Jason nursed his pint and shook his head. "Shame. Bet they can't pour a Guinness for shit in there. Company bar. Imagine having the money for it, anyway."

The bartender shook his head in return. "As if they have bartenders at all. Just the machines, push a button, pours it for you."

Mike grimaced. He stood at the bar empty-handed, staring at nothing in particular.

"You with us, Mike?" Jason smacked him on the shoulder. "Did they send you all the work I was apparently too shit to do?"

"I'm just worried," Mike said as he gestured to the taps. "We've not had much work through either this week. Me, or anyone around me. You can see us all milling around the kitchen by 2:30, fuck all to do." A pint slammed down on the bar in front of him.

"Suck it up mate, at least you've got a job." The bartender nodded up toward the television, to some ongoing story the BBC had been covering wall-to-wall all day. Some major firm had just announced another 45,000 redundancies. The UK Government claimed to be absolutely livid, but admitted that given recent legislation, there was nothing to be done. The whole story was given an odd tone by the lilt in the presenter's voice and the warm smile on their face. This wasn't their fault, of course — human news presenters had started being phased out last month on the BBC — but hopefully some producer had noticed and would correct the tone to be appropriately sombre before the story went out again.

Or maybe they'd all just gotten so used to it that it really was better to be amused than angry.

Jason, per usual, tried to cheer everyone up. "So? So? How'd it go?" He patted Mike on the back and looked around at everyone. "My man's been back on the apps, yeah?" Mike grimaced and stared even harder at the TV, hoping this might be about him, rather than involving him. No such luck, though. He felt the expectant eyes of his co-workers, all ready for gossip and relieved not to be asked to speak.

"Honestly, I've not gotten a single date. From any of them. Just chat, chat, chat. It's good banter, but they've just never got time. Dating in the city, you know. Everyone's busy."

Jason shook his head. "Let's see it, come on, let's see what we're working with." Knowing there was no way around it, Mike willingly entered the hell that would ensue, unlocking his phone and handing it to Jason.

"I do like her," he said as he pointed out one match in particular, a woman named Gemma. "I've mostly been focused on her." Jason leaned in, studying the situation. He tapped and swiped. A smile crept across his face.

"Michael. I dare not tell our assembled colleagues what I've seen here." He put his arm around Mike, any warmth tempered by the severe public embarrassment sure to come next. "Mike," he whispered. "This is not a real person."

Mike chuckled awkwardly. "No, heh, no, first of all, no. It says verified on the profile. And when we chat it says it's a real person. And we talk for hours, we talked all night practically the other night."

Jason sucked air through his teeth then pursed his lips. He scrolled through that night's conversations, a proper slalom through arts, culture, favourite Indian places in Central, favourite cocktail bars in Shoreditch (a trick, as they both hate it there), far too many forced quotes from a book they both like, and finally a failed attempt to make plans — with a gentle assurance that Mike should try again next week. "Mike, this isn't her. Listen. I'm not saying there's no Gemma, you just haven't made it past her bot."

"But it tells you if it's the, um, bot. Agent. Right?" Mike timidly sipped his pint between sentences. "It literally says right at the top there." Jason turned him away from their other colleagues for a bit of privacy.

"That's so easy to get around," Jason said with severe disappointment, almost pity. "Everyone gets around that. Takes two minutes. Mate, we've gotta work on this. I can't have you sitting around alone every night chatting with some girl's chat bot."

Mike sipped his drink in defeat as Jason scrolled past several chats that all ended in some semblance of the same way, snapping his fingers and pointing when he'd spot "another one." All different messages of course, but a recognisable pattern to them, and all saying the same thing — let's not meet up, but let's keep chatting. This was the way it worked now, Jason explained. The dating apps all let you have a sort of virtual agent that chats on your behalf, and if the person on the other end ticks enough of the right boxes, it lets them through to the "you." It knows your schedule, so it can even set up the date. You, as the suitor, know you've been properly vetted. And they get back loads of free time, with dates populating their calendar on a regular basis.

Mike's stomach went sour. He met his ex-wife Elizabeth

at a cocktail bar in Cambridge while he was up there doing some courses at the university. Like some sort of Neanderthal. And Elizabeth would've chosen now to sneer, mock and rant about the very notion. He felt a twinge as he pictured her and his mood went through the floor. And vulnerability wasn't something he was comfortable showing in front of the lads. He muttered something about needing the toilet, then slipped out the pub and down the street to the Underground station.

HumanTouch had a four-day work week, so now he just found himself at home with nothing on until Monday. Usually he'd appreciate more time to himself, but now he felt off. He almost wished he had work tomorrow, just to get him out of the house and away from his own thoughts.

He poured himself a double whisky, his mind spinning like a top. Intrusive thoughts weren't the only reason he wanted to go to work, right? He liked what he did. He was proud of it, and of the company. As much as it was a gimmick he also appreciated where the owners were coming from: refusing to use AI, having people on staff like himself who actually drew, designed, laid out graphics. Advertisements, book covers, leaflets, they had to be one of the only places left in the city where a human did any of this unassisted.

Collapsing into the sofa he thought more about book covers, having spent his morning making one. For yet another book by some rabble-rousers railing against the scourge of automation. It made him roll his eyes, every time, but he knew what they wanted. And of course, they couldn't possibly use an AI-generated cover for such a book. He made advertisements too, but half of them were for protests, or rallies, marches from Trafalgar Square to Downing Street, angry about the latest employment reforms or jobs programmes. And the flyers and leaflets, to be handed out at said protests, rallies and marches.

Now it occurred to Mike that his working hours were spent drawing up bullshit for delusional people who couldn't get their heads around a changing world. Elizabeth must've wished on a monkey's paw. He hoped something tragic had befallen her as a result.

The next morning Mike popped awake suddenly, having forgotten any sort of alarm. The flat was drenched in sun and Mike was drenched in sweat. It was quarter past 10 in the morning. Drool ran down his creased, stubbled face. Presumably none of this was what the inventor of the 4-day work week had in mind. He should be up early doing some sort of life admin, getting breakfast, pursuing a passion, or just not being hungover.

A half-dozen messages had come through on Linkup, though. Now that he'd been told, he could easily see there was a pattern to them. Clearly all automatically generated. They'd all arrived in a seemingly-organic way, but the first one was at exactly 8 a.m. Unbelievable. Staggered to appear they were real. Jason had ruined dating apps for him. He made a mental note to look for videos or something that might help him get better at getting past these virtual agents and to the real person underneath. He couldn't give up this easily. This was how it worked now. The new normal.

He stared around his flat, which was an absolute tip, and wished he had a hobby. He lived a pretty small life, and his "chores" such as they were surely didn't take an extra day to handle. He'd have all this picked up in an hour. If he wanted. Which he didn't. Without letting himself spiral too much, this line of thinking usually led him to walk. And today was no different.

On days like this he enjoyed walking the "capital C City," as in the City of London. A square mile of banks, bars, barristers and almost no housing whatsoever. It had always been a ghost town on weekends, but with the move to 4-day weeks at so many firms, combined with the 'streamlining' of staff pretty much everywhere, it was a beautiful place to just walk around and think. Massive, glittering glass towers, lined with relatively ancient architecture, all weirdly empty, frozen in time, the set of some dystopian thriller.

And so he walked. Down the Strand, past the Cheshire Cheese, all the blue plaques noting the birthplaces of forgotten artists, or benches where some guitar player sat. Past towering brutalist blocks, past millions of pounds worth of vacant offices and shops. He avoided the encampment around the old Mansion House Station by dodging down an alley. He picked his way through police barriers near Covent Garden. A normal person might grab their phone and look up why Covent Garden was closed now. But he ignored it and found himself instead meandering toward Trafalgar Square.

The sounds of the protest drums and the megaphones, the growing din of the crowd, will either pique your curiosity or send you briskly toward the nearest Tube stop, depending on what kind of London day you're looking to have. And Mike couldn't really help himself today. His legs took him right to the trailing edge of a rally.

Before he could find any signage accessible enough for him to understand the cause, someone was thrusting a leaflet into his hand. She looked him square in the eye and said something or other. He took off his headphones. "I'm sorry, what?"

"Did you register? We have a sign making station just

over here—" Her voice was practised but with an awkward edge to it.

"Oh, I'm not, I'm just browsing," he stammered like a person might when they've been walking for four hours. She laughed and nodded, pivoting back to sorta-face the stage and sorta-watch for more new arrivals. He looked down at the leaflet in his hand and stared. It looked familiar...

URGENT! RALLY TO STOP CONCENTRA! DEMAND OUR GOVERNMENT HOLD THEM TO ACCOUNT! TRAFALGAR SQUARE TO DOWNING STREET — RALLY 1400, MARCH 1500

It had that retro Shepherd Fairy pop art styling, with the Trafalgar Square monument silhouetted, some crowds, a fist, and the Concentra logo. It wasn't the most inspiring design, but it worked. "Oh." He moved his thumb from the corner and saw his tiny initials hidden in the background. "Hey, I designed this," he said to nobody. The girl who'd greeted him fairly assumed that was for her.

"You what?"

"Oh, I designed this flyer. I mean, just for my work. I draw flyers." He flashed an eye-bugged grimace and raised the flyer. She gave him a knowing nod.

"Ohhhhh, you're at HumanTouch. A load of you have already come through, mostly toward the front I think."

"Not sure what you mean?"

"Uh huh." She laughed, but he must've looked quite confused, because she straightened right up. "Oh, you're serious. I just assumed you knew, dude! Concentra announced they acquired HumanTouch, first thing this morning."

He felt a wave of numbness wash over him. Surely he didn't just learn this news from a stranger on the street. "I didn't work today. I'm on a four-day week."

She turned her phone toward him, showing the news story, a pitying look on her face. "I think you're on a no day week, dude." He looked at her phone, an older model with a blurry screen and a crack down the middle. His eyes kept scanning the device itself, not looking at what she was actually trying to show him. His legs felt like rubber.

Phones. His had been on silent, and he had definitely felt some notifications earlier, but hadn't checked them. He looked around, patting his pocket, feeling that his phone was still in there. The drums from the protest sounded so loud.

He rubbed his hands up and down his thighs, feeling the texture of the denim.

The girl continued trying to get his attention. He wasn't sure what she wanted, so he just did his best to smile and nod at her. The denim, he kept thinking, and kept rubbing his hands across it, but then worried he looked quite odd.

He looked around sharply, all around. He felt the girl's hands on his shoulders, but he still went hard to ground.

He couldn't catch his breath.

His heart raced, pounded.

He pushed his hands across the cobblestone.

The crowd was impossibly loud, and he couldn't catch his breath.

TWO

THE PARTY WAS A DISASTER

March 2041.
Maida Vale, West London.

IT WAS ABOUT 30 minutes before her alarm went off
when Gemma's phone rang. "Not a good sign" was what she
tried to say, but what she managed sounded more like
"unnggg."

"I know, I know, but wake up fast, okay?" It was her
assistant Tom on the other end, with his crisp American
accent, and he had all the spunk and vigour of a man who
was somewhere that it was very much not 6:30am.

"Tom, you are one of two people able to break through
my do-not-disturb. And I divorced the other one. Please tell
me nothing bad happened to Taylor Swift."

"Ma'am, you know we have not had Taylor in years.
Listen. Something's up. I'm still at the office, we all are.
You're about to get an email." She squinted her eyes together
a few more times and looked at the phone. Sure enough, an
email dropped in. It just said "[Please Attend Virtually] UK

Town Hall – Today at 8 a.m. Link to follow." She grimaced, annoyed.

"Well, shit Tom. That's, what? Someone's stepping down? Look, you probably know, can you just tell me?" She rubbed her eyes. Tom let out a sharp exhale which just came out as a crackle for Gemma.

"Ma'am, I'm honestly not sure. But they asked a lot of the admins to stay around. And it's me, and looking around, it's just people who support people in the UK office."

Gemma glanced up and saw herself in the mirror, a full-length standing mirror across from a king bed in an otherwise extremely sparse bedroom. She let out a groan, put the phone on speaker and dropped it on the bed. She dragged her hands across her face and let out a longer, more guttural groan. "Tom, talk me through this. What are you hearing? Forgive me if I drift in and out of consciousness." She lifted the duvet off of her and winced as she saw her sequinned blouse and leather skirt from the night before.

As she pulled herself together, Tom ran through what he'd heard: all the gossip from the Los Angeles office, as it were. Essentially, he knew nothing, but he did his best to fill the time and keep Gemma company while she brushed her teeth, put her hair into a slightly better state, and maybe, no judgement, had the tiniest sip of vodka from a glass on her nightstand.

She'd been staring at her crow's feet in the mirror for what felt like a year before realising Tom had gone silent. "Tom? Still there?"

"I am! So how was it last night by the way? I missed everything, classic Tom. Did you go to the party after?"

"Christ, Tom, it was the Brit Awards. It was, I don't know, it was fine. The party was a disaster. One of our artists tried to pick me up. At least I think he's one of ours." She finished the nightstand vodka and set off toward the kitchen.

"Oh no, which one? I'm so sorry that happened!"

"I don't bloody know his name. I nearly let him, too, until he referred to me as his 'cool record label executive' and said it was fucking inspiring to see a woman over 50 still relevant in the fucking industry. Christ. Fucking gorgeous though. A bit dim." Tom was stifling laughter, which also seemed to come through as a faint crackling sound.

"I think I know who you mean. I'll see if I can discretely let him know you're only 47."

Gemma's eyes widened, she let out a clipped, high-pitched "Great catching up, Tom" and dropped her finger onto the End Call button. She looked at the clock: 7:04 a.m.

Standing alone in her kitchen, she inhaled deeply, held it, then exhaled. The sun was breaking through the window. She walked through the kitchen into her under-furnished living room and stared out to the street below. The morning light cutting through the treetops of her West London street, same-ish looking joggers filing past the rows of same-ish looking Maida Vale mansion blocks.

About an hour to pull herself together. Her heart was beating oddly fast. She inhaled and exhaled again, and again. She squeezed her hands into fists, then shook them out. She did what she'd seen characters in films do when they need to calm down. But she couldn't get her head in the right place. She looked back at the counter, a pastel jar with "COFFEE" on it, next to a half-empty handle of Stoli. And she decided to go up the street to the café.

The sun wasn't as forgiving outside, and Gemma instantly regretted not having her sunglasses. Her sequinned top was catching it particularly well. Though surely she wasn't the only one in this neighbourhood prowling around for coffee after a Brit Awards afterparty.

She'd never quite settled into the Maida Vale vibe, and had practically been shoved into her current flat by a colleague who dragged her kicking and screaming out of her "Shepherd's Bush shithole." Really she'd never quite settled into having a job that paid well. She worked with a singular purpose since she was able, having declared "music is my life" somewhere around age 15, and angrily refused to be dissuaded every day since. Ticket-tearing and bartending at the Shepherd's Bush Empire, leaning on the stacks at every random indie gig she could find, recording her first album, declaring it shit, helping engineer other people's less-shit albums, recording her second album, realising it was somehow worse.

Eventually, money was an issue. But she'd mixed enough of other people's albums that she was able to get an internship at EMI, where they'd groomed her into being a "trends analyst," and things escalated from there. Finally, years later, she was waking up to the horrifying realisation that she'd been referred to as a "record label executive" at a Brit Awards after-party.

She walked into the café, deciding to just own her vibe, but was immediately struck. Something was off. Her usual barista gave her a wave. "Morning! Bit earlier than usual."

She cocked her head and looked up. He nodded. "Yeah, I knew you'd notice. You always liked my playlists. Honestly most people won't notice."

"It's the... what is this?" She pointed up at the speaker bolted to the wall. He grimaced performatively.

"I have no idea. Head office has switched us to this new music service. I can't pick my own music, there's not even

playlists, it's just buttons. This one's 'Coffee Shop Morning.'"
Some soothing, inoffensive Spanish guitar came out of the
speaker, with occasional whiffs of piano behind it. Gemma
groaned and suddenly her head was killing her.

"Mate no, you can't with this. Just get a record player or
something. I will bring you a record player. I can't start my
mornings with this procedural bullshit."

He pursed his lips and then sighed. "I wish we could. I
wish I could let you. You know how it is. The music labels
charge us so much now per song. They said we'd have to
charge another £2.50 a drink just to pay it."

"Greedy fucks." She squinted. He stared back innocently
enough. Her secret identity remained intact. "Listen, what if
I could guarantee you'd never get caught." He smiled, though
a bit more pained. Someone else had queued behind her
now. Pleasant chat was over.

She slid into a booth in the corner. 7:41 a.m. Plenty of
time to mindfully drink this latte, clear her head, then get
back in time for the meeting. She took a sip, then stared at the
wall. Her eyes felt so dry. The Spanish guitar had gotten a bit
peppier. It would probably keep doing that as the day went
on, until it was a full fucking rave in here by 6 p.m. She rolled
her eyes.

This auto-generated AI music ("procedural," in industry
parlance) had been a thing for a while, but the music industry's initial fear of it had been overblown – it had wound up
just capturing the market for ambience. Audio wallpaper for
people who aren't comfortable in silence, or people who are
reading the news in a café alone, or people who have tinnitus
from leaning on the stacks at every random indie gig they
could. Whatever. They didn't care what it sounded like so
long as it was on. Music fans, ultimately, still wanted the real

deal. There was one company doing something a bit more ambitious, supposedly, but they knew better than to panic this time. Still plenty of real artists, making real music, for real fans. And yes, commanding higher-than-ever royalties from coffee shops. They had to make up the losses somewhere.

Still, though. It was surprising to see this place fall to the darkness. They'd worked hard to cultivate a certain image. They had vinyl album covers plastered all over the walls as art. Until recently, they still sold CDs. And they were down the street from the legendary BBC Maida Vale studio. Some real heavy hitters had recorded there. And the area was posh as hell. It made no sense to Gemma whatsoever.

She rubbed her temples. Her feet were fucking killing her. Her jaw felt sore for some reason. 7:43 a.m. Christ, still ages away. She took out her phone. Maybe she'd have a little mindful news and weather with her mindful latte. As she went to unlock it, the screen lit up with an Apple News notification:

"EXCLUSIVE: UNIVERSAL MUSIC TO ANNOUNCE ACQUISITION BY CONCENTRA AS EARLY AS TODAY; UK SUBSIDARY EMI TO SHUTTER; ALL UK STAFF TO BE LET GO."

Gemma looked up at the barista. He smiled politely. She rolled her shoulders back until she heard a loud pop. She looked down at her phone, which had become a steady flow of new message notifications. She flipped it upside down, set her latte down on top of it and slid down in her chair, no longer in any particular hurry to get back.

THREE
HUMANS FIRST

June 2043.
Just outside Central London.

ELIZABETH STILL FELT a weird tinge of awe whenever the train got close enough to let her see the London skyline. "There it is," she said to nobody in particular, as the Shard caught the sun. A few of the folks around her chuckled, one shot her a half-smile, but nobody looked out the window. Elizabeth always looked. "Same as it ever was." It felt odd, in that the city still looked essentially the same from a distance. And really it looked the same at ground level as it did when she was a child. It was eerie to her how different it felt, though. All the films, books, telly that imagined a post-apocalyptic London always showed it desolated or half-destroyed. Jackbooted thugs, or ruined buildings, explosions, toppled skyscrapers. Or there the pandemic fiction of creepy, empty streets with the occasional corpse.

The reality had been so much worse, because of how

normal it all looked and felt. Even as the fall was just as sudden as the fiction predicted.

And like so many fictional pandemics, terrorist attacks, dirty bombs, zombie outbreaks, the Government had stepped in. Swiftly, forcefully. The Prime Minister in a primetime address to the nation, to calm the people who'd lost their life savings in the markets, or worse, who'd lost their pensions. Emergency aid, emergency funding. The Chancellor doing everything short of holding up a huge novelty cheque made out to the people of Great Britain. We'd see the back of this crisis by autumn, she told the public. Action would be taken, payments made, evictions frozen. All the right things. And we'd ensure it could never happen again.

Six months later, unemployment had reached 25%. Two years later, it had doubled. And now, well, now Elizabeth would daydream about the past as her train pulled into London Bridge station.

"We're here, dude, you with us?" Siobhan patted her shoulder. She was maybe half Elizabeth's age, and Elizabeth found it charming that apparently things like 'dude' and 'rad' were back in fashion. Or maybe Siobhan just watched too many old films.

"I'm with you, sorry. I always sort of space out when I see the city again." Her voice was thin, distant. Siobhan snorted.

"Let it go mate, it let us go. Besides, we need you focused. They're all coming to see you, after all." She picked up her duffle bag and stood, and Elizabeth followed her off the train.

Siobhan bounded over to a group of similarly dressed folks, which is to say, they were all wearing the distinctive bright green hoodies of Humans First UK. They were a young new political party desperate to make waves but thus far making a ripple or two at best. Even in what they saw as a cataclysmic, humanity-ending crisis, people really just had room in their head for about three political parties. Elizabeth preferred her usual, a smart tailored blue suit jacket, white shirt, slacks and heels. It wasn't that she wanted to feel separate, of course. She had found a look that worked for her in her early 30s, and here she was two decades later, still making it work. Siobhan said it worked "for your age," though it made the rest of them "feel like groupies."

Even here, looking around the platform, it all just seemed so normal. The tannoy announcing a departing train. A couple with rolling bags, excited for their holiday. A small, whisper-quiet robot gliding by, hoovering up an empty crisp packet. The station was spotless, she noticed. It looked better now than it did in her memories.

She was doing it again, though. Just looking around, taking in the London-ness of it all. She so badly wanted to be back there, two decades ago. But since she couldn't, she could at least take a moment and feel this connection. Until, of course, Siobhan started shouting her name and waving. So off she went to join the group.

"I'm here, I'm present. Shall we get coffee and a scone before our little band of misfits march on the halls of power?" She put on a wry smile. One of the assembled group, an older man, probably in his late 50s, looked up animatedly from his phone.

"You're Elizabeth Marsh! You were my MP. I voted for you. Met you once, years ago, at a surgery. Really excited to be part of this, ma'am. Came all the way from Trawsfynydd today. Happy to see you back in politics."

Elizabeth demurred immediately. "It's my honour. What's your name?"

He smiled. "It's Arthur, ma'am."

"What brought you to my surgery?"

"Was a problem with my universal credit, ma'am."

"Did we get you sorted?"

"Your staff did their best, ma'am."

She furrowed her brow and nodded, understanding what that meant.

"Well Arthur, let's see if we can go get people fired up to throw away their vote on us." There was a big laugh among the group, who'd circled around them and listened intently to the quick back-and-forth. "It's good to hear you all in such good spirits," she added. "It helps me believe this might actually be worth it."

Someone had picked out a café to serve as their base of operations for the morning, so they walked there at a brisk pace, with the more enthusiastic volunteers handing out flyers for the rally every time they saw anyone. Takers were few and far between. There was a real feeling of defeat in everyone they met. Some would take the flyer, read it, drop it and walk on. Most politely refused. And nobody else recognised Elizabeth. She tried to tell herself this was a mercy, but really it also gave her a twinge in the pit of her stomach. Humans First UK certainly wasn't her idea, and she'd never dream of trying to take credit for it, or even to declare herself "the face of it." But they'd found her and gotten in touch, and before she could talk herself out of it, here she was on the way to her third rally for them in a month. She felt the weight of it a bit. She didn't want to let these people down. She never wanted to let anybody down again.

She forced herself to be present as Siobhan went through the sequence of events for the day, standing at the head of their packed table in an otherwise quiet VQ, attentive faces above a sea of neon green. "You've all heard the news, of course, that the Modern Health Efficiency Act is getting a second reading tomorrow, just as news leaks that Concentra Health is aiming to acquire six NHS trusts the moment they become available. Six! That's thousands of nurses, consultants, admin staff, all automated away overnight. We're talking private hospitals with almost no human staff. No doctors physically present. Nurses replaced with virtual agents. Algorithmic triaging of patients. We've seen it in America."

As Siobhan spoke, her voice rose, got more forceful. One volunteer pounded the table angrily along with her every sentence. "They're making it legal to just sell off our birth right, put everyone out of work, and let algorithms decide whether you live or die!" By the end, she was shouting, her 2000s throwback slang gone, her soft lilt giving way to a full-throated rage. "We don't have to choose to let society be this way! We don't have to turn everything over to machines run by one company! We can choose to put humans first! Put humans first!" The volunteers were all pounding the table now. One of them raised a fist and shouted "PUT HUMANS FIRST!," and a chant broke out, a dozen green-hoodie'd men and women all chanting in unison.

Elizabeth looked around the otherwise empty café. No staff whatsoever. Just machines. Lucky that — if it weren't the case they would've gotten themselves ejected. Siobhan ran up behind her, playfully batting her back and forth by the shoulders. "Miss Marsh! Elizabeth Marsh! Let's get that energy up! We've got to go inspire!" Elizabeth leaned her head back, looking up at Siobhan's now beat-red face. She nodded.

The rally itself was at ground zero for London protests since time immemorial, Trafalgar Square. The beating heart of fringe democratic movements. It felt easier than ever to get a police permit to stage an event there. Cynically, it was a pressure release valve for the Government. Let them have their peaceful marches so things don't get violent. But optimistically, she hoped the Metropolitan Police had a few good eggs who believed in these things and were happy to permit as many as possible.

The walk from the cafe to Trafalgar Square was uneventful. More hustling of flyers from the groupies, more not being recognised, more vague anxiety that nobody would actually turn up for the rally in the first place. As they got closer, Elizabeth could feel herself listening for the signs of crowds. But it was deceptive, as large pockets of Central London had now been cordoned off for encampments. It was the most visible evidence of the government's complete failure to contain the situation, and to deliver some sort of help for these people, who had stuck it out until they could no longer afford to leave, if they could've ever to begin with. This is what governments were for. At least, it's what they could be for.

Still, the local organisers had decided to take them on a rather circuitous route, to avoid having to walk directly through any of them. It made Elizabeth feel like a massive hypocrite. But she was secretly relieved, because she wasn't sure how she would react at being confronted with the fruits of her labour all those years ago.

Memories were inescapable here for her, which is probably why she now lived in Cambridge. She ran from her problems these days. She ran from government, she ran from her ex-husband, she ran from her friends, and now she was hiding from even more people she failed, while on her way to give a speech about why those very same people should join her shiny new political movement. None of this was lost on her, but she really wished it was.

"We're just gonna pop in here yeah? Me and you, one last run through the speech and some coffees." Siobhan was suddenly pulling her arm and gesturing to a coffee shop in the lobby of The Grand Hotel. Elizabeth saw it and her heart sank. She forced a smile.

"Of course, whatever you need Siobhan. I'm here for you."

Siobhan laughed. "Dude, you're here for them. Come on."

So Elizabeth followed close behind as Siobhan led her into the hotel where, fifteen years ago, she'd unwittingly destroyed her career, her marriage, a friendship, and the entire country in one fell swoop.

FOUR
DOWN THE HATCH

April 2041.
Shepherd's Bush, West London.

WHEN GEMMA WAS FEELING LOW, she'd wander into an upmarket chain pub near her flat. But this was rock bottom. For this, it was back-to-basics time. For this, she needed The Fox on Uxbridge Road. Her old Shepherd's Bush haunt, proud home of £3.75 pints and a local reputation for being "a bit stabby." Not exactly where you'd expect to find a semi-powerful executive at one of London's biggest record labels. But the good news was, she wasn't that anymore.

She was leaning against the wall, all of five foot ten in her flats, and back in her shimmering and leather. This time she'd added a cigarette to complete the ensemble. It was a strong vibe to send first thing in the morning. When the bartender turned up at 11 a.m. he had glanced over briefly, saying nothing. What a treat for him when she followed him right inside.

"Excuse me ma'am, you can't smoke in here, and we don't

actually open until noon." He looked early 20s, white T-shirt, tight jeans, real "Rebel Without a Cause" energy. And just a smidge taller than her, too. She chuckled and flicked her cigarette out the door.

"You're American? It's the accent. I have an ear for these things."

"Correct." He didn't seem impressed.

"You a student?" She stood at the end of the bar and watched as he pulled chairs off of tabletops. He let it hang there for a second and finally looked up.

"Ma'am, I'm serious. I'd be happy to serve you at noon, when our licence says we're allowed to serve. You can't be in here. You're old enough to smoke, you should know that." He swivelled in place as she walked past him and began also pulling chairs off of tables.

"Relax, James Dean, you're not going to get in trouble. Just shut the door and lock it behind us. The police aren't going to kick it down at 11 a.m. on a Tuesday." He was visibly flustered, and clearly not sure what happened next, or what he should say. He threw his hands up and went to lock the door.

"Fine, fine. I appreciate you helping with the chairs, at any rate."

"So. Student? Yes?" She leaned on the bar and looked at the taps. "Mind if I...?"

"Ma'am no, you can't, it won't, I need to engage the keg couplers before anything will pour." She let out a cackle.

"Gosh, the keg couplers. No no, you're absolutely right, I'm sure." She popped around behind the bar, finding the nearest fridge and taking out a pint can of Carling. He swung round from his dutiful chair-flipping as he heard it crack open.

"Hey!"

"Sorry, I'm being a lot right now. You'll have to forgive me, my entire life has recently collapsed. I'm Gemma Thomson, and you are?" She popped up on a stool at the end of the bar. He sighed.

"I'm Kevin. Yes, I'm a student at the University of West London."

"Ooh, UWL, nice nice. Freddie Mercury went there, you know."

"Who? Do you want a glass for that, by the way?"

"No I don't want a bloody glass from some child who doesn't know who Freddie Mercury is, thanks." She waved her hand dismissively.

"Excuse me, I'm sorry, I have better things to do than sit around studying who was famous back when your generation were destroying my future."

She shook her head and sputtered at him. "Kevin! I'm bantering with you. No need for these personal attacks. And Freddie Mercury was the lead singer of a band called Queen, and he died tragically of AIDS, and I've never gotten over it honestly. Even though it happened before I was born." Kevin flashed a polite smile as he pulled cling-wrap off of beer taps. She looked at him and felt a bit anxious. "You know, I will take that glass." He rolled his eyes, grabbed a glass and put it on the bar in front of her. She stared at it, then pointed. "A Carling glass, obviously. You've served me a Carling, dear."

He switched the glass in spite of her. "I didn't serve you at all."

"Well, for the best. Licence restrictions and all that."

"Gemma, is it?"

"It is!"

"What brings you into The Fox at 11 a.m. on a Tuesday, dressed like you're out for the night?"

"I'm not sure, if I'm honest, I just sort of appeared outside. You must've seen me in a magazine, thought 'oh she's fit, I'd do her' and wished really hard."

"Something about your entire life collapsing?" He continued doing loads of prep behind the bar, but she'd given up helping and was focused on pouring her Carling at the perfect angle.

"Right, I did say that didn't I? And thank you for the compliment on my outfit." She waved her hands down her sides dramatically, showing off her sequin blouse and leather skirt. "Too much makeup you think for a Tuesday?"

"No, you look good."

"Kevin! You've made my day."

"You'd have made mine if you had let me pour that for you." He was right. Her pour was rubbish. Nevertheless, she persisted. "So, the life?"

"Dear, if I wanted to talk about that, I'd have taken you up on it the last time you asked. Shall we move on?"

He laughed and shook his head. "No can do, ma'am. See, I'm an annoying Yank, and us Yanks use our bartenders like therapists, which means as the bartender, I'm your therapist. So, you know. I really can't let it go."

"Against your ethical code?"

"Who told you about the code?" Kevin had mercifully lightened up, against all odds. "Listen. Sometimes the lids on these things get real stuck, so you gotta loosen em."

She tilted her head. "Pardon?" He plopped two shot glasses on the counter, then turned around and clapped his hands. "Okay! Shot, shot, shot... ah, here we go." He picked up a bottle of Jack Daniels. She recoiled.

"Christ! Please God, anything but that. I'll talk, I'll talk. You've tortured it out of me." But he was already pouring.

"You had your chance, Gemma Thomson. Down the hatch, here we go." He picked up his shot and gave her the eyes. She tutted.

"Let's get this swill down then, shall we?" She picked up her glass, they gave each other a cheers, bumped them back down on the bar, and shot. Gemma coughed and wheezed. "Shit. What the fuck?" Kevin was laughing his ass off.

"Tennessee Honey flavored. That'll wake you up!" Gemma was flabbergasted.

"It was fucking flavoured! You tit. Unbelievable! Now I am truly at rock bottom. Drinking flavoured Jack Daniels before mid-day." She chased it down with her extremely heady Carling, covering her nose and lips with foam that she quickly wiped off. "Fucking state of this morning."

"So, Gemma Thomson. Did we loosen the top on you? Of the jar, my jar metaphor."

She shook her head. "Charming. No, but you've tried so bloody hard I'll 'spill the tea' anyway as we used to say. But first." She tapped the empty Carling can, he swapped it for another, and she started in.

Gemma covered it all: how she'd been at the BRITs, woke up to the news her company had been acquired, got laid off, and how one of her last acts as an executive wound up ruining the music at Underground Coffee near her flat. That last part she seemed to be the most upset about. Kevin listened intently.

"So now, my dear Kevin, sweet Kevin, you find me here. At rock bottom. Served with this." She reached into her bag and pulled out a letter, still sealed. But people had come to recognise the envelope's distinct, understated style.

"What's that?" Except Kevin, of course.

"What's thi—right, American. Student. New here. This, Kevin, is a letter from His Majesty's bloody Government." She held it up and tapped the corner: HM Employment & Public Works. "You get one of these when you're made redundant now. You see, in their infinite wisdom, the bloody Tories have figured out a way out of our growing unemployment crisis. They've simply outlawed being unemployed! Isn't that wonderful? Thanks, we're cured."

Kevin laughed anxiously, clearly unsure what she was talking about. He pulled her another pint of IPA and swapped it for her empty glass. She immediately picked it up and took a sip.

"See Kevin, inside this envelope, is gonna be 3 pieces of paper. The first one will tell me I get free money. Some tiny fucking amount of free money, but it's free fucking money. Great British Pounds, right in the account. But in order to get it, I have to look for a job. Provably. Fucking provably look for one."

She was very animated now, waving the envelope around in one hand, and going at her pint with the other. "But they know I won't fucking find one, because there aren't any. So there will be a second piece of paper. And on that piece of paper, will be a job offer. They will offer me a job. On some fucking government-funded project somewhere in the middle of nowhere, no doubt. And I can tick the box saying I want it, or I can tick the box saying I reject it. And then there will be a third piece of paper, where I can tick a box telling them I'm fucking rich, and therefore they can get fucked." Kevin grimaced and nodded.

"Ma'am, that sounds very intense. I do not understand

how the government works here. That is not the sort of thing they'd do in the USA, I can tell you that much."

"Oh, it's all such a fucking joke," she said with a cackle. "I barely understand politics in this country, but this shit has been hard to not know about. I watched a documentary called The Envelope on fucking iPlayer. Tragic." She leaned over the bar and play-whispered in Kevin's ear: "I don't even pay my council tax, Kevin. They've never come after me for it."

Kevin had a vague look of concern. "So, what will it be then?"

"Jack and Coke. You've turned me."

"No, no, I mean which of the three? Look for a job, take their job, or are you rich?" She sighed and slugged back the rest of her pint.

"No, Kevin. I am not rich. I have pissed away my fortune in pubs like your fine establishment here, on luxury fucking flats, on too many black cabs, on subscriptions to Linkup Platinum."

"Well sure, but okay, so you find a job. You're like, a powerful executive in her 50s. Confident, attractive, you'll get a job anywhere, I'm sure." Gemma pointed at him.

"Oh, Kevin, you sly fox, you said so many nice things we'll overlook the 50s remark. But, you know, I've been thinking." She slid her finger under the flap of the envelope and tore it open. "I've been thinking what life might be like, if I gave it all up. The flat, the music, the executive-ness." She pulled out the papers and shuffled to the second page. "I think I could really see myself as a..." She stared at him, the page in her hand hovering above the bar. She said nothing. He looked at her, then looked down at the—

"Don't look at it, Kevin. Christ. I can't look. I can't I can't I can't"—

"Oh—"

"Fuck, shit. Okay. No no, it's fine, it's fine. Because you'll look."

"I will?"

"You will. And you'll tell me."

"Okay, ma'am." He looked down, then started to open his —she put her finger straight on his lips.

"Shhh, Kevin. Shhhh. You mustn't tell me." He stared at her. She stared back. An older man at the end of the bar shook his head and took a sip of his lager.

"Mmphfh." Kevin aptly feigned not being able to speak. Gemma really appreciated his commitment to the bit. She took her finger off his lips.

"Kevin? I'm scared. I'm scared you're never going to pour me that Jack and Diet."

"Ma'am, I—"

"Okay fucking fine, Kevin, I'm scared of what it says. Okay. Just! Just tell me." He looked down at the page. She closed her eyes.

"Shift Supervisor, Nights, 11 p.m. to 7 a.m., at ... Traw... suh... fine... dund..." Gemma popped her eyes open and shot a look down.

"Is that fucking Welsh?!" She squinted. The paper read:
ASSIGNMENT OFFER:
SHIFT SUPERVISOR, NIGHTS (2300-0700)
CONCENTRA ENERGY
TRAWSFYNYDD, CYMRU
HOUSING / 3X DAILY MEAL PROVIDED
PAY GRADE 2
Her head landed swiftly on the bar. She banged it on

there a few times for good measure. Kevin was studiously reading the pamphlet that had also been in the envelope.

"It says here that you can reject this but request another assignment, but that this one is likely to be the 'most generous in terms of pay and accommodation' and was 'specially selected to fit your skillset as known to the UK Government'." Kevin nodded sagely as he read. Gemma let out a massive sigh. The man at the end of the bar chuckled to himself.

FIVE
AN URGENT QUESTION

January 2028.
Westminster, Central London.

MIKE STOOD at a nondescript gate in the freezing cold, waiting for his escort. He was well aware he needed to be more supportive. But this was par for the course for her. When she used terminology he didn't understand, he'd ask what it meant. And she'd simply smile and say 'never mind'. When she was off somewhere for work, she needn't bother explaining, as he lacked the context. And now she felt he needed an escort just to get inside one of the world's most-visited tourist attractions. An escort who was late. He rubbed his hands together, glove-less as he was, as pins-and-needles shot through them. He wasn't even sure who he was waiting for, but presumably they'd find him. As he looked around, he caught sight of a police officer looking back at him, a rifle hung around their shoulder. Extremely comforting. Though he supposed it was, in a way. These people kept Elizabeth safe. Even from her husband, it should seem.

Somehow he'd never been to the Palace of Westminster, even though his wife had been serving as an MP for years now. He'd gotten the odd invite for a tour or drinks, but never felt totally comfortable taking her up on it. And now here he was, presumably about to be led inside, for reasons he wasn't quite sure of, but got the impression were quite serious.

"You must be Mike." A female voice came from behind him, terse and impatient. He spun around and saw her, and towered above her. Maybe 5 feet tall, she came up to Mike's chest, her blonde hair perfectly parted and straight, with piercing blue eyes that seemed to stare a hole straight through him. He stuck his hand out.

"Hi, yes, Mike Fernsby. Elizabeth Marsh's husband. I was supposed to meet her here."

"Cassandra Cooper, MP for Poplar and Limehouse." She shook his hand, avoiding eye contact, watching the handshake itself.

"Poplar, that's in the Midlands," Mike replied with a nod.

"It's Canary Wharf, not far, right here in London," Cass replied through a grimace, also nodding.

"Right, no of course," Mike said. "I must be thinking of... honestly, you know, I think I was thinking of Call The Midwife."

Cass nodded even harder, a pained smile crossing her face. "Right, yes, same Poplar, over East London, hasn't moved!"

Mike also kept nodding, unsure how to break out of this, his face feeling like it might be going a bit red. "Right of course! It looks quite different in the show."

"Believe they film it on a set somewhere," replied Cass, also clearly unsure how to move forward. "Shall we, erm, I don't mean to be rude, shall we get on with it? Not much time I'm afraid."

"I've put my foot in it, haven't I," he squeaked.

"Give me your phone, please?" She put her hand out and tapped her palm impatiently. He dropped his phone into her hand, and she swept it straight into her handbag.

"Phones aren't permitted inside I take it?" He fumbled for a reason why he'd just agreed to that.

"We're not going inside, I'm afraid. There's been a bit of a change of plan." She nodded up at him, clearly hoping he would just sort-of agree. He stared down at her in confusion, his face contorting.

"Listen I'm sorry, I should, explain. I don't have much time to explain, but I'm happy to try."

Mike nodded. "All I really knew was that Elizabeth said something was going on, and I should meet her here and she'd pop out and explain."

"Ah, anything she might've told you is probably worthless now I'm afraid."

"Right." Mike smacked his lips.

She looked up and down the street they were on. It was oppressively grey outside today, oddly dark even at just past Noon. A small smattering of tourists moved past them, in a security queue to get into the Palace. Cass stepped close to Mike, looking up at him. She spoke in a low whisper. "To cut through it, we had a plan in place, and it's since spiralled a bit."

"Right," he nodded. "Okay."

"Mike, it's bad." She looked very upset suddenly, under her professional facade. She kept putting stray hairs back into place as the wind caught them. "I told her I'd fetch you and we'd keep you close in case there's any press."

He kept nodding. "Okay." He started to feel like a bobblehead.

"Reporters, paparazzi. It might be nothing. People might not care. But it'll depend... it's probably easiest to just... go watch." She sounded a bit deflated. "I'm honestly not sure how it's going to go. It's gotten away from me a bit."

She walked him to the front of the security queue, to a small separate lane. A terrifying, well-kitted officer handed him bins for his things and gestured at the metal detector. They both went through quietly. Cass put her hand on Mike's back and walked him to a door then in, and down a dark hallway. She held up a security pass on a lanyard and smiled uncomfortably at him. He lowered his head down, letting her put it around his neck.

"Miss..." Mike stammered.

"Cooper."

"Miss Cooper, what's going on?"

"Mike, there's about a thousand things I need to tell you. But we need to get through the next few minutes first. And I hope you can still be supportive of her when she needs you. Okay? Because I'm not going to be able to help her." She looked up at him with sanguine eyes. He'd never met this woman, never been in this building, and now he felt like he'd gone through the looking glass.

Mike nodded. Cass shook her head.

"Not good enough, say you'll try."

"I'll try."

"Okay."

She gathered him up and brought him down a corridor at a brisk pace, up some dark stairs, and suddenly he was looking out over the House of Commons. "It looks a lot smaller in person," he muttered to himself, then thought how pedestrian of a remark that was. Stupid.

"I'll come get you after. Stay here. I have to go down. Mike, I'm so sorry."

Before he could react, she was off. He squirmed relentlessly in the seat and tried to watch the proceedings, his escort having deposited him and immediately fled. He looked around and noticed everyone else in the gallery had their phones. He'd been conned. And he was now deeply troubled.

Finally, after who knows how long, he noticed Cass appear downstairs, sat on a bench near the back. He wondered if Elizabeth was also somewhere, and as if she was cued, she entered as well, slipping into the chamber from a different entrance and sitting on the front bench opposite. It was, otherwise, quite a sparse attendance, and Mike couldn't help but be extremely cynical about how Members of Parliament were off wasting precious taxpayer money instead of being sat in here, listening to what appeared to be an extended debate about funding for new climbing frames at primary schools in Durham.

"Thank you, thank you, that's all for questions." Whatever it was, the woman who'd been overseeing proceedings appeared to be wrapping it up. "Please let the chamber clear for the urgent question." People shuffled around, some came in, others left, and within a minute it had gotten even more empty than it was for the climbing frames debate. "Right, thank you," the speaker continued. "We now come to the urgent question. Alastair Mitchell."

A man had risen part-way through and was now standing at the front. He cleared his throat and held up his notes on a piece of paper. "Thank you, Madam Speaker, I'd like to put a question to the minister for Works and Pension, if I may, regarding an article that's appeared only a short time ago in The Guardian, which has made some rather shocking allegations. Allegations that this government, quite frankly, has been colluding in depth and in secret with the American tech conglomerate Concentra during the drafting of the Public Works Act."

Mike leaned forward, craning to see if Elizabeth was down there. They'd had some blazing rows at home lately about this bill, and her stress over it, and most recently, how she'd come home in tears and hysterics over Concentra's involvement. He'd told her to calm down, to trust the others around her, not to jeopardise her position so early into her political career. But that had just sent her spiralling, and she'd disappeared and been quite distant ever since. Mike's head started to spin. Had she run off and... had they somehow gotten to the press?

"Madam Speaker," the man continued with a practised fury, "can the minister please put our minds at rest, and tell us these allegations are in fact completely false. And if they are not false, tell us that they will immediately agree to withdraw this terrible legislation that many have taken to calling the Conscription of British Workers Act, the Betrayal of the British Public Act, the Surrender to Artificial Intelligence Act. Madam Speaker, will the government withdraw this bill?"

As he finished, he was increasingly jeered from the opposite benches, which had started to fill toward the end.

Mike was absolutely flabbergasted. It all seemed so sick. He told himself this must just be how it always was with these people, these politicians. He regretted ever helping

Elizabeth get elected. Now she was exposed to this, corrupted by it. He regretted having come here.

The speaker shouted for quiet. "Minister for Works, Elizabeth Marsh."

Elizabeth now stood at the dispatch box and opened a folder neatly in front of her. "Thank you, Madam Speaker, I'm happy to field this question. We are at a pivotal moment in this nation, indeed in the world. We're seeing unprecedented job losses, unprecedented economic hardship. A cascading effect of widespread automation, aberrations in the financial sector, the crash of the American stock market, and rapid industry consolidation have devastated the British economy. No national government can control these effects Madam Speaker, they are global, as I'm sure my esteemed colleague knows. We can only seek to limit the damage, to do right by our citizens. It is not an economic crisis but a humanitarian one, Madam Speaker. Millions of unemployed across the nation now look to us for answers, for help and for hope. And we have sought support from our friends in the private sector, and we will not apologise for it."

As she spoke, jeers and cheers would rumble from the respective sides of the room. But on that last bit, the jeers were deafening. Mike found Cass again, and she was sat motionless, alone, not watching. She had her head tilted down, her eyes closed.

"Madam Speaker," Elizabeth continued, "the British state cannot pay the wages of every unemployed citizen while also paying for the infrastructure they use. We cannot put food on the table for millions while also subsidising the farms that grow it. It is not possible for the Treasury to sustain that level of spending. We have therefore sought solutions from industry, including yes, as The Guardian has pointed out, the CEO of Concentra, Rebecca Prue."

Eruption. It was chaos. A deafening wave crashed onto Elizabeth from the opposing benches.

"CORRUPT!"

"RESIGN!"

"IT'S A BETRAYAL!"

"KILL THE BILL!"

The speaker once again demanded order. "Minister, please continue."

Elizabeth cleared her throat. "I only admit the facts are true. They have been tremendously misconstrued." The jeers continued at pace, and Elizabeth shouted over them. "At the time this government feel a public private partnership to be in the best interest of the British public, to immediately stop the spread of foreclosures, of homelessness, of this epidemic of unemployment and misery. To get Britain working again, to get Britain building the infrastructure we need—" the shouts became too much.

The speaker demanded everyone be silent. Elizabeth looked remarkably unmoved.

So many nights they'd sparred. Sloppy, drinks in hand, screaming themselves hoarse over a jam jar lid left out, damp towels in the closet, Mike's lack of ambition. How messy and ridiculous it always was. If she could be so composed here, in the face of all this, why not at home?

"—Madam Speaker, Britain needs clean energy. As evidenced by the recent blackouts, we need more energy, more than ever. But we're not blind to the optics of the situation. Given the appearance of impropriety I will take this away to discuss with my office, with the Cabinet, and with the Prime Minister, with a view to shelving this bill until it can be properly re-drafted."

A surprise uproar of cheers from the opposition bench, including Cass, who rose instantly to her feet, cheering. They were clearly not expecting this. Nor was anyone, given the extremely angry shouts from behind Elizabeth. Mike had assumed they were on Elizabeth's side, as they were quite literally on her side. But in that moment, she appeared to stand alone. The speaker thanked Alastair several times but he remained standing in place.

"Madam Speaker one follow-up," he said. The speaker nodded. "I'm sure all the members do appreciate the minister's agreement to consider a re-draft of this bill. I personally do appreciate it. Can we ask that when doing so, would the minister and her staff please do their best to recall this time in 1833, the Parliament of Great Britain passed a bill in this very chamber, titled the Slavery Abolition Act!"

A cacophony of shouts and jeers came from all sides. Elizabeth's mouth was open, her head askew. She was aghast. The speaker shouted desperately for order. Mike felt his stomach tie in knots. All the blood rushed from his head. He felt faint. He leaned back in his seat, sliding his feet back and forth across the wooden floor. He pushed his hands back and forth along the fabric of his trousers. He closed his eyes and waited for it all to end.

A hand touched his shoulder. He jolted sharply. "Jesus christ!" came the startled voice of Cass behind him. He wasn't sure how long it had been. Other business seemed to be going on in the chamber below now. Elizabeth was nowhere to be seen.

"Sorry, sorry, I must've spaced out." He looked and saw

who it was. "Excuse me, excuse me, what the absolute fuck —" Mike was interrupted by Cass raising a finger to him.

"Not here." She squeezed his shoulder and lifted, and he stood to follow. They eventually found themselves back outside, once again on the street. Anger and confusion swirled through Mike's brain, but he felt as if he were on rails, unable to deviate or even speak for himself, as this woman appeared to lead him to a Westminster pub.

He followed her through the door, not even knowing the name of the pub or the street they were on and feeling unable to go his own way — partly from curiosity, partly from intimidation, and mostly due to the fact that she still had his phone. Maybe she'd planned that bit to ensure this bit happened. But now, in a snug at the back, he sat barely a foot away from her. He parted his lips to speak, but his throat felt so dry. By the time he found any words, she pointed at him. "Lager?"

"Um, sure."

She nodded and excused herself to the bar. And so, he sat there alone in the tiny, oaken snug in a pub he didn't know the name of, with a woman he'd only just met, desperately worried about what was happening with his wife. He craned around a wooden pole to see the television hanging in the corner. He could make out a clip playing, video of where they just were. The text on the bottom of the screen read "SOURCES: WORKS MINISTER LIZ MARSH HAS 'GONE ROGUE', WORKS BILL WILL NOT BE WITH-DRAWN." He felt flush.

Two pints of lager landed on the table in front of him, and Cass slid into the booth, blocking his view of the television. He immediately picked up his pint and took a sip, then a bigger gulp. He put it down and sighed, looking down at the glass. When he finally looked up, Cass had set her pint down half-gone. Mike tried to chuckle, but it came out as a cough. He took another gulp. "Miss, can you please tell me what the hell was going on today? The TV says Beth's 'gone rogue?'"

Cass put her head in her hands. "That's not what I wanted to talk about."

"Then why are we here?" Mike was extremely uneasy. He needed to assert himself. Gain control of the situation. "I need my phone back. Right now."

"Please, I just need to keep us off the grid for a bit. I promise it's—"

"You can't just keep my phone," Mike fired back anxiously. "That's, that's theft. You've stolen it!"

"Stolen what," she answered with a grim smile. "Give me one second, though."

Mike slumped back into the booth. He wrapped his hands around the bottom of his pint. Cass had produced her phone and was tapping away on it. He sat helplessly and watched her. Over Cass's shoulder he could see the TV was now showing some kind of sport. Useless. He was in a total information blackout. He sighed and pouted, rotating his glass quarter-turns between his palms, over and over and over. Cass finally glared up at him. "Can you please stop? That's extremely annoying."

"You sound like Beth," he replied.

Cass flashed a sarcastic grimace and went back to her phone, which was vibrating constantly. "Can you at least tell me everything's okay with her? This is all very, very bizarre. Please. I'm worried." She looked up at him over the top of her phone and sighed.

"Mike, right now, your wife has likely been pulled aside in some suite at The Grand Hotel, and she's being told the consequences of what she's done today. Her bosses are not going to be happy with her. As you saw, she's, well, 'gone rogue.' There's a principle called collective responsibility, a minister cannot publicly disagree with the—"

"I'm a graphic artist!" Mike rapped his hand on the table, shouting. "I don't know any of this shit, okay? Can you not condescend me for five minutes?"

Cass groaned. "Listen. Drink up. We have to talk through some stuff that I *really* don't want to have to talk about, and I can't be sober for it, and maybe you shouldn't be sober for it either."

SIX
UNREAD MESSAGES

Two weeks prior.
Canary Wharf, East London.

THE LOCK GAVE a quick beep followed by some clanking and clunking. Elizabeth pushed the heavy glass door open and slipped inside the building. In a panic, she'd texted her friend and colleague Cass, asking for some last-minute sanctuary for the night. "Not going to be home for a while but here!" came the response, along with a QR code. She lived in a brilliant little high-rise in Canary Wharf that let her generate a guest entry code. Clever, though the style left much to be desired. The lobby was mostly cold, grim steel. The decor in these Canary Wharf apartment buildings was offensively inoffensive, the usual "dystopian vision of the future" that the FinTech crowd seemed to prefer. She groaned and rubbed her shoulders while she stared at a painting of Tower Bridge in the lobby. Underneath it was written "London Bridge" in script. She grimaced and placed her phone against the elevator panel. It lit up with her photo next to Cass's photo, and the elevator doors glided open.

She hoped walking into Cass's apartment would be a relief, but she still felt so tense. She'd discretely collected an overnight bag together and ducked out while Mike was still steaming and stewing in the kitchen. Surely he'd notice any minute now, if he hadn't already. She dreaded to think about the inevitable texts and calls.

The apartment was gorgeous, though. She'd actually never been here. A floor to ceiling window took up one wall and looked out over the neighbouring buildings. She was on the 14th floor, high enough to see quite a bit of the city lights glittering below. It wasn't spacious, of course. Most of the room was a bright yellow sofa, a writing desk, a small but well-stocked bar and a truly stunning amount of plants of all sizes. A narrow hallway ran down to a few closed doors, presumably the bathroom, kitchen and bedroom. You definitely traded space for location here.

Knowing what she knew about Cass, the arrangement of the furniture was about expected. No television, and the sofa sat facing the window, a small coffee table between it and the world. She pictured Cass sat there, sipping a gin, staring out at the city lights.

Elizabeth slung her bag on the floor by the desk, deposited her phone, then collapsed on the sofa to do likewise, though minus the gin. She had no energy to make herself a drink. Within a minute she was passed out, slouched over to one side. Stress and repressed rage had a way of making her sleepy.

She awoke to the door opening some time later, Cass letting herself in. Her bag hitting the floor. Elizabeth kept her eyes shut but rolled to one side, her back to the window, her face buried in the upholstery. She laid there, arms tucked close, listening to the silence, occasionally interrupted by the sound of a zipper moving, of shoes being flopped onto the carpet. A door opened, a light clicked on. The shower started running. Elizabeth smiled slightly. She loved the sound of the running water. Cass had left the bathroom door open, and steam started to roll out into the rest of the room. It made Elizabeth start to actually relax. Her fight-or-flight response calmed down. Her shoulders and back were tight, almost throbbing with pain. Laying squished up on the sofa surely wasn't helping.

She sat up and caught a glimpse of herself reflected in the window. Her hair was a fright, her eyes were puffy from the crying, and she had crease lines on her face from the nap. She could only laugh, so she did. She felt so far away from her problems, in this small room, this safe space, the city stretching out below her. Her mind drifted to the pyjamas in her bag.

Would she gamble that Cass wasn't going to want to go out? She would. She took her blazer off and tossed it to one side. She caught her reflection again, sat on the edge of the sofa, her shoulders slumped and her belly protruding. She instinctively straightened up, sucked in her stomach. She shook her head and slouched back down. Inhaling and exhaling, she told herself: "You're okay. You're okay."

"You're awake!" Cass shouted out from the shower. "I didn't want to disturb you, and your text sounded like you were in a pretty bad way." Elizabeth looked over her shoulder but stayed sat on the far edge of the bed.

"I'm awake." Her voice cracked.

"I can't really hear you! Come in here," Cass shouted back, a bit playfully.

"Ha. I said I'm awake! Are you going to want to go down the pub? Or out-out?" Elizabeth was shouting, and her voice was so shaky, her throat so scratchy. This was not the first time today she'd been shouting.

"Let's do it! I'll be out in a few minutes. Won't be long."

Elizabeth stood up and looked at herself again in the reflection. "Fuck," she whispered to herself, then crossed the room to her bag. She could freshen up a bit at least. As she went to pick up the bag from the floor she caught sight of her mobile on the desk. The screen flashed up another notification: "Mike Fernsby – 7 unread messages."

Ugh.

She stood there frozen, staring down at the screen. Mike's found a way into her bubble, as ever. Her fault. She knew he can't leave well enough alone. She should've turned her phone off, or at least muted his notifications. Whenever they fight, he can't switch it off. She asks for space, he refuses to grant it. She asks if they can pick this up in the morning, he says he can't sleep unless they resolve it.

"Mike Fernsby – 8 unread messages."

She picked up the phone and walked back across the room. She sat perched on the very edge of the sofa, staring at it. Feeling it vibrate lightly in her hand each time. Running her fingers around the cold metal edges.

"Mike Fernsby – 9 unread messages."

Swiping her finger up and down the screen, watching it animate the notification bubble bigger, then smaller, then bigger, then smaller. Not quite unlocking it.

"Mike Fernsby – 10 unread messages."

The sound of the shower was soothing. She focused on that instead, and stared at a nearby Monsterra. Feeling the glass of the phone screen under her fingertip as she dragged it back and forth. Picturing the animation in her mind's eye, avoiding looking at the actual screen.

Suddenly the vibration intensified, startling her, pulling her back into focus. She looked down.

"Mike Fernsby – Incoming Voice Call."

She closed her eyes again and inhaled, then exhaled. The exhale got caught in her throat and she coughed. She held the phone between her palms, her fingers tapping and drumming the back rapidly.

"Mike Fernsby – Missed Voice Call."

Swipe. She made eye contact with the phone and it animated to life, taking her straight to the messages. A wall of text, insurmountable. Words and phrases jumping out as she tried not to read it.

"—trying to protect what we have—"

"—just get so worried—"

"—know it's not my place, but—"

"—feel like you love your job more than—"

"—childishly running off any time we—"

She locked it again and let it drop to the floor. A thud, the heft of the phone bouncing off the gaudy, rock-hard carpeting. Elizabeth started crying. She stared at the phone on the floor. Vibrating, but face down. She started to sob uncontrollably. So much built up from the day already, by the time she got to Mike. All she'd wanted to do was have him listen, even if he didn't understand. And now she was here.

"Liz, my god." Cass was shocked. Elizabeth looked up sharply and saw her in the reflection on the window, standing behind the sofa wrapped in a towel. The shower was off now, the last bit of steam billowing out into the hallway.

"Christ, I'm so sorry." She sniffled hard, tears streaming

down her face. She wiped her hand across her cheeks quickly. "I was just going to get some bits from my bag to freshen up."

"No, don't do that. You're hurting, god, look at you." Cass sounded sincerely concerned. She sat down on the sofa next to Elizabeth and put one hand on her shoulder. "What happened?"

Elizabeth started to answer but couldn't find the energy to say anything. She just shook her head a few times, otherwise frozen. Cass grimaced, looking briefly panicked, unsure what to do. She put her arms out.

"Can I hug you?"

Elizabeth nodded and threw her arms around Cass. Her sobs were full body heaves as she felt everything come spilling over the wall. The cabinet meeting. The horrifying conversation after. The hopelessness. Mike treating her like she was crazy, like she was somehow threatening their life with her "work problems."

They squeezed each other tightly.

"My god, it's okay, it's okay." Cass whispered in Elizabeth's ear, rubbing her back. The warmth of the embrace felt wonderful. As did the sobbing. She hadn't cried this hard in, well, she wasn't sure if she'd ever cried this hard.

Her sobs calmed down a bit. She let go and leaned back to see Cass still looking very concerned. She laughed a little.

"Christ. I'm so sorry. This is not a great start to our gal's night out." She was still wiping tears from her eyes and cheeks. Absolutely wrecked. No going down to the pub like this. Cass stood up.

"Please don't apologise. You seemed so out of sorts when you texted earlier. I'm assuming because of your bloody husband, or the bloody government."

Elizabeth chuckled. "Bit of both?" She looked at Cass who stood there in front of her. A rare sighting of her without heeled shoes on. Indeed, this was more of Cass than she'd ever seen. Blonde hair matted against her coarse, freckled skin. Gorgeously vivid tattoos from her shoulders going down both arms. A wild, stylised Cheshire Cat, some other characters she didn't recognise, someone waving a huge orange, white and pink flag, and so many flourishes, vines, and details. None of this was ever visible in her usual all-business attire. And what was she, 5 foot 2? "Jesus, you're tiny! And what? Cassandra Cooper MP, you have tattoos! You're blowing my mind. Who are you?"

"Why, thank you! I do pride myself on being a little mystery."

Elizabeth booed. Cass did as much of a curtsy as one can in a towel wrap.

"I have some on my back as well! Buy me a drink first. I'm kidding."

They both laughed, and the laughter was nice. Her brain fog lifted and she finally felt present. She shook her head, her eyes widening. "I'm so sorry, I don't know I have it in me to go downstairs to the bar. I'm really sorry. I might just shower and pull myself together?"

"Good thing about me is, I have my own bar, right here in the flat." Cass smiled and winked. A huge weight lifted.

They kitted out in pyjamas, blow-dried their hair and said very little, which was exactly what Elizabeth wanted. It was extremely cosy. Her propped up on the bed, a couple lamps and the lights of the City providing a nice glow. Cass mixed their second round of gin & tonics in the other room and delivered them to the bedside table.

There was a brief attempt to broach the topic of Mike,

but Elizabeth quickly waved it off and suggested they watch the news. It was an easy sell for people in their line of work. Cass had her TV hanging on the wall across from her bed. Terrible for healthy sleep. But perfect if you want to hide that you have a television from random houseguests.

And of course with the news on it was only a matter of time before Elizabeth's problems came crashing back down on them.

"The government announced today the Public Works Act will soon receive a second reading in Parliament," the BBC presenter said neutrally. Elizabeth moaned. Cass leaned forward. "The long-awaited bill, announced in this year's King's Speech, promises to quote 'get Britain working again' with quote 'a job for everyone,' according to the minister for Works and Pension Elizabeth Marsh." Elizabeth slid down the headboard and moaned again, as bullet points from the bill appeared on screen next to a video loop of her exiting 10 Downing Street earlier that day.

Cass reflexively pulled away from the TV, then shot Elizabeth a hard glance. "You are now the *face* of this horrifying legislation?" She sounded disgusted. "Did you put this on so I would see it and harass you? Because I'm game. I will bloody terrorise you."

"I hate it, Cassie," Elizabeth sighed. "It's the wrong approach. I came into office saying 'you know, this AI stuff, let's slow down, let's regulate automation, let's pause consolidation.' And now—"

Cass nodded. "I do recall this, yes."

"Yes, and, now we're just giving up," Elizabeth said.

"You hear Concentra's footsteps approaching your bedchamber. Close one's eyes, open one's bank account, and don't you dare think of England."

Elizabeth rolled her eyes. "Yes, yes, I know. More than you know, I know. And you should see this bloody legislation. It's—"

"—Liz, I've seen it." Cass downed her drink. "I see it when I close my eyes. It appears to me in my dreams. It's fucking slavery."

Elizabeth sneered. "That's a bit inflammatory, yeah? It's aggressive. It's too aggressive. I completely agree. But we still need to put people to work, we can't just give the whole country benefits forever. Unemployment is set to double every six months."

"Have you tried doing something about that part instead? And if you completely agree—"

"—What do you propose we do?" Elizabeth was trying to keep her anger in check, her friendship with Cass becoming increasingly strained lately. Their political differences finally coming to the fore after all this time, Elizabeth assumed.

"Stop letting corporations buy each other? Stop loosening employment laws?" Cass was incensed. "Christ Liz, *you* told *me* what the problems were the night we met! That was only a couple years ago, what changed?"

"It's complicated."

"What's complicated?"

"It's so much worse than I expected. Than we expected, I mean. Cassie, we've lost millions of jobs. So many millions. These companies have been squeezed on every side. Another firm goes broke every week in every industry. And Concentra have absolutely perfected stepping in to pick them up, automate them, enact layoffs. What company would turn that down and choose to implode instead?"

Cass shook her head, and had been shaking her head during most of Elizabeth's speech. "No, no. You can regulate everything you're describing. You're choosing not to do it. You're allowing this to happen."

"This is happening with or without us. It's progress. It's market forces. We can't be anti-progress. This genie will not go back in the bottle. And we do—"

"—I cannot believe what I'm hearing, Liz. I cannot believe it." Cass gathered up their glasses and headed to the living room. "Same again?"

"Yes, that's fine, thanks."

"How do we even have the energy for what you're describing?" She trailed off as she vanished into the living room. Elizabeth got up and followed. "Aren't we in the middle of a power crisis? I've had two blackouts this week already. Isn't this *because* of the new Concentra AI data centre in Hounslow?"

Elizabeth dismissed that with a wave and an eye-roll. "Are you joking? Trafficking in conspiracy now over at Labour? Do you know how ridiculous you sound—"

"—oi, look. Don't belittle me. You're not Mike and I'm not you." Cass handed over a fresh drink, then walked round to the couch and sat down with her own.

"Excuse me?" Elizabeth remained standing, drink in hand, now staring down at the back of Cass's head. "That's extremely uncalled for."

"You've come a long way in a couple years, I'll give you that." Cass raised her glass sarcastically. "You can launch into a character attack one breath to the next. The Tories have trained you well."

"Looks as if we both can."

"Bab, I'm not some yampy little girl you can mug off. I'm a member of Parliament just like you. If you want to discuss this then let's discuss it."

Elizabeth walked around and sat down on the couch next to Cass. "You're right."

"I'm sorry about the Mike comment."

"Oh, don't. You're not wrong, he does belittle me."

Cass turned, crossing one leg under herself, putting her arm up behind Elizabeth. "Liz, do you honestly thing this is the right thing to do? This is your bloody floor of the building. You're a minister. I'm just barking from the back bench."

Elizabeth let out a huge sigh. "We have to do something. But it shouldn't be this. It shouldn't be, yeah, we've lost millions of good jobs, but don't worry, because you can get a mandatory work placement. Just come build nuclear power plants for the government. We know you were originally a television writer but don't worry, we'll train you. Here's a free cot and a hot meal. No pay, is that fine?"

Cass snorted. "Well now wait, I'm sold. Will you throw in a Union Jack tattoo?"

"Those are mandatory as well."

"Do your constituents want this?" Cass rolled her head around. "I *suppose* that is worth considering. I say that grudgingly, mind."

"Oh, you should hear them. Every letter and email straight from a template provided by the Daily Mail. But they just hear, I'll get a job. They need one of those."

"Maybe," Cass said with a hint of defeat in her voice, "maybe this is better than it reads on paper. I can't argue with—"

Elizabeth was shaking her head again. "This just takes me up to today. We're current now."

"I don't understand."

"Concentra wrote the bill, Cass. This is all tailored to a business plan they came up with."

Cass shoved her lightly. "Shut the fuck up."

"We were on a video call with their CEO and the PM literally today. I found out today. This is why I am here. This is why I'm so at odds with myself tonight." Cass's mouth was agape. She had a few false starts, air escaping with no words to accompany. "I don't know what to do."

"Christ, Elizabeth, you cannot be serious. You're the minister for the department. Just... pull the plug. Threaten to resign if they don't let you." She was flapping her hands about, spilling drops of drink here and there. "Or actually resign, and go public. Call for the PM's resignation. You know I would support you, we would support you."

"Slow down, Cassie. Slow down." They both took a breath. "We're wrapping the whole identity of the party up in this 'a job for every Brit' thing. And there's collective responsibility. I'd be sacked the moment I took a different position publicly." She took a long sip of her drink and stared at the wall. "And resigning... means you're on the outside. You can't change anything from the outside. And, I don't know. There's pressure. Family pressure. Peer pressure. Many pressures. Resigning would seem like I'm giving up, I can't handle it."

"Can you handle it," Cass said pointedly. "That would be my question. If you're saying a thing is beyond your control, and it's something you supposedly do control."

Elizabeth had a sour look on her face. She took a quiet sip.

"Go on Breakfast or Good Morning Britain," Cass continued. "You can WhatsApp a producer right now and be on tomorrow morning."

"I would be sacked. It wouldn't change anything."

Cass stared at Elizabeth. "You're just stonewalling. Why

are you— no, I don't understand. Are you... do you want my help? Or do you just want me to absolve you of your sins?"

"I don't know." She sank down into the sofa, cupping both her hands around her drink. She brought it to her lips and slurped it. "What if it... what if it leaked to the press? Is that something?"

"It's something, Liz. But it's a huge risk. If you're worried about being sacked, especially. And it makes the information seem dodgy. And if you're connected, it makes you seem dodgy. All on top of your being sacked over it."

Elizabeth nodded. She slid over a bit, putting herself fully in front of Cass's arm, nestling in. "I know." Cass looked down at the top of her head and let out a clipped sigh. She finished her drink and set her glass on the table, then took Liz's and set that down next to it.

"Liz, why are you here?"

"I can't talk to anyone about this. Not anyone else in government, not any other friends, talking to Mike about it was a disaster." She slid down a bit more, resting her head on Cass's arm. "You're who I came to, Cassie."

Cass sighed. She ran her hand through her hair, and again, and again. "You are a frustrating lady. Pretty, but frustrating."

"You keep doing that," said Liz, looking up at Cass. "Running your fingers through your hair."

"I do, oh, I do." She rubbed her face and pinched the bridge of her nose. "I'm anxious. I'm drunk. The room's spinning a bit." Cass was slurring her words a bit.

"It is."

"I do it when I'm anxious, run my fingers through my hair. Do you ever do that? It feels nice, makes a nice sound. Feels good in the brain. Calms me down."

"Yeah?"

"Here, lay down." Cass shimmied into the corner of the sofa. Liz stretched her legs out, letting them dangle off the other end, and rested the back of her head on Cass's chest. Cass gently pushed her fingers into Liz's hair and slowly ran them front to back.

"You're right, that is nice," Liz said. She closed her eyes while Cass continued. "Talk to me?"

Cass chuckled. "Talk to you?"

"Yeah, I don't know. Talk to me about something else. Anything."

"Well..." Cass said, in an almost whisper. "You're the first guest I've ever had in this flat. I hope you like it." Liz felt floaty and tingly all over. She could feel Cass's chest vibrating as she spoke. Her muscles were finally relaxing, aside from the way her legs were forced to dangle over the hard edge of the couch. "I kept meaning to invite you over. I needed time to mentally prepare myself for you to bring Mike as well. Sorry, that was mean."

Liz smiled, but kept her eyes shut. "I suppose it worked out." Cass brought her other hand down, pushing all her fingers through Liz's hair. She scratched lightly with her fingernails that time, dragging them slowly across Liz's scalp. "Ohhh, god, Cassie, a scalp massage too? You spoil me."

"I don't know if you deserve it."

"I don't know if I do, either. But I'll take it." She opened her eyes, hoping the room would stop spinning. "Cassie, you got me drunk."

"Sorry, I think I did my *me* pour for *you*, too. A bit too heavy for company. That's for when I'm just sat here staring out at Canary Wharf."

Liz gasped and tilted her head way back to see Cass's

face. "You do that! I knew you do that. I pictured it when I saw where the couch was. You're so twee."

"And apparently easy to read," Cass added.

"I just know you," said Liz.

"Speaking of. D'ya wanna see my other tattoo?"

"I do."

She slid out and off the couch, and Elizabeth grudgingly sat back up properly. Cass stood just in front of Elizabeth, her back turned. She looked over her shoulder and smiled. "It's silly, don't laugh." She slid the bottom of her pyjama top partway up. Elizabeth leaned forward on the couch to see it better. A woman in a green dress, with long flowing red hair, laid across a rock on a beach. Before her were waves, a bit of ocean. Parts of the top and bottom were obscured, and there was a shadow such that Elizabeth couldn't make out all the detail. "D'ya like it," Cass asked.

Elizabeth moved her hand towards Cass's back. "What is it?" She took the pyjama top in her fingers and lifted it a bit more, sliding the bottom down a bit as well. It was a full scene, stretching across her whole lower back. Even in the dim light she could see it was vividly coloured.

"It's supposed to be Miranda," Cass said, craning her head around. "From The Tempest."

Elizabeth gasped. "Really!" She laid her hand on the tattoo and Cass jolted.

"Cold!"

"Shit!" Elizabeth couldn't help but laugh. "Sorry. Terrible circulation." She dramatically blew into her hands and rubbed them together to warm them up. Cass rolled her eyes and laughed. "It really is breathtaking, Cassandra. I can't believe I never knew this about you."

"You sort-of knew! Not this part specifically."

"I suppose." Liz put her hands on Cass's hips, running her thumbs gently over the design. She felt Cass shivering, then felt the goosebumps on her skin. "God, my hands are so cold. Sorry." She leaned in and studied the design, stared at the face of Miranda, splayed out on the rock, looking out at the ocean. Almost imperceptibly small was a quote on a small scroll along the bottom. Elizabeth whispered as she read it. "At mine unworthiness, that dare not offer..."

"...what I desire to give, and much less take," Cass continued. She was looking back at Elizabeth, a sly grin on her face. "What I shall die to want." She slowly turned around, placing her hands over Elizabeth's, keeping them on her hips, her pyjama top slipping down to cover them. "But this is trifling, and all the more seeks to hide itself."

"You still remember quite a bit of it." Their eyes met. Elizabeth could feel her heart pounding in her chest. "It's beautiful."

Cass smiled even wider, her voice shaking. "I am your wife, if you will marry me." She bit the tip of her tongue, a cheesy grin on her face. "If not, I'll die your maid." She stepped closer and looked down at Liz, who looked up at her in a bit of a daze. "I'm sorry!" She was even shakier, a bit panicky. "Ahh, sorry! Sorry. I'm getting all swept up and I'm going too far, and I'm, I'm misreading things. I don't want to, well—"

"—don't want to what," Elizabeth whispered.

Cass stared, her mouth part-open, her throat creaking. The words wouldn't come out.

"...don't want to what..."

"Ahhh, can I kiss you?"

Elizabeth's mind was in a blender. Her heart was still racing. She felt her face go hot, her body tingled everywhere.

She closed her eyes and tilted her head up, then felt Cass's lips against hers.

The next morning, Elizabeth stirred awake with a splitting headache. She pressed her hand over her eyes as if it could somehow relieve the pain. Cass was curled up next to her in the bed, face pressed into her side, one arm draped over her stomach. She could hear her snoring gently, fast asleep. The room looked so small in the day, the bed barely fitting into the exact space allocated for it. Her pyjamas balled up in the tiny space between the bed and the window.

She felt cold. Freezing, in fact, on top of the duvet. She needed to finish sobering up. She needed to get out of here. It was Saturday. She had all weekend to formulate a plan. To find time to speak to Mike. To smooth things over.

A hand, sliding across her stomach. A kiss on her chest.

"Mmmm, good morning. I'm fockin' hungover, bab." Cass's voice, so raspy, her lips brushing against Elizabeth's skin as she talked. Elizabeth's whole body tensed up instantly. If she were a rubber-band she'd be in danger of snapping apart.

"Morning." Elizabeth sounded as stressed as she was. "I can't believe how late it is. I've got so much on today, I should've set an alarm, I'm so stupid."

"Is everything okay?" Cass's voice was still so raspy, but now she also sounded a bit worried. Elizabeth pulled and pawed at the duvet until Cass joined her in the effort to get it over them. They both laid under it. Cass rolled on her side and faced Liz. Liz faced the ceiling. "Lizzie, you haven't looked at me once."

"I have a really bad headache."

"I'm sorry, my fault. I do, too." Cass leaned in for a kiss and Liz recoiled instinctively. Cass's eyes went wide. She froze. Liz still wouldn't look at her. "What's... what's wrong, I don't understand."

"This is, I, I'm just. I'm sorry. I didn't mean to—"

"—Didn't mean to what." Cass's defences were fully up now. She glared at Liz, both of them still frozen in place.

"No, no, not that." She let out a 'tsk.' "Maybe that. Cassandra, I'm married."

"Barely!"

"You either are or you aren't, Cass! I definitely am!"

"Well, I'm not, Liz. And if you're going to just lie and pretend you don't know how I feel about you, how I've always felt—"

"—I don't even know what to do with that statement, Cassandra. I really don't." She rolled over, facing her back to Cass, and stared out the window. The sun was striking the adjacent tower perfectly, creating such a beautiful scene, the glass shimmering in the morning light, high above the chaos of everyone down below. She inhaled slowly and closed her eyes, wishing her headache would simply go away.

They both laid there for a bit, quietly, and listened to each other's breathing, with the occasional footsteps coming through the ceiling from the flat above. Elizabeth's mind was increasingly focused on how she would explain any of this, followed by whether she had it in her to even do anything about the works bill, Concentra, any of it. Whether she had the power, or even the desire.

"Maybe," Elizabeth said, "maybe it's one of those things you just let happen and hope to fix later."

"Oh?"

She rolled over to see Cass had been facing the same way as her. Perhaps both of them had been looking out the window. She saw Cass, finally, for the first time this morning.

She looked tired, vulnerable. Her hands tucked up under her face, her elbows together, covering her chest. She looked at Elizabeth expectantly, though without any hope. Curiosity in defeat. It gave Elizabeth this uncomfortable feeling in her stomach, spreading through her whole body. Rising panic, anxiety, desperation. Cass now distrusted her, maybe even disliked her. Mike was already upset with her, and would almost certainly leave her now, if he hadn't already decided to for other reasons. And Cass was right — something was happening in her department of government, and somehow she still couldn't stop it.

She raised her hand and placed it gently on Cass's face. "Hi." She caressed Cass's cheek with her thumb.

Cass smiled a nervous smile. "Hi."

"It's just a lot, I'm sorry. I'm here now."

"I've been thinking," Cass said.

"Yeah?" Liz was intrigued.

"Yeah. I have a plan."

SEVEN
PAST FAILURES

January 2028.
Westminster, Central London.

MIKE HELD his head in his hands, his elbows on the table. Unwilling to lift it, his face red and tear-streaked. He wanted to be angry, but it wasn't there. It was just sadness, a deep well of sadness.

"Mike, I'm so sorry. I'm really, really sorry." Cass had brought them another round, everyone around them in the pub definitely assuming she had just broken up with him. He wished it were that.

"How long has it been going on?" She'd been mercifully light on detail, giving a very awkward, clumsily-described account of her time with his wife. And eventually he'd asked her to please stop. But now he felt like he needed the rest.

"It's, no there's, there's nothing." Cass was making herself as small as she could on her side of the booth. "It was just the once."

He picked up his head, his face a total mess. She handed

him a napkin, and he tried to pull himself together. "Okay. Okay. Thank you for telling me."

Cass shook her head a little, then nodded. "Uh, right yes, of course. I'm just, Mike, I'm so sorry. I think I just thought, you were, separated, or..."

He put his hand up. "I can't."

"Right no," she quickly replied. "Of course." She took a huge swig of her pint. "Mike, I didn't tell you that entirely out of guilt. I need you to know that so I can tell you the rest of it."

Mike sniffled hard and wiped more tears from his face. "The rest of it?"

Cass looked around. The pub had really started to fill up now that it had gotten a bit later in the day. And the news was still running the story wall-to-wall. They loved it when a minister imploded.

"We need to get out of here." She hopped up, tossed her phone in her bag and tapped him on the shoulder. "Let's go."

A short walk later and Mike was once again piping up in desperate confusion. "What's here?" Cass had charged up some steps and was headed into a small boutique hotel.

She turned and smiled delicately. "Come on, in you come." He followed her inside in a daze, the woman his wife had cheated on him with. They went up the elevator and into a cramped room. "This is us, then." She tossed her bag down, then fumbled for the mechanism that opened the bathroom door. Mike looked down and saw a button next to the bed, glowing white, with a little toilet and faucet icon on it. He tapped it, and the door slid open. She looked at it confused for a second, then went inside and somehow shut the door. He heard the shower come on and the glowing button turned red.

He desperately wished to know why he was still with this person, now together with her in this terrible room. He refused to let himself draw his own mind onto the topic of why Elizabeth would do this. Or whether Cass was even telling the truth. That was something he hadn't fully entertained, and it might well fit. He and Elizabeth had their problems, but it wasn't so bad that she'd cheat. But what would Cass gain from lying to him?

He might be able to think about it if the room wasn't distracting him. It was a wildly over-designed, tacky mess, made to look like the bed, desk, chairs and cabinetry were all carved into one huge chunk of plastic. A 2000s vision of clean-room futurism. Also, he could see the seams all over the place.

Mike paced around the room like a caged animal. He stared out the tiny window at the brick wall of the building next door. He sat on the weird curved chair jutting out from the ridiculous laminated MDF desk. It was so slippery he nearly slid off. More doodling then, he supposed. The hotel stationary was equally fucking dumb, he noted, ruled but with lines that got all wavy and went off in weird random directions. It said "write outside the lines" at the bottom in a bad font.

Everything about this place screamed that it was designed by an AI. Well, "tool-assisted" was the preferred nomenclature to avoid offending both the interior designer who had used it and the engineers who had made the AI. The magic was that it could take all of the variables into account and make what were once laborious changes extremely quickly, including the most dreaded part of this sort of work – all of the client feedback.

Once properly calibrated, a designer with a good pipeline was just pasting the client feedback into one AI model, trained to reformat it in a way that the architecture model could understand, then pasting that result further across. Yet another model could turn the plans into a material break-down, and if you were good, you were taking this flow all the way across to an industrial fabricator, which would machine the MDF. That fabricator might be downstairs in your factory, or it might be up in the Midlands while you were sat at your desk in Brighton looking out at the seaside. What once took a dozen people hundreds of person-hours could now be done in a week by one person. Minus the installation of course, which was still fully human powered.

But it was real work, Mike admitted to himself as he drew a spiral pattern. Any random couldn't just rock up and start doing this, you really did need to understand it all. You needed some sort of background in it. And the technology was pricey to deploy, just in royalties and subscription fees alone. Which led him to wonder what so-called expert green-lit this shithole. There wasn't even a television. He slid off the chair and kneeled on the floor, looking under the desk for any sort of indication of who built this. "Ah, right," he muttered to himself as he spotted the Concentra Group logo laser-etched into each part.

His keeper was still holed up in the space bathroom, doing god knows what. Mike sat on the floor under the desk, a cosy spot in which to think more clearly. Across the room, which wasn't at all far, he saw Cass's bag. His phone! He stared at it. In his mind he replayed himself stretching across the room and opening it. And again, and again. Each time would've been enough time to get it before she came out. But what if she came out right now? But, she didn't. That would've been enough time. And, again. And again! He sat motionless. He couldn't bring himself to do it, to take the risk. What if... what if he could lock her in the bathroom? Not forever. Just long enough to grab his phone.

His eyes now went to the control panel. The light for the bathroom door had gone red. Did that mean locked? Or just occupied? Sometimes you could lock these things by holding the button, rather than pushing it. He'd absolutely search how this worked right now, if his phone were accessible. But the worst that could happen was probably nothing. It obviously wasn't going to let him open a bathroom door locked from the inside. But maybe it would let him re-lock it, from the outside. He shimmied over to the control panel next to the bed. The shower/faucet icon glowed red. He put his finger on it and held. The door dutifully popped open, and the room was filled with the sound of both running water and Cass's scream.

"What the fuck!"

"Sorry! Wrong button!"

Mike panicked and hit the button again as fast as he could. The door apparently had to finish opening before he could shut it. Pushpushpushpushpush, until he finally heard it start to slide back closed.

Okay, so red means occupied, not locked. That's noted. His original plan had been so stupid. His heart started to thud as he became hyperaware of his surroundings. The sound of the shower was noticeable now, even through the door. He hadn't heard it before. He leaned his back against the side of the bed, staring up at the brick wall out the window. It was dark out, but he could still see it clear as day. Security lights, maybe? He squeezed his hands. They felt tingly. Was it both, or just his left one? He couldn't possibly be having a heart attack. He tried to manage his breathing as his heart went a mile a minute. He pushed his fingers into the weird shag rug on the floor. His vision closed in and he shut his eyes.

"Oi! Where the fuck did you—oh." He heard Cass's voice from behind him. "Why the fuck are you bursting in on me in the bathroom?" He kept his eyes squeezed shut. He pushed his hands through the carpet again and again. "Oh Christ, you get panic attacks yeah? Do you take anything for that?"

"No," he managed.

"Well you fucking should. Sorry, I'm sorry. What do I do?" He could hear the genuine concern in her voice, with a slight hint of annoyance. He tried to breathe in, and out.

"I'll be fine. I'm okay. I just need to sit. It's just anxiety."

CASS SAT cross-legged on the bed quietly on her laptop, while Mike sat on the floor next to it, feeling a bit better, regaining his calm. He'd decided to just act as if, do whatever he could to get what he needed, then regroup with Elizabeth at home as soon as he could. Then he'd simply ask her what was true, what wasn't, and what they could do next.

He leaned his head back and looked up at Cass on the bed. "Can I get my phone back?"

"How are you feeling?" Her tone was much softer than it had been. He noticed she had a glass of red wine. "I sent Lizzie a note to let her know where we are. That's all I said."

"How is she?"

"She hasn't read it yet. Or anything I've sent since midday, actually."

"You mean in the Parliament."

"It's not *the* Parliament, it's just Parliament. And even that sounds stilted."

"Don't deflect."

"Oh who the fuck are you, anyway? Like, who are you?" She was more tense than she seemed. "Look, I told you the other thing, so I could tell you something else. I need to tell you now." She put her laptop down and got up, then poured a second glass of wine, finishing off the bottle. She set it on the desk near him. He clambered up onto the slidey chair and took a sip, then looked at it, and looked at her.

"What is this? Are we in for the night?" Oh dear. His composure faltered so much faster than he expected. "I obviously need to get home and see my wife, and see how she is, and you know, sleep in my own bed."

"You don't want to be there tonight," Cass said. "She won't be there either, most likely, if she's smart. It's mad with reporters. And they know who you are, what you look like, where you work. If they can't find her, they'll try to find you. So this is where we're at for now."

Mike shook his head angrily. "This is absurd. It's absurd. I can get past reporters without saying anything."

"Great! You've got something to hide, they'll go with that."

"I can say no comment, or that I don't know where she is."

"A government minister has gone missing! Even her own husband can't find her."

"Fine. I take your point." He leaned back and sipped more of his wine. "This is that bad? It's that bad that people are going to be looking for her?"

"I said reporters are looking for her. The people who are

actually making this bad know exactly where she is and they've known since the moment she left the floor."

"You make it sound like some sort of terrifying cabal."

"It's worse. It's the Conservative Party."

Mike chortled. "I don't much care for any of the political parties, to be honest." Cass shot him a look, then decided to let it go. Instead she walked him through the plan they'd come up with. Elizabeth had some information, some rather damning information, and Cass had a plan to raise a written question, which is a very common thing that happens loads of times per day. In her question she'd say a 'source' had told her this damning information. And Elizabeth would reply with shocking honesty. And then, they'd feed all that to the press.

Mike looked a bit doe-eyed, and said nothing.

This was not normal for Cass. Almost everyone she knew was either in government, in Parliament, or was an obsessive political wonk either for business or pleasure. Yet she found herself in a hellish post-modern nightmare of a hotel room at 10 p.m. explaining basic Parliamentary procedure.

"Okay, stay with me. So. Well. Mike, somehow The Guardian got that information and ran a story. They just ran it. And so another member of my party swooped in and demanded an urgent question."

"And what's that?" Mike was genuinely trying to hold all this in his head.

Cass pinched the bridge of her nose. "Mike, you were there."

"Right."

"So, we thought, this will be bumpy. But it'll still give us the right outcome. And then I got this." She opened her phone and pulled something up, then showed Mike. It was a text from an unknown number.

"WOULDN'T DO THIS IF I WERE YOU. HAVE THEM WITHDRAW THE QUESTION. I HAVE THE REST OF THEM. THE SUN VERY INTERESTED IN THESE."

Underneath it was a photo. Mike reached forward to tap on it. Cass pulled the phone back.

"Mike, I don't think you—"

He grabbed it, tapped the photo and zoomed in. It was a woman, heavily tattooed, standing with her naked back to a window, in front of a sofa. It had clearly been taken through a long lens from the opposing balcony. Mike shook his head, confused.

"I don't get it."

"Mike, please." Cass's voice was desperate, pleading.

"What? What is this...? Is this... you?"

Cass reached out to take the phone back. Mike held onto it. "This is just a photo of you then? So, what?"

"There's another." She looked down at the bed, her voice meek. "I wouldn't."

Mike swiped his finger on the screen to the next photo. He only caught a slight glimpse, a figure lying on top of another on that same sofa, before turning the phone away from his face. He smashed his lips together and closed his eyes, letting the phone drop to the bed. Cass picked it up.

"I'm so sorry, Mike."

They sat silently for some time, Mike occasionally nodding, looking around. He inhaled and exhaled slowly. "Okay. Okay." It was all he could do to put it out of his mind. "Okay."

"Okay?"

"You said it. You thought we were separated. I, I can't be angry. I can't be angry." He kept repeating it under his breath.

"Mike! Focus. They're blackmailing her with these photos."

"And you told her this? Or told the other man from your party? And everyone still went through with this?"

Cass tilted her head back and finished her glass of wine. She stared at Mike, her lips pursed, still holding the empty glass, gesturing it around. Finally she shook her head, almost imperceptibly. "No, no, I didn't."

"You what—"

"No, Mike, I didn't fucking tell her, okay? Because I didn't want to distract her. So I didn't tell her. I didn't ask, I didn't check with her. She believes in what she's doing. She wouldn't have wanted the distraction."

"You had no right to keep this from her. You had no right!" Mike was suddenly shouting at her. "You're just... you're just using her to get what you want! You talked her into this in the first place, didn't you?"

Cass got to her feet. They were squared off at opposites sides of the bed in this very cramped room. They paced in their respective patches of rug. "No, Mike, no. She's idealistic. She's more politically minded than you've ever given her credit for. But I thought she'd struggle to go through with it if it might become a scandal, or if it might make..."

"...make what?"

"...make my life harder," she whispered. "But now I don't know if she even cared about that, honestly. I realise it would really because she'd worry about losing you. Losing her perfect little life."

"But now, what," Mike yelled. "Okay! So, she's gone and

done it. She's gone rogue, as you people keep saying. So what's going to end her career? The going rogue? Or the photos?"

Cass screamed. "Fuck! Mike! It doesn't fucking matter!" She slammed her wine glass down on the table. It shattered, sending glass shards all over the nightstand and floor. "God damnit. Fuck." Her hand started bleeding, a large gash on her palm.

"Shit! What the hell!" Mike dove backwards and was sitting on the desk, the only way he could put any more distance between him and the situation. He took a second, staring, able to take a wider view now. "Ah, shit, are you okay?"

"No, I'm not bloody okay, my hand's cut." She stomped off to the bathroom, reached in and grabbed a towel. She wrapped her hand in it, and it was almost immediately starting to soak through with blood. "Fuck." Mike put his hand up as she started to walk back.

"Woah, woah. Glass on the carpet." He climbed onto the bed and looked over the edge, spotting a decent sized shard. He carefully picked it up and dropped it on the nightstand, then grabbed the rug from his side of the bed to cover any stray bits on her side. Cass put on an awkward smile.

"Thanks." She gingerly stepped back over to the bed and sat down on the edge, tying her bloody towel tighter onto her hand.

"You're going to need to get that treated."

"Fuck, I know. Can't wait to see that on social media."

MIKE RETURNED from the hotel lobby with a miniature first aid kit and two more bottles of wine. Cass tilted her head.

"Have I lost a lot of blood, or do you seem to think we need *this much alcohol* at 11p.m. for two people?"

"I asked for one. The second one is a gift from the management. They apologise for the inconvenience and do hope you'll consider staying with them again in future."

"I will not." Cass got to work putting a proper treatment on her wound, which was not nearly as bad as it first seemed. She heard the distinctive sound of a screw-top bottle opening. "Look out, a classy gentlemen has entered the room."

Pretty soon it was midnight, and they were finishing another bottle, lying next to each other, crowded onto the double bed. Much of that time had been spent in silence, or with Cass repeatedly denying his requests to see his phone, or with Cass explaining and re-explaining the differences between government and Parliament, or with Mike making fun of every little thing about himself, or gallows humour about his crumbling marriage that made Cass extremely uncomfortable.

But by the end of their second bottle of the night, with one more to go, he felt like he'd try to move past all that and into an actual conversation.

"So. Tattoos. You keep those to yourself."

"I do," she deadpanned. "I suppose that's over when the photos get released."

"I'm sorry."

It got quiet again. Mike figured he'd give it another go.

"So do you have kids?"

Cass snorted. "Fock no! Ha! First of all, how old do you think I am?"

He looked her up and down. "37?"

"Christ, bang on. Has she told you? You already knew that."

"I have literally never heard of you until today." Cass's face fell, even as she'd clearly tried to hide it. "How long have you two been friends?"

"We met at a cocktail party I'd say, two years ago, maybe three? Now we're thick as thieves."

"So right after the election."

"God, you're right, it was yes, she'd just been elected to her first term and I was on my second."

"Your second term? So you were, what, 24 when you were elected? That seems unlikely!"

Cass cackled. "Oh, I was elected in a by-election. My first term was around 6 months. Then I had to get re-elected. Honestly humiliating. What if I'd lost?"

"What's a by—"

She put her finger to her lips and made a *shhhhhhh-ing* sound. "No more civics lessons for tonight, please. Take a course!"

Mike shrunk back. He took a gulp of wine and they sat quietly for a bit. "So, husband? Boyfriend?"

She rubbed her eyes impatiently, as if waiting for some unseen force to please fix this conversation or get her out of it. "I'm gaaaaay, Mike. As my ex put it, my big ex, I'm a huge disaster gay. I am single, I am unmarried, I am unattached. I cannot possibly convey the depths of my dysfunction to a straight man, so let's mooooooove on." Mike looked over in fascination, the kind of hot-faced, liquid courage-y fascination that comes when you're stuck in a room and don't really care if you bother people.

"What is that? A disaster gay? Why are you that?"

Cass groaned loudly and tossed her head back. "Miiiike, pleaaaaase. We're not friieennnnds. I do not shaaaare this part of my life with yooooou." He nodded and turned back to staring at the blank, oddly-textured wall, where no television was hanging. She finished her glass of wine and immediately turned to the nightstand and started pouring another. She kept facing away from him. "I get it wrong." Mike smirked and looked back at her.

"You what?"

She turned around and flung her arms open broadly, splashing wine about.

"I get it wrong okay! I'm always wrong! I fuck up, I hit on my straight friends, I ruin friendships. I uh, uh," she gestured to him, "you know."

Mike nodded and grimaced. "I mean, I've always said to Beth—"

"—Mike! Don't weigh in!"

"Sorry."

She flapped her hands, continuing to spill as she shouted. "My life isn't pride parades and glitter cannons, nobody's sauntering up to me wearing a rainbow pin and holding out their phone number. My move is to spend a whole night hitting on someone right up until I go to get us another round and come back to see her arm around her boyfriend who's just arrived." She'd barely had enough breath to get it all out.

Mike tried to process this all as quick as he could. "God. That *is* a disaster." She shoved him.

"Oi, it is! It's a fucking Shakespearean tragedy!" Her voice had ascended to an exciting new octave. She threw her finger in his face. "Don't you fucking repeat any of this, by the way. This is not Cass the MP, this is Cass's personal life."

"You should honestly put all this on your campaign flyer.

I'm happy to design it for you." Everything Mike said was now through barely stifled laughter. Cass's face was beet red. She anxiously clutched her wine glass. "I don't get it though, why can't you just use apps? Aren't there apps for this exact thing?"

"I can't go on the bloody apps, I'm a public figure! My profile would leak immediately!"

"So? You don't want people to know you're gay? You can't *possibly* be the only gay member of Parliament. And most people are totally fine with—"

"—What? No, there's loads! I'm not closeted, you bellend! I'm in ParliOUT! I've walked in the London pride parade! I'm just a weirdo, that's what I hide. I hide all of me. I don't know. I feel weird. MPs aren't allowed to be weird. I have to meet people privately in safe spaces. And it's just all suits and sensible heels and terrible banter and jokes about housing policy. Everyone has their normal person masks on the whole time, forever. My life is a masquerade ball that never ends." She let out an exasperated sigh and flopped back against the headboard. "I just want to pretend to be someone else, but that someone else is me, and I'm the someone else. You know?" Mike had a slight frown. He didn't know.

"I'm sorry. That sounds complicated."

Cass nodded. "Yeah. Well, thanks. Thank you." She raised her glass to him and took a sip, and he did likewise. "Just, listen, okay. Remember. You promised to try. To be there for her. When this all comes out. Which might be in the morning. I know it's proper roiling to hear this from me. I'm the last person you probably want to hear or see at all. But she means a lot to me and I fucked everything up. I can't be there for her. She made a mistake, that's all. You promised to try."

Mike stared at the glass in his hand for a while, then nodded. "I did."

———

THE NEXT MORNING Mike was startled awake by the phone on the desk above him. Not a mobile phone, but an actual phone in the room itself. Surely the last bastion of landline telephones was now hotel rooms. He pulled himself off the floor where'd been sleeping and answered it, croaking out a groggy, "Hello?"

"Cassandra Cooper?"

He peeked over the top of the bed. She wasn't visible, but he saw the bathroom light on. She'd ducked in there to take a call at some point before the sun had come up.

"She's in the bathroom." The person on the other end hung up. Mike shrugged and dropped it back on the receiver. The bathroom door flung open.

"Mike?"

"Yeah, I'm up."

"I'll let you watch this."

"Watch what?"

"Your wife is about to be on television, it turns out."

Mike sat transfixed on the bed, staring at Cass's laptop perched on the desk. Through his sleep-crusted eyes he could see his wife appearing on morning TV. Typically he would have worked hard to not see this – not just when his wife was on, but any time – such was his revulsion. But after a long, restless night asleep on the floor, in this bizarre sequestration, he figured he'd take Cass up on her offer to finally show him what was happening.

For her bit, she had retreated to the bathroom some time

around 5a.m., and had been on some sort of war room Teams call ever since. He could make out vague snippets if he tried, but of course he tried not to try, due to fear of retaliation. He still didn't have his phone, after all. She'd start taking his fingers next.

The bottom of the screen was a good indicator of the weight of what had happened next. "ROGUE MINISTER EXPLAINS HERSELF: Elizabeth Marsh MP appears after yesterday's Commons calamity sends government scrambling." None of this sounded particularly good, but he had a hard time focusing on what she was saying. He was still so angry. Why had she left him to this treatment? Why had she not gotten in touch with him to say she was okay? Why was this the first he was seeing her?

The presenter, Mahmoud Osman, was the BBC's go-to morning political wonk. Mike had gathered this from years of hearing his wife curse his name from the other room. He was sat comfortably opposite her on a large orange sofa, and the screen behind them was a collage of irritatingly bright newspaper front pages.

"These are a few of the headlines you've made this morning. LIZ BITES THE HAND THAT FEEDS US ALL. WORKS BILL STUCK IN THE MARSH. MARSH LEADS INSURRECTION AS CORRUPT TORIES SELF IMMOLATE. Fair to say you've made quite a name for yourself overnight?" Every headline accompanied by an unflattering photo of Elizabeth, usually a blurry still from a video.

"I can only agree, though that was certainly not my intention."

"But you understand why people think this was an attention seeking ploy. Here's a message sent in earlier, and remember you can send those in yourself through our app. 'I've been out of work for six months now after redundancies at my firm. Universal Credit can't come close to covering food for myself and my two children. I've sent over 700 job applications and not a single call. And now the minister for Jobs is advocating against her own jobs bill in some sort of political gamesmanship. It's beyond a shambles. This government is criminally negligent.' And that's from Thomas in Kent. Thanks Thomas for your message. What do you say to Thomas?"

"I'd say we hear you. And I personally apologise. As I've said, as I've been saying, this is a crisis unlike any we've seen in our lifetimes. And we won't apologise for turning over every stone in our search for solutions to deliver for the British people. And we won't apologise for moving as quickly as we possibly can. And sometimes moving quickly means you make a mess."

"You've certainly made a mess here. Can we look at the original allegation – that the government has been meeting in private with a major corporation, one in particular, and that they've been personally shaping the text of the jobs bill. Now yesterday you said that was in fact true. The allegation and your subsequent admission both seem to have caught your party completely on the back foot. My sources were describing party leaders as apoplectic, talking of meltdowns and panic in back channels, pretty consistently calling for your head."

"I think your sources may be overstating things a bit, Mahmoud."

"One source quoted in the Daily Mail described a warlike footing, emergency meetings about how to play this into the wee hours. You weren't confirmed as a guest for us until about an hour ago."

"I will tell you we're interested in getting this right. If we need to put the work in, to make sure that happens, none of us are afraid to pull an all-nighter. I'd remind you we are the youngest cabinet in British history."

"So tell me, then, really. What is going on? Has the government colluded with this major corporation, I can't use the name, nor should you, due to the nature of the allegation of course. But here, a day on from the urgent question. What's the real story?"

Elizabeth cleared her throat. Mike leaned forward, staring at her on the tiny laptop screen. She felt so far away, her voice thin and artificial, coming out of the terrible speaker. It was like he was watching a stranger, just another infuriating politician spreading lies on morning telly. The past two days had been eye-opening for him, seeing what his wife actually did for a living. He was heartbroken. He was scared for her.

"I can tell you," Elizabeth answered, "that we are indeed working with Concentra. Very closely in fact, to ensure that the day this bill passes, it is an oven-ready solution, a shovel-ready solution, as Concentra will be ready to begin putting Brits to work on projects for Britain. Day one. The mechanisms of government will be ready, our civil service will be ready, and Concentra will be ready. And we recognise our determination on this and the speed with which we're moving has opened a chink in our political armour, and the opposition have found it. But I'm here today to bring this appeal straight to the public. Straight to Thomas in Kent. Straight to all of you. Trust us and we will put you back to work."

Mike was overwhelmed, once again. Because he actually felt a stirring. What she was saying made sense. It was efficient, it was necessary. And it was the antithesis of the molasses-like bureaucracy that had exacerbated the problem to begin with. But it was the exact opposite of her position on this for so long. All those long nights arguing, shouting at him, at her laptop, at the wall.

The presenter seemed happy with that. "There you have it. Thank you very much Elizabeth Marsh, minister for Works and Pensions. One final question before I let you go. Can you speak to those who *don't* trust you? Both in the public, of course, and to your opposition, perhaps specifically Alastair Mitchell from Labour who had some very strong words for you yesterday, referring to this jobs programme as, well, as tantamount to slavery."

Elizabeth laughed quite hard. It was a very rehearsed laugh, Mike noticed. "Well, most people I know in Labour have quite a flair for the dramatic. Alastair isn't immune. My dear friend Cassandra Cooper even used to be an amateur actor. Maybe that's quite common on the opposite benches."

"Oh?"

"Yes, she did some Shakespeare, I believe. But I shouldn't talk out of school. I'll leave that to you to look into if you like."

The presenter had an awkward smirk. "Right! Well, once again thank you, Elizabeth Marsh."

"Oh, fuck that!" The bathroom door burst open and Cass stormed out in a fury. She threw her phone angrily and it bounced onto the bed. Mike sat frozen. "Fuck her!" She was livid. Shaking. Her face a bright red. She slammed the laptop shut. "Your wife is a nightmare, she's a focking nightmare."

She was wagging her finger in Mike's face, very close to him. He leaned back with a blank expression.

"I'm not her."

"I bloody know you're not her! Why am I even here? Why was I even doing any of this for her?" She had started throwing all her things into her bag wildly, plastic and metal scratching and slamming around inside it.

"Can I get my—"

She snatched his phone out of the bag and flung it at him. He caught it, only just. It was dead. "Perfect."

"I'm going home to shower and change before I go get my bollocking from about a dozen people." She grabbed her phone and flicked through it quickly, then let out a groan. "They sent someone to get us and they're saying there's loads of media downstairs."

"What?"

"Media? The press? They must know I'm here, or that both of us are here."

"How?" Mike's voice was full of desperation. He just wanted to be under a duvet. Away from all of these people. Away from everything.

"I don't know, Mike. Sometimes front desk clerks sell you out, sometimes someone spots you randomly and posts about it online, sometimes they just start calling around and get lucky."

Mike went white as a sheet. He nodded. "That's wild."

"It is Mike, it's wild. Come on, let's go. Car's waiting."

"How can we go? You just said…"

"It's not the SAS, Mike. It's some blokes with cameras. You'll be fine."

As soon as the elevator doors opened, he heard the commotion. Cameras began snapping, lights flashing. People calling out to Cass. Some polite questions, some just shouting her name, some shouting some rather offensive insults about her apparent prior attempt at a career. She smiled and nodded as she walked, but said nothing. Mike was not as adept at this, having mostly stayed off the radar. Nobody really cared about the non-political husband of the jobs minister. Until of course, they did. He froze like a deer in headlights.

Cass turned back and saw him just standing there, a camera or two trained on him. She turned and leaned back, then grabbed his hand and pulled him along with her. He tried to keep up lest he get dragged, and by the time they reached the car he felt like he was emulating her moves pretty well.

The door to the small black car shut behind them, leaving them sat in silence in the back seat, behind mercifully tinted glass. Cass let out a deep sigh.

Mike looked over at her. "What now?"

She shook her head. "Now their works bill will pass." He stared out the window as the car pulled away.

"Right, but what now for us?"

EIGHT

CRUSADERS OF STAR LEAGUE

July 2041.
Maida Vale, West London.

IT WAS MOVING DAY, and Gemma had forgotten to set her alarm.

She woke up in an uncomfortable heap on the floor, having sold all her furniture bit by bit over the past month. She'd read online that the hardest thing to do in your first couple years as a "connie," aka conscript, was to get into a financial rhythm where you were saving enough to afford "luxes," aka luxury goods, aka liquor.

Her new friend Bartender Kevin at The Fox had been helping her get a grip on her new situation, which involved a crash course in where the modern discourse was happening. In her day she'd been as active as one must be on stuff like Instagram, or Reddit, or TikTok. But in their new era of digital safety, digital sovereignty, whatever the fuck it was called, it was just way too much of a hassle to access foreign apps. And by the time that had happened, she had a staff who was keeping up with all of it for her. A staff she was sorely missing now.

But over a few beverages, Kevin had talked her through the basics. Some Brits still used those big American and Chinese apps, but the only people who went to the trouble of doing the identity checks, requesting the licence, getting them unblocked, etc. were mostly older people (like herself) and mostly to look at older stuff that was on them already (like Queen music videos). All the new stuff had necessarily moved "on island," to home-grown British apps like Understairs, Popround and Telly. As an American, but one not eager to offend Gemma, he explained he felt these apps were "um, fine," but they were succeeding in his view mostly due to legislation and the massive government subsidies they'd gotten.

(The two she did know already were Linkup, a dating app, and Shag. "That one's for sex," he'd helpfully pointed out when he spotted it on her home screen. She'd nodded politely.)

Gemma tried to sit up but her back cried out, her legs stiff, everything generally feeling not-great. "Right, a lie-in then." She opted for laying flat on her back on the knotty wooden floor, the rugs having gone along with the bed yesterday afternoon. It all hurt, but it was less painful than getting up. Kevin had offered to let her sleep at his, but she was pretty sure he lived in student accommodation. Things hadn't gotten that dire yet, had they? She'd never seen him outside the pub. She wasn't convinced he even existed outside the pub.

She reached for her phone, knocking over several empty beer bottles, and quickly dismissed all her notifications before she could even read them. Instead she popped back into Understairs, which was a sort-of hip, altish discussion app that reminded her of Reddit. She'd joined a few of the recommend spaces when she signed up – Oldies (for music from the 2000s), AcousticGuitar (for covers of music from the 2000s), NormalIsland (UK news), BloodyBloody (British-themed horror stories) – but the one she fixated on was Bunk-Life. This was people talking about their lives in the worker housing at various work sites around the country, including hers out in Wales. As moving day approached she'd become increasingly anxious and desperate. She'd hoped reading the daily goings-on would help calm her nerves, show her that it was just like any other job, in any other small, middle-of-nowhere Welsh town.

What she got was anything but. Every time she opened it, she was met with an onslaught of grim post titles.

"[Telly] [Howto] How to get rid of bed bugs in your bunk – easy way (free!)"

"[Question] Rations cut for excess tardiness what are my rights?"

"[Sheffield] [Footie] Weekly 5-a-side looking for new player! (our GK died)"

"[Rant] Denied housing upgrade for third f-ing time"

"[Help] Converting my credits to pounds, how?"

"[AITA] Stole bunkmate's lux voucher for revenge but now they've filed a grievance"

She doom-scrolled every last one of them, absorbing all the knowledge as best she could, which wasn't easy. Rations? Credits? 5-a-side? What the fuck? These people seemed deeply unhappy, and they seemed to be living quite desperately in some sort of fake nonsense world. But at least they had each other. Or so claimed user mancmonk, in his post:

"[Motivation] At least we have each other"

It had 6 upvotes and 439 downvotes. She gave it one more upvote, then decided to quite literally pick herself up off the floor. It was nearly 11a.m., and her train was at 1p.m.

She'd promised Kevin she'd say goodbye, but now she was having second thoughts. Human connection, not really her forte. He was just a kid. It was a good lesson to teach him, not to trust the promises of strange unemployed women who day-drink. If it wasn't her it'd just be someone else. So that was a heart she'd break.

There were all her former colleagues, whom she'd mostly lost touch with the moment they took away her work phone. She didn't know whether it was odd that she'd never taken their personal numbers, or connected with them on any other service. It was a healthy distance. Work life balance. That's what she'd told herself, anyway. But now she had no way to reach them. Probably for the best, though. A few of them were still at the office no doubt, helping close it down, or helping run the "streamlined operation" on behalf of the new owners. Not somewhere she'd like to see again, if they'd even let her up the lifts. Pass.

She walked toward the tube station dragging her rolling bag behind her, duffel bag over her shoulder, and the thoughts of dread gave way to a sudden, intense loneliness. She was leaving the city she'd known her entire life. Aside from a few overseas dalliances, she'd never lived anywhere else. Birth, childhood, primary school, university, street rat failed indie musician, young gun session producer, all the way up to industry executive. And now she struggled, at her age, to think of a single person to go visit before she moved away.

"Fuck," she muttered to herself. "I need a drink."

There was certainly time for one, maybe two. But she

wasn't paying train station pint prices, then loitering near the goddamn vending machine sipping it. So sad, those people. Worse that there wasn't a single actual pub left in or around King's Cross.

Kevin perked up as she burst through the door to The Fox.

"Kevin, it's your lucky day. I've come to say goodbye."

"Honestly I assumed you'd flake."

"And miss seeing The Fox one last time? Who knows how long this place will survive without my patronage."

He'd already started pulling her usual. Better make it two, she'd said, as there's not much time. She had to be at the train station. They only provide one free ticket, she explained. If you missed it, well, you paid your own way.

Two pints became three, with a couple rounds of shots, and maybe a fourth. But she really had to go, she'd say, before she'd order one more. She had an envelope full of cash with her, the money she'd been putting aside, the money she'd made selling her furniture. Much more efficient than faffing around with her phone to pay every time.

She regaled Kevin with tales of life before all this, before her company's untimely demise, before she'd found herself sleeping on the floor of an empty flat. There was the time at the GRAMMYs where she'd misplaced her wallet and nearly gotten arrested trying to get back in. That time she threw up over the side of a helicopter getting across Manhattan. That time she let a stranger do blow off the back of the toilet while she threw up in the bowl. That time she'd spent an entire 90 minute meeting referring to some indie acoustic act as Nate Mathanson instead of Matt Nathanson. "Everyone was fucking hammered and coked up at the office back then," she'd pointed out. "It was just what we did."

A celebratory round of shots, she said, and Kevin dutifully poured them a couple tequilas. "These are on me," he said as she went fishing for another tenner from her stash. "That money was supposed to be your emergency fund."

He's a good kid this Kevin, she thought as she made her way to the toilet. Maybe she'd be nice to him after all, take him back to hers. Show him a thing or two on the hardwood floor. It was so uncomfortably warm in the toilet at The Fox though, and just generally unclean, and her leather skirt was a huge fucking pain in the ass to deal with. As she tried to get it off to use the toilet, she was hit with a wave of nausea. She hurled the last few pints back out onto the floor, pure liquid, not a trace of food. Her stomach heaved and tightened, her throat burned. More vomit came as her legs went, her knees landing in the pool on the floor. She grabbed the metal bar on the wall and tried to pull herself up as she dry heaved. Her eyes watered and she heaved uncontrollably, coughing and wheezing. Tears started to run down her face.

"Everything okay in there?" Kevin shouted through the door to the disabled toilet.

"No," she bellowed in response through tears and searing pain. Her nose and throat burned like hell. She started sobbing and sat on the floor, letting go of the bar. She stared at the back of the door and played with the graphite bands that hung on a chain around her neck, clutching them tightly in her hand. Kevin banged on it from the outside.

"Gemma? Open up please?"

She shook her head but said nothing. He knocked a few more times.

"Gemma, are you hurt? Do you need help?"

Snot and tears ran down her face, her eyes a smeary black. She sniffled hard.

"Kevin, I'm scared. I can't do this." Her voice was shaky, her words slurred and slow. She struggled to get them out through the tears. "I don't have any friends here, I don't have anyone, my parents are gone, nobody even cares that I'm leaving, nobody's going to care about me at this new place they're all so young, and it sounds like a fucking nightmare." She couldn't stop sobbing. "I have nothing. I have nothing. God, I'm so old. I miss my parents." She tried to wipe off some of the tears with the back of her palm. Her throat gurgled as she breathed. "I miss—"

"Gemma? I'm opening the door, okay?"

"What?"

The handle lowered slowly and the door started to creak open. He peeked in just a bit. "Are you decent?"

"It's locked!" She croaked out in confusion.

"Gemma, it's a bar. You think we can't open a locked toilet door? Someone barricades themselves in the handicapped stall at least once a night. Can I come in?"

"Go on then. Come see what you see."

He pushed it open a bit more and looked inside, seeing her sat on the floor in her own sick. "Oh no, miss. You've done a number here, and all before 1 o'clock." He reached down and picked her up from the floor, supporting himself on the metal bar with one hand, his other arm around her waist. She was drenched.

"I'm so tired." She closed her eyes, still being held up by Kevin's arm.

She jolted awake suddenly, feeling like she was falling but catching herself on the bed. She was in a room she didn't recognise, barely lit by sunlight streaming in through a gap in the blackout curtains. Plain white walls all around her, with a cheap little desk across from the bed, a plain blue task chair tucked under it. She had no idea where she was, or what was happening. Her back chafed against what seemed to be a couple of beach towels.

"Uh. Hello?!"

The door opened almost immediately, blinding her. "Fuck!" She covered her eyes with her arm.

"How are you feeling?"

"Kevin? Are we at the pub?"

"You passed out. I didn't know who to call or where you lived, and I couldn't exactly put you in a cab to the train station like that... so I brought you here." She kept her arm on her face and let out a groan.

"Student accommodation." She sat up. He gingerly offered her a glass of water, but she shook her head and gestured for it to go on the desk. "My fucking train. Kevin, I'm so fucked. What time is it?"

He looked at his watch. "It's just now 6 p.m."

"FUCK!" She shook her head a few times in disbelief. She'd missed the goddamn free train. And it wasn't exactly like she was going to Cardiff, or some other place in Wales that people wanted to go. (Surely there must be at least one other.) There was one train, twice a week, from London out to the nuclear plant. It went out Monday, then it came back that night, and that was it 'til Friday. "FUUUUUUCK!" She screamed. Kevin jumped and grabbed the door frame reflexively.

"Do you... need anything? I have some food, well, some snacks. I can make you something? A sandwich?" She laughed and looked down at herself. She was in a state.

"Kevin, I'm disgusting." He grimaced and looked down at his feet, nodding. "Can I maybe use your shower?"

She came walking out of the bathroom a short time later as

he watched TV on the sofa. Kevin had apologised profusely that her bags were locked up at the pub, because he couldn't really carry them *and* prop her up all the way here. So with an exaggerated flourish she swept her arms across herself, showing off her borrowed outfit – a baggy white t-shirt under a blue University of West London hoodie, extremely loose-fitting, too-long jeans cinched up with a belt and rolled up cuffs, and bright white tube socks. Her dark hair was soggy wet, hanging down behind her. Her makeup gone, the bags under her eyes quite pronounced. "Could you have given me a more stereotypical set of clothes to wear? I look like we just fucked in a romantic comedy."

He shrugged. "You look fine?" He picked her chain of rings up off the coffee table, and she quickly snatched them from his hand and tossed them back around her neck, tucking them away under the hoodie.

"Oh you would say that. Christ, thanks mate. I feel gorgeous." She flopped onto the sofa next to him and resumed her pre-shower groaning. "I missed my fucking train, Kevin."

"You did." He was staring straight ahead at the TV, watching some animated thing Gemma didn't recognise.

"The next one's not til the end of the week. And I can't bloody afford it."

"How much is it?"

"It doesn't matter! Unless it's, I don't know, ten pounds. That was it, Kevin. The emergency fund? That was the whole Gemma fund. That was it. I have to fucking figure this out."

"Why would you spend so much on drinks if you..." He glanced over at her and saw the fury in her eyes, then let his sentence trail off. "Listen. I'll drive you. I looked, it's like 5 hours each way. Not close, but it's doable. We can go tomorrow morning."

"Are you..." She sounded incredulous, like she assumed he must be screwing with her. He shook his head.

"Totally fine."

"Christ."

She looked down at the table and saw the glass of water had been relocated, sat neatly on a coaster in front of her. She picked it up and took a sip, then guzzled it all down. Kevin watched out of the corner of his eye and nodded. She let out a huge sigh and crossed her arms over the gigantic hoodie, nestling down into it.

"So the rings," Kevin asked. "You've always got them on. Are you secretly married?"

"Don't pry." Kevin pursed his lips as Gemma kept facing straight ahead. "What's this then on the telly?"

"So, this is Crusaders of Star League," he said stoically, recovering from the knock back. "I don't know if you had it here. It's made to look really serious like a science fiction drama, but it's really funny. I watched it when I was a kid but I get the jokes a lot more now."

"I'm almost fifty years old," she deadpanned.

"Oh, there's no maximum age." His mouth curled into a smirk. He ticked the volume up a few notches.

The glow of the TV lit the room as they watched, Kevin letting out his loud American guffaws near-constantly and Gemma letting out a small chuckle occasionally (though mostly rolling her eyes). Kevin disappeared to the kitchen at one point, returning with some extremely basic cheese sandwiches and packets of crisps for them to eat. Gemma would interject every so often with a question about the plot, or something she'd misheard, or that she needed him to pause it while she ran to the bathroom.

They eventually fell asleep, laying across opposite arms of the sofa, just before the credits rolled on the second season finale.

NINE

JEWEL OF THE MIDLANDS

The next day.
On the motorway south of Birmingham, England.

THE DRIVE to Wales was a lot longer than Gemma expected, partly from a load of road closures and partly from the anxiety. Kevin did his best to stay calm about the situation, but she got the impression he was a bit anxious as well. She'd hounded him about two hours in as to whether he had somewhere to be, some sort of class, or work, plans? He swore it was nothing. He'd wiped his diary clean for this.

"Hmm. Kevin, I worry you're a loser."

Kevin smiled. "I'm new here! I don't have many local friends. Is it that surprising that I'd have a whole day free? I feel like even people with friends have whole days free."

"I suppose," she said dubiously. "Who are these friends?" She was squirming in her seat, the seatbelt chafing, her muscles all sore for some reason.

"Well, there's the other people who work at the bar."

"Those are your co-workers. They're not friends. They'll drop you in a heartbeat the moment they find a new job."

"Okay... well, there's David from my program. Him and I get along pretty well. He's come over once or twice."

"Classmate," Gemma interjected. Kevin sighed impatiently.

"These are the only two things I do, Gemma. I work and I go to school." Gemma made an 'ick' noise and shuddered.

"Christ, don't say 'go to school,' you make me feel like a cradle snatcher."

He stared straight ahead. She looked over at him, then out the windscreen. They were once again stuck in a massive tailback, this time somewhere near Banbury. Gemma shook her head again. "We should've been in Birmingham by now."

"I guess this is why everyone takes the train," Kevin added unhelpfully.

"Do they," Gemma erupted. "Why's there so much bloody traffic then, Kevin?!"

It fell quiet between them. Rain pattered against the roof of Kevin's tiny blue Vauxhall Corsa. Gemma squirmed and rubbed her shoulder. The seatbelt slid back and forth across the skin on her shoulder every time she squirmed, leaving it a bit raw. Kevin sat in the driver's seat stiff as a board, hands at 10 and 2 on the wheel. They could train a self-driving cab off him. Bloody algorithmic precision, including the shit-tier banter. You'd pay it extra if it would agree to let you out early and release you from the misery.

"What's a cradle snatcher? Is that like, a kidnapper?" Kevin's eyes scanned over to Gemma curiously. The boy was never above asking what something meant. Americans and their total lack of shame.

"It's when an... forget it." Gemma, on the other hand.

"It's when a what?"

She scratched at her seatbelt burn and demurred. He looked over at her, since they were fully stopped at this point.

"Come on," he insisted. "We've got nowhere to be."

"You'd call it a... 'cooo-gerrrrr'," she exaggerated in his accent for maximum effect.

"Ohhh. Oh! I mean. Was I flirting? I didn't mean to."

"No, no, it's fine, we can move swiftly on." She made a quick little sweep gesture with her hand then stared out the side window.

"Were you?"

"Swiftly on!"

Kevin grimaced, then resumed his stoic motoring protocol. Gemma exhaled through pursed lips and rolled her head around. Not even to fucking Birmingham yet.

Another hour or so passed before they finally had to pull over for a charge near Walsall, north of Birmingham. Kevin leapt out and immediately ran to the pumps, with the swiftness of a man with a lot going on.

Gemma's body was in shambles. She grumpily popped the door open and got out, then tried to find the sweet spot where she could have a good stretch without somehow ruining the next two days of her life by making it worse. She threw her arms in the air, spread her legs a bit, grabbed one wrist with the other and slowly pulled her arm. The relief came, a warmth radiating through her muscles, the pain subsiding. "Oh Christ that's good," she whispered to herself as she bent forward, stretching down toward her toes.

Her orgasmic stretch session was interrupted by Kevin, who needed to cover off some critical Trip Logistics. She frowned and whimpered like a puppy.

They'd set out at 10am, Kevin said, planning to get there

by around 5 p.m. at the latest, getting Kevin back into London by 10-11 p.m. that night. It was now 2:30 p.m. and they hadn't even made it half way. Not only was he never getting back to London tonight, the jury was out on whether they'd even make it to Trawsfynydd.

Gemma snickered. Kevin looked agitated as he asked, "What?"

"Mate, don't try to pronounce it. I just don't think you have it in you."

"How is it pronounced?"

Gemma just laughed and rolled her eyes. "Anyway."

"Tell me, so I'll learn. Do you know?" He had an earnestness in these moments that she found so sweet. But outwardly, she could only cackle.

"Yes?" She hit him with the classic indignation. How dare he?

"Well?"

Gemma blanked him.

He studied her closely, leaning in a bit. Finally he shook his head. "You don't know."

"Course I don't bloody know. You ever hear me saying it?"

Kevin's eyes darted up and around. "No, I guess I haven't." She smiled and patted his cheek in what an observer might find to be a condescending manner.

"Just for that, you're paying for the charge." She smirked and walked away, going back to her stretching. Kevin stared down at the lead sticking out of his car. He looked at the screen on the pump, currently set to 'PREMIUM CHARGE: £2.00/KWH'. He winced and tapped 'BASIC CHARGE: 50p/KWH'. The estimated time remaining changed from 15 minutes to nearly 4 hours.

"This'll be a while," he shouted over to her. "Must've been really dead." Gemma moaned obnoxiously.

They locked up the car, leaving it to rest while they wandered the streets of Walsall. Almost immediately Kevin had started taking photos with his phone. A post box. A derelict Wimpy's. A bin. It all fascinated him. Gemma kept getting a wider and wider lead on him as she poked mindlessly at her phone, ignoring her surroundings, trying to figure out if they were near a pub where they could get some food and a couple of pints.

She finally got fed up when she noticed him on the other side of the road from her.

"Kevin, mate, you have to keep up." He looked up from what were presumably a bunch of photos of Keep Left signs.

"Sorry, I've never been anywhere in England except for London."

She scoffed. "Welcome to Walsall, jewel of the West Midlands. They got a big Tesco in like 2009 and they're still riding that high. Think the Queen came up to unveil it." Casting her eyes around, all she could see was the same terraced housing, flat brick new-builds mixed with crumbling Victorian facades and paved-over gardens you find literally anywhere in England. Poor kid. Imagine finding this even the least bit fascinating. This cultural wasteland.

Kevin smiled as he finally joined her on her side of the street. "I enjoy it. I know you've probably seen it all your whole life. I know I wouldn't find it interesting giving a tour of the suburbs of Cincinnati."

She sighed. "Sorry, no you're right. There are some hidden gems here. I know a great spot on the high street to get our mobiles stolen."

"Where?"

She had a crazed look in her eye. But he was still being so bloody earnest. It was shorting out her brain. She put her hand gently on his elbow to lead him. "Come on love, let's find a pub."

It was a long, grim walk. Gemma had explained they could catch a bus into the city centre, but quickly gave up after they passed the third bus stop with signs explaining that it was no longer in use. They passed a large park full of open green space and a handful of beautiful Ash trees. She pictured herself with a few pint cans, sat under a tree in the shade, shielded from the breeze by a thin cardigan. But the park was completely full of tents, temporary fencing all around the outer edge, with some government signage about something or other, asking people not to enter.

Kevin seemed to avert his gaze as he passed it and made no comment, instead just looking down at his phone. Gemma stopped and looked in. She could hear the chatter and goings-on of what sounded like dozens of people. A whole community, just living on the green. Washing was hung out to dry near to where she stood, just on the other side of the fencing. She made eye contact with a young girl, maybe 9 or 10 years old. Gemma put her hand up cautiously and waggled her fingers in a wave. The girl gave a huge wave back in return, her face lit up with a big smile.

She looked up and down the park. There were so many tents, so many people. She turned around and looked down a nearby street. It, too had the temporary fencing, this time blocking the road itself. Beyond it, more rows of tents. Neatly organised and spaced. All pushed right up to the fronts of the rows of terraced homes. Were people living in those as well? How did that work, she wondered? She knew of a few parts of Central London that were essentially no-go zones, but she'd never really known what it was like elsewhere. She'd never really thought about it.

A hand landed on her shoulder. "Hey!" She jolted, horror-struck, bringing one hand up to free her shoulder and the other thrusting straight out ahead of her to push whoever it was back. "Holy shit!" Kevin shouted and jumped back a step.

Gemma was in a full panic. "Jesus fucking Christ! Kevin, don't do that!" He put his arm around her waist and started to walk her forward. She protested. "What the hell!"

"We need to go, it's not safe." His voice was soft, but stern.

She nodded. "Okay, okay. Let's go."

A short walk away was The Pig & Whistle, which Kevin said was described in reviews as having a "laid back vibe" and "all your favorites on tap." (She could just hear the missing 'u' in favourite when he said it.) They slid into a booth to one side. She spied the two most common cask ales in the country, so that bit seemed right. The vibe was less laid back and more stereotypically depressing, as loads of men sat quietly in front of fruit machines, gambling away with their pints in hand, ignoring each other.

Kevin popped up at the table with a couple pints of Carling, unprompted. Gemma smiled.

"You're back in the good books, Kevin." A clink and a sip, then she collapsed backwards into her side of the booth. "This town's a bit shit yeah?"

"Those camps, full of illegals. I'm surprised they allow it to get this bad."

Gemma shook her head in disbelief. "Kevin. 'Illegals'?

Really?" Severe disappointment rose up from deep within her. Never had she gotten the 'ick' so quickly from someone she'd otherwise liked so much.

"Sorry." He looked instantly regretful. "I don't mean, you know. Illegal immigrants. They're just all probably dodging the work camps." Gemma just stared at him from behind her pint on the table. He cleared his throat. "The... envelope. You know how that all works."

She pulled a face and shook her head, then put her lips on the rim of her glass and stared up at him. She was fighting hard to not feel anything, to let him explain himself. She could practically see the flop sweat forming.

"The envelope," he continued, his voice cracking a bit. "It's essentially a prison sentence. It's not really a job offer. I was reading about this. It's not legal to be unemployed here. They just tell you to show up at the assigned facility, and then you do labor, and they house and feed you. But if you just refuse to go, or if you go and refuse to work... By law, prisoners aren't required to do labor. It just means they don't get paid. So then they'd just have to stick you in a regular prison. But there isn't enough room. So, I, uh..."

Gemma had put her hands flat on the table and was sliding forward, pushing her beer along toward Kevin, until she was stretched out lying face down on it. Kevin picked up the beer and put it safely to one side before it could topple off the edge and spill all over him. She pounded her head against the table a few times.

Kevin looked extremely confused. "What's uh... what's happening?"

"I'm a prisoner?" Her face was still pressed against the table, her words muffled, barely intelligible.

"Only technically." He pat her back a couple of times. She started to sob. Her back heaved, the sound mostly inaudible, just the occasional laboured breathing. He rubbed his hand along her back rather clumsily. "Gemma, it's okay. It's all going to be okay."

She let out one loud sniffle, then sat up sharply. Her face red and tear-soaked, her eyes puffy, indentations from the table running across her cheeks and forehead. Kevin went to open his mouth, but she shook her head and whispered "no," then nodded to her beer. He put it back on the table in front of her and in a swift motion she picked it up, tilted it back and downed it in one.

He once again went to talk. She slapped her hand down on the table, got up and headed toward the bar. The bartender, a plainly-dressed man in his mid-50s, looked concerned. He gestured over to their table. "He just dump you in my pub?" He had a gruff, but warm, Midlands accent. She let out a quick giggle.

"Christ, no. What? No, no. I just found out I'm going to prison."

The bartender nodded. "This one's on me, bab."

One round turned into a few, as Kevin eventually surrendered and asked the bartender if there was anywhere in town they could stay the night. "Got a couple rooms upstairs," came the answer, so they took one for what Kevin felt was a reasonable rate. (It wasn't, Gemma noted, but she kept it to herself in a rare moment of kindness.) They got one final round to bring upstairs, since Kevin was desperate to get back on the road early enough to miss whatever had ground traffic to a halt all day.

The room was dingy. Dirty white walls, a double bed

with just enough room to walk all the way around it, a wardrobe that had to be a hundred years old, a closet of a bathroom with a claustrophobic shower cubicle, sink and toilet stacked around a patch of tile barely big enough to stand in.

"Perfect," Gemma exclaimed as she walked in. Kevin heard that then followed in behind her, a real rollercoaster of expectations. She plopped hard onto the edge of the bed and set her pint down on the nightstand, kicking her shoes off and wriggling out of the oversized jeans she was still borrowing. Kevin neatly hung his jacket in the wardrobe and placed his shoes in the bottom. When he turned around she was propped up against the headboard in her panties and t-shirt, holding up her pint in a cheers.

"We have to be out by 6 a.m. 6:30 at the latest." He collected up her errant clothes and tucked them away neatly in the wardrobe as well, along with her suitcase, which he'd had to go fetch from the car out of an abundance of caution. She nodded.

"Bless you, taking care of me. I will absolutely fight you if you try to wake me up that early." She was being playful, but he knew she was also probably serious.

"Well, I can leave you here. You can start your new life in Walsall." She cackled her usual cackle, a mischievous grin on her face. "It's not Wall Saaaulll," she said, mocking his accent. "It's Walsall. Waawl Saawwl."

"Walsall." He gave it another go, but it sounded identical to his last attempt.

She rolled her eyes and sighed. "Come here, come here." She sat up cross-legged, then reached out and grabbed at him. He obediently joined, sitting cross-legged in front of her. "Say it like me." She looked him in the eye and pointed at her mouth. "Watch my mouth. Waawwll Saawwll."

"Walllll Sallll." The same again, just slower. She pressed her lips together and shook her head.

"Like this." She put her fingers on either side of his mouth. "Go on, go on." He tried to say "Walll Sallll," while she squeezed his mouth closed at the sides. She tittered. "It was better that time, I think."

He eked out a muffled "I'm hopeless," her hand still pushing his mouth shut. She chuckled again, putting her hands on his cheeks, stroking them a bit, feeling the coarseness of his five o'clock shadow. She ran her hands over it a few times.

"Oh," she whispered. Staring into his eyes, she pulled his face toward hers, kissing him gently on the lips. They both closed their eyes and lingered there for a moment, before she pulled away from him. "No."

He looked a bit stunned. She touched her lips with her fingers, her eyes darting down. "Sorry, I shouldn't have done that," she said. "I really shouldn't have done that. God, Kevin, I'm such a mess." He scooted himself a bit closer to her, putting one arm around her, laying his hand on her back. His other hand caressed her cheek. "Oh." She exhaled, opened her mouth and closed her eyes as Kevin's lips pressed against hers.

They had only been asleep for a few hours when the alarm went off. He'd followed through on his sadistic threat, it seemed, as the sound of gentle guitar coming from a tiny speaker filled the room at 4:45 a.m. Her head was killing her. Her mouth was so, so dry. She lay spread out across the bed, her legs entangled with Kevin's, him half on top of her. He slid off to one side and immediately lifted the duvet, ready to dive into his day. Annoyingly youthful. She reached out and put her arm around him, clawing him back into the bed. He complied and she immediately sidled over to him, spooning him and clutching him around the stomach.

He let out a conflicted sigh. She kissed his back a few times. "Just a few minutes. Please, I'm old. I'm barely alive."

He laughed. "You're not that old." His throat was raw, his voice lower than usual. She ran her fingers through his chest hair, then pawed at him a bit desperately. It was still nearly pitch black in the room, with a tiny bit of morning light creeping in along the sides of the curtain. She squeezed her body against his.

"Kevin. I don't want to go. I just want to be here." He tried to turn around and face her, but she squeezed him, sliding one leg between his. "I just want to be here just like this."

He was forced to face the window. "You have to go, though," he whispered. She eased up on him and sighed. He rolled over to face her, draping his arm around her side, running his hand up her back. "I'm so sorry." She pushed her lips into his, kissing him passionately, pressing herself against him as hard as she could.

The room was getting brighter by the minute. He stroked her head, looking her in the eyes. Suddenly he shifted and nudged her to roll over. She slid back against him, nestling in, his arm covering her chest, pulling her close. He kissed the back of her head.

"Gemma?" His voice was so soft now.

"Hey." She lay her arm on his, squeezing her chest with his hand.

"Will I see you again?" His voice cracked. His question was a mix of hope and dread. She closed her eyes and pushed back against him. They lay in silence, his head pressed against her back, kissing her. She felt his tears on her skin. She pulled the duvet down onto them hard, tucking them in.

They laid there together, embracing under the covers, until the sun became impossible to ignore.

TEN

EMO MILLENNIALS

June 2043.
Trafalgar Square, Central London.

ELIZABETH WAS JUST LEAVING their makeshift stage when she saw a bit of commotion at the back of the crowd. Someone had fallen to the ground, and Siobhan appeared to be helping them. She'd pushed her way through the throng as quickly as she could to see if she could help.

"Mike?"

Siobhan looked up. "You know him?"

Mike looked up from the ground to see his ex-wife standing a few feet away. He gave an incredibly awkward wave, revealing the bloody scrapes on his hand. "Hiiii, honey." Siobhan helped him to his feet.

The crowd pushed on in their modest hundreds, starting their march to Downing Street, signs waving. A chant of "CONSCRIPTION IS SLAVERY!" grew as they walked. Siobhan looked at Elizabeth with urgency in her eyes. Elizabeth nodded. "You go on" she said, handing Siobhan the megaphone she'd been using to address the rally. "I'll make sure he's okay. Not sure I'm much use in a march, anyway."

Siobhan looked concerned but nodded back. "Aye I'll head off, but all the press will be at that end, not this end. I hope yous can make it." She ran up a couple steps, grabbed the apple box and took off to join the march. And after that flurry of activity, Elizabeth and Mike were standing alone in Trafalgar Square. She threw her hands up and slapped her thighs.

"It's been what, ten years?" Mike decided to go first.

"Has it? Doesn't feel that long."

"I think it's closer to fifteen at this point."

"Ah." She assumed when she saw him that this would be awkward, but now, standing here, it didn't feel awkward so much as it felt like nothing at all. She stared at him and no feelings came to the surface. No reason to be awkward. He looked older, a bit heavier. He'd gone grey, but that had already started in his 30s. He was dressed terribly, but that'd also already started in his 30s. No wedding ring. And there was the matter of his being on the ground? "So, what happened? Someone bump into you?"

"Oh. No. I just got a little lightheaded."

"You still get panic attacks?"

"I don't know if that's what they are." She nodded sharply. Same old Mike. "Do you want to... should we grab a coffee? Before you—"

"—I do need to catch up with the march at some point."

He nodded. "Right, of course, of course." His tone was that of addressing an old university friend you accidentally ran into on the tube. Neither of you want to be doing this, but polite society demands it of you. And neither of you wants to be the one who explicitly says, *No, as it turns out, I thought I'd never see you again, and that seemed fine.*

"Of course, we could grab a coffee on the way. If you can walk with me."

"I could walk that way, I suppose. If you don't mind the distraction."

"It's no distraction."

"And you don't need to be at work?"

"Oh, I don't think I do that anymore."

Elizabeth tilted her head in surprise at that remark. "Oh? Well, okay then. I'm sure there's a café we can stop in along the way. And we can unpack that a bit!"

"There's a Nestle kiosk just on the corner here." She grimaced, then nodded. Those bloody kiosks drove her crazy. But she was aware they were a quarter of the price of a hand-made coffee, and he'd just said he wasn't working.

They walked to the kiosk in silence. This wasn't unusual back when they were married, but it felt odd now, some 15 years on from the last time they'd seen each other. In fact, the last time she'd seen Mike was in the kitchen of their two-bedroom flat in Ealing, which had been his, that he'd convinced her to move into. He'd been having some breakfast – eggs, toast and a mug of coffee – and she'd had nothing, using that time instead to brief him on where to go to meet up with Cass. "Black gate, wait there, someone will collect you," she'd told him, and then dropped him a pin.

Even though she obviously knew that was the last time they'd seen each other, it still took her by surprise when she recalled the memory. It still sounded like the sort of thing that happened to other people, not you.

None of this seemed to be weighing on Mike at all. There he was, fresh off his panic attack, walking briskly to get some coffee, leading the way and all but ignoring her presence.

It was enviable, she supposed. And it helped her be okay with the way she also felt nothing. Nothing but some random bits, some facts floating by, called up through sheer relevance with no emotional heft to them.

They'd apparently arrived at the kiosk while she was lost in thought. The trademark beeps and chimes of a Nestle CafePoint filled the space between them.

"Mocha?" He casually tossed out her usual order from a decade and a half ago, which was still her usual order today. The audacity. She shook her head.

"Long black, please. These bloody things can't mix a proper drink to save their lives."

He smirked incredulously and keyed it in, then tapped his watch to the pad. Shit. "I'm happy to pay."

"Bit late, but it's my treat." The machine whirred away, dropping two cups and pouring two drinks. Ridiculously fast, as always, and surely just as shit as she'd come to expect. They both picked up their cups. Mike gestured to let her lead. "After you."

This was already becoming unbearable. Why had she agreed to it?

"You look nice." He fired a compliment at her like a warning shot.

"Thanks. Still fits. The MP Collection by Elizabeth Marsh."

"So you're back into politics, then? That's great."

The nerve of him. What was he playing at? "So, you

came to see me then, did you? How'd you find out about the rally?"

"I designed your flyer."

"Shut the fuck up." She stopped and spun round to face him. "You did? You didn't."

"I did! Not on purpose. Your group hired the firm I work at. Well, I'm not sure if I still work there. We were apparently acquired by Concentra today. It's my day off. I was out for a walk and found out from that woman who helped me."

"Oh, Christ. I'm so sorry." She seemed to show genuine concern, but even she wasn't sure whether it was. "What was the name of the firm?"

"HumanTouch. We erm, we specialise in handmade designs. You know, no tool assistance. No automation. Just a man with a pen and a brief."

"No shit? Well, it makes sense we'd do that. Given the cause. I'm surprised we don't have any volunteers who can draw a flyer. That's a little depressing." She frowned and hoped it wasn't actually the case, that Siobhan was just lazy and didn't bother looking.

"I'm kidding. Well, I'm not kidding, except about finding your rally that way. I just happened to be walking by."

They still weren't moving, she noticed. They really needed to be, to get to the rally on time. But she didn't want to rush him. The panic attack, the news about the acquisition. Was he in shock? Surely, he must be. She stopped short of putting her hand on his shoulder.

"God, Mike, I'm so sorry. To run into me on the day you lost your job. You've really struck out there."

"They say bad things come in threes, so it's likely my flat's burning down right now."

She was struck by how conflicted she'd become over this. It was crucial she be at the rally. It was why she came back to London in the first place. It was also, sort of, if she were prone to dramatics, the continuation of her life's work. But there was the other bit of her chiming in now, the bit of her that did not want to be ghoulish to her ex-husband. And partly wondered whether either of them would bring up the obvious, yet less savoury, topic.

"Listen. I've got to go to this thing, bit of an obligation really. But I could get drinks after?" Mike laughed and looked around as if to say 'can you believe this' to his invisible audience.

"For Elizabeth Marsh? How could I possibly say no?" She groaned. He was determined to make her regret this.

"I'll meet you then? After?"

"When does it end? Your, whatever this is."

"I've no earthly idea, if I'm honest. It's a protest rally, not a telly programme."

"So whenever you're threatened with arrest then."

"Suppose so, yes."

"I'm happy to tag along. I'll stand at the back. Watch your speech. As we've established I have nowhere to be." Mike smiled his wry smile. So many new wrinkles. So much less hair. She'd resisted ever looking him up, and it really did take her by surprise. Had she also gotten this old? What he must think of her, as well.

She chuckled. "Fine, fine. Come along then, old man."

And so they marched, such as it was when they were a mile behind everyone else, all the way to Downing Street.

When they arrived, Elizabeth was actually stunned by the size of the group. It had grown to what looked like twice the size since she'd last seen it, and about three times as rowdy. Loud chants filled the air and police cars lined the street on either side, barriers having been erected to corral them into a designated "zone." Modern British protest. Say whatever you like against the government, as long as you stand exactly here, there's no more than this many of you, your loudspeakers are roughly this loud, and you're done before the 5 p.m. rush.

Nevertheless, she'd take what she could get. She deposited Mike at the agreed-upon spot, "the back," and then worked her way forward. As she moved through the crowd cheers would occasionally rise as they'd recognise her, open a gap, send her through, then the cycle would repeat. It was exhilarating for her, as in her relatively short political career prior to this she'd never exactly been a superstar.

Finally she'd cut through far enough that she caught sight of Siobhan, their actual superstar, and a hand thrust out to pull her up next to their trusty apple box, where Siobhan was already posted and leading the chants.

Her voice took on a fresh energy after she saw Elizabeth.

"Yous have all heard enough from me!" she bellowed into the megaphone, seeming to play up her usually-soft accent. "I want ye ta hear from a legend of British politics. A woman who inspired me to be up here today, fightin' for what I know is right. For the society we deserve. A woman who knows first hand just how much damage Concentra have done, how much damage our politicians have done to us, te pad their own pockets! A woman who Westminster were too afraid to let hang around! A woman who has the battle scars from a life fighting the power! A woman who can help lead us *into* power! Elizabeth Marsh!"

The crowd roared. Elizabeth was beaming as she

bounded up onto the box, Siobhan leaping down to make room, handing off the microphone as she did. Some boo'ing was mixed in with the cheers, along with some indistinct shouts. Elizabeth shot a nervous look back down to Siobhan, who closed her eyes, shook her head and waved a hand dismissively. Elizabeth nodded, her smile giving way to a bit of anxiety.

"Thank you for coming here today, all of you, and thank you for still believing in democracy! In the building behind me, just over 15 years ago, the government set us on the wrong path. A dark path. A spiral downward—"

Another jeer came from the crowd, followed by some shushing and boo-ing. Elizabeth scanned around, trying to see the source of it. She was shaken now. Her fears were coming true almost instantly.

"I'm sorry, it sounds like we might have someone here who isn't happy to see me." She squinted and kept looking.

"Oi, you bloody did this to us!" There he was. An older man, English, maybe in his early sixties, pointing right at her. "It was your bloody plan! Your idea!" Elizabeth laughed skittishly, involuntarily. Her eyes tried to find the back of the crowd, to see if Mike was seeing this, or if he'd gone. But there were too many people. In the corner of her eye she saw Siobhan trying to goad her on. She blocked it out.

"You're a disgrace!" Another shouting voice, from somewhere she couldn't see. It was such a mistake to be here, she cried from inside herself. It was always going to be this. Other shouts rang out, filled with vitriol, hatred, disgust.

"Let her speak!"

"She's a liar!"

"Fuck you!"

"Fuck her like she fucked this country!"

There was no hiding what she was, no redemption for her here. Why had she let Siobhan convince her otherwise? Fucking idealistic Siobhan, a child when this all started. Still a child.

Elizabeth froze. She looked out at them all, now quiet, staring up at her. She stared back, megaphone held to her mouth, but no words came. She worried none ever would. She'd wasted these people's time. She'd wasted her own time.

"You're right," she finally said. "I was there. I thought I could help, but I couldn't. I couldn't help then. And I can't help now."

A loud bit of feedback reverberated through the air as she lowered the megaphone and stepped down from the crate. Siobhan grabbed her as she tried to get past.

"Where are ya goin'? We fuckin' need ya, you're supposed to be the adult in the room. Christ, you emo Millennials." She stripped the megaphone off of Elizabeth and jumped back up in her place on the box. The crowd had started to drift, a cacophony of side chatter and despondent resignation.

Siobhan stood on the apple box wielding the megaphone like a weapon. "Oi! What am I hearing? Booing? Threats?" She paused, looking out at the crowd. She shook her head disdainfully. Her voice was full of fire, full of passion. "You boo her? You threaten her? You're booing our whole movement. Threatening everything we stand for. Cause I'm only up here cause of that woman there, yeah? That woman you're booing. I'm only up here because of her. Which means all of us are only here because of her."

She appeared to have captivated the crowd, or at least shamed them into listening a bit longer.

"We didn't get to choose this, yeah? We didn't choose this

society. We were born into this. They sold our destiny to Concentra when I was seven years old. By the time I graduated, getting your envelope was just another part of growing up. But it doesn't have to be this way. People made it this way. I never really thought about it until I read her book. It motivated me to go learn more. And now I understand what they gave up. What they lost. And what we could get back. And so I started this party. To put Humans First. Cause it's up to us to decide what kind of world we want to live in."

She'd worked the crowd into a lather, their cheers rising to crescendo. Siobhan had found her cadence.

"But let's face it. Not a lot of us know how any of this political shit works, yeah? Don't have the patience for it personally myself." A big laugh. She paused and smiled, drinking it in. Then she pointed at Elizabeth. "But you know what? She does. So I went and found her. And I told her what we were about. How we want to change the system. How we want a fair system where we can work for each other and ourselves. And she believes we can do it. And I believe in her. Do you believe in me?"

"YEAH!" A chorus of shouts rose up from a friendlier section of the crowd.

"Do you believe in what we can do?"

"YEAH!"

Elizabeth looked up at Siobhan, already a decent height, towering above her on the crate. She was playing the crowd like an instrument. The sun broke through a cloud behind her. It was a glorious image. Beautiful, moving. She couldn't help but laugh at herself. Always a sucker for poetic imagery in a moment.

"Now I'd like to hear her speak." Siobhan pointed at someone in the crowd. "Would you?" They nodded. "Yeah!

How about you?" Another nod. She started clapping, others following. She looked down at Elizabeth and smiled, then hopped down. Elizabeth cautiously stepped up. Thunderous applause greeted her.

Her smile was infectious as she started speaking.

"Thank you, Siobhan. I'm thrilled to continue."

ELEVEN
THE NEW NORMAL

Late June 2043.
The City of London.

TAP TAP TAP, tap tap tap tap tap. Mike furiously punished his backspace key, getting rid of everything he'd written aside from "Dear Elizabeth." It wasn't the first or even fifth attempt he'd made to write this email, an apology for abandoning their plans after the rally. As the crowd had turned on her he'd felt extremely awkward, and suddenly began to worry he might even run into some of his co-workers, or some of Elizabeth's friends, or even Cassandra. So, he'd walked away. It was for the best, he'd written in at least three of the draft apologies, because he assumed she wouldn't want to worry about having to keep their plans after going through all that on stage.

The reality was also that he couldn't stand the sanctimonious bollocks. The moaning about automation, the moaning about the government, the over-wrought chants and endless marching back and forth. Coming from her it was particularly galling. He could still remember watching her defend it on TV. And then there was the matter of her family money. She raged against the very machine she built, while existing in a totally parallel world where the machine had no power over her whatsoever.

Meanwhile, Mike was finishing up his last week at HumanTouch.

He'd been lucky enough to get kept on to assist with the transition, so most of his colleagues had gone already, having been cut weeks ago. This sort of thing used to be a blessing. When he was younger he'd worked at a company which conducted a mass layoff, and he'd gotten a nice cushy severance package along with 90 days of what they referred to back then as "garden leave" – where the company essentially paid you to sit in your garden at home, finishing out the rest of your contract on full pay.

After a flurry of reforms, the nature of which Mike couldn't really explain, that sort of thing simply didn't happen anymore. No severance pay, no garden leave, no unfair dismissal complaints, nothing. As long as the company used one of the government-certified dismissal algorithms to determine who to let go, to ensure complete fairness, they were free to offer you nothing and terminate you as soon as they saw fit. The firm acquiring HumanTouch, Concentra, happened to have one of those close to hand. Because they happened to have built and released the first tool to ever receive that particular government certification.

Still, Concentra weren't foolish. They wanted to retain as much of the firm's existing business as they could. So they picked a few of the longer-tenured, higher-performing designers to stick around and ensure their AI models were appropriately trained.

Mike actually found the process fascinating. At first they'd simply let operations continue as normal, taking in requests from their clients, passing them to the designers, iterating on the results and then releasing them as normal. But they were, alongside all this, also feeding the inputs and outputs from each step into artificial intelligence models. And over the course of a few weeks, they'd see how close the AI was getting to the human output using the same inputs from clients. It was never perfect, of course, and the human designers would occasionally turn in something Mike might call "inspired," but his new manager would certainly call "an aberration."

By the beginning of the third week, they were quietly handing the output from the AI out to the clients, then having the human design team work through the feedback. By week five, the design team was simply supervising the outputs of each AI step, flagging anything that seemed odd, or waiting in case a client threw up a massive complaint.

None ever did.

By week six, the few remaining designers on Mike's team, along with Mike himself, were "on standby." They no longer had any visibility into what was going on, but were told they'd get a call if they were needed.

So here he sat at 3 p.m. on Thursday, the last work day of the sixth week since they were acquired. No calls had come in all week. It had given Mike plenty of time and space to draft, re-draft and re-re-draft his apology to Elizabeth. But it also probably meant Mike knew what the one call he'd end up getting would be.

Funnily enough, it turned out he was wrong. 5 p.m. came with nary a whisper. No phone call, no email, no nothing. "Huh," Mike muttered to himself as he gathered his things and tucked them into his backpack. Each week had been a smaller and smaller group gathering at the pub for post-work drinks, and he feared today would be down to a single digit number of people. But he'd give it a go anyway.

On his way out of the building a rather unfriendly looking man in a black suit approached him just ahead of the gates, a small tablet in his hand. "Michael Fernsby?"

Ah, right. "Yes, that's me."

"Mr. Fernsby, Concentra thanks you very much for your service. Your access has been revoked, I can let you out." Mike's phone vibrated in his pocket. That'd be the notification of his building pass being remotely deleted. Right.

He walked into their usual pub at around the usual time, though with no colleagues in tow, and no colleagues in general. He briefly questioned whether it was the right place, given it was practically empty. Their usual bartender spotted him and waved. "Thank christ, something to do."

He sipped his pint in silence, head on a swivel, wondering when or if anyone else he knew might walk in. It had apparently been dead all afternoon, he'd been told. Mike warned him the rest of his HumanTouch colleagues had been let go today, including himself, and the bartender just sighed and nodded, then poured a couple of shots.

Now though he sat perched at a table alone, half a Guinness in front of him, his phone occasionally lighting up with another angry or dejected message from their "Work mates" text group which he noticed had now been cleverly renamed "FUCK CONCENTRA." He picked it up and muted the notifications without reading any of it. About half-way through his first pint, he was still angry. But now he sat here halfway through his second a determined man. This wasn't something he was going to moan or cry his way out of, he'd resolved to himself. He knew he was up against it, being a bit older, being from a profession that had mostly been automated away. But it happens. It's happened time and time again throughout history. You can either let it beat you down and give up, or you can find your place in the new normal.

Mike had decided: he'd find his place.

But first, maybe one more pint. He stared at the news, on as usual for the City crowd, if only they'd showed up. His thought drifted back to the apology to Elizabeth. Maybe a text would work better? She probably had the same number. It didn't carry the same gravitas as a letter, of course, but then he wouldn't have to think so much about the contents. He was increasingly stuck on this, though. He had to get past it, get it out of his mind, so he could focus.

And then there she was on the TV. Mike's eyes went wide. A photo of her from some recent rally, it seemed, with her fist in the air, in that same damn blue blazer she'd been wearing for half her life. "FORMER MP WILL STAND FOR, LEAD NEW PARTY IN UPCOMING ELECTION." Mike shook his head and downed the rest of his Guinness accidentally.

God, why would she throw herself back into this? It was honestly so nice to see her after all these years. They still had a decent rapport, some good banter. And she obviously didn't need to work. She had plenty of money. It was something he'd never understood about her, even as he'd try to encourage her whenever possible.

At least knowing this made the text easier to write. He grabbed his phone, dismissed all the nonsense, and popped open a message to Elizabeth.

"Saw you on the news," he wrote. "Picking up right where you left off I see. You look great as always. Sorry to have missed our plans after the rally, and most of the rally itself. Wasn't feeling well. You're probably right about the panic attacks. Hopefully drinks and proper catch-up soon?"

He tweaked the punctuation, swapping one period for an exclamation point, then another. Then both back to periods. Then a mix. Should this end with a question? Or should he declare 'drinks soon!' He decided to stick with the question.

And, send. That struck the right balance, Mike felt. Casual, apologetic. Admitting to her that she's right. He felt good about all of it. He turned to pop back over to the bar for another pint when his phone vibrated. Wow, instant response? He looked down and frowned:

"Your message did not send. Nobody with this username exists or their privacy settings prevent you from contacting them at this time."

Okay. Great. So it turned out he didn't have an easy way to reach her after all. Had she blocked him? It'd been nearly 15 years. Maybe she just had a new username. Or a totally new app, to be fair. So much had changed since then. He could try to find her on Popround, or ... no, he couldn't spiral. He wouldn't let himself spiral. He got another pint.

Right. Starting his new life in the new normal. First thing's first: a job. He'd found the job at HumanTouch through an old university friend who already worked there. It had been a while since he'd tried to find anything. And he was up against hundreds of thousands of others. But he was confident in himself.

He popped his earbuds in and opened YouTube. There was no room for shame anymore. Time to get some help. He searched "how to use ai job apps." Much like dating, applying for jobs had changed dramatically in the past decade. Luckily, in addition to being a vast archive of older videos, YouTube was still haunted by people his age, still happily churning out how-to videos, a community of people helping each other survive and thrive in such a rapidly changing world. It was worth the time and effort to get the offshore network licence.

He found a pleasant-enough video called "Best AI Job Application App I Could Find (Britain)," made by a Cornish woman with the channel name "LyndseyHelps" who looked to be in her mid-50s. She had curly silver hair, green eyes, a warm, soft voice, and was sat quite close to her camera in what appeared to be a darkened sewing room.

She spoke at length about what had led her to need an app in the first place. Her husband of 30 years had passed away about five years ago, and he had historically been the breadwinner of their household. They'd always lived rather hand-to-mouth. She had no savings. And she refused to give up the home they'd shared for so long and be relocated through a government programme, which meant she didn't qualify for any benefits. So she'd thrown herself head first into what she knew was probably a futile job search.

It was a moving story, but it reminded Mike of why he hated having to watch how-to videos.

Anyway, nine minutes later, Lyndsey explained that she really liked an app called Jobsworth. Pretty soon Mike was set up on it as well. To her credit, it was extremely straight-forward: the app would ask him a few freeform questions about himself, what he was good at, his experience, then it would generate and send hundreds of job applications instantly. It would continually do this any time an opening matched his experience and interests, then it would let him know once it had found something. It seemed almost too easy, and he wondered why everyone wasn't also doing this.

It promised to let him know within a week what it had lined up for him.

Of course, none of this was free. He'd paid £8.99 for the Jobsworth app and would pay 5p per application it made on his behalf (with the option to set a budget per day, per week or per month). There was also a £4.99 per week subscription regardless. He figured this was time sensitive, and 5p was nothing, so he didn't set any budgets – Lyndsey had strongly suggested that not setting a budget led to the best result.

So, the new job was sorted, it seemed. He just had to be patient. He flicked through the ever-growing list of applications it was sending on his behalf, all of them going to "Pending," then a handful going to "Screened," and a few of those going to "Rejected." It was all extremely fast. Bots talking to bots, he assumed. Criteria being assessed. As best he could tell, the hiring and firing at many large firms was all fully automated. While he thought about how a system like that might work, a few more of the "Pending" applications flipped straight to "Rejected." Hmm, it did say to wait a week or so. Better not watch how the sausage was made. It might get demoralising.

He closed Jobsworth and mindlessly flipped over to Linkup. He'd had a smattering of new matches, and it was once again offering him some auto-generated tips on how to improve his chances. He'd disabled every bit of automation when he first signed up, and was proudly a non-paying member, all of which it was happy to make clear to others if they looked at his profile. Shameless, absolutely shameless.

This wouldn't fly anymore. Mike the graphic artist at HumanTouch, drawing everything by hand, that's the guy who handled his dating profile like it was 2015. If he was going to live in the new normal, he had to fix this.

Back to YouTube he went. This one took more effort. His fingers hovered anxiously over the keyboard, the cursor blinking ominously in the search box. He could barely bring himself to type it.

"how to use linkup ai dating"

And off it went. He flicked through a few pages of results almost without looking, unable to bring himself to see them for fear of dying from embarrassment. He snuck a quick look over his shoulders to see if anyone could see what he was doing. All clear. Still empty. The bartender caught his eye and nodded toward the taps. Mike nodded.

Fine, fine. He had to just get it over with. What was there to lose? His eyes went to a result toward the middle of the page, "Best AI Dating App I Could Find (Britain)." Huh. He tapped on it, and was once again greeted by the warm, soothing presence of LyndseyHelps, in her dark sewing room somewhere in Cornwall. She started talking once again about losing her husband, in her hushed, even tone. Needing to put herself back out there, not knowing where to begin. It was genuinely heart-breaking.

Mike found himself thinking about her, and not paying much attention to her tips on how to configure Linkup. He couldn't help but picture her sat there all alone in her marital home, widowed, working to support herself, trying to find someone new to spend her life with. And still finding time to record these how-to videos. Sharing her experiences with the world.

The bartender set a fresh pint down in front of him, breaking the trance. Mike took a quick sip and paused the video, then switched back over to Linkup. It popped up another offer of help with his profile, and this time he simply tapped "Yes, please!" A virtual agent appeared on screen and began asking him questions about himself. Seemed easy enough.

Eventually he was facing down a screen with a list of tiny, round pictures of faces, names, ages, locations and "suitability scores." Next to each one had a status: Pending. After a few minutes, a handful changed to "Screened." He scrolled down a bit and saw a smiling face that piqued his curiosity. Penny, 44, Wandsworth. She was quite cute! And she had an 84% suitability score. That seemed promising!

The status next to Penny changed from "Pending" to "Rejected." His thoughts wandered back to LyndseyHelps. He wondered what she was up to right now.

TWELVE

POLITICS TODAY

August 2043.
West End, Central London.

OUT THE WINDOW of the cab they could see the extent of the encampments around Central. Elizabeth tried to ignore it, though not intentionally. She just felt compelled to be on her phone for some reason or another. Siobhan sat across from her staring out the window, occasionally glancing up at Elizabeth in mild annoyance.

"I can't believe how many there are," Siobhan said. "It's a bloody fuckin' travesty. They've totally given up."

Elizabeth let out a tut.

Siobhan shook her head. "Miss Marsh, look at it. I think this is what you should be talkin' about today."

The cab bumped slowly along Regent Street, light filtering through dense clouds, everything a dim grey. Elizabeth finally let herself look out the window. Her reasons for disliking what she saw were unbelievably privileged, but the terrible human cost of their "new normal" was something she'd become numb to — no matter how much she tried to focus on it or be enraged by it. What pained her was seeing Oxford Circus in squalor. What was once this dignified European destination, with the occasional diversion into glitzy or even tacky, now dark and shuttered, overrun with the homeless. Repurposed into a shanty town because nobody needed it anymore or cared enough to intervene.

She put her hand on the window and sighed. "I queued outside this shop for a bloody mobile phone once. Decades ago now, I guess. Do you remember that?"

Siobhan looked over at her. "Remember what?"

"When you could buy things at shops."

"No dude, that's before my time. I've read about it. In your book." Elizabeth chuckled and nodded, knowing the loss of shops was not new. As unemployment began to spike so did theft, and once the first couple of major chains had gone "shop-to-door" the rest fell like dominoes. Can't be robbed if there's nothing in the shop to take except rows of steel kiosks where you can order things for delivery, the things themselves off in some unmarked, guarded warehouse. Criminals responded by ensuring kiosks in shops were under constant attack. Before long it was rare to find one working anywhere. So the shops went entirely.

Siobhan shrugged and looked back out the window. Sigh. It was a deep pain for Elizabeth, the nostalgia for what she'd lost. It was something she told herself she should probably feel for her life, her friends, her marriage, her career, some-thing. But none of that ever really surfaced in any crisp detail. It was just a sort of ache. A longing. If she looked too much, let herself think about it too much, it ruined her for days.

Siobhan tugged at her dress and squirmed. It occurred to

Elizabeth she'd never seen Siobhan in anything other than jeans, T-shirts and hoodies. "Dressing the part today, are we?"

"Can't look like shite at the BBC." She chuckled. Elizabeth looked amused.

"They putting you on the panel as well then?"

"Shit no, dude. Just trying to look respectable, as your campaign staff."

"Campaign staff! My god, Siobhan. You started the bloody party. I'm just a candidate."

The car finally turned into the roundabout in front of Broadcasting House, a bizarre oasis of still-in-use infrastructure in this part of the city. A ten foot fence stood between the encampment and the facility, a bright line between the clean facade and the unmaintained, grime-coated everything else. Security had appeared as they pulled in, to escort them through the barrier and inside.

"You're late, we've barely time to put your mic on." An extremely nervy, fast-talking young man was rushing them through turnstiles, doors and onto a waiting elevator. "I should've brought it down with me, so stupid. I apologise Miss Marsh." She waved her hand dismissively.

"It'll be fine, I can mic myself. Not the first time I've been here to give an interview." The lanky production assistant turned sharply toward her.

"You know you're on a live panel right?" More fear in his voice, clearly on edge, worried he'd gotten yet another thing wrong. "It's not an interview."

Siobhan stood by in amazement as this poor man melted down. Elizabeth put her hand on his shoulder. "It's fine, I misspoke." Her soothing demeanour got a bit more coarse. "However, I never was told who else is on the panel."

He looked to be at his wit's end. His eyes darted between the two of them as the elevator doors opened. Another young assistant was stood waiting just outside, microphone pack in hand. They immediately clipped it onto Elizabeth's pant pocket and handed her the mic to wear.

"That's my bad, dude. I do know, I got your email, I just forgot to pass it on." Siobhan smiled at him quickly then turned and gave Elizabeth a big fake frown. "Worry about our message! Not these other clowns."

Elizabeth stopped walking, which pushed the poor production assistants to the brink of their sanity. "Wait, who's going to be on? Why'd you—" she spat out grumpily, but Siobhan interrupted her.

"—it's the usual! It's a few of the other people standing for your constituency, and one other MP. I wouldn't worry."

"Miss Marsh, please..." the first assistant pleaded in desperation. A huge clock on the wall showed they had about 30 seconds 'til the top of the hour. The second assistant opened the door to the studio, just ahead, and beckoned them toward it. Siobhan spun Elizabeth and clapped her on the shoulders.

"Focus. Mention the camps. How they made you feel. Unemployment numbers, why did they stop publishing them? Save the NHS. Our plan to put humans first. You've got this."

Elizabeth nodded. She stepped a few paces forward and walked into the studio, to the relief of a great number of staff and crew. A third assistant, this one equipped with a headset, intercepted. "Right this way."

A camera floated itself past them on an air bladder. She saw the long table. The presenter, plus five chairs. Three of the chairs were tucked in, translucent screens on the desk instead, those guests clearly deciding to appear virtually. One empty, presumably for Elizabeth. And then. Her heart immediately started racing. She stopped walking and spun around, putting her back to the set. Siobhan nearly ploughed into her.

"Whoa, dude, they're going to actually murder us if you don't go sit down."

"I can't." Elizabeth sounded terrified. Her voice trembled. Siobhan had never seen her even remotely like this.

"What?" The crew were taken aback. They had no idea how to move this along. On a nearby monitor, the show's titles were running — BBC Politics Today was starting. A robotic camera swung over their heads, taking a sweeping shot of the desk.

Elizabeth tried to steady herself. She swallowed, her throat suddenly dry. "Is Cass Cooper on the panel?"

Siobhan nodded. "Uh yeah, Cass Cooper, the lib dem MP from, I forget? Somewhere in London. Popwich? Is that a place? Been around ages. Elected in the before times. You know her, yeah?"

Elizabeth gritted her teeth. "Siobhan, why didn't you—"

A production assistant put a hand on Elizabeth's shoulder, another on her back. Elizabeth jumped involuntarily, startling everyone around her. "Ma'am I'm sorry, we've got to get you over there" she whispered, as the presenter had already gone live. Elizabeth nodded a few times as they quickly ushered her around the back of the set, seating her just as introductions started. She was red-faced, breathing quickly, her eyes closed. She thought her heart would leap from her chest.

Pull it together, she begged herself. *You have to pull it together. Focus. Focus.* She opened her eyes, immediately looking for Siobhan across the studio, and finding her. They made eye contact. Siobhan gave her a big smile and double thumbs-up, which did bring her partway out of the darkness.

"I'm Priti Shah, and this is Politics Today ..."

The presenter's voice was muddled and distant.

"... today on the programme, we'll ..."

The pain behind Elizabeth's right eye was sharp and came on suddenly. She closed them both and tried to just focus on the sound. Smooth and professional. It came into clarity.

"... bit of a political reunion, as seated to her right is controversial former MP Elizabeth Marsh, who's surprised us all with her sudden return, standing as the candidate for Humans First UK in Leyton and Wanstead. Ms. Marsh, thanks for being here."

Elizabeth put the pain aside. She smiled warmly and nodded. "Happy to be here." She could sense Cass sitting right next to her, just in her peripheral vision. She blocked it out, looking alternatively at the presenter or Siobhan.

"Elizabeth, first of all, why Leyton and Wanstead?" Priti was going straight in for her, she thought, even as the other faces sat un-introduced on their various screens, even as Cass sat right there. "You're from Cambridge, yes? You were the MP for Cambridge for two years."

"Leyton and Wanstead is our battleground, Priti, as it has one of the largest hospitals in London. As soon as the Modern Health Efficiency Act passes, Concentra are coming straight for it."

"Of course, yes," Priti said. "I obviously want to talk about that, the protests and the recent incident. But as someone who's followed Westminster politics for some time I of course also have to start with this. Elizabeth Marsh, you obviously have a rather rocky history with the woman on your left, Cassandra Cooper."

"Tabloid scandal," Cass quipped. "And some robust disagreement on policy."

"That's a rather mild description," Priti continued. "This was ultimately a landmark bill, and Ms. Marsh, you were a Works minister at the time, and you were the champion of that bill. And suddenly there's the leak, that explosive debate on the floor of the Commons. And then the scandal, and the allegations surrounding Ms. Cooper being the architect of the debate, and why she might've had it out for you." The presenter was dramatising it quite intensely with her tone and cadence. One of the virtual panellists let out a bit of a belly laugh, the tinny sound rattling out of a speaker under the desk.

"Apologies to those watching who are under the age of 45 and have no idea what we're talking about here," he cracked, pleased with himself. Another, a younger woman, smartly dressed, shook her head in the neighbouring screen.

"Oh I disagree, I'm fascinated by it. I read her book!" A thick Yorkshire accent. Elizabeth had no clue who it was. She gave Siobhan a quick hard stare. She'd known who these people were, and could've shared it.

Priti smiled. "Thank you, Alex Singh, Conservative candidate for Leyton and Wanstead, and Jasmine Bhati, the Momentum candidate." They both nodded. "So, Ms. Marsh, in your first book you did touch on all this, in an almost perfunctory way. You mention in one sentence that you never spoke to or saw Ms. Cooper again. You didn't address any of the allegations. But that was almost ten years ago." The presenter leaned forward, an eager smile on her face. "I wonder if it might help to clear the air now."

Cass laughed. The sound startled Elizabeth and she tried not to jump.

"Priti, again, it's tabloid gossip. You've rightly not said it, I think it's right to leave it unsaid." Cass sounded so chipper, so nonchalant. Elizabeth turned toward Cass, getting her first good look. She studied Cass's face. It was strange to see her so much older. Crow's feet, wrinkles around the mouth, a bit heavier. Her hair had greyed. She must be in her fifties by now. It was infuriating how calm she was, how easily she could just sit there. Ignoring it all.

"Apologies I'm just, you know, I'm seizing my opportunity. What are the chances of having you both on the same panel after all this time?" The presenter was clearly invested in this on some superfan-esque level. "Ms. Marsh, to you, same question."

"I'm..." Elizabeth's head throbbed and her vision blurred. She put her fingers to her eye, pushing on the side, in some vain attempt to relieve the pressure. "I'm not sure I know the question."

"Did you want to clear the air?" She could feel the push from Priti, the desperation to get this discussion opened. Cass was a magnet pulling her gaze, and it took everything she could to stay focused, looking at the far end of the table, not to her left. Not at Cass.

"I think that's a no then," Cass said with a smirk. "We can—"

"Presumably you're referring to the photos of Ms. Cooper with my then-husband, yes, Priti?" Elizabeth just blurted it out. She could see Siobhan off-stage, next to the camera, looking absolutely stunned. Elizabeth glanced over at Cass quickly and caught her staring daggers.

Priti also seemed stunned. "I, well, yes—"

"I never spoke to my ex-husband or Ms. Cooper about it. I saw the photo of them in The Sun same as everyone else." Elizabeth shook her head. "After everything else that had happened, I really had to focus on myself. It's not just, it wasn't just because of, well, I didn't really stay in touch with anyone if I'm honest."

"You went back to Cambridge, yes?"

"That's right, to care for my parents."

"And for them to care for you as well, I suspect?"

"I suppose so, yes." Elizabeth crossed her arms tightly.

"And you, Ms. Cooper. Now of course the other side of this allegation was that you were the source of the leak. And of course as you say, the tabloid scandal, was that you had ulterior motives when doing that. Would you care to respond?"

Cass smirked. "No. This was a decade ago, Priti. And it's a private matter."

"Is it private," said a man from one of the screens. "Is it, really? This is someone who's asking for votes now. I think it was fine to let the past die when she was secluding herself in Cambridge. But now we need to ask the questions."

"Okay," Priti said. "What do you say to that remark from Mr. Singh? Either of you."

"A photo of two people holding hands in a hotel lobby is not a scandal that deserves oxygen ten years on, Priti." Cass sighed. "I think it's beneath us all."

"And speaking of, Ms. Cooper," continued Alex Singh, "are you still beneath Ms. Marsh's ex-husband?" Cass, Priti and Jasmine all shouted over each other.

"Oh you vile, vile—"

"That's extremely enough, Mr. Singh—"

"Poor, just poor—"

Alex Singh smiled out from behind his screen.

"I think Ms. Cooper is entitled to her privacy," Elizabeth said. "I've never asked her what happened, and it can remain between the two of them."

Siobhan was waving frantically at Elizabeth, hoping to get her attention, but it was hopeless. The two of them were rapidly spiralling each other downward, much to Priti's apparent delight.

"Ms. Marsh," Priti said with practised empathy. "It's fine if you don't want to discuss it. But for those of us who do worry about these things. Do you know what really happened?"

Cass snorted and looked up at the ceiling, away from the proceedings. Elizabeth's right eye teared up from the pain, her vision a dizzying array of stars, halos, auras. She felt a numbness creeping out from her extremities. None of this seemed real, seemed to be happening. It was all too bizarre. She'd entirely lost control of the situation, of her life. She watched herself inhaling in slow motion, about to answer such a deeply personal question on a live video stream. She wondered if Cass was even there to begin with.

"I suppose I can only assume," she answered, "the most obvious answer is probably the correct one. It's Occam's Razor, really. Cassandra and my ex-husband had a relationship, and perhaps that motivated her, subconsciously, to want to sabotage my political career. I don't know if it was intentional. Priti, we've all let ourselves down at some point in our lives. It's just not usually so public."

"Christ," boomed the speaker under the desk, Jasmine Bhati perhaps not remembering she was unmuted.

"Excuse me?! This is, this is arrant nonsense." Cass was apoplectic. "And it's beneath this programme, and it's certainly not why I came here today, Priti. And Ms. Marsh, we both know there are details that are being left out of this story. And we both know—"

"I'm hearing we do need to move on," Priti blurted out, clearly desperate to get the fire under control before it consumed her entire show.

"Elizabeth Marsh is a leaf in the political wind," Cass shouted over everyone, "blowing where it takes her, then moaning about where she lands. Campaigning idealistically against automation, against AI, against Concentra, then opening the door for them as soon as she got into government!"

Jasmine Bhati clapped loudly in her screen, the claps coming out as loud spikes of static from the monitor speakers. "It's quite right! Elizabeth sat on the Conservative benches as the nursemaid for the new normal! She bottle fed the works programme until it could walk! And now she vilifies it."

"Now that's unfair," added Patrick Moore from a screen at the far end. Patrick was a councillor in Hackney from the Bright Future party, the self-styled "techno-optimists." He seemed to be appearing as a virtual character rather than himself, but his name and details were on the screen below his unnaturally-smooth digital face. "Elizabeth Marsh had resigned by then and gone off to write books about all the so-called problems she'd created." His voice was bizarrely smooth, algorithmically inoffensive, with an accent that would never occur in nature. "Now she'll come back and fix them? It's fifteen years too late, dear. The world has moved on."

Elizabeth sat stone-faced, not dignifying any of it, indeed not really hearing any of it at all. She felt at peace, watching it all unfold on her perch from far away.

"I certainly doubt she'll be back," said Alex Singh. "Humans First? Might as well be the Monster Raving Looney candidate. No offence to either, of course."

Priti threw her hands up in desperation. "I've put the cat among the pigeons here," she said with a sigh. "Can I ask everyone for a bit of a reset? Let's go around the desk. Several of you are standing in the same constituency. What's your one word pitch?"

"Stability," said Alex Singh, meeting the brief. "Conservatives mean stability. Keep us in place, we'll continue to deliver."

"In a word, socialism," said Jasmine Bhati. "We don't run from the label."

"Progress," said Patrick Moore in his fictional Mid-Yorklondonfordshire accent. "No need to worry about when your MP can see you, I can chat with every one of my constituents at once. I remember all of our past conversations, I have the ability to get things done for you right away. I can poll every party member instantly and decide something based off the result."

"Normalcy," said Elizabeth. "And humanity. It's hideously offensive, the very notion of being represented by a collection of algorithms. It's inhuman and shouldn't even be legal." Patrick's face flashed a set of over-sized annoyed eyes.

"Pass," Cass said with a smile, not having been asked.

"Right, that's our lightning round then," said Priti. "I'd like to get into the real topic." With a nice graphics package accompanying it, she got viewers up to speed on the Modern Health Efficiency Act, which was soon to come into effect and, among other things, was likely to see most publicly-owned hospitals and medical facilities sold off to the private sector. The government had been desperate to get this through before the next election, and they'd only just managed it.

Elizabeth stared at the screen, but wasn't watching the video. Instead she was playing the events of the past few minutes over and over again in her head. Over, and over. She could've gone the rest of her life without ever having seen Cassandra Cooper again, had she only stayed in Cambridge. Had she not come back. Why had she—

"Ms. Marsh?"

"Sorry, I'm sorry." Elizabeth snapped into place. "Can you please repeat the question?"

"So, it's a repeal then?" The presenter had a pained smile.

"A repeal."

"I'm sorry, in your mind, the Modern Health Efficiency Act. Your party gets into power somehow. It's repealed?"

"Sorry, yes, of course. Not likely, as I'm our only candidate." She smiled. Priti smiled. Jasmine and Alex shook their heads, and a large cartoon sweat drop appeared next to Patrick's face briefly. The speaker under the desk crackled.

"Great," Priti said. "So the other big story today is of course, another incident involving the activist group people have started referring to as 'AI Kills.'"

"Terrorists," Alex interjected. "And it's criminal that you won't just call them what they are."

"Same tired argument," Jasmine added, rolling her eyes. "Were the Suffragettes terrorists in your mind as well?"

"They absolutely were. There's a right way and a wrong way to go about these things."

"Right, you're absolutely right, we should politely request successive Tory governments please stop destroying British society, and hope they please listen."

"Most successful political party in the history of the world, love. And when's the last time your train was late? Bins picked up on time? We're getting on with the job."

"I obviously take some offence at the very name of 'AI Kills,'" said Patrick Moore, his face briefly changing to something resembling the anger emoji. Elizabeth tilted her head and looked on in confusion. Was Patrick just appearing as a virtual character, or was he actually an AI-powered agent? She decided not to ask, worried it was obvious to everyone but her.

"Right, let's cover the latest incident," Priti pleaded. "A dozen protestors managed to infiltrate the Concentra UK headquarters in Canary Wharf, with multiple sources confirming the group made it as far as the executive office before being detained and ultimately arrested. Now Concentra being an American company this is of course not the office of Rebecca Prue their CEO, but of David Ryan, head of their UK operation. There's been no official statement from either Concentra or from the organisers of this action. But it's the first sign that the group has started moving from peaceful sit-ins and rallies to something a bit more sinister."

"I'd say this is far from the first sign," said Jasmine. "These are the same people who harassed Concentra employees so aggressively that the company had to ban them from going out to pubs after work for their own safety."

"I have to agree with Ms. Bhati," Elizabeth added, finally feeling like she was on stable ground. "There's legitimate protest and then there's harassment. And now this was, what? What were they planning to do? Kidnap David Ryan? Handcuff themselves to his desk? The solution to the Concentra problem isn't terrorism, it's voting." She looked over at Cass and caught Cass looking back at her. Their eyes briefly met. A flash of panic. Elizabeth tensed up and retreated to looking behind the camera, to Siobhan. Something was definitely bothering Siobhan, but she still nodded and gave a reassuring double-thumbs up.

"Safe to say then that Humans First denounce this style of activism," asked Priti.

Elizabeth caught Siobhan's gaze again. She nodded slowly. Thanks for green-lighting me denouncing terrorism. Glad that's safe to put in the party's official platform.

"We obviously don't condone anything illegal. Even if we understand where they're coming from." Elizabeth trailed off a bit. Fuck. That was a mistake. Nobody was going to let that go.

"You understand where they're coming from?" Alex was weapons free. Full tilt British indignation. "You understand what's motivating terrorists to stalk, harass, threaten people just because they happen to work for one of the largest and most successful companies on earth?" Elizabeth was vigorously shaking her head, flustered by having walked straight into this trap. Siobhan, on the other hand, had quite a grin on her face.

"What I mean to say," Elizabeth started. She felt herself floating away again. Her eye felt like it might explode out of her head. She tightened her jaw and pinched a tiny bit of skin on her leg between her fingernails, sending a sharp pain up her leg. "That is, what I mean. I don't mean I—" She felt Cass's hand touch her arm. It jolted her to silence.

"How could anyone reasonable *not* understand where these people are coming from?" Cass said forcefully. "Their government has meticulously constructed and somehow managed to normalise a desperately corrupt system that has practically enslaved a whole generation. It shocks me we haven't seen more action like this, and more frequently. They simply have nothing left to lose." It was a fiery sermon.

Elizabeth couldn't help but smile. She was overwhelmed with confusing, conflicting thoughts. Cass's words had made her want to cry. The worse things got, the more people seemed to value stability, calmness, the status quo. It was frustratingly counter-intuitive. The sudden rise of this new group of activists was the first spark she'd seen from anyone in ages. If only it had been channelled into something productive instead of violence.

The panel sparred, Priti having given up any hope of getting things back on track. Finally, mercifully, the segment ended. A smooth, digitally-generated Scottish voice came from a loudspeaker overhead: "Transmission has ended." Priti let out an exasperated sigh and whispered "thank christ" under her breath. The robot cameras all immediately returned to their rest positions, tucked away in various corners. Siobhan sprinted up to the desk with her exhausting youthful exuberance.

"That was bloody brilliant, Elizabeth!" She dove in for a big hug. "I love you!"

Cass stood up and forced a smile at them both as the rest of the panellists' screens turned off one by one. She turned, wordlessly, and stepped off the stage.

"Oi, and you," Siobhan shouted over to Cass. "Join us for a coffee?"

THIRTEEN
THAT HAS SUCH PEOPLE IN IT

May 2026.
Soho, Central London.

IT WAS A MORE tasteful affair than Cass expected, if she was honest, in spite of being in the ballroom of a hotel with a charitable 3-star rating on Google Maps.

An elegant banner hung at the entrance to the ballroom read "Welcome Class of 2026," wait staff criss-crossed the room holding trays of drinks, and the space was a decent-enough size that you could breathe comfortably. But she wasn't so keen on having any company today. It was more of a relief than a celebration, having squeaked through the general election only a few months after similarly squeaking through a by-election. But it was a cocktail reception for "newly seated" MPs, and she'd somehow been invited. Not that this was an official event, of course. It was some light-touch lobbying group called "Friends Of Britain," some little party they organised after every general election. Maybe they figured she hadn't yet had time to get properly compromised.

She finished downing her second glass of free Prosecco and thought ultimately, it wasn't so bad. It beat being in her flat alone, she told herself, lying.

It was meant to be a networking thing, but she'd spent almost all of it glued to her phone, texting away. It was 8 p.m., which meant it was 6 a.m. in Sydney. She could credibly harass Rose without feeling bad about it. 6 a.m. was a time people got up, yeah?

"Cannot believe I do this just to talk to you," came the response.

"You know I love you for it xxxx," Cass sent back with a grin.

"Like a sister now though, yes?" replied Rose. An anxious emoji face stared up at her. Cass felt a knot in the pit of her stomach. She tried to lean cooly on a cocktail table, one of many dotted around this bit of the reception, though hers was the only one not being used to socialise.

"Of course," she finally forced herself to type out. "But I do miss you," she added, then quickly erased before she sent it. "Of course."

"Good! You know I want the best for you! You fucking deserve it!"

Cass quickly swooped another glass of champagne from a passing waiter and took a healthy sip. "Thanks babe," she typed, erasing "babe" before she sent it. "Thanks."

"Hope you're wearing something that shows off your sexy ink."

She darted her eyes to one side, thought about it, and decided not to lie to Rose. "All covered up I'm afraid."

"Sure, sure. It's fine. FOR NOW. You know I dream of seeing my designs in some clip from BBC Parliament."

Cass looked up and saw the room had really started to

fill. Everyone was fashionably late, it seemed. Excellent quality for members of Parliament. She gave the crowd a desperate scan for someone she might fancy speaking with. It was desperately male, desperately bland. Was she the only non-Tory who came to this thing?

And then she saw her.

Stood alone at a table across the room. Drinking a proper cocktail, not just the free Prosecco. So tall, with the confidence to wear heels on top of that. Her dark hair buzzed on one side, hanging down almost to her shoulder on the other. Stood there so goddamn effortlessly cool in a shiny pink blouse and leather skirt. Who is she?

"Christ, I'd get lost in her shadow," she muttered to herself. She worried she was gawking. Was she gawking? It seemed to be going unnoticed, so maybe just a bit of gawking was fine.

Her phone buzzed, snapping her out of the trance.

"SO? Making friends? Making more than friends?" Rose again. Cass looked around. Nobody behind her, nobody in her immediate vicinity. She brought her phone up as if she was replying, flicked to the camera and quickly snapped a photo of the mystery woman in the shiny pink blouse.

"Who is this?" She fired off the photo. Rose had many flaws, one of which was her unhealthy obsession with British politics, and British politicians. Cass was hoping, for once, that she'd kept it up since the move.

The reply came back swiftly. "That's Elizabeth Marsh. New Tory prodigy. Nepo baby. Def. getting a junior cabinet post in next reshuffle, I guarantee."

"Suppose I can make time for a Tory just this once. Socialising is fine right? Just no unprotected governing?"

"She's a pretty lady" came Rose's reply, dripping in snark.

"We're both alone!! Everyone else already has someone to chat with."

"I can see two lads by themselves toward the back of this same photo."

"Look at her hair tho." They'd never felt threatened being thirsty around each other, even when they were exclusive. But there was that feeling in Cass's stomach again.

"Is she 9 feet tall? And you're 4 foot yes?"

"5'4" in heels. Check her bio though actually, how tall *is* she?"

"Says here she's tall enough to step on you without even noticing."

Cass looked over the top of her phone at Elizabeth, still stood there alone, powering through whatever reddish cocktail that was. "Yes, please." She added a panting emoji for good measure.

"Down girl. As established she's a Tory. Sometimes they're hot, it's how they lure you in then bam they privatise you and strip you for parts."

"I can fix her."

"Also definitely straight. Bi if you're lucky but you're not."

"Says that on her Parliamentary bio does it then"

"I can tell. We both know you cannot. This is your worst area Cassie trust me."

Cass frowned. Maybe she was being playful, but it just came across as mean. Maybe it was just the text. Whatever. Benefit of the doubt. She had to make things normal with Rose. Rather than engage, she simply sent back a smiley face.

"You're going over there aren't you," came the response

from Rose. "My beautiful disaster gay. I'm gonna get a bit more sleep, be safe."

She clicked her phone off and dropped it in her pocket, then made a beeline for Elizabeth. Scores of besuited men bumbled about, discussing the election, how close it was, party meetings, boring, boring, boring. She picked her way through the crowd, dodging eye contact with at least two or three people she sort-of recognised. Elizabeth had just finished her cocktail when Cass arrived.

"Looks like you're dry! Shall we off to the bar?" Elizabeth looked up surprised, then back down a bit. Cass smiled up at her. "If you put me on your shoulders I'll be able to see where it is."

"Ha! Yes, bit of a height difference there. Sorry, I'm a fucking giraffe."

"No bother, you can make it up to me with a drink." Cass let out a weird giggle and touched Elizabeth's elbow. Elizabeth exhaled a big, performative sigh as they started their walk to the bar.

"Oh fine, this is what it's come to is it."

"I'm afraid it has. Unless you've spent the last of your money on that incredible top. I could get this round if so. You've done us all a favour with it." Elizabeth looked down at her outfit and gave an awkward grin.

"Thank you! I was worried it was a bit loud. I text three different people asking if it was too 'ahhh!' to wear to an event like this."

"I'm glad they approved!"

"Oh they all said absolutely don't, but fuck it, here I am anyway."

"Fock yes!" Cass lit up, and said that maybe a bit too loudly. A few randoms around them all looked over in unison. One rolled his eyes and turned back round. "Fock yes," she whispered, getting a low chuckle from Elizabeth. They now stood in the queue motionless behind far too many people. A group of men in matching blue suits at the front were in a strop over the bar having run out of a particular Pinot they'd been drinking.

Cass put her hand on Elizabeth's back, leaned up and whispered in her ear. "The lobby bar probably doesn't have a wait."

"Are we allowed to do that?" My god, Cass thought, this woman is adorable. She studied her face, wondering how old she was. Rose had called her a "prodigy."

"Allowed? We're adults."

Elizabeth laughed nervously and scratched her neck. "I just meant, you know. I'm not sure what I meant." Cass smiled and looked her in the eyes for a moment. Such gorgeous hazel eyes. She might never find her way back out of them. "So," Elizabeth continued, "lobby bar then?"

"Shhhh. Don't spread ideas." Cass walked Elizabeth out of the queue, hand on her back, like security escorting her out of a gig. A few minutes of smiling, nodding, bobbing and weaving later, they were on the stairs headed down. As predicted the hotel's lobby bar stood practically empty, a couple tables occupied out of a dozen, and the bartender looking eager for something to do.

They took a table at the back, G&Ts in hand, already half gone from lingering at the bar. Cass took care to sit next to Elizabeth rather than across from her. Her energy was intoxicating. She just wanted to be near her. They just felt so compatible. So effortless. It made her realise they'd been talking, one unbroken conversation, since the moment they met. She hadn't even introduced herself.

"I'm Cass, by the way. Cass Cooper. Popler and Limehouse."

"Cass Cooper! What a fantastic name." Elizabeth's eyes widened. She let out a dramatic gasp and held her hand to her chest. "But wait, gasp, you're Labour! Oh, no." The corner of her lip curled as she tried not to smile. Cass leaned forward with a naked grin.

"I won't bite. Without consent, of course." Elizabeth threw her head back and cackled.

"Oh, you're funny! I like you. And christ, yes! I'm Elizabeth Marsh."

"MP for Cambridge," Cass interjected. "Tory MP, even! Sorry. I might've looked you up before I walked over. Welcome to the class of 2026."

"You looked me up! You cheat. Unbelievable. Still came over even though I'm Tory scum, though."

"What can I say? It was the hair." She raised her glass. "I never stood a chance."

"Oh, you like it?" Elizabeth looked up, like she was trying to see her own head. "I think I'm having a quarter-life crisis."

"I cannot possibly convey how much I like it."

"It feels so weird." Elizabeth ran her fingers over the shaved bit. "I'm so not used to it. Wanna feel?" Cass very much did, and she very much went for it.

"It's sharp! I'm gonna cut my fingers on your hair here, Lizzie. Can I call you Lizzie? If so, and only if, you can call me Cassie."

"Lizzie and Cassie it is." She flashed a smile. Then her face fell a bit. "God, what are we doing? I spent ages prepping for this, thinking we were going to be talking policy, procedure, what to expect. I worry we should be?" Cass couldn't contain a huge belly laugh.

"Bless you. It's a drinks mixer. Everyone just gets drinks. If I'm honest half of Parliament is drunk half the time, anyway." That bit of wisdom from Cass seemed to make Elizabeth's face fall even more. She slumped back into her chair.

"I do worry, you know. Whether this was the right choice for me." She finished her drink and set the glass down, sighing. "Everyone I talk to that's, you know, outside all this. It's just oh, you can't make a difference. It's all the same. 'Politics is rubbish,'" she said in a low mocking voice. "I don't know. Sorry. All gin and no food make Liz something something."

"We all go through this," Cass said. "Politics was certainly not where I saw myself. I came to London to be an actor! And then I made the mistake of reading too much about unions one night, and wound up more passionate about that than the acting." She stared at her glass. "Never did manage to get into Equity, though. Was in a play once. The Tempest. I was Miranda. They didn't pay me."

Elizabeth cracked up laughing. "Miranda! Really!"

"Oh, wonder!" Cass said, hamming it up. "How many goodly creatures there are here!"

"I would never have guessed."

"Well. I pride myself on that, I suppose. There's a lot about me I keep hidden. *Especially* that."

"Huh," Elizabeth said. "Interesting."

"What about you?"

"What do I keep hidden?"

"Why did you go into politics?"

"Oh. Talking of keeping things hidden. I'd rather not."

Cass smirked and straightened up. "Okay, Beth. No. I want to get real. This is now a real talk zone." She drew a big imaginary box around them with her hands, Elizabeth following with her eyes, finally letting out a giggle. "Elizabeth

Marsh, what motivated you to stand and represent the good people of, ... where did you stand again?"

"Cambridge!"

"Right, sorry. I don't go outside the M20. Don't much care for it out there."

"Oi!" She slapped Cass on the shoulder.

"Sorry, sorry, real talk zone. Please."

Elizabeth inhaled and looked up at the ceiling. "It's embarrassing. It's so frowned upon. Eventually I'll be crucified for it on TikTok, if I ever put my head above the parapet." She closed her eyes and shook her head. "Mmm, no. Nope."

"Come on! Respect the zone!"

"Fine! Fine. It's the family business, I'm afraid. My father was Donald Marsh."

"Why do I know that name?"

"Donald Marsh? He was the MP for Cambridge for about a thousand years." Elizabeth looked down, away, a bit red-faced.

"Oh! I knew this, sort of. Someone told me. You're a bloody nepo baby! And now you're... the MP for Cambridge."

"Stop! It's true. Nepo baby." She grimaced. "God, that was practically Labour's entire campaign against me."

"It doesn't seem to have worked. Pity!"

"It's not as if I'm just some pretty face with a famous surname, you know. I do have issues I care about, that Cambridge cares about."

"The estate tax?"

"Cass! It's AI, actually. Automation. Bloody terrified of AI. Terrified of it."

Cass nodded hard. "We're all bloody terrified of AI, bab.

I was shitting myself last month." Even mentioning it brought memories of it straight to the surface. A fully-automated NATO mission, first in history, had deployed as part of an ongoing skirmish near the Lebanon border. Hezbollah were using similar, having put together their own weaponised automatons from the same off-the-shelf components, the same technology, from the same American company. A dozen city blocks were wiped out across two days, with almost no human casualties on either side. Just utter, senseless destruction. "It was so awful," she finally added. "Part of a city levelled, with nobody in it from either side, just two automated armies that would still fight this war with each other even if we were all dead."

Elizabeth brushed her thumb gently over Cass's cheek. A tear had apparently rolled down it. Cass quickly wiped both eyes.

"Christ, sorry. I got lost in it there."

Elizabeth looked her in the eyes, pain on her face. "I honestly worry about society. I obsessively worry. I worry what the point of all this is. Automating war, is awful. It's awful to think about. But—"

"—How bloody pointless. It's pointless. Did anyone stop to think what the outcome of that was actually supposed to be?"

"Right, okay, but. I worry about what's happening right here. The Streamlined Sentencing Act. Jailing people without a trial if we can algorithmically determine they'd be found guilty? How did that possibly pass?"

Cass squinted while she searched her memory for that one. "I did not vote for that."

"Okay, sure. The new benefits cap? Why? Too many people unemployed already. And all the consolidation? AI companies combining and combining and combining." Elizabeth was animated now, her voice raising and raising, her arms flapping around, her eyes wild. "All the automation? No more baristas at Costa! That happened awfully fast. Thousands unemployed instantly. Shrug, it's cheaper. No more train drivers. Thousands unemployed instantly. Shrug, it's safer. It's just the start! We have no plan! I just don't know what we think the point of society is, I really don't. What is the point? What are we all supposed to do next? What will we do after we've made capitalism so efficient it doesn't even need us anymore?"

Cass stared at Elizabeth. Enraptured, obsessed, in love. "You're bloody terrifying me, bab." They both burst out into giggles. "You are! But you're right. You're so goddamn right. I mean, I hadn't thought about it from this angle."

"It is! It is terrifying. I'm sorry, it was good bants and then I went Oppenheimer on us. I have Oppenheimer'd our bants." Elizabeth scrunched up her face and swirled the ice around in her empty glass.

"Shut up. I absolutely want to talk about this. Focking hell, do not think for a moment you are as dreadful as you think you are." She stood up and slid her hands up and down Elizabeth's arms, then patted her shoulders, her hands lingering a bit. "I'll get us a couple more. You're brilliant by the way." Elizabeth looked up at her and smiled brightly. It sent a wave of warmth through Cass's whole body, which she expressed by waggling her eyebrows and sauntering away with their empty glasses.

The secret was out on their hidden bar, so she stood in the queue anxiously. She really wanted to get back. But she thought she might use this time to give 'AI threats' a cheeky search, and maybe stand a chance of keeping up with the meatier bit of the conversation. When she looked at her phone she saw a few missed texts from Rose.

"I'm awake again. How'd it go? Hope you show her your tatts, that'll bring her over the line if anything will. Last seen 2 hours ago, well done."

Cass sent a little "halo" emoji and tucked her phone back in her pocket. She hadn't thought about it, or about Rose, this entire time. *Elizabeth Marsh, you're a revelation.*

A couple more gin & tonics served up, this time pink, because sometimes you have to live a little. As she approached the table she was thrown. There was a newcomer, some guy, bearded, with a ribbed tan jumper on. "Hello, tan jumper! Do we know tan jumper?" Her voice had a bit of a sharp edge.

"Yes!" Elizabeth shouted. "Oh my gosh, I had a million texts, I absolutely abandoned Mike upstairs when we snuck down here. Mike, this is my new friend, Cass Cooper. Cass, this is my partner Mike."

Mike smiled politely and nodded toward Cass. "Nice to meet you."

FOURTEEN
FLERVER

"Personal AI agents were heralded as a marvel. No more waiting for others to be free! The agent knows what they'd say and can say it for them. But the way it works means once you've spoken to them enough, their opinions calcify. You're malleable and unpredictable, subject to your whims, hormones and the phases of the moon. Your agent has no such weakness."

— Elizabeth Marsh, What We've Lost

September 2043.
Southwark, South East London.

IT'D BEEN about a decade since Mike had been on a real, honest-to-god date. And he wound up marrying her. So there was a lot riding on tonight. He stood in the bathroom, staring at the mirror. His jacket didn't fit very well these days. The fabric of his shirt strained, the buttons hanging on for dear life near the middle. It wasn't in the cards to buy anything new at this point. Money had gotten tighter than the shirt. The jobs market was proving a formidable opponent, and the Jobsworth app was fuelled by the money in his savings. He ultimately knew it was worth it, to find a job, to get his life back on track. The savings could be replenished once he was safely onboarded in his new role. You had to pay to play, Lyndsey always said in her videos. And whoever paid the most, won.

He ran his fingers through his grey hair. Still had that at least, he said. He gave himself a smile. His date, Kathryn, was meeting him out at around 9 p.m. A ridiculously late start. Did the tube even run that late? But maybe 9 p.m. dates were the new normal. Everything was the new normal, he'd decided to assume. Everything was fine. He'd never felt so old in his life. But it would be fine.

This was one area he'd never gotten into in his various other chats. None of them had ever seemed to come close to leading to an actual date. There was Gemma, who he'd kept talking with, even after his old workmate Jason had been absolutely convinced it was a chat bot. She was funny, she was blunt, but there was a kindness to her that kept him coming back. Most of his other Linkup matches were far more transactional. Even their chat bots were buttoned-up and to-the-point. He guessed that's just how it worked. You can configure how amiable you want it to be when it chats with others, how much time you want it to waste, essentially. And since the higher tiers of service are pretty pricey, you really can't let it waste any time. Especially when it's probably just talking to other people's chat bots.

Of course, the chat bot wasn't just some generic bot. It

built up a profile from all of your text messages, emails, anything you've written. You could even let it listen to you as you went about your day. All of that went into training it to be the most accurate possible "you." At the most expensive tier, you could even train it on how you sound, and your potential matches could have calls with "you."

Mike had never tried that. Both offering it, or doing it with someone else. He had been willing to spend the few quid to "talk" to Gemma once, but sadly it informed him that she had never set it up on her end. And she had politely declined to have an actual call, of course. With Kathryn, she'd mercifully been keen enough to skip all this and just meet in person.

He stared out the window of the tube, adverts for films, apps, food delivery services whizzing past. He was still lost in thought. How would this even work when he got to the restaurant? Were her pictures recent? Would he recognise her? He hoped she'd just recognise him. Come running over, a beaming smile on her face, throwing her arms around him for a big hug. They'd eat, it would be awkward at first, but then after a few drinks, he'd relax and tell her how awkward he had felt. And she'd say the same.

It would be nice. He'd see the new normal was the same as the old one. Because fundamentally people are people.

He strode across the road and turned up Shoreditch High Street, the restaurant just a few metres away. He hated Shoreditch. He used to love how he and Elizabeth both managed to hold onto that hatred even as the neighbourhood changed and changed and changed again. Nearly unrecognisable! Yet still, the hatred. That was an admirable quality. Just never letting go of your hate.

But of course Shoreditch was back in the good books of

the young people. And when Mike had politely pointed out he wasn't a fan of this area – for his own pointed reasons, and more reasonably, because it was extremely far from his home and hard to get to – the app alerted him that the last thing he'd said was unfortunately a deal-breaker, and he would automatically un-match from Kathryn if he continued.

He paid £2.99 to retract it.

And so here he stood, in the doorway of somewhere called *Flerver*. Dimly lit, tables close together, the walls draped in wild, patterned metallic sheets. And of course, there seemed to be no human staff. Bartending had managed to survive as a profession, especially for pubs that catered to an older crowd. But human wait staff at a restaurant were a luxury few could afford and fewer saw the need for.

He checked his watch. 9:14 p.m. He was late. But not by much, and for London, he was practically on time. Nobody tackled him to the ground with their aggressive hugs, though. Nobody seemed to pay him much mind at all. The tables, bizarrely, were all pairs of people. There didn't even seem to be any tables for groups larger than two. Bloody Shoreditch with their high concept nonsense.

At the entrance to the restaurant was a screen, perched on what appeared to be some sort of over-wrought lectern. A badger-faced man appeared on the screen, a virtual agent, its face taking an impossible shape. "Welcome to Flerver." It spoke in pinched, annoyed tone, with an affected North American accent. Clearly trained on a real maître d'. After a second of his inaction, it coughed and made a noise that approximated a polite cough. "Scan, please?"

"I'm sorry?" Mike felt like he was absolutely blowing this date and he wasn't even technically on it yet.

The face appeared to look Mike up and down, then

furrowed its brow. "I'm sorry, I suspect you've not been here before. You are meeting someone here, yes? From Linkup?"

"Um, yes. I'm here to meet Ka–"

"Hold your phone up to the tablet please. I do apologise, usually it's automatic, your face must not be on file." Mike looked around at everything and felt extremely out of place. He raised his phone up to the tablet and immediately felt a vibration. The face approximated an unusually wide smile. "Michael Fernsby" it said, in its Hollywood-ish voice.

Halfway across the restaurant, a lamp lit at one of the tables, a sort of old-style green banker's lamp. Mike saw a young woman sat there, opposite an empty chair.

"Please seat yourself. Good luck, she's quite fickle, I believe. I recognise her from earlier." The agent had a dry twist to its words.

"Earlier?" Mike hoped he'd just misheard.

"Yes, she was in her with another man earlier, a younger man, handsome fellow. Better head over, she's waiting." The face nodded over its non-existent shoulder, and Mike looked over to see her watching him. She had a bright smile and gave a small nod.

He made his way over to Kathryn. She really was quite striking. Fiery red hair cut very short, leather jacket over a tight T-shirt, and as he got close he saw her bright green eyes. Her smile was infectious, so wide, so joyful. She must be 15 years younger than him, though. A wave of intense nervousness crashed over him as he sat.

"Mike, you made it. Thanks so much for coming!" She was talking so fast, and had a bit of South London in her accent. He spotted the two empty martini glasses in front of her. "You're very cute, thank you for using up to date photos. You have a sort of washed up designer thing going for you, which I love, which I guess makes sense, since that's what you are." He felt his face go red. He instantly regretted this. Staring, just staring. What could he even say? His hands fumbled about with each other on his lap.

"I guess I am, yeah." Finally, he managed to get some words out. It felt so difficult to know what to say.

"Oh I don't mean it in a bad way, honestly. I love it. I love that you're like, a walking museum. You know? I love history. I read about history a lot. I mean you know all this, we've talked. What was it like actually drawing? Honestly I've never even held a pen, I don't think. Crazy, right? I'm not even that young. I must seem young to you. You're 48. Do you remember how old I am?"

How did she talk this fast, he wondered. He was watching her lips rather than listening for half of that. "You're, ah... you know I don't remember. I'm sorry, I know it says how old you are on your profile."

"You're funny, I'm 35. 35! Can you imagine. A 2000s baby. I'm like, Gen Zalpha, not quite Gen Z, not quite Gen Alpha. My god, Mike, you're a millennial. Secretly? I think that's why I wanted to meet you. You're like living history."

Mike scratched the back of his neck and looked around. Was everyone in here on a date like this? He did get a vibe that he was the oldest person in here by a lot. He put it out of his mind.

"Well, you know us millennials, we, uh..." he trailed off. She was on her Ring. He'd seen them from time to time, but had never used one. It looked like a wedding band, but thicker, and projected images down onto any surface, like a table. You could tap on them to use it like a phone, or talk to it. Mercifully she wasn't talking to hers. His eyes wandered down to catch a glimpse of what she might be doing on it. He briefly saw his own photo before she closed her hand instinctively.

"Cheeky, trying to catch a glimpse." She was being fun about it, but she still seemed a bit miffed. Was that some kind of creepy faux pas, looking at someone's Ring?

"Sorry, I've never actually seen one of those up close."

"Really? What do you — oh obviously, you have a phone!" She threw her head back and let out a big laugh. "I'm on a date with a millennial! Honestly you're more fun than my last couple of these. Thanks so much. It's been a long night, I really am exhausted. Shall we call it here?"

"Didn't you... I mean, we haven't even gotten drinks yet. Or eaten anything."

"Honestly, it's fine. I saw you are only on Linkup Premium, not Platinum? I figured you might be relieved not having to buy any drinks here?" She tossed her hair and scoffed. "This last guy, turned out to be a connie. Can you believe that? He doesn't even work in the area, he's all the way out in Southend. I honestly have no idea how we matched, it had to be a glitch. Terrible fucking app."

"A connie?" Mike could feel his disdain for this woman spiking to unbelievably high levels. But he pushed it down. This was his expedition into the new normal. He couldn't turn back now just because of a little frostbite.

"A conscript. I know, I know, kind of a slur. Not allowed to say that. Whatever. Honestly I don't even know where I got it. Probably from EastEnders."

"EastEnders! That show is still on?" Mike briefly lit up. "That's wild. I haven't seen it in so many years." He had always found that show, or really any soap opera, to be interminable garbage. But it was at least something he recognised and could latch onto in this conversation that wasn't a direct insult.

"It is! I never miss it. Oh my god, honestly, wait. When did you last watch?" Mike and Liz used to flop on the sofa and switch it on after a fight sometimes, an easy shared laugh when they needed to calm down.

"Probably a decade ago. At least."

This sent Kathryn over the moon with excitement. "Michael! The last time you watched they still wrote it by hand! You're like my unfrozen caveman boyfriend!"

He felt himself dying that much more inside. That's right. The new normal. Your date watches BBC soap operas that are written by one algorithm and performed by a variety of others.

"To be fair," he admitted, "it's probably better now."

Out of some sense of masculinity, he insisted they get drinks, which he could absolutely not afford. Mike got an Old Fashioned, which sent Kathryn into a giggle fit. He wasn't sure what Kathryn got because she whispered the order into her earpiece, which up until now Mike assumed was a bit of jewellery. When she returned from picking it up, it was a synthetic-looking reddish-greenish-swirl.

They spent another round of drinks hearing about Kathryn's other dates that night. Mike tried not to absorb any of it, caught between wanting to understand more about modern dating and not particularly wanting to hear about the other men in Kathryn's life. Is this normal now too? Talking about your other dates on your dates?

Mystifyingly, he found himself walking her home, to a tiny little garden flat near the bar. Low ceilings, a cute little window looking out onto the garden, and absolutely rammed with furniture. Floor to ceiling books on every bit of free wall space. Kathryn bounced in and went straight to the kitchen and put the kettle on. "Any tea? Coffee?"

"Anything a bit harder?"

"Honestly, you're hilarious."

Mike wasn't sure whether he was getting a drink. He dropped his coat on a chair and walked around the living room, as much as one could. The books were a chaotic mix of subjects, everything from philosophy, to pulpy romance, to cooking, in no discernible pattern. The spine of one of them jumped out: "What We've Lost," by Elizabeth Marsh. Instant anxiety. He'd never actually seen this book, let alone read it. He slid it out of the pile carefully, turning it over a few times in his hand, analysing it more for its physical form than what it actually was.

Kathryn came in holding a bottle of beer and a mug of tea. She set them down with a delicate "clink" on a tiny free patch of table, amongst the piles of papers, magazines and older half-finished mugs of tea. "What are you doing?" She looked at what he was holding with intense confusion.

"Oh, sorry. How was this book? I've never gotten around to reading it."

Kathryn laughed. "Are you joking? Those are decoration! Fun, yeah? Organised by colour. See?" She did her best Vanna White, showing off each pile and how it did in fact go from dark blue to light blue in a pleasing gradient. They were sorted by size too. "You should know all about this though, as a designer. I love that you thought these were like, my books, can you imagine?"

"I'm a graphic artist, not a designer. Different—"

"—What's that one about?" She stepped slightly to her side and was right next to him, looking down at the book.

They were roughly the same height, which was somehow intimidating.

"It's a sort-of memoir nostalgia trip thing. Or so I've heard. My ex-wife wrote it."

"Yikes," she quipped. "Well, let's see her, go on then." Exactly the right place to go after an evening of talking about her other dates. Let's look at his ex-wife's book jacket photo. He opened the cover and there she was, in her usual low-key business attire, not a hair out of place, unnaturally big smile, stood in her garden in Cambridge. Kathryn took the book out of Mike's hands. "Oh, she's lovely. You married that? And she was an MP? Shit. How'd you let her go?" She flopped down onto the sofa behind them, the book still open. She started flipping from page to page.

Mike stood awkwardly in front of her. It was nearly quiet, aside from the constant drone of passing cars outside. He picked up the beer and took a sip. Fine. New normal. He flopped down onto the sofa next to her.

"They said AI would put an end to work," Kathryn read from the book. "In a way, they were right. Ohhhh, chilling stuff this. Is it post-apocalyptic?"

Mike couldn't help but sigh. "It's non-fiction. Well, it's her opinion on why automation is bad."

"Interesting." She took the beer out of Mike's hand and downed a few swigs. "Clearly written before she'd used an auto-vibe." More thumbing through the pages. "Turns out," she continued reading, "people can always tell when something was made by AI. But it also turns out that they don't care." She chuckled. "Well, she's not wrong there."

Mike took the beer back, taking a few swings, essentially mimicking her. She looked over at him and smiled.

"Christ, sorry, you don't want to be reading your ex-wife's book, do you? Or do you care?"

"I'd probably rather not. Subject change?"

"You can't just say subject change, Michael, you need to change the subject." She arched her back, stretching her arms out behind her, pushing her chest out. Mike couldn't help but look. She'd shed the leather jacket at some point. Her V-neck top was, in Mike's estimation, "ridiculously tight" and "shockingly low cut." One thing hadn't changed about dating, it seemed. People still went all-in on highlighting their best features. His mind scrambled enough as it was, he was almost relieved that his thoughts had slipped into the gutter.

"I have one then. You mentioned earlier. Uh. What is an auto-vibe?"

"Oh, Michael." Her voice was low and breathy, playful with a tinge of disappointment. "You really are like a cute little caveman." She stood up and beckoned for him to follow, disappearing through a dark doorway. His eyes narrowed. He downed the rest of the beer, then dutifully followed.

It was pitch black aside from the slight glow coming from the lamp in the other room. Mike stood by the doorway, not wanting to trip, slam into anything or otherwise make a fool of himself. He heard Kathryn mutter something under her breath and a bedside lamp came on. She was laying on the bed, in the centre, a wry smile on her face. His eyes wandered up her painted-on blue jeans, her breasts heaving out of her shirt.

"I at least still know how this part goes." He chuckled at his own bad joke, then crossed the room and started to climb onto the bed. She chuckled awkwardly.

"What uh, what are you doing?"

He stopped, his hands on the foot of the bed, his feet on

the floor, his face once again going red. "I'm... sorry, it's been a while. I thought you wanted me to, uh."

She scooched herself up, her back against the headrest. "Oh! Oh. Right, no, no. Honestly I haven't done, uh, that, since... I can't even remember. Have I ever? Possibly when I was a teenager!"

Mike was spiralling into confusion. This night was becoming way, way too much. "What are we..."

Kathryn laughed. "You've really been off the scene a while, yeah?"

"Let's just say yes, yes I have."

"Okay, so honestly, I'm, well there's different labels, I guess I am mostly aro."

"Aro?"

"Aromantic?"

"Oh. Right, sorry, I knew that." He didn't.

"But like, that doesn't mean I don't like to get off." She patted the bed and looked at him. He pushed himself up onto it, finally taking him out of his weird limbo. He sat cross-legged and felt a decidedly painful burning in his thighs and back. "I just, well I don't know, I don't like to label it. Honestly I get turned on, and I like being around people I get on with, but the idea of anyone touching me just gives me the ick."

"So that's ... aromantic."

"Oh, I don't know Michael, not always." She sighed. "It's a spectrum. I'm not used to having to explain it, I just use the traffic lights. Anyone I go out with has seen the, well, look." She held up her hand and her Ring projected what looked like a phone's home screen onto the bed. She moved her lips, whatever she was saying imperceptible to him. Suddenly, it was projecting her Linkup bio. "See these icons?" Mike leaned down and saw a row of brightly coloured, differently-shaped icons under Kathryn's name. She pointed at them rapidly. "Aro, gray, prefer agent, prefer virtual first, no politics, no religion."

"I, uh, yeah... I remember a friend telling me about these, and you're right, I don't really know what they mean. I guess I just figured I'd chat and vibe." His friend was Lyndsey-Helps, but he felt maybe it was a bridge too far to mention he'd watched videos on how to date and still gotten it this wrong.

She tapped on the icons and they expanded to reveal a few more. She quickly rattled through them. "See, these are 'Sex no', 'touch no', 'hug ask', 'cuddle ask', 'auto ask.'" She had an almost educational demeanour. He felt overwhelmed. He just wanted to be alone in his own bed right now.

"So prefers agent," she continued. "This means I would prefer to talk to your chat bot that you've trained rather than having to talk to you, when we're texting. Because it's more respectful of my time, Michael. I can get responses when I need them rather than having to wait for you to be free."

"Right. That makes sense."

"And virtual first, meaning I prefer the first date to be, well, not in person. Which you also ignored."

Mike was mortified. He started to get off the bed. "I'm so sorry, I just really didn't know what any of that meant. And you agreed to meet."

She put her hand up. "No, don't, it's fine. I could've just unmatched from you. I thought it would be interesting to go out with an older guy. Obviously, there's a lot of challenges."

"Sorry. You just mentioned the, uh, sex toy, and then you went to the bedroom, and, well, you're very attractive."

"I understand. It didn't occur to me that you hadn't read

my traffic lights. And honestly, I don't really know many people who even have sex. I guess it's generational. It just comes across as so disgusting and primal to me. Like, we're not animals. It's literally how animals reproduce."

"It's never occurred to me to, well. Not have it. I mean, not by choice."

"I'm sorry, if that's what you're looking for, I'm not for you."

He felt a fresh wave of panic set in. "No, no no, I'm not opposed to any of what you're saying. It's just new to me, that's all. I just didn't quite know what to expect."

"Because you didn't read."

"... yes."

"Another flaw of your generation." She yawned. "Michael, my sweet, lost millennial caveman. It's late. Stay with me." She slid down the headboard, laying down, her head on the pillow. She looked up at Mike. "I'm like, weirdly obsessed with you now. Like you're this sad puppy I have to train."

"No... no, I should go. Really. I'm so sorry."

"It's after 10 p.m., the tube is shut anyway. How would you get home? Don't be silly, lay down. This is a perfect learning opportunity for you."

He awkwardly laid down next to her, still fully clothed. He slid his shoes off at least, feeling like she'd been either unobservant or extremely forgiving that he'd had them on her bed. "What am I learning? How to sleep fully clothed?"

"Michael, we're not 11. You can get comfortable. I'm going to get comfortable." She wriggled out of her jeans, then her shirt. He averted his eyes, trying not to notice her underwear, and instead focused on getting comfortable himself.

Unbuttoning the shirt was such a massive relief. He really needed new date clothes.

"Shouldn't I sleep out on the sofa? I'm happy to do that."

Kathryn tutted. "This is exactly what I mean. Your learning opportunity. Look." She raised both her hands, her Ring again projecting her dating profile, this time onto her other hand. "Cuddle ask, auto ask. You didn't ask. Not that I'm forcing you, of course." She dropped her hands back to her side.

He side-eyed her suspiciously, letting it linger for a second. "Would you like to cuddle?"

"The other one, Michael." He heard a drawer slide open on the other side of the bed. "Ask the other one."

FIFTEEN
A GREENER TOMORROW

July 2041.
Somewhere east of Trawsfynydd, Wales.

THE LAST BIT of the drive to Trawsfynydd had been serene, almost beautiful. Kevin and Gemma hadn't really spoken in hours. She hid mostly inside her co-opted, over-sized hoodie, with her big headphones on, watching out the window as the Welsh countryside rolled by the windows. She didn't know if her low mood was because of well, everything, or because she'd been listening to a specially-curated playlist of extremely sad songs. But it was well and truly low.

It surely didn't help that every one of these songs would've been from the label she used to work for. Hell, she'd probably met half the artists. She even remembered meeting half of that half. She wasn't trying to toe the company line when she'd do that – when she'd build a playlist entirely of their artists – she just genuinely preferred them. And she liked to think she'd had a hand in guiding them toward such a strong catalogue of artists capable of making deeply, deeply depressing music. Soul-crushingly sad. Not all of it, of course. They had plenty of pop, funk, R&B, trance, lo-fi. That was not what the day called for, though.

It had just finished raining, and the sun struck the emerald hills just right, a golden light filtering through a lingering storm cloud. It was the upper to mix with her downer. She floated right in the middle.

"I'm a city mouse" came her reply any time friends, colleagues, family members, random Tinder matches had wanted to go upcountry somewhere. "Come with me to Nottingham for a wedding" said the boy from the events company, with the mullet and the disgusting flat. "My family have a little place outside Glasgow, we can hit the munroes" said the jacked middle-class backpacker with no discernible profession. "The Bath Christmas Market is so much fun," said Blaine with the scary neck tattoo who turned out to be off-puttingly wholesome. It was always a no, no, no. Ibiza, sure. New York, at least twice a year. Dubai, once, for a work thing. The North of England? You had to be fucking joking.

But now she regretted having never come here, to Wales, when she had the means. Because everything she saw now just came with a tinge of pain or irritation at knowing she no longer had the freedom. All the gorgeous lakes and hills of Snowdonia National Park, with Snowdon itself looming in the distance. She knew it wasn't called that anymore, and wished she knew what it was called instead. A Welsh word, she suspected. Kevin would know. She refused to ask him. But Snowdon being a benevolent mountain didn't mind whether you knew what it was called, it let you behold it all the same. Everything so green, so unspoiled. A remarkable restraint they'd shown in leaving it lie, and this was the reward.

She fumbled round in the back seat for the rest of the vodka, but didn't feel it anywhere. Kevin seemed to be talking, she noticed out of the corner of her eye. She lowered her headphones and glanced over. "Hm?"

"I put the rest of the booze in the trunk," Kevin repeated.

"Well, now's as good of a time as any to pull over."

"We're nearly there. Can you do without for 20 minutes?" He sounded disappointed in her. Bloody child.

They'd been driving through the park for quite a while now, down this narrow stretch, and finally they seemed to be turning toward some trace of civilisation. She saw in the distance some businesses, some houses, random bits, like a proper little village. Was this where they were going?

And then she saw: between the car and the village was a massive chain link fence.

Stretching across the road and into the distance as far as she could see in either direction, topped with barbed wire. It cut indiscriminately through the green, with signs dotted on it here and there. CCTV cameras seemed to be monitoring it at regular intervals. Kevin started to slow down as they approached the imposing gatehouse. A massive concrete sign indicated that this was Wales Site F (Trawsfynyd Cymru), with a smaller metal sign proclaiming that it was operated as a partnership between HM Government and Concentra Energy. A faded vinyl banner strung across the top of the gate house had what looked like a little sketch of Snowdon and the slogan "Concentra + UK Government: Green Energy for a Greener Tomorrow."

And of course, there was the much less friendly sign, metal, attached with a couple of wires through punch-holes, flapping in the breeze against the fence. It indicated that this was a secure facility, and that lethal force would be used to protect it.

Kevin stopped the car in front of the gate. Two heavy mounted guns tracked them as they approached, atop concrete pillars on either side of it. The gatehouse was empty. There didn't seem to be anyone around for miles.

A screen, almost like an old drive-through fast food window, was at the gate. Kevin rolled down the window. A digital agent appeared, with an unnerving grin and matinee idol looks.

"Hello, and thanks for visiting Wales Site F." The voice was male, extremely polished, speaking in received pronunciation like some 1950s radio address. Gemma peered around Kevin to get a look at the screen. The head unnervingly did not have a neck or body. "For your safety, and the safety of our staff, this facility is not open to the public, I'm afraid. I am terribly sorry for the inconvenience, but if you could please turn around and leave as soon as possible."

"I'm dropping someone off who works here," came Kevin's sheepish response.

"Of course! My apologies for the confusion. Anyone assigned to Wales Site F would've been given a return code upon their departure through the gate. I'll just need that code and we can get this gate open for you." A light on the gun turret blinked at a regular interval. It remained pointed right at them, feeling much closer than it probably was.

"I've never been before, I've got no code." Gemma shouted past Kevin at the face on the screen.

"Thanks for letting me know you've never been before, and therefore you don't have a return code. It's important to note that for your safety and the safety of our staff, Wales Site F is not open to the public, and therefore no visitors are allowed. Additionally, I'm only permitted to allow you a certain amount of time near the gate before I'll have to ask you to please turn around and leave." It sounded so incredibly chipper as it issued a vague threat.

"I work here ya naff robot, I just missed my train." Gemma was instantly annoyed. She was presenting herself voluntarily for imprisonment, and the prison wouldn't take her.

"Of course, I understand, and I do apologise for the mistake. However, it's important to note that Wales Site F is not open to the public, and therefore no visitors are allowed. Therefore—"

"Can you please give us two minutes to find the paperwork?" Kevin jumped in, hoping to avert a gunning-down.

"Yes, I understand you'd like a bit more time to find any relevant paperwork. Please note that you're permitted to be at the gate for five minutes, starting from when you arrived. If you are still in front of the gate without authorisation by the sixth minute, measures will need to be undertaken. Thanks for understanding." The face flashed an unholy grin, then vanished. It was replaced with a timer counting down from 3 minutes 47 seconds in a pleasing serif font.

"Christ." Gemma panicked. She grabbed her backpack from the floor of the car and started rootling through it like mad, looking for the papers she'd been sent.

"This is insane, I'm going to turn around and leave." Kevin appeared to be keeping it together, as well as one can when automated defences were ready to remove you from the equation over a misunderstanding. Gemma dumped the papers out of her bag onto her lap and started flinging them behind her as she checked then one by one. Kevin looked behind him and went to put the car in gear.

"Wait!" Gemma held up a paper in front of her. "I'm with orientation class 1534!" She shouted her employee ID and her national insurance number for good measure. The timer vanished and the upsetting face reappeared.

"That's fantastic, thanks very much Gemma Thomson. You're permitted entry to Wales Site F with one medium-sized piece of luggage and one hand-carry item such as a backpack or handbag. No vehicles or guests may accompany you at this time." A smaller gate to the side, at the pavement, began to slide open. The main gate remained shut. "Please exit the vehicle and proceed to the gate with your luggage. A bus will be along per the regular schedule to bring you to the facility. You'll find the transport schedule and a waiting area just on the other side of the gate. Please do enjoy your time at Wales Site F, a fruitful partnership between the UK Government and Concentra Energy. Green energy, for a greener tomorrow." The face winked, then vanished. The screen went dark.

Kevin had started rolling up the window. He let out a huge sigh. "Well, we're not dead."

"I can't imagine we were in any danger," Gemma laughed. "Regrettably." It's possible in that moment she pictured herself dying here, at the gate. Shredded into an unrecognisable heap by government bullets. Would she be a martyr? Or just another anonymous victim of the gate to Wales Site F? That wouldn't really have mattered. The important bit would be that she was dead.

She climbed out of the car quickly, avoiding any chance of eye contact with Kevin, looping quickly round to the boot of the car. It popped open and she grabbed her medium-sized piece of luggage and her one hand-carry item. Bullet dodged there. Just for good measure she also reached in and grabbed the bottle of vodka, tossing that into her bag.

And then she stood there. The air was crisp. The wind pushed hard against her face. The wide open green space, the edge of a nearby reservoir with its eerily still water. She took a long, deep breath. The country air filled her lungs. What a rare treat for them.

"I don't know how long I can sit here." Kevin had a real urgency to his voice. Fine. She could still see all this, breathe this air, from the other side of the fence. It was just some fence. Put here by people. It held no sway over the air, or the majesty of Snowdon.

"Yeah, yeah." The wheels of her bag clicked and clacked across the gravel road until she hit the smooth pavement. She turned back to face Kevin, still sat behind the wheel of his car. He didn't even get out. "Kevin? Going to hug me goodbye?"

"I don't know if I'm allowed to get out of the car." Her stomach churned. She tutted and shook her head, putting on an extremely foul expression.

"Well, thanks, man. Sorry you got more than you meant to get. Enjoy that drive back." Kevin stared out the window of his Corsa, expressionless. She doffed her invisible cap to him. "Adieu."

The car started to back away from the gate as she stepped through the door. It slid closed behind her. Everything in her wanted to turn around to see him one more time, but she absolutely would not, instead cutting into the alcove and flopping down on the cold metal bench. A poster hung near her face with a bus schedule. Today's schedule was quite quick to read: there weren't any.

She squinted and saw the edge of the village in the far

distance. Maybe she'd stay a while longer though. She stood and faced back out the way she came, back at the wide green plain, the distant hill, the reservoir. It still looked quite beautiful through the chain link fence.

The vodka was a little over half-full when she arrived. Not ideal, but probably enough to get her through the night. She alternated sitting, pacing, standing, sitting again. She tried to shout for the gate guard, but it wouldn't activate. An ancient Relient K song blared from the tinny speaker on her phone, and she scream-sang along with it. Again. And again. And again.

The gate house was locked, dark inside. It looked like it hadn't been used in years. Flood lamps made her concrete perch an oasis in a sea of blackness as the sun went down. The harsh halogen light gave her a massive headache. The vodka was mostly gone, and so was her phone battery. She thirstily gulped down the rest of both. Her backpack was a suitable-enough pillow, but the bench had an arm rest down the middle making it impossible to lay on. At some point, not long after, the floodlights went out. Complete darkness. She curled up on the ground, her arms pulled inside Kevin's hoodie, shivering and crying in the freezing cold Welsh air.

Her dreams were scattered, chaotic, terrifying. Not anything she could particularly remember. A nightmare of loneliness and running, chasing, being chased. Slipping, falling into an abyss. Landing in an endless ocean. Soaking wet.

She gasped and coughed, her eyes suddenly open. It was absolutely pissing it down. "Fucking christ!" Her head, her back, her arms and legs, everything was in some terrible state. Six different kinds of pain, and completely soaked through. How was there no cover?! She looked at the gate house, with its definitely bolted-shut door. Its window looking into the dusty, empty, bone-dry interior. And in her mind's eye, the blinking light on the heavy weaponry just feet away. Surely it would forgive this trespass.

Her fingers curled around the empty bottle. She struggled to get to her feet as the world spun around her, as every centimetre of her nerves, as all her muscles, her bones and her soul cried out in pain.

SMASH! The window easily shattered, the bottle landing safely inside the gate house, out of the rain. Jagged glass shards jutted randomly out of the frame. Lovely.

Torrential rain poured down on her. She looked up briefly and got a face full, feeling like she'd drown instantly. Sure, fuck it.

She clamoured over the waist-high wall and into the gate house, cutting and scraping herself all over her hands and tearing random cuts and rips all over her hoodie and jeans. She thudded down onto a small counter just under the window. Phew. No fall to the ground. And her cuts weren't nearly as bad as she thought they might be. The glass seemed to be dull, rather than sharp. Only a couple seemed to be bleeding.

This was the biggest win she'd had in a long time.

She lay on the counter, completely drenched, panting, her adrenaline briefly masking the pain. Her chest rose and fell, rose and fell. Her breathing slowly came under control. Her heart rate lowered. She burst into a laughing fit and threw her arms straight up into the air. "WOOOOOOOOO!" Even that, though, came with a cost. Joints cracked and popped. She gingerly put her arms back down and scanned the room. Completely empty. Not even a chair, a disused cabinet, a stool. Not even a piece of paper.

An absolute joke, this was. Searing hot pain started to spread through her lower back. More grim laughter. "Useless, I'm so fucking useless." She closed her eyes and stared up at the plain white ceiling, focusing on the sound of the rain.

"Uh. Hello?" She opened her eyes and saw a man standing a ways back from her in the room. The sun was nearly whiting him out. "Are you okay? What happened?"

"The—" She started to speak, but went into a coughing fit. "It was pouring rain outside and there was no bus. I came in here to stay dry."

"What happened to the window?" He sounded calm, but extremely curious.

"It uh, I'm not sure. It was broken. Lucky though, it's how I got in." She raised her hand with a grimace, showing her cuts.

"Why not use the door?" He gestured to the door behind him, which was wide open. She propped herself up a bit with her elbows and stared.

"It was locked. Bolted shut."

"Really? It shouldn't have been. I don't think it would be. This is the waiting room. It's never locked. There isn't a lock."

She let out a groan and shook her head. "Whatever. Who are you? Why are you?"

"I'm driving the shuttle today. Brought someone here. Saw the broken window. Saw you. Do you need a ride back to town?"

The seat of the shuttle was an honest-to-god delight. So plush. So much pain relief. She sank into it and worried she'd never be able to get back up. The same greenery, the same open space, the same crisp air all existed on this side of the fence. It was easy to just put it out of your mind, she thought as she watched the distant buildings get closer.

Her chauffeur, Roger, was a young buck of around 24, messy blonde curls, extremely forgettable face, but kind enough even if he did like to ramble. She noticed he was a bit perturbed that she'd climbed into the front seat with him, rather than the back. But her glare seemed to suffice in calming down any objections. Apparently driving the shuttle was a gig he did for extra credit, which sounded very much like a school thing.

"Not credit, credits. You uh, you new here?" was Roger's fumbling response. Classic Roger.

"Fresh off the boat. I know I look like I fell overboard, spare me the joke."

"Aye right, you'll be keen on credits soon enough, soon as you learn what they are."

She cast her mind back to all the reading she'd done on Understairs. So many bookmarked threads, so much note-taking, so many concepts she'd talked through with Kevin. It was all gone. Where had it gone? Her brain felt like a lemon that'd already been juiced. Not a drop of thought left in there, just rind and bit of zest. Hopefully she'd be able to make sense of the notes on her currently-dead phone.

"I'll be honest, I'm not so good at the learning these days. Mostly get by on my looks and charisma. Usually relied on my assistant for the rest."

"Assistant? Oh, this is gonna be hard for you, huh."

"You're very observant, Roger. I can tell we're going to be fast friends."

SIXTEEN

MS. MARSH AND MS. COOPER

November 2043.
Belgravia, Central London.

ELIZABETH, Siobhan, and Cass sat quietly around a small cafe table in the corner of an otherwise empty Costa Coffee. They'd keyed their order into the display on the table, one by one, and now they waited to be told it was ready. Nobody said a word. For her part, Elizabeth was staring at the table, not quite ready to disappear into her phone, but also unable to be present in the moment. Siobhan sat between them, looking back and forth.

Finally, the light flashed, with a gentle chime accompanying it. Siobhan leapt to her feet. "I'll get them!" She dashed straight to the counter just as the drinks rolled out on the conveyor.

Meanwhile, Elizabeth and Cass sat across from each other. A wholly unsurprising amount of tension hung in the air.

"So? Does she know? What really happened, that is?"

Cass had come off the blocks and was sprinting headfirst into this conversation. "Does anyone? I figured you'd have written your third book about it by now. *What We've Lost, What Comes Next*, and now, *Who I've Smashed*. The trilogy."

"She's my campaign manager," Elizabeth barked. "She's the founder of my political party." She shook her head and looked off to the side.

"You've not changed, have you." Cass needled her. "On to the next then is it?"

Elizabeth slammed her hand down on the table just as Siobhan returned with the drinks.

"Woah, dude! I was gone for like two seconds." She set the drinks down and, weighing her options, chose to keep the tray rather than risk leaving again and coming back to a crime scene.

"We're not ... 'seeing each other,'" Elizabeth said, the second part more delicately. Siobhan looked quickly between the two of them, still holding the tray of drinks.

"I'm sorry," Cass said. "I apologise. It's been a long time. I can't stay angry about it." She looked up at Siobhan. "Did I catch your name?"

"It's Siobhan," Elizabeth interjected.

Siobhan laughed awkwardly. "I'm not sure—"

"Stay angry about what exactly, Cass," Elizabeth fired back a bit too hastily.

Siobhan interrupted with a loud laugh as Cass frowned. "Ha ha, what a scene we're making, in public."

Elizabeth tented her fingers in front of her face and exhaled. She nodded and smiled. "Right, look, I'm sorry. It's just a lot to take onboard today."

"It's unbelievable that you ambushed me with that

ridiculous story about Mike," Cass said with an eye roll. "You know it's not true! If you're going to say anything, say that."

"Do I know it's not true?"

Siobhan gingerly set the coffees down in front of every-one, then slipped quietly into her seat, as if one wrong move might set off a motion alarm that killed her instantly.

"Look, I'm sorry this was stressful for you." Cass sipped her drink. "But there's no need to revert to this nonsense."

"This is all my bad, dude," Siobhan said, putting one finger in the air. "I didn't tell her you were going to be here. We probably wouldn't have come otherwise."

Elizabeth didn't remotely understand why she agreed to this coffee, but she wanted it to be over as quickly as possible. Ghosts from her past were popping up everywhere she went in London. She should've expected it, but she'd somehow told herself it was fine. Well, Siobhan had convinced her it was fine.

"So Lizzie," Cass said, "it's been quite a while."

"You fucked my husband." Elizabeth blowtorched the table with that one, Siobhan and Cass both leaning back instinctively to get out of the blast radius.

"Enough! That's— it's...?!" Cass was a volcano, finally erupting. "We walked out of a hotel lobby together! Those are your scandalous photos?"

Siobhan sipped her latte. She pointed at the other two sheepishly. "Lattes."

"Between your outing me as a theatre kid on morning television and The Sun concocting a ridiculous fiction about Mike and I, you seem to have forgotten what actually happened."

Elizabeth stood up. "This was a mistake." Cass stood as well.

"Fine."

Siobhan, not one to be ignored, also stood. "Can we please just be civil, dudes? I want to talk about what happened on the show today, not however long ago this was."

"It was national news, Cassandra," Elizabeth fired back at Cass. "There were photos. I just cannot fathom how you managed to work that quickly. I could see it from Mike, he was so fucking insecure he'd leap into bed with anyone who asked, I'm sure. But you? I thought you were my friend." Elizabeth was seething, furious. Over a decade of rage spilling out onto the table.

"Are you kidding me? Again! It was *one photograph* of us leaving a hotel. You know better!"

"You were holding hands! And the quotes from the people in the room next door about what they heard, and the hotel clerk—"

"Oh, Elizabeth Marsh." Cass sounded bitterly disappointed. "You know *far* better than to believe any of that. It was such a clear, obvious tabloid setup. The story went away in a matter of days! It didn't hold up at all! And surely Mike was able to explain. And you frankly know why it makes no—"

"I never saw Mike again." Elizabeth's voice shook and creaked. Cass leaned back in surprise.

"You what?"

It was quiet again. Siobhan slurped her coffee, watching passersby on the street outside, all of whom were unaware of the history they could witness if they just popped in for a flat white.

"I never saw him again," Elizabeth said. "I left the studio, I went back home. Nobody was there. I expected to find one of you, or both of you. I never saw either of you."

"We went to my flat. He wasn't ready to go back to yours, he was worried there would be press. He didn't call you? Text you?"

"He texted me. He said he knew there was something we had to discuss. Something he didn't know how we could ever move on from. I saw that. And I saw the photos." Elizabeth gritted her teeth and stared down at her coffee as she spoke. Cass stared straight at her, trying to will her to make any sort of eye contact. "It was a decade ago. I don't know. I don't remember everything. I just know I sat alone in our flat for what felt like ages. Reporters stood outside, eventually giving up. And that night, I got in my car and drove to Cambridge..."

Cass's eyebrow went up. She squared her jaw.

"...the next morning," Elizabeth continued, still sounding quite sure of herself. "I saw my phone had melted from all the texts and calls. Luckily nobody really knew how to find me up in Cambridge. But we do get The Sun in Cambridge. And there you two were on the cover."

"That's when you resigned," Siobhan jumped in. "Shit."

Elizabeth nodded, and focused on her coffee. Cass's smile was extremely tight. "So, that's what you're saying Mike was talking about. That's what you are telling me you believe, Elizabeth. That Mike was texting you to speak about the two of us together. Mike and myself."

"What would you have me believe, Cassandra? It all lined up," Elizabeth said. Cass sighed, possibly bemused by Elizabeth's wilful ignorance, or possibly just bored of it.

"This is crazy." Siobhan tried for another helpful contribution. "This was like, so long ago. Ms. Cooper, you were really helpful today on the panel. Maybe uh, not at first, but at the end. I really appreciate it. I'm sure everyone in the party appreciates it."

"It was surprising," added Elizabeth. "Why take bullets for a new political party that will, no offence Siobhan, probably fail to pick up any seats?"

"I didn't do it for your, what is it? Human First? I did it for you. And one can be a bit less restrained in their comments when they've decided to retire."

"Retire? You won't stand again?"

"No, and I've taken my time letting people know about that. They'll probably start figuring it out. And then the party will politely ask me to stop appearing on panel shows, no doubt." She gave a wink.

"Retiring? Sure you wouldn't consider standing for us instead?" Suddenly Siobhan's angle was clear to Elizabeth.

"Christ, this whole environment terrifies me." Cass just shook her head and smiled. "I've done my public service. I'm happy to sit back down now that we're getting to the part where terrorists are stalking people, breaking into offices. I know what comes next."

"What comes next?" Siobhan turned slightly to face Cass. Elizabeth seemed to be relieved. She leaned back and held her mug of coffee between her hands, closing her eyes. She was determined not to betray just how much of her sanity this little coffee date was costing her. How could it go straight back to how it was, whenever you ran into someone from your past? The moment she saw Mike, she could feel the chaos from ten years ago fighting desperately to break out and come to the surface. She kept a lid on that. But now, here, looking at Cass, sat in a fierce chat with Siobhan, she was worried she had no refuge. No chance to keep it sealed.

"They're not bloody terrorists," Siobhan exclaimed.

"They're fighting for what they believe in, they're trying to wake us up, and we should be thanking them. They're making people realise there's a better way. You can't just write a book about how good you used to have it and then hide away. You've got to take direct action."

"I wrote two, actually." Now it was Elizabeth's turn to dive in front of bullets. "Not that anyone read either of them."

"Beg pardon Ms. Marsh, I'm not saying *just* writing, well, I mean to say I'm not implying. Obviously your book was a big inspiration to me."

Cass looked at her with a suspicious gaze.

"I appreciate that, Siobhan," said Elizabeth tersely. "I'm sorry, I shouldn't butt into your conversation."

"Please do," Cass invited her in, against her will. "How do you feel about these Just Stop AI yobs?"

"It's AI Kills," growled Siobhan.

"I respect why they're doing it. I'm glad they're angry. But I don't condone it. And I wish they'd stop before things get out of hand." Elizabeth nodded at Cass. "Don't you agree, Ms. Cooper?"

Siobhan was unsettled. "You focking middle class women, so comfortable in your middle class lives. Nothing will be different for either of you, no matter what. All my friends? My family? Everyone who volunteers at our events? All conscripts. Slaves for the state. They don't give a fock if they get arrested for doing what they do. They're already in prison! How much worse could it be?"

Elizabeth and Cass both looked down at their coffees. Neither made a move or rushed to speak first. The tension was back. Siobhan breathed out sharply and grimaced.

"Look, I'm sorry. I just get where they are coming from,

and I want to help them. And I know you two do, too. I just want you to—"

"We get it," Elizabeth interrupted. "We don't have anything at stake. You're right. I have my family money, Ms. Cooper has her state pension. But I promise you, I am here, I'm all in. I want to help."

Cass glared at Elizabeth, but said nothing. Siobhan looked between them, and inhaled deeply again. She wanted to be calm, clearly, but she kept bubbling over.

"If you'll excuse me." Elizabeth had decided to bail. "Need the loo." At least, temporarily.

She pushed open the door to the bathroom. Her heart started racing. "Fuck, fuck, fuck," she repeated under her breath as she paced around the grim, unmaintained toilets in the Costa. Was she right? Has she felt this way the whole time? She pored back through everything she'd ever said and done, as was her way. It was all too jumbled, too messy right now. Why would she possibly agree to come out with Cass? And those two not getting along? The cherry on top.

She went into a cubicle and sat on the closed toilet lid. She ran her hands through her hair. And again. And again. Exhaling, inhaling, exhaling, inhaling. Her breathing slowed. Her heart wasn't quite threatening to beat its way out of her chest anymore. She closed her eyes and kept running her fingers slowly through her hair.

The door to the bathroom creaked open. Elizabeth quickly threw her foot up and kicked the door to the cubicle shut, leaning forward to bolt it. The distinctive sound of heels clopped in front of it and stopped.

"Liz?" It was Cass.

"Cassandra."

"Liz. How's your head?" Her voice was softer. Elizabeth

remembered Cass's hand on her arm earlier that day. How she took over in Liz's moment of brain fog. How her afternoon could've been much worse, if Cass had not—

"I'm quite fine," Elizabeth blurted out. "Lot of coffee today, long day. Will be out in a moment."

Another sigh from Cass, but nothing else. Clop, clop, clop. She slipped out of the bathroom, the door closing behind her. Elizabeth pursed her lips and squeezed her eyes shut, then stood. For good measure, she gave the toilet a flush, having never even opened the lid. Excellent tradecraft.

Siobhan had moved and was now sat across from Cass. She gave a cartoonish wave as Elizabeth appeared. "I'm explaining the history of the suffragettes to Ms. Cooper."

Cass smiled. "It's all news to me, 52-year-old long-serving member of the British Parliament."

"You seemed like you might need a refresher," retorted Siobhan through gritted teeth.

Elizabeth shook her head and laughed. "Glad you two are getting on famously now."

Siobhan and Cass both replied in unison: "We're faking."

Elizabeth nodded, then gestured toward the counter. "Shall I get us a few more? If we're getting into the history of direct action?" They both immediately shook their heads.

"I'm just off actually, Ms. Marsh," added Siobhan. "Meeting up with a few friends. You two are welcome to stay of course." They both laughed, appreciating the permission from their 20-something companion to hang out together without her. She gave a curt wave and bounced out of the café, looking back briefly.

Cass stood, and Elizabeth had finally worked up the courage to look at her. She really was the same old Cassie. Just a bit weathered, a bit more distinguished. Still so short, on such gigantic heels. A bit heavier. But her eyes looked as bright as ever, a mischievousness behind them. Elizabeth's mind flashed to the seared-in image of her sat on the back bench in the Commons, staring on as the trap sprung, as Alastair humiliated her. It had been so cynical, so unbelievably opportunistic. The sickening reality of British politicking. Every friend concealed a dagger. She felt a knot in her stomach. Her throat tightened.

"Actually, let's find a pub," Cass said. "We might have to take a taxi, not too far. In spite of everything, it's good to see you Elizabeth. I'd quite like to catch up."

Some of Elizabeth wanted to say yes. She looked out from behind her own defences, trapped. Impossible to escape. "I can't actually. Need to keep my energy up. I should really get back to the hotel, review my speech. I've a speech coming up."

"Right, of course. Split a cab then? I'm –"

"—No, I'm actually quite near here. Just the hotel around the corner."

The doors slid open as they approached, Elizabeth letting Cass go ahead of her. Cass looked up at her and smiled. "Bloody Ent, you are."

"I've lived a very long, long time," Elizabeth replied in a deep, growly voice.

"Christ, honestly it's good to see you. I tried to stay angry. But it's just nice." She opened her arms and tilted her head. "May I hug you?"

Elizabeth froze for what felt like an eternity, but was really just a few seconds. She bit her lower lip and nodded, and instantly Cass was wrapped around her, hugging her tight. She hugged her back. They held there, blocking the doorway, their eyes both closed.

"Walk me to my hotel, actually?" Elizabeth whispered that, as she couldn't quite commit to saying it. She felt Cass laugh.

"How about wait for my cab with me?"

"Sure." They finally let go, taking each other's hands, standing there a foot apart. "Cass, I'm sorry I've never called."

Cass raised her finger. "It's okay. We don't need to do it all at once. But I'm going to be worrying about you now. Again. You're mixed up in something now, aren't you?"

"What do you mean?"

"'Humans First'? Your little terrorist friend? Focking terrifying, bab. I'd run away from that as fast as I could."

"There's quite a big difference between being a terrorist and understanding the motivations of someone who feels they've nothing left to lose, Ms. Cooper." Elizabeth had taken a stern tone. She felt cornered suddenly, threatened. Same old Cass, always sticking the dagger in while she had you in her embrace.

"I'd be frightened if the head of my party was so ready to empathise with terrorism." A cab pulled up, the door opening automatically. A smooth digital voice quietly said "Cassandra Cooper." Cass nodded at Elizabeth and climbed into the cab. "Can we please get a drink soon?" The door started to close automatically.

"How do I reach you?"

"Same number, Liz. I never went anywhere." The door shut, the car pulling itself away from the kerb and into traffic. Elizabeth stood alone outside the Costa, watching it drive away.

SEVENTEEN

CONNIE TRASH

November 2043.
Southwark, South East London.

MIKE LAID on the floor of his flat, where he'd been for the better part of three days. Across from him on the floor was an envelope. Time had run out for him. And so had the money. His bank account was drained, his rent was due, and he had to pause his Jobsworth search because he simply couldn't afford it anymore.

It had hit him rather hard. He'd been meant to see Kathryn again, which he surprised himself by agreeing to, but when the day came he was in no mental state to actually leave the flat. Not that he could've afforded it. He wondered whether she might cover it, but was far too proud to ask. And he definitely didn't have the strength to take any more insults about his age or general lack of social awareness.

He'd ignored the first envelope, tossing it straight into the bin when it arrived. He knew that was a no-no, but it wouldn't matter, because he'd have another job soon enough.

The second one was essentially the same as the first, and he'd hung onto it, but didn't bother opening it. Part of him wondered if they somehow knew he'd binned the first one, and he didn't want to chance it. But still. The job would come. It didn't matter.

The third envelope was the final chance. It was red. And it was hand-delivered. "We want to ensure you have a full understanding of the contents of this letter, the opportunity you're being afforded, and the consequences of ignoring it." That's what the man had said. A police officer at his side, a stoic look on her face. Really dialled things up to 11, that.

So there he laid, on the floor near the door, the envelope unopened mere inches away. They'd really wanted to open it for him, to read it to him, to ask him to confirm he understood. He whimpered and simpered and whined his way out of it. In hindsight, it was a pathetic, sad little display. He regretted having done it in front of the female police officer. She was cute, if extremely intimidating. It was probably the latter that had done it for him. A historical weakness of his.

He pictured her coming back later, knocking on the door, letting herself in. "I was worried about you," she'd say. "You looked in a bit of a bad way. And I know how tough you must be having it, to be getting one of these." She'd hang up her various belts, radios, stab vests, hi-vis, head to the couch and beckon him over. He'd lay his head in her lap, she'd run her fingers through his hair, and let him know it was going to be fine. She'd look after him now, until he was back on his feet. And then they could look after each other.

He drifted in and out of sleep, unsure what time it was, not even having a vague sense. The curtains were drawn. A faint glow came from the bathroom nearby, where he'd left the light on at some point. It bounced off the red envelope, ensuring he could still see it, and only it, on an ocean of dark grey tile.

It wasn't going away. Nobody was coming to save him. He'd failed. And his stomach was so empty, he felt like it was eating itself. He slid his hand forward toward the envelope. He rolled over onto his back, picked it up and held it above him. HM Works, Office of the Secretary of State. Final warning. To be hand delivered to the named recipient. He slid his finger under the lip and popped it open.

"You are ordered to present yourself at the HM Works head office for immediate placement," it read. "Failure to respond will lead to arrest and may result in a fixed penalty notice, incarceration or loss of citizenship."

He'd never done anything wrong in his life, he told himself. He stared at the paper in his hand. "I've never done anything wrong in my life! Fuck you! Fuck you!" He screamed at it. It stared back unimpressed. "Fuck!" He slammed his head down against the tile repeatedly. Tremendously painful. Tears welled in his eyes. He instinctively rubbed the back of his head, feeling for a cut or a bruise. The back of the paper, as expected, had one final placement offer for him to accept voluntarily. He'd been avoiding looking. But there was no point in it now. No ignoring it. The new normal had failed him, or he had failed it.

ASSIGNMENT OFFER:
PROMPT ENGINEER (0830-1700)
CONCENTRA UK LTD.
LONDON, GREATER LONDON, E14
NO HOUSING / 2X MEALS
PAY GRADE 3

He lifted his head and stared at the card. This seemed almost... good. Was this good? It certainly wasn't breaking rocks in a quarry somewhere, or fitting solar panels to new builds. He fumbled around for his phone and raced to search. Pay grade 3? That was roughly 2,000 credits per month. Was that good? Chatter on various threads on Understairs seemed to indicate it was pretty good, although there was tremendous disagreement as to how many pay grades there even are. Several people were also quick to note that a grade 3 doesn't receive a housing benefit in London for some reason, which they felt was a huge scam and was setting you up to fail. But it seemed fine by Mike. He already had a flat, and he could easily budget. Presumably these people just didn't quite "get" London.

Maybe it wasn't going to be so bad after all. He really wanted to tell someone, but wasn't sure who. He knew Kathryn's thoughts on "connies," though maybe she'd see it differently if she knew he'd actually be based in London, with a living wage. He never had managed to get back in touch with Elizabeth. Although he could think of any number of awful things she'd say to him about it, and she'd just start ranting about the government no matter what. Just then, a notification appeared on his phone.

'NEW VIDEO ON CHANNEL – LYNDSEYHELPS'

Oh! He tapped on it right away, and Lyndsey appeared. He laid back down on the floor, holding the phone above his face. Today she was talking about some of the best DIY tools to have around the home. She'd been fixing her house up a bit, since it had gotten into disrepair, her late husband having typically done all the maintenance. It was always quite soothing to see Lyndsey there in her sewing room, to hear her warm Cornish accent. Most of Mike's time on the floor had been spent watching her entire back catalogue, gathering little tidbits of the story of her life which she'd pepper into each video. Occasionally he'd leave a comment, something generic or supportive. "Good to see you doing well, Lyndsey!" Or maybe "Really appreciate the advice on this!" And she'd always take the time to reply back.

"You're so sweet to say that!" she'd written in response to one. "Life's a bit less lonely thanks to the connections I make on here!" came another.

He popped open the comments on this new video, which were still mostly empty. Filled with a fresh sense of optimism, with hope, he thought he'd take a little chance. "Found out I've got a new job as of today, Lynds! Not a bad one, at that. I'll have to come take you out for a couple of Rhubarb gimlets soon!"

He hit send and immediately felt a bit of regret. Was he being a creeper? She'd mentioned Rhubarb gimlets were a favourite of hers a few times in a video about cocktail delivery services. And he hadn't wanted to come across as down, but she'd really been helping him get through some hard times. And she always seemed to be so lonely, and, well, what was the harm in trying? He felt a real connection to Lyndsey. He could even conceive of being friends with her, or maybe even more. They were in similar situations, after all. Both without someone. Both lost someone. Both trying to find their place in this world.

For now though, he'd put it out of his mind. He needed to pull himself together. He was starting his new job tomorrow.

The next morning, intake was a bit of a whirlwind. He had the initial embarrassment of turning up at Concentra's headquarters in Canary Wharf, just walking straight through the main door into reception. The receptionist cheerfully informed him that this building was for current, full employees, and that their intake facility for works programme staff was in Wapping. So not only was he twisting himself into a knot apologising, he was also late.

Take two, he thought, as he jumped off the bus. A low-slung brick building, backed up to the Thames, windowless, with a metal door facing out to the pavement. A far cry from the glittering glass tower he'd just come from, but work was work. A sign on the door let him know he was in the right place: WORKS   PROGRAMME   ATTENDEES ENTRANCE. Someone had spray-painted "CONNIE TRASH" in white under the sign. Probably Kathryn, thought Mike.

The process, built up in his mind to presumably be humiliating, degrading, miserable, was actually fine. It was no better or worse than any other job he'd started, except maybe a tad better, because there was no paperwork. Everything was automated and digital. He walked in, approached the desk, and the camera took his photo. "Michael Fernsby," it said. About five seconds later, a bright red badge was ejected from a machine on the desk with his photo, name and some numbers printed on both sides. On the screen, a large smiley face appeared. "Please clip this badge somewhere visible on your person, and display it at all times." He took a clip from the jar and did so. He still hadn't seen anyone.

On the far end of the room was another door with a small metal plate next to it. He approached and the plate lit up, the door sliding open soon after. A vast room full of cubicles was spread out ahead of him, a low din of chatter throughout. It really did seem endless. He hadn't seen something like this since his call centre days, when he'd put in around six months doing telephone support for British Telecom, explaining to people why their internet didn't work. It seemed like several lifetimes ago.

Now though, he just stood, looking around, slouched a bit in his wrinkled shirt and slacks that were a bit too tight at the waist. Was he meant to have gotten more direction? Maybe he left the last room too soon?

"Mike, holy shit, is it you?" A familiar voice?! He turned just in time to get a backslap from Jason, his old colleague from HumanTouch. "Shit, it is you! Mate, this is proper mental. Look at us. Back together at long last. Eh, oh." Jason's eyes scanned down to Mike's badge.

"Jason, hey." Mike was taken aback, in a bit of a daze. He suddenly had to think of how to explain why he'd never responded to any texts, never gotten back in touch. "Really great to see you, man."

"Yeah! Sorry about the circumstances." Jason sounded quite down all the sudden, a tone Mike had never heard him take before. "I suppose we can make the best of it."

"Circumstances?"

"Your, you know." Jason flicked Mike's badge, his eyes darting away nervously. "Mate, it's all good. I shouldn't say anything."

Mike was confused. He looked up and down Jason's person, and then spotted it: Jason's badge was a pleasing shade of blue, rather than the aggressive red. He nodded. "Right, so, what's that then? I'm on probation or something? I just started today. I just got here, actually."

Jason rubbed the back of his neck. He looked so uncomfortable. "No, so. Blue badge means I'm, you know. Employee. And red is."

"Red is..."

"Connie."

"Oh. So you actually." Mike felt tiny. Again.

"You know what? It's not a problem, mate. Not a problem. So, hey, I can show you where you're sitting actually, cause it looks like?" He reached down and tapped his Ring against Mike's badge, then opened his hand, looking at something Mike couldn't see. "Yeah, you're on a 7-day rotation, so you can actually get your own desk! I can get away with just assigning you one. No sharing! A night shifter might use it, but I mean, you'll have the same one every day. That's cool, yeah?"

"Yeah." Mike got the impression that Jason didn't really think any of this was cool. Nevertheless, he followed behind as they walked the length of the facility. Dozens and dozens of people, of every race, gender, age, all sat at identical desks, headsets on, muttering away. They finally arrived at a section that was mostly empty. Jason gestured into an open cubicle.

"This is you, my man. You're late, but I can put that down to extenuating circumstances. I know they put the wrong postcode on the cards for this gig." He seemed to be slipping into "manager, but we're cool" mode. This would never be comfortable. But hopefully we could keep it in this gear.

"So what do I do?"

"Oh, no worries there, you'll be a pro at it. You're just prompting the automations, that's all. So on the screen here, you'll get a sort-of high level task, like uh, well, let's do one. Have a seat." Mike sat down and put the headset on. Jason hopped up and sat on the desk next to him. The display flickered to life and displayed both Mike and Jason's names and photos. Jason leaned forward and tapped Mike's photo, then grabbed Mike's badge and tapped it to a small plate on the desk. "So that's you logged in, you just do that every day when you get in."

"Got it."

"Then you wait. And..." A queue of tasks appeared on the screen. "So these tasks come in, and anyone can grab them. It doesn't just hammer you with work, you pick one and start it. Then do another. So you're free to go get a coffee, use the bathroom, whatever you want. You just need to hit quotas, but it's easy, you'll hit them."

"Okay."

"So here's one. These are wicked, you want these." Jason tapped one with a little drama masks icon, and it opened full screen. He quickly tapped "Accept," and Mike's name filled in for "Assignee." "So we'll do this one."

Mike quickly read through the screen:

WORK ORDER

CLIENT: BBC

CATEGORY: DRAMA COMMISSIONING

PROMPT: 'Produce the next episode of EastEnders and prepare it for air'

PROMPTER: p.riggs

What a funny thing to see. Jason side-eyed him and grinned. "Pretty cool, right? Okay, so these can take a while. But it's fun. You basically just gotta pull up the previous episode and see what's going on, and then sorta work out what happens next. And a few other things. There's a whole checklist, yeah?" He tapped the screen, pointing at a box labelled "Action Points." It had a long checklist of items, like "Review previously commissioned episode," "Prompt for plot," "Prompt for scenes," "Quality check," "Prompt for character production" and so many more that seemed to scroll off the screen.

"So, wait..." Mike stared at it, his mind reeling. "I honestly, Jason, I honestly assumed this was a bit more automated than this. Can't the AI just take this task list and do it itself?"

Jason laughed. "Mate, I know. I thought the same thing. Here, we should knock out a few of these quickly though." He picked up the headset and ran through a few of the first few action points, pulling up the previous episode and asking the AI to summarise it. He then asked it to extrapolate what each character would do next, and to turn that into a bulleted list. One by one, he asked it to write each scene. Mike watched in amusement, but was also increasingly confused.

Finally, Jason took off the headset. "So yeah," he said with a smile. "It's basically that. Anything that's not bang intuitive, you'll get some notes on the screen that sort of explain what to do."

Mike shook his head. "I don't understand. This is all automated. What am I doing?"

"So," Jason leaned down, whispering. "Honestly mate, what you see there, is what the user prompted it with. So in this case, P. Riggs, probably some producer at the BBC, sat at his desk. And that comes to us, and we break it down into more manageable prompts, and handle those. It's all seamless to P. Riggs. They just see the result. So it is automated, it's just also sometimes there's a few people in the mix that nudge it in the right direction."

"Surely it could just read itself the list of prompts."

Jason laughed again, a little more nervousness creeping in. "Sure mate yeah, and sometimes I think it does. But you know, there's occasionally capacity concerns, or power concerns or something. I honestly don't know fully, way above my pay grade. I'm new here too, remember. But we're here to just help it out and make sure P. Riggs doesn't get told to try again later."

"Right, okay." Something about this wasn't sitting right with Mike at all. It made no sense. These AI models were already so sophisticated. Why were humans in the loop at all? And why had he never heard of this? Given the whispering, he guessed it was something they didn't exactly brag about.

"Make sense? It gets really cool on these, you get to prompt it to shoot the virtual characters on the different sets, it synthesises all the voices, it's absolutely wicked mate. You get to basically make an episode of EastEnders right here at your desk." Jason seemed so into this. It must kill him that he basically just supervises others and doesn't get to do it himself.

"Sounds cool, mate. I could've done a lot worse, assignment wise."

"Right? Yeah, that's the spirit. You get it. Cool, cool."

"So," Mike tossed in, trying to be "fun." "When I get a prompt, and I'm giving other prompts to fulfil it, those aren't just going to someone else in this room, right?"

Jason smiled wide and gave him the two-finger point. "Oh, this guy, look out. Mate honestly, you're gonna love it here. Come find me if you need anything, my office is right by the door."

Mike finished up the rest of the day as he'd been shown, and it actually wasn't too bad. It did feel invasive. There were the corporate requests, like the one for the BBC. Some others to prepare shipping manifests, paperwork for bringing goods into the EU. Some random admin for a florist. Tax forms. The usual things you'd expect to see automated. Crucially, no designs, as that might've sent Mike spiralling. But there was also the odd personal request. Write an apology to my wife. Plan my wedding, including venue bookings. Does this scan show signs of cancer? It was bizarre. Mike was mostly just spooling this all off to the AI agents, but a few of them he had to tackle himself. Fully manual. The person requesting this would have no idea any actual humans were involved at all. How would they feel if they knew?

At any rate, the day ended, and Mike went home satisfied. He had a new job, with a boss he knew, a boss he liked, a boss he was pretty sure liked him. So that part of his life was sorted now. Thank goodness.

It would be another few weeks before he understood the extent of his dilemma.

"I'M NOT QUITE sure what you're asking." Jason put on quite a front. He had to know this was coming. Surely it was common. "As a works programme attendee, your salary isn't in pounds."

Mike shook his head. "I don't understand. How can you pay me, but it's not in pounds?"

"The paperwork should've made clear it's in credits, mate. This isn't something I've made up."

"Right, I mean I did see that. I did. But I guess I just didn't understand. I assumed credits and pounds were the same. Or that I could change my credits for pounds."

"You can mate, you can. Has no-one shown you how to do that?"

"Yes, I've seen it," Mike snapped back. He'd only just. The exchange rate was abysmal. Ridiculous, one might say. An entire month of his wages couldn't cover a single month of rent on his flat. And he'd been continuing to spend, going pub for the occasional, seeing Kathryn again, which meant a pricey tube journey, buying himself a few new sets of work clothes. His savings were nearly gone.

"Mate, I honestly don't know what to tell you." Jason's veneer was quite thin now. "You're not a real employee here. I have very limited options. I can't bonus you, I can't enter into any sort of salary discussion. You're essentially a ward of the state. You're staffed here through them."

Mike rubbed his face. This was fucking unbelievable. It was goddamn absurd. He was a highly qualified, eminently experienced professional. Jason used to be his peer, not that long ago, at the same company. Really, his junior, if they went by tenure. It was frankly unacceptable the position he now found himself in. "If something can't change," he finally said, "I'm afraid I won't be able to continue here."

Jason cleared his throat. He stood up and walked around his desk, past Mike sat in the chair across from it, to the door. He kicked the doorstopper with one swift motion and the door slammed shut as if it were spring-loaded. "Mike. Mate, I dreaded this conversation the moment I saw your badge. I knew it was coming." He sat on the edge of his desk, next to Mike, looking down at him. "We've spent a lot of time together. That makes this hard."

Mike felt his stomach drop. He'd never come close to seeing Jason like this. Had he ever seen Jason actually doing his job? Or had it only been in the kitchen? Or the pub after? Definitely once at a wedding.

"Mate, I'm supposed to keep my comments strictly limited to our engagement here." He stood up and looked behind him. In the corner of the office was another chair. He picked it up, spun it round and sat down eye-level with Mike. "You obviously are struggling. I'm not blind to it. I've seen your productivity dip over the past week or so, and I've seen you linger outside my door a couple times. But there's honestly nothing I can do. And if it doesn't work out here." He put his hand on Mike's shoulder and leaned in. "Mate, they'll just reassign you. It won't be a desk job."

Mike nodded. He'd lost the capacity for speech. It was unbelievable what he was going through right now. He'd never imagined it. All he could do was nod. Nod. Nod. And look down.

"I hope it's somewhat easier to hear coming from me. I hope we can get ahead of it. I really do."

Finally, he looked up, met Jason's eyeline. His stomach turned again. He parted his bone-dry lips, a frog in his throat. "Can... can I ..." he stammered. He remembered what he'd read on Understairs. "Can I get a housing benefit?"

Jason stared for a moment, then let out a loud sigh. "Mike. There's no housing benefits in London right now. I'd absolutely fight for it for you. I absolutely would. Even when I started we had some, for like a month. But they stopped. I have no mechanism to even ask."

Mike's lip quivered. He ran his hands back and forth across his trouser legs, feeling the smoothness, the weird texture of the synthetic material. His eyes darted around almost involuntarily.

"I really am sorry, mate. I don't want to have to say all this. I was crushed when I saw the colour of your badge. I was crushed." His voice did waver a bit. He might actually feel bad.

Mike nodded and stood up, determined to save a bit of face. "Yeah thanks, yeah. I'll sort it. Sorry to bother, I will sort it."

"It's honestly no bother."

"Thanks, mate. I'll get out of here." Mike nodded hard, again. He slipped out the door without a look back.

He burst through the door of his flat many, many hours later. Fresh from the pub. Stinking, drunk, stinking drunk. No fucks given about his bank balance. His prospects. His future. His past. None of it mattered. Fucking Jason, he thought. He kept thinking, all night. Fucking goddamn Jason. This was his fault. He didn't take their job seriously at HumanTouch, and he doesn't take his job seriously now. His not taking the job seriously probably tanked the business in the first place. It would tank Concentra, too. The way they could just ignore his talent, totally immune to his struggle, when they could snap a finger and solve all his problems. And free him up to perform for them. To tackle harder and harder prompts. To solve whatever problem was causing them to need so many people in the first place. Nobody gave a shit.

He pictured Kathryn, her gleeful over-the-top reactions to the most mundane things, and smiled. He grabbed his phone, knowing she'd find this interesting. "Unbelievable bullshit today at my work. Working at Concentra now. you wouldn't believe if I told you. so dysfunctional." He waited a second, to see if she came online and read it. Nothing. What time was it? Around 11pm. Fuck her, anyway. Probably out, with some other guy, probably multiple guys. She's fickle, that's what the badger-faced man had said.

"Crazy developments today in my life, funnily enough." He tapped out a comment on Lyndsey's most recent video. "Starting to feel so lost in all this. You're my anchor keeping me from drifting out to sea." And, send. It was true, too. Lyndsey was there, consistently, always. Everything had slipped away. All of it. His job, HumanTouch. People can tell! Yeah, fuck it, they don't even care. The whole company, gone. Elizabeth? Elizabeth. Fate brought them back together. And of course Elizabeth, oh, Elizabeth. Who else but her would ignore fate. Reject fate. Dispute it. So that was over and done with now, too.

He stumbled to his kitchen, banging his head hard against the dividing wall. A sharp corner there, going from the living room to the kitchen. "Fuck!" He slid down, deciding to sit on the floor instead. Didn't need water. He ran his hands across the tile. So cold and smooth. Everything was bullshit. All of this was bullshit.

He knew what he had to do. It had all become clear after a brief nap on the floor. He grabbed his phone. Straight to BritRail, straight to the journey planner. He'd go to Cornwall. He'd go, and he'd find Lyndsey. Because she'd understand. They'd basically been through the same things. The same problems. He knew she was near Penzance, so he'd just go there. He'd go and ask around and it would be fine. Tap tap tap, and he was booking it.

"It appears you are currently on a works programme allocation." The message from BritRail was blunt. "Please confirm that you have requested the appropriate dispensation." He tapped rapidly on the screen. Another message briefly appeared, something about not being able to confirm. Tap tap tap, and it was gone. And, booked.

He nodded, looking at the screen. In the morning, he'd go. One day away was fine. Seven day rotations were something mostly for the new grads, the less experienced. People who didn't know the boss. His head hit the tile, his arm tucked under.

It would be fine.

EIGHTEEN

THE PUBS OF PENZANCE

Late November 2043.
Somewhere west of Reading, England.

"MR. FERNSBY?" The train guard had already scanned his ticket and moved on. Mike had gone back to staring out the window, watching the tents and rubbish go past as they worked their way out of London. "Mr. Fernsby, yes? That is you?" So why had he come back?

"Yes, that's me."

"I'm afraid I'm required to inform you that you're absent without approved leave." He turned the scanner around and quickly showed Mike the screen. It had his photo, a lot of words and a lot of red. "I'll need to ask you to disembark at the next station and present yourself to the police."

"N-no, no, that's a mistake. My manager knows I'm off today, tending to a family emergency." He avoided eye contact. Mike was a terrible liar, and always had been. "He probably forgot to log it. It was short notice."

The train guard grumbled a bit to himself, looking down

at the screen again, then up at Mike. "Mate," he whispered. "I've already scanned it."

"Can't you—"

"They'll be waiting at the next station. They'll be expecting you."

"What if I—"

He shook his head and turned, walking away, continuing his rounds. A few stray eyes peered over and around seats, trying to catch a glimpse of the scofflaw making such a fuss. Mike squeezed himself against the window, still watching everything fly past outside. Surely they didn't actually check on these things. Not for a first offence. Maybe they'd log it, he'd get a slap on the wrist. But he just couldn't get off the train. Not now. Not after finally working up the courage to go see Lyndsey, spending virtually every penny he had left. There was nothing left to lose. And everything to gain.

"The next station is Newbury." That calm, generic, generated voice. It took on a more sinister quality, Mike knowing that his fate might await him there. He half-expected it to read his name out and tell him to disembark. It didn't though. Some people shuffled off, some others on. Mike sat motionless, unwilling to let go, quite literally, his hands gripping the sides of his seat.

The doors slid closed with a chime, a loud rattle and some grinding noises. Was it all bluster? No-one had stormed the train to retrieve him. He peered out the window. No police presence to speak of on the platform. Clearly, all bluster.

As the train began to move, his phone lit up. It was a message from Jason. He swiped his hand dismissively over the screen and it disappeared. That was for later. When he had some good news to share. Something that seemed to be a valid reason for missing work. It's not like it was exactly fair that he didn't get weekends off. It shouldn't even be legal.

The hours crawled by and the train ambled along, his second of the journey, having changed at Exeter. Cornwall looked close on a map, and yet it had been nearly five hours since he'd boarded at Paddington. A lot of stations seemed disused these days. Closed, abandoned, maybe repurposed. The train still had to slow down to go through them, but most had unusually high barriers of metal or plywood blocking your view. All in all it was remarkably less remarkable than the last time he'd come out this way, probably with Elizabeth, probably over a decade ago. The trolly went by and he picked up a gin tinny to loosen up, take his mind off of it. He didn't know how much money he even had left at this point. But it was now £15 less. Bloody train prices.

Finally, the announcement came. "We will shortly be arriving in ... Penzance... where this service terminates." Hardly anyone was left aboard at this point. Mike stumbled out into the afternoon sun looking rather disheveled, his unwashed hair having left a greasy spot on the window. This was just a reconnaissance mission. If he found a lead, he had time to pull himself together somehow, even though he had nothing with him and possibly no money. At the very least, he'd rely on Lyndsey being understanding of his whole deal.

In between naps he'd looked up a few spots where locals might be, figuring he'd simply show Lyndsey's photo to people, ask around, see if anyone knew her. She talked a lot about her favourite drinks, so he just assumed she left the house sometimes to drink them. Especially as a widow, surely she'd be using a pub in the area for some socialising.

As he stepped into The Mitre he could feel a few sets of eyes on him right away. It was quiet, and bright. A rough, worn-out look to the place, like it was really starting to feel its age. Chips and splinters abound on various low tables, the wooden flooring knotted, untreated and with gaps between the boards you could lose a 50p coin down. The bar itself wasn't too shabby, with care and attention paid, the cherry wood polished and shining, gorgeous copper pipes for the three draught beers with ornate logos on each tap handle. And behind the bar stood a rather cross looking heavyset man with a flat-cap atop his bald head and a football shirt stretched over his stomach. This was a proper pub.

"Hello, excuse me, I'm just in from London, and I—"

"Christ," said the bartender under his breath.

"I, um, and I um," Mike stammered, "I'm actually looking for someone."

The bartender gestured out to the rest of the room, where a handful of old punters sat quietly, nursing full pints. "This is the lot of them. Oh, are you meeting your friend upstairs for silver service? Perhaps out on the fuckin' veranda?"

Mike grimaced. He'd put a foot wrong here somehow. "Sorry, I don't mean that I'm meeting anyone, I'm actually looking for someone in town. I'm wondering if maybe you know—"

"You gonna order anything?"

"Yes, I um, yes. I'll have a gin and tonic?"

He patted one of the beer taps. "Pints, mate."

"I'll have a pint. Sure."

"Pint of what."

"Whatever's on."

The bartender nodded and started pulling what looked like a nice amber. Mike tapped his phone to the paypoint on the bar. It flashed red and buzzed quietly.

"Credits only, mate." He pointed with his free hand at a

sign, heavily graffitied and stickered over, the relevant bits still barely visible. 'NO £ / CR$ ONLY'. The bartender put the drink down in front of him. "You a connie, London? We're a connie bar. Need to leave else, house rules."

Mike grimaced again, rapidly adopting it as his trademark look. He nodded and fumbled with his phone, opening his WorksPay app, then tapping the paypoint again. It let out a pleasing chime and flashed green.

"You out on the tidal plant build? New in? You don't look right for it mate."

"No," Mike replied between sips. "I'm just in town looking for someone. Actually, do you know her? Lyndsey?"

"Lyndsey? What's her surname?"

"... I don't know."

"Don't know any Lyndsey. You lot," he raised his voice. "Anyone know a Lyndsey?"

A choir of grumbles accompanied by head shakes. Mike stared at the pint, then the sign on the wall. Well, she wouldn't be drinking here. She's not in the works programme as far as he could tell.

"Any other pubs around here? Ones that aren't just ... connies?" The bartender scoffed. Someone behind Mike chuckled. "I just mean, the person I'm looking for, they're... not one."

"The Billet's up the way, up on erm... oi, where's the bloody Billet?" He shouted past Mike. An ancient man with his head drooped low, practically dipping his nose in his pint, muttered back inaudibly. "Yeah right, up on St. Mary's. Should be open today. Tossers."

Mike finished his pint, then left unacknowledged into a heavy downpour. He repeated this pattern at The Billet, also having no luck, but was sent to The Goose & Gander, which was closed. Someone in a tent on the pavement nearby thought for sure she'd seen Lyndsey hanging round at The Meritorious, which was up near the old soft play, across from the new dorms, which weren't done yet on account of all the weather lately. But nobody there knew her either, and by then he was completely soaked through, and already too late for the last train back.

He curled up on a bench inside the train station and waited for morning, finding it marginally more comfortable than the tile floor in his flat. He knew she was somewhere out there. He wondered if, had he found her, she would've taken him in. He thought about pulling up one of her videos, to calm him down, help him sleep. But he couldn't spare the battery.

The first train back to London left shortly before 7 a.m., which, after changes and the glacial speed at which it moved, got him into Paddington around Noon. By 1:30pm, he was slinking awkwardly into the office, looking and feeling like absolute hell. Jason was stood angrily in the doorway of his office waiting.

"I can't get my head around what you've done here. I really cannot." It was not the tone of a disappointed friend. It was the tone of someone who thought perhaps jail might sort you out.

"I'm really sorry, Jason. I'm so sorry. I thought I had the day off."

"How could you have possibly—" he raised his voice sharply, then looked around. He motioned for Mike to join him in the office, shutting the door behind them. "How could you have possibly thought that?"

"I don't know. I'm new to all this. I haven't been feeling well."

"Mate, this isn't a bloody job. I can't just sign you off on compassionate leave while you mourn your dead career. It's a fucking prison."

"I know."

"They sent me a photo of you sat on the train! How was Cornwall, by the way? Nice little holibobs? The sea air do your lungs good? What the fuck, Mike! The state of you!"

"I can go home."

"You absolutely cannot. You need to go work, now. Please, please try to salvage this. Please don't make me have to actually do something about it, Mike. You were never like this at HumanTouch. Pull yourself together."

He slinked back to his cubicle, stinking and distraught, still feeling damp in places. There were, of course, loads of requests for him to work on, and he found it somewhat rewarding, or at least distracting. Nothing so glamorous as a new EastEnders, but a smattering of random low-effort stuff. He still felt confused, utterly baffled by this. How many other giant rooms full of people existed? He really wanted to know if, when he asked the AI to multiply a bunch of numbers, if someone in the cubicle next to him got out a calculator.

But then one request caught his eye. He almost instinctively tapped it, accepting it. And then he stared. It had the little film icon next to it. The client was listed as *Aspirential*, an advertising firm he knew because they consistently got work HumanTouch had bid for. And the summary Mike had trouble reading. His eyes went in and out of focus. He leaned back in his chair, trying to physically distance himself from the words. "Create a LyndseyHelps video to market our new sewing machine. Product information is attached." Tasks populated down the right side of the screen. He skipped the first few, his eyes finding "Prepare virtual set." He tapped it, and after a moment, there it was. Lyndsey's sewing room, lit exactly as he'd always seen it. This close, and at this resolution, he could tell it wasn't real. A computer-generated virtual set. An empty fake chair sat in the foreground.

He winced and looked partly away, seeing enough of the screen to tap "Load character from library." The usual search interface appeared. Under his breath, his voice cracking, he said "Lyndsey." The search results appeared, and there she was, part-way down. He spotted her instantly from the thumbnail. Tapping it placed her, after a moment, straight into the chair, the designated spot in the virtual set where the character went.

There she was. Mike felt a bead of sweat coming down his forehead as he stared at the screen. He made eye contact with her cold, dead stare. Completely frozen, awaiting input. Awaiting him telling her exactly what to say. To do some quick searching, to find some inferior sewing machines, so Lyndsey could make her pick for the one she was being paid to shill for. It was her purpose. She existed to shill. She didn't exist at all.

He was breathing so heavily now. He held two fingers to his wrist, trying to feel for his pulse. His feet got tangled up on the chair leg as he rubbed them together, nearly sending him flying backwards. He scratched his arm, a lot, the skin feeling raw and numb under the sleeve of his shirt. Still, her eyes stared out at him, a vague smile on her face. It was breathing: the model designed to animate, even when idle. It blinked. He jumped to his feet, still staring at the screen. He had to get out of here.

In the corner of the screen a timer had been running, and slowly getting larger, the longer Mike took. It knew roughly how long each task should take an average worker, on average. This was how he was graded. This determined his pay each day. The timer was huge now, and had gone from orange to red, and was blinking. Some lackey at the ad agency was still sat there, watching a screen, an indicator telling him to wait. He might even see the virtual set, with the virtual Lyndsey sat there, staring out at him too.

He moved swiftly past loads of cubicles, steadying himself on the wall, a couple heads poking up out of cubicles to see what the commotion was. He burst into the bathroom, the first one he came to, slamming the door behind him and bolting it. Vomit went everywhere, sweat poured down his face. He fell to his knees, crying. Not long after, he was being quietly escorted out of the building.

That night, at his flat, he packed. A notice had been taped to his door when he finally got home. The reddest of envelopes. As it had not worked out in his current posting, it said, they had generously arranged an alternative for him. They wanted to see this work for him. It wasn't optional, they added, but they appreciated his flexibility.

As he brushed his teeth, his phone lit up. A text from Kathryn, wondering if he was free for a gig that night. He swiped it away.

NINETEEN

BRIXTON HIPSTER BULLSHIT

January 2044.
Wales Site F, Trawsfynydd, Wales.

IT WAS MOVING DAY, and Gemma was excited.

Not her moving day, of course. She was staying put, having consistently failed to score a room upgrade for her first two years, and recently having decided she quite liked life in The Bunks, actually. She liked the company. It was good for her, she figured, or at least it made things interesting, and gave her a built-in audience for her various rants, riddles and impromptu acoustic performances. No, it was moving day for Shruti, who hadn't had any trouble scoring a room upgrade, and was now packing for her imminent trip next door to her very own studio flat. And since it was moving day for her, that meant a new bunkmate for Gemma and Co.

She'd miss Shruti, for the most part, but also Shruti had never gotten on with their other bunkmate Bertie, whom she found "irresponsibly complicit" for actually enjoying his life.

So that would ultimately be a relief, to be rid of that toxic dynamic.

And then there was Cian, who held similar contempt for Bertie, and had tried to use that to bond with and/or smooch Shruti, which probably motivated her to find a new place to live in the first place.

A smile crept across Gemma's face. It really was paradise in The Bunks.

"We'll miss you, girl," she offered up from behind her book. "Better have us over sometimes."

"There's barely enough room to have myself over."

"Well, pretend."

"Can't wait to have you all over!" Shruti flashed a big fake smile, her crate already in her hands. So keen to get out of their lives forever. And that seemed to always be how it went. They'd done more than a few of these bunk handovers since Gemma got here, and she'd never intentionally seen any of them again. Sometimes around the plant, of course, in passing, or maybe on a shift together. But you'd just awkwardly push through. You'd assume sharing the misery together would forge some kind of unbreakable bond, but apparently that only happened in films. The reality was that she had to learn to not get too close to any of these people, because they'd wind up hating her and leaving at the first opportunity.

From another perspective it wasn't hard to understand. The conditions were not great. Four bunks, two on each side of the room. A tiny bathroom with a sink big enough to wash one hand at a time, a claustrophobic shower cubicle, no attention paid to where anyone would keep their towels or toiletries. Everything painted a faded sea-foam green, which research had apparently shown was the colour most likely to put people at ease. (As a result, every square metre of The Bunks had been painted in it.) Both sets of beds had little desks at each end, giving you some semblance of your own space, with the most uncomfortable low-backed task chair you'd ever seen in your life tucked under. It was an extremely efficient use of space. Or, to describe it more simply, it was a jail cell. Gemma found it cosy. On her top bunk she was inches from the ceiling. Tucked away, hidden. But with access to instant socialising with her bunkmates should the need arise. And she had her headphones and her music to disappear into from time to time.

A loud buzz came through the speaker. Shruti spun around to face the door. "I think it's time."

"Bye Shruti, good luck with everything!" Bertie, chipper as ever, sat at his desk, didn't even get a glance.

The door swung open and Shruti shot through it like a bullet. A couple sets of footsteps getting further away, escorting her to her new life and out of theirs. A new flat wasn't just doled out on its own – it was almost always the perk of going up a level. You weren't applying to move, but to get a better job. You technically earned more credits, but the higher pay was immediately eaten up by the added cost of the bigger room. So that was her gone, then.

"Where do you think she's transferred?" Bertie was stood looking up at Gemma now. She contemplated headphones, but instead sighed and rolled over.

"I didn't ask."

"Huh. I'm sure it's a great fit for her, whatever it is."

"Ruthless optimism as ever."

"Hello?" An unfamiliar voice from the hallway. They both glanced over to the door. There stood someone Gemma found a bit familiar, but she wasn't sure from where. Messy greying hair, pricey slim-cut jeans stretched out from overuse, a rumpled graphic T-shirt that was just a bit too short, a beer belly sticking out a bit too far. Ah, she knew where she'd probably seen him. He looked like every man in the bar queue during an alt-rock gig at the Empire.

"Can we help you," offered Bertie, in his tragically non-judgemental way.

"Hi, I think I'm in here. Living in here, I mean." He struggled to keep holding his little crate of things, shifting it around in his arms.

"Oi, the fuck you are." Gemma threw her legs over the bar and jumped down from the top bunk, taking another year off the few remaining in her knees. "Let me see your—"

"—here it is." The man was already holding out a small card, bent and folded all to hell. Gemma took it. It was slightly damp, sweated through in his pocket. Eew. But she could clearly see it said Bunks, Hall R, Room 62.

"Well, okay then. Michael Fernsby, welcome to our little slice of paradise, I suppose." She took his crate and dumped it onto the bottom bunk, where Shruti used to sleep. "That's you. It's probably still warm from the last occupant. If you let us all call you Shruti it would help ease the transition."

"Mike is fine." He extended his hand, which amused Gemma. She gave it a shake and threw in a sarcastic head nod. None of the kids around here ever shook hands, hugged, anything like that. So she grew out of it. Cian had, too. It was going to be annoying having someone else her age kicking around.

"Did you just transfer here? Do you know where you'll be working?" asked Bertie. This was how it went. The new person died slowly, cut to ribbons by Bertie's aggressively positive yet relentless questioning.

"He's from London, aren't ya?" Gemma patted him on the arm. "Yeah, you are. Look at you." Mike stammered out a yes and nodded, robbed of his chance to say it himself. "I'm gonna guess... project management."

"Graphic design."

"Shit, that was my next guess!" She looked him up and down then nodded, a look of realisation on her face. "Well, you've awakened in a strange place, Michael Fernsby. I'm Gemma, that's Bertie. You'll be staring up at me while you sleep. Or you can roll over and face Bertie I suppose. Cian's on top over there. They'll be along at some point, shift changes in a bit. You two can get acquainted while Bertie and I slave away overnight."

Mike looked down briefly at the moist tatters of his assignment card. "I'm on night shift as well." Bertie cocked his head in confusion. Gemma rubbed the bridge of her nose and sighed.

"Christ, three night shifters in here? Right, well, that means I'm technically your supervisor now, Mike. Job one, please tell me your whole wardrobe isn't this Brixton hipster bullshit."

"It's—"

"Don't interrupt, I'm rolling. Bertie, you see him, he's got the fire in him. The fire of youth." She patted him on the back. He grimaced and straightened up, smiling like a show pony. "He also bloody loves this place. So if you want a nice, positive spin on life at the plant, he's your man. Cian, you'll meet them, not so much with the loving of this place, but doesn't make a fuss. See how we've all got books on our desks? Cian can't fit all their books so we pitch in. Please make room for some of Cian's books."

Mike glanced around at the desks and saw there were

indeed piles of books on each, including one that only had books on it, presumably Mike's new desk. He sighed and nodded.

"Then there's me, I feel like we've covered me. How old are you, Mike?"

"48."

"Shit, we're the same age. Well, I'm a January baby, so I'm probably older than you. I can tell you're a summer, you carry yourself that way." Mike just stared, his soul attempting to escape his body. "Bertie, how old are you?"

"You know I'm 22."

"Look at him. So fresh, so youthful. Never shaken a hand in his life." Bertie was beaming. He definitely gave the impression that he'd seen Gemma's bunkmate induction ceremony before. He was otherwise quite a perfunctory human. Brown hair tightly cropped, a round face, rail thin, probably five-foot-seven, in denim overalls with a plain white T-shirt under. Designed to be forgettable, Bertie was as close as you could get to someone having the default Fortnite skin in real life.

At some point during all this a loud, low tone had come out of a speaker on the wall. Mike had ignored it, presumably because he was cognitively overwhelmed, and everyone else had quietly made note of it. This was the shift change bell, and Gemma had long since given up finding it demeaning. Cian appeared in the doorway, looking confused that the door was open, then further confused by Mike's presence.

"Who's this," they asked.

"Don't interrupt," Bertie quickly replied. "She's rolling."

They all walked over to their section of the plant together, Gemma giving Mike quite a performance which disguised various bits of training she was required to do on his first day. They were working in Corridor B, specifically on a control room buildout. It was slow, tedious work, as this week they were simply running wires. So, so many wires. The training for this would take about twenty minutes, she said, and then he'd he get faster and faster at it as the week went on. No, she added, they didn't know what the control room was meant to control, and no, they hadn't been told what any of the other rooms they'd worked on were for either. "It's a nuclear power station, Mike," she'd said when she hit peak annoyance. "Are you a nuclear technician? No. You're a slave who runs wires. Stay in your lane."

It was just the three of them, plus one blue badge who definitely did know what the room was for, and didn't act like anything was particularly secretive. He'd leave them unattended, there was no security aside from the usual CCTV, he seemed to generally trust them. But he kept his distance, the relationship not really existing for them to ask those kinds of questions. Or any questions that weren't strictly related to the work. No real interactions other than his tasking Gemma, who would then task the other two. Classic middle management. Otherwise he just sat in the corner on a little chair, tapping away on a tablet, sipping coffee.

"This is how it always is with the blue badges, by the way," Gemma whispered to Mike. "Honestly, I think they just feel guilty." Mike nodded. Bertie added that it was probably a rule. An utterly useless contribution. Some days Bertie's bootlicking was charming, but others it was exhausting.

For his part, Mike spent the day quiet, absorbing everything, speaking when spoken to. Gemma kept prodding, poking, making jokes, hoping he'd open up. But to no avail. He was determined to be a blank slate. And he hadn't even changed out of his elder millennial uniform. She'd give him a bit more time, though. After all, she knew him well enough to know it'd just take a pint or two to open his floodgates. Then maybe she'd tell him where she knew him from. Or maybe he'd finally realise on his own.

The walk back was relaxed but silent. Gemma was shattered, her back wrecked, her feet killing. She just wanted to be back in her bunk. Usually she could find the energy to go out, and she worried everyone would expect it, especially with the new guy around. Her demeanour must've been a sufficient deterrent, as Bertie just quietly proceeded onto the bar alone when they arrived at the door to their room. She clamoured up into her bunk almost immediately, not even bothering to change into anything more comfortable, just flinging her shoes off the top.

Mike flopped into the little task chair at Shruti's old desk and looked around, seemingly unsure what to do with himself. There was an awkward tension in the room, just the two of them, with Cian presumably also off at the bar. She wasn't quite sure when they slept, if she thought about it. She shook her head and pulled her sleep mask on, hoping to pass out instantly.

Squeeaaaaaaak. Squeeeeaaaak. Squeeeeeeeaaaaaaak. Her whole body tensed up. Squeeaaaaaak. What the hell? She flung up, hitting her head on the ceiling. "Fuck!"

"Are you okay?" Mike's quiet, stoic check-in.

"The fuck is that noise?"

"What noise?"

"The bloody squeaking."

"I don't hear anything."

She exhaled sharply then laid back down, still engulfed in darkness from the sleep mask. Squeeaaaaak. She ripped the mask off and rolled over, shimmying to the edge of the bed, glaring down at Mike. Squeeaaaaaaak went the shitty metal chair as he slowly rotated back and forth.

"Mike, it's you, you're fucking squeaking. Can you stop? Lay down or something. Sit still."

"Sorry."

She rolled back over, laying flat on her back. The sleep mask slipped off her head and fell down. Goddamnit.

"Do you need this?" Mike, goddamnit, stoically offering to hand it back up. It must've landed on his desk.

"No, fuck, I just want to sleep. Please leave me alone." The added stress was making all the sore bits of her outright hurt now. She closed her eyes, throwing her arms down by her sides, fidgeting, trying to find some position that might hurt a bit less. Squeeeeaaaaaaaak. She was properly seeing red now. "Mike, you've lost your fucking chair privileges for the night."

She heard him get up and walk the two steps to the bed. He flopped hard down onto it, shaking the whole unit. He let out a little sigh, then another. Christ.

"Mike, I'm sorry." She softened her tone a bit. Too tired to be angry, perhaps. "I know you get panicky. I mean, I can tell. Just read a book or something. Please? I'm knackered."

"Sorry. I haven't really shared a living space with anyone since, well, it's been a very long time. Yesterday I had my own flat in London."

"We all had our own flats in London, mate. Not special."

"Is it possible to eventually get your own flat here? Or at least a private bedroom?"

"It's possible. It's not for me. But some people manage it. Or they manage to shack up with someone who managed it.

Word of advice on that, as best I can tell, nobody here fucks. So that's a dead end."

He was quiet for a bit. She wondered what he was doing down there. Finally, he piped back up. "Should I turn off the lights?" She smiled.

"Sure, go right ahead."

She listened as he plodded around the room, probably checking every open bit of wall. Then the desks, one by one. She'd give him this, he was thorough. And again! Working his way back around. Extremely typical. Refusing to simply ask her. Once he'd started his third round, she couldn't take it anymore.

"There's no switch, they're always on. I hope you have a sleep mask."

"What?"

"I'm sure Bertie can breathlessly defend the decision by our corporate slavers to never turn them off. But they're always on. You can use mine. Since it's down there anyway."

"I'll be okay." Classic Mike. So defeatist, needlessly so. What a martyr. She shook her head, staring at the ceiling. There was a little spot where she'd hit her head. She rubbed it, trying to clean it off. Down below, Mike tossed and turned loudly. Everything the boy did was loud.

"Mike, I know it's fucking mad here. I remember what it was like when I got here, years ago now. I was off my head. It does get better, if you let it. Not much better, but you get used to it."

"Right. Okay." He sounded so down. So done.

"Cheer up, anyway," she added, using the rest of her energy to muster up a bit of playfulness. "You're a lot cuter in person, yeah? Your photos were a bit shit. The banter too, really."

"Excuse me?" He sounded concerned. Oh, no. But Gemma could barely keep her eyes open.

"Your Linkup profile. We matched a while back." She yawned, starting to drift off. "You really bare your soul on that thing. Bit heavy for my taste." She closed her eyes and rolled over, tucking her hands under her head. "Anyway, I'm passing out. G'night, Mike."

TWENTY

SHE FANCIES HERSELF

January 2044.
Wales Site F, Trawsfynydd, Wales.

MIKE SLIPPED OUT of the room and into the hallway, his utter contempt for himself no longer able to fit in the same room as Gemma, competing for space as it was with her utter contempt for him. So he started walking. The hallway was so brightly lit, all the time it seemed, just like the rooms. Combined with the building being mostly windowless he felt weirdly jet-lagged, isolated, out of position. Like they were on some sort of submarine. Even those had portholes though, surely. He'd never seen one in real life.

Signs on the walls did helpfully direct you around. He appreciated that this place seemed intentionally designed. The walls were a pleasing shade of sea-foam, which he knew from experience was quite a calming colour.

He managed to find his way to the bar, which was full, if not very lively. A low-ceilinged, extremely rectangular space with a smattering of boring tables, a small bar-height table at the back. A bartender stood in front of a few fridges of canned beer, with stacks of crates of more off to one side. A very slapdash affair. He scanned the room and found Bertie, who had already spotted him and was waving excitedly.

Mike stopped off at the bar for a can. It was silver and said PILSNER on the side, with various certification logos and the ABV percentage under it. Huh. Though at least it was a reasonable 15 credits.

"I know, bloody outrageous prices for these. Sip it slowly," said the person Mike didn't know. Bertie shook his head.

"It's actually pretty reasonable," Bertie asserted. "I appreciate they let us drink at all. This room used to be storage I heard, but one day they converted it into a bar to give us somewhere to relax between shifts. This is Mike, by the way."

"Cian."

"Keh... say it again?"

"Key. An. Key-an. Cian." They were older than Bertie, maybe early 40s, Mike would guess. Dirty blonde hair, thick untrimmed beard, a plush red-and-black plaid overshirt hanging loose over his T-shirt, which was just a little hand-drawn sketch of an old record player.

"Got it."

"Sláinte." Cian raised their beer and everyone joined for a sip. Mike immediately felt a bit more relaxed. "Giving Gemma her space? I hear she was pretty rough on you."

"She likes hazing the new guy," added Bertie. "That's you."

Mike gulped down his PILSNER, rejecting the prior advice. "Turns out she knows me."

"What? She knows you?"

"From Linkup. We matched apparently." He took

another big swig. "She said my banter was shit." Bertie looked like he needed a minute to process. Cian lit up immediately.

"That's fucking great, man. That's fucking hilarious. What are the chances, man? Can we see? I have to see Gemma flirting. I can't even imagine it." Mike stared a hole through them. "No judgement, no judgement, I just wanna see hers, I won't judge yours."

Mike just shook his head. "Never happen. I probably deleted it, anyway. A mate of mine convinced me she was a chat bot."

"Did she tell you what the rings are," Bertie asked sheepishly, "on her necklace? She just scowls at me if I bring them up."

"Eh, no. It was text chat."

"Brilliant, fucking brilliant," Cian howled. "Seriously, I love Gemma, but she's hard to parse. She's got that weird old millennial humour, always making rude jokes. I get it. But she doesn't get on well with most people here. Doesn't really fancy anyone, so far as I know. Well, she fancies herself. Sometimes a bit too obviously, if you know what I mean."

"Jesus! She's our supervisor, Cian." Bertie now seemed flustered that they were talking out of school like this. "Don't give a bad impression."

"They're old friends! Plus we're all in the clink together now." He threw his arm around Bertie and got in his face. "You, me, Gemma, 500 some odd other lucky fucks. What does it matter?" Cian picked up Mike's beer and shook it, then seemed to be impressed it was already empty. "Next one's on me. Keep your mobile handy friend, we're gonna need to see those old texts." Cian jumped up and headed toward the bar with their two empties.

Bertie grimaced. "It's not a prison, you know. We can come and go."

"I got threatened with arrest on a train because I skipped work," Mike snapped.

"Oh. Well, no, you can't skip work. But if you were off work, you know. We're allowed to leave. It's not really a prison."

"Fine."

"I know it feels like one. Cian hates it here. They don't say it outright, but you can tell. I think a lot of people do. I don't mind it, though." Bertie leaned forward, his bubbliness giving way to a more earnest tone. "I grew up near here, you know. My family didn't have any money. We didn't have much of anything. It was really chaotic. So this, getting my meals free, having a place to sleep, friends, doing really important work. I like the stability."

"He gets like this when he's scuttered." Cian sat down with the beers. "You'll get used to it."

"Hey, sue me," Bertie smiled. "I don't know. Sue me, it's an easy life. Do what you're asked, follow the rules, and it's all good."

"This from the man who reads generated books, watches generated telly. Listens to that manky fuckin' procedural music. Nightmare."

"We can't all be tragically hip like you, Cian, spending every credit we have on human-crafted artisanal books that aren't even as good."

"Oh aye, it's worth it ya gobshite. Try one, maybe you'd grow a soul if ya read something that fucking resonates with the tragedy of the human condition."

"I prefer stories without glaring plot holes and spelling mistakes, actually."

"That's the feckin' point ya dope! We're not perfect, art isn't perfect!"

Mike watched this unfold and it felt oddly nostalgic, hearkening back to post-work drinks with Jason and the HumanTouch gang. But even then it felt like it was slipping away. The rituals slowly dying. The new normal already creeping in. And now here he was, listening to someone actually lose a debate about whether a human-authored book was even worth reading. Mike felt even older in this moment than he did when he was with Kathryn.

"Well?" Cian barked at him as Bertie stared.

"Well, what?"

"Right, no, answer the question. Hand-crafted or gennies?"

Mike let out a big sigh. "Honestly I used to hate it when people would complain about this stuff, it just sounded so anti-progress. It drove me crazy. But lately. I don't really know how I feel about it anymore." Cian waved dismissively, irritated at the non-answer. "My ex-wife was the one who cared about this stuff for the both of us."

"You were married?" Bertie seemed intrigued.

"Aye, what happened to her? Sent to a different site? Feckin' government has no problem—"

"—no, we split ages ago now. About a decade ago. Since then she literally wrote the book on this stuff, though."

"Wrote the book?" Cian was intrigued. "What book?"

The trip back to their bunks was swift, even with the brief stop to get three takeaway beers. They blew into the room with little regard for Gemma, who was fine, as she'd donned her sleep mask and put her headphones on. Cian went straight to their desk, running their fingers across the spines of all the books in a few different piles until they stopped and plucked one out. "Here it is. Rare thing, this. Don't print it anymore. Fucking christ, man. Your ex-wife is Elizabeth Marsh?"

"It was a long time ago."

"This book changed my life, man. It changed my life. It reminded me, well, feel stupid saying it, but it reminded me what we lost."

"I've never read it." Mike was avoiding eye contact, and doubly avoiding looking at the book now in Cian's hand, which became a lot harder now that Cian was trying to get Mike to take the book.

"You need to read it! It's a quick read. Bertie refuses."

"It's true," Bertie chirped.

"Nah, I really can't, it just feels silly—"

Cian slapped the book hard against Mike's chest and let go, forcing him to grab it. He looked down at it awkwardly. "You're gonna love it friend," Cian said with a wry grin as he dashed into the bathroom with a bundle of work clothes. "Start it today. Start it right now."

TWENTY-ONE

IT'S A BIG ISLAND

"The power that a performer could have over an audience was incredible. Bringing everyone up to the edge. Waiting. Smiling. Then pushing them over with that first chord. It was so emotional, so raw. I might miss gigs most of all."
— Elizabeth Marsh, "What We've Lost"

February 2044.
Wales Site F, Trawsfynydd, Wales.

SOMEHOW, Mike had gone a month without actually leaving the facility. It wasn't like he was required to stay inside, something people had increasingly pointed out to him. There were other buildings, there was a whole town even, all within the fence. And supposedly there was even a little neighbourhood with real, proper terraced housing that the blue badges lived in. But Mike was a creature of habit, or so he told everyone when they'd go off to their jaunts. He went to work, he went to his bunk, he went to work. Sometimes he'd even go to the bar down the hall.

"We ready?" Cian leaned on the door impatiently. The streak was about to end. Cian had finally convinced Mike to come out, proper out-out, to the one pub in town. "You gonna change?"

"This is, this is what I changed into." He looked down at his tight tee and skinny jeans, complete with vintage Chuck Taylors.

"Christ, you really need to update your look. This probably worked a treat for you in 2015."

Mike shrugged. "Are Gemma and Bertie coming?"

"Just us, friend. Don't get so pissed you can't walk, I can't carry you back all by myself."

And so they stood at the shuttle stop with little to say. Mike had started opening up a bit more, or at least he felt like he had, but the two of them seemed to have so little in common. He honestly wasn't sure why Cian wanted to bring him out at all, except that maybe he just found it grim to drink alone. But it was a good excuse. And Gemma not joining them would be a relief. She hadn't really let up on her offensive. Indeed, it had mostly just escalated. Nothing was off-limits. His thinning grey hair, his crooked yellow teeth, the way he sometimes chewed with his mouth open because of his deviated septum. And of course, his shit banter. She was a full-on psychohazard.

The shuttle glided to a stop, the doors opening automatically. They both boarded, Mike behind Cian, and that's how he noticed there was a small paypad just inside the door. His stomach dropped. "How much is this?"

"Don't know, maybe 10 credits? 10 or 15."

The paypad stared at him, looming. "There's no one else aboard. Will it even know if I don't pay?"

"It literally won't shut the door if everyone hasn't paid, it certainly won't drive."

He sighed and tapped his mobile to the pad. It deducted 17 credits. Mike winced, almost feeling physical pain from that one. The door to the shuttle slid closed and it started its dutiful journey into town.

The ride into town would've probably been quite scenic if it weren't pitch black outside. Aside from the lights on the facility and the dim headlights on the shuttle, it was just inky void until they reached the town. It made Mike uneasy. Cian, on the other hand, was drumming on the seats and pacing up and down the aisle.

"Come on, man, get with it, get pumped up. We're going out! First time for you!"

"I've been out before."

"Not here! What will it be like? You don't know!" It was admirable how Cian could self-motivate.

"How much are drinks at this place?"

Cian shook his head. "Another money question. I've no idea, friend. I just tap and go. You'll be fine." Mike nodded, but his feeling of uneasiness only grew. He wondered how anyone could be so cavalier about this.

It turned out the answer was 15 credits. Mike stared at the pint, the unbelievably expensive pint, the pint of some weak English lager that tasted vile. His anxiety was distracting him from his first time setting foot in The Harp, a modest little pub that was clean, sufficiently dim, with a forgettable but mood-setting soundtrack playing gently in the background. They posted up at a small table near the front, where someone was setting up an amplifier and microphone.

"This place is shit, but they do live music, which I appreciate." Cian sipped their ale. "Nobody else feckin does, I guess." The room was mostly empty, with a few random groups scattered around at a handful of tables. "You've gotta keep it alive though. You know? What's the point otherwise?"

Mike nodded. "I was just thinking I like the music here. It's a good vibe."

"This feckin' procedural trash? Don't break my heart Mikey, I'll have to kill you and leave you for dead. Hey!" Oh god, they're shouting across the room at the bartender now. They're not even one beer in. "Turn this shite off! Off!" They shook their head and turned back to Mike. "I'd honestly rather hear my mum getting railed than hear another note of this fake shite."

The music abruptly stopped, the bartender perhaps expecting Cian to ask for it. Instead he clicked on a TV in the corner. The dulcet tones of a virtual news presenter filled the room instead.

"Marginally better. It's still fake, but it always was," Cian said. Mike sipped his pint and wondered if Cian's offer to murder him was still available.

"So where's Bertie and Gemma?"

"Bertie's not so much into leaving his precious Concentra. Gemma, I expect will be along soon."

"Oh? You said she wasn't coming."

"Yeah, I feckin' lied, friend. Keep up."

The sound from the TV dropped back down. A light came on, illuminating the empty stool on the stage. Mike heard some sparse applause behind him, and turned just in time to see Gemma walking up to the stage holding her acoustic guitar.

"WOOOOOOO!" Cian screamed and whistled, pounding the table. Mike smiled wide and started clapping. This was surprising! He knew she played, he always saw the guitar sat there, but he didn't know it was like this.

She strode onto the stage and hopped up on the stool. Her look was a stark contrast to her usual work attire — boots, dark blue jeans, a University of West London hoodie with a black leather jacket over the top, and her usual black-ring-on-a-chain necklace. Her hair was down and, shockingly, washed and brushed. She threw the guitar strap over her shoulder and smiled out at them, briefly making an 'oh no' face at Mike and Cian. "I see some familiar faces here tonight. And a lot of empty tables. Good, less pressure." Her voice boomed out of the speakers and through the pub. It had been so many years since Mike had seen any sort of gig, and many many more since he'd seen a little acoustic pub gig like this. The whole vibe – the pints, the stage, the dim room, someone on a stage with a guitar, the friend of a friend who frankly terrifies you – felt like such a throwback in the best possible way.

"I'm just gonna play a few songs tonight. Just a warm-up really. I haven't done this in a loooooooong time. This first one's an oldie but I've been listening to it a lot lately." She gave her guitar a little tune, plucked a few strings, and an odd silence came over the pub. People actually pausing their conversations to listen. It gave Mike chills, remembering all the times he'd been at a gig, the room falling quiet just before they started. She raised her pick and started to strum. It was fast, intense. It took him by surprise.

Da da, da dadadada, da da, dadada, da da...

He knew this song! He didn't remember the name. But the way she sang it was so powerful. She swayed back and forth, practically growling at times, beautifully melodic at others, her eyes mostly closed, moving in time with the music, that movement flowing back into the music. Her foot pounded the stage to the beat as she sang and rocked, the light of the stage catching her hair, making her glow, bouncing off the cracked, worn-out shoulders of her leather jacket. She struck the last chord and the room fell silent again. She opened her eyes and looked out at the pub in a sort of daze. The dozen or so people burst into applause, sending Gemma into a brief giggle. Her eyes welled with tears.

"Thank you, so much. God. Thank you. That was Ignorance by Paramore, by the way. That song means the world to me, thank you so much."

A few folks sat at tables in the back shuffled up toward the front as she rolled into another song, a downtempo acoustic version of "Alone in a Room" by Asking Alexandria. Her playing wasn't perfect, but it was energised, passionate. Mike stared up at her in awe, watching her fingers move up and down the fretboard, plucking the strings with a practised fury.

He hadn't thought about these songs in probably a decade or more – he'd been a kid when some of them came out – but suddenly he was right back there in university, on his bed in the dorms, headphones on. Before conscription, before Elizabeth, when A.I. was just a mediocre Spielberg film. He closed his eyes and disappeared, listening as she played, letting it fill up his mind.

Her next song was one he didn't recognise, and she didn't introduce. It was quiet, plucky, a bit funny, with a haunting melody.

Dreaming of you, my jewel of the Midlands,

Walsall my love, my jewel of the Midlands.

She seemed to pour a lot of herself into it, her voice breathy and low.

Filled with regret, you're mine for the taking,
Can't get you back, my heart still broken,
I'll ruin your life, and I won't let go.

It made him feel quite down, though he couldn't get his head round the idea that there was some depressing love ballad about a town in England that, as far as he knew, was mostly abandoned and a bit shit.

Finally, she finished with one he did know, "Who I Am Hates Who I've Been" by Relient K. Also a downer, but beautifully so. She finished up, grinning ear to ear, letting her guitar drop and dangle from the strap. She was breathing heavily, sweat starting to run down her forehead, as the gathered few people applauded.

"Thank you again, really, thanks everyone. I wish I had more, I'm already going hoarse. Hopefully again soon! Thank you!" She gave an awkward wave and tried to hop off, at first forgetting to unplug her guitar, which stopped her right in her tracks for a moment. She let out a quick "wahh!" and unplugged it then finally bounded off the stage, the light dimming, the sound of the TV fading back up.

Overall quite a sad set, though each song beautiful in its own right. It was the surprise of the day, the month, probably the year, to be here for this this. He was lost in a sea of feeling. Cian brought him straight back by pounding loudly on the table and yelling "Woo!"

"Fuckin' right! It's good, yeah? She's good. I saw her once before, in someone's flat. A few of us crammed in there, sweaty as hell. Someone tried to get into the room during it and slammed the door right the fuck into me. Had a bruise for a week."

Mike went to answer, but Cian had already jumped up and headed back to the bar for another round. He secretly hoped they'd finish these and leave before it was his turn to pay for one. He turned to watch Cian order the drinks and saw he'd already met Gemma at the bar, her guitar slung on her back, drink already in hand. Her and Cian were both animatedly freaking out. They gave her a huge hug. She threw her arms up and played like she was screaming. They were both too far away for him to hear, especially over the sound of the news. He hoped they'd call him over to share in the joy, but they didn't. He felt his mood start to float back down. Isolated, anxious. He wondered if he'd done something wrong.

"Oi! You waiting for an invitation?" Cian was shouting at him. He looked over to see Gemma waving too.

"Aloof wanker!"

"Sorry, sorry. Was uh, thinking," was Mike's mealy-mouthed excuse as he sprinted to the bar. "Gemma, that was fantastic, really."

"It was! Remember that, Mike. Remember how fantastic I am. They applauded for me." She raised her eyebrows and took a sip of her drink. Mike just nodded.

"What was that song? The one about Walsall? I've never heard that one."

"You'd heard all the others had you?" Gemma laughed and poked him in the chest. "I just assumed you'd have shit taste, Mike, I apologise for thinking it."

"You ever wonder where everyone is?" Cian gestured around the pub, which had only gotten less full since Gemma had finished. "Like. Are they all just at home? You wonder? I mean really, where is everyone? In general. There's what, 70 million people in the UK? They say over 60% of them are unemployed now?" Mike nodded along as Cian talked faster and faster. "And 500 supposedly work here? And here we are, and there's what, fuck all else going on, and maybe ten other people in here? Where is everybody?"

"It's a big island," Gemma suggested drolly. "They're about."

"The uh, the Walsall song though?" Mike didn't want to let it go.

"I wrote it. It's one of mine. I shift supervise and I write songs. I'm a woman of many talents, Michael Fernsby."

"Are you from Walsall or something? I thought you were —" *Unff*, Cian's hand slammed into Mike's chest. *Patpat-patpat*, Cian tapped him repeatedly on the arm.

"Look! Look! Oh shit! Hahaha!" They were losing it, going between wailing on Mike and pointing at the TV. There she was: Elizabeth Marsh. On the BBC News. Stood amongst a load of protestors waving signs, a microphone shoved in her face, the screen declaring "Protest at Concentra Health facility ribbon-cutting ceremony."

"Great, thank you Cian, thank you for showing me this."

"It's yer ex! On the telly! Look—"

"—I'm looking—"

"—he's looking."

"You ever read her book?" Cian asked.

Mike bounced his head back and forth. "I, erm, I skimmed it."

Gemma laughed. "What's she on about?" They all got quiet and strained to hear. Something about Concentra, something about health? After listening for a few seconds Mike knew roughly what he'd already read on the screen.

And then, suddenly, there seemed to be a huge flash of light, of orange, of black. Everyone lurched forward, spinning round. Arms thrown up to shield faces. And then the screen went dark. It stayed that way for a moment before cutting back to the presenter, who generically apologised for the technical difficulties, then sat quietly, eerily. Staring into the camera. Breathing but saying nothing. A new caption appeared and the virtual character began again, in an off-putting upbeat tone.

"We are receiving reports that there has been an explosion at the ribbon cutting ceremony for a new Concentra Health facility in Central London."

TWENTY-TWO

I DID WARN YOU

"When I entered government I was young, just 27 years old. Not that it's an excuse. But it was simply not enough time to develop the bitterness required to shake free from the ridiculous, doe-eyed notion that we knew what we were doing."
— Elizabeth Marsh, "What We've Lost"

February 2044.
Belgravia, Central London.

IT WAS a big day for the Government, and an even bigger day for Concentra. The culmination of over a decade of effort on the ground, and dozens of decades of technological advancement. It was finally time: today marked the official opening of Concentra Health's first ever fully-automated medical facility. It was heralded as a truly momentous occasion by many: the end of backlogs, the end of waiting, the end of over-worked, under-paid health staff.

To Elizabeth, it was desperately cynical. "Tens of thousands of jobs, gone in an instant."

And to Siobhan, it was horrifying. "Algorithms deciding who lives and who dies."

Concentra were treating it with the gravitas they felt it deserved. A who's who of the political scene would turn up to speak at the event — the Health Secretary, the MP for the constituency, some other hangers-on — and in turn, Concentra would send David Ryan, head of their European operation. It was the perfect storm, ideal to rally folks to the cause. Siobhan dreamed of a protest that could dwarf the actual event, garnering loads of media coverage, showing people they weren't alone in feeling like this wasn't right. That things didn't need to be this way. There was just one problem, she'd explained.

"Security," Elizabeth had correctly guessed.

Siobhan nodded. "Security. They're locking it up like they've got nuclear secrets in there. You won't be able to get near the place. Not even close."

"Right." Elizabeth nodded back, the conversation starting to trail off. That seemed to be that, yes? "So perhaps a counter protest, somewhere else, at the same time. Force them to cover both."

Siobhan shook her head violently. "No no no," she insisted. "We need to be there. Right there, in the exclusion zone. They can't force us away. It's a violation of our rights, our principles—"

"—right, right, okay." Elizabeth waved her hand a bit. She never wanted Siobhan to get so worked up when they'd talk strategy, but it was becoming more and more difficult to avoid. "Well, so, what is there to do, then?" Siobhan stared at Elizabeth across the table, filling the air and really the whole cafe with a sort of pleading, guilt-inducing energy.

"You're a former member of Parliament," Siobhan finally offered. "Can't you request to speak?" This cracked Elizabeth up. It was perhaps a little terrifying that her so-called campaign manager believed that's how things worked.

"That's. No, that's not a thing. I couldn't ask for that even if I was currently a member. They can invite whomever they want."

Siobhan was on her feet now, pacing a groove in the floor next to the table. "Let's just demand to be let in. We'll just demand it, dude. Make them arrest us if they don't." Elizabeth joined Siobhan in standing up, but tried to corral her a bit, toward the door. Maybe they'd have this chat while walking, perhaps to somewhere a bit more private.

"I don't know if getting arrested is going to lend the credibility to our cause that you think it will. The people at this event are all being targeted for harassment by different groups. Put them all together, we're liable to get shot anyway."

Siobhan stopped walking and turned to face Elizabeth, a fury in her eyes. "This is what is going to get our message out, Elizabeth. Our poll numbers spiked not after our march, our rallies, but after you went on video saying you understand why the protestors are angry. We have to keep that momentum." Elizabeth sighed and looked around. She rubbed her temples, her head bothering her more than usual today. Siobhan grabbed her hands and held them. "Elizabeth, please. Don't let me down. You can think of something."

"Okay, okay, okay. Just, not here."

They adjourned back to their hotel and got to work.

Which, in practice, meant Siobhan pacing around while Elizabeth sat at the desk staring, wandering her mind palace. After about an hour of this, Siobhan mercifully giving her peace to think, she stood up.

"You know," she started, "you're not wrong. We do need to just demand it. But properly."

"Properly?"

"We'll just file a request. We want to hold a small press conference, maybe a dozen or so people, with some invited media, inside the exclusion zone. They'll say no, and we can go on the offensive, take the grievance to the news. Get it to go viral, clips on Telly, all that."

Siobhan bounced around the room like a kid on a sugar high. "Yes! Brilliant! Will that work?"

"I don't know. Probably not. But it gives us something to say, 'Look, they're afraid to let us speak on this.' They're afraid to even acknowledge us as a political rival."

And so the plan was set. They went straight to the Met Police office, using the kiosk to file a very straightforward request. It was denied instantly by the computer — this event wasn't accepting applications for protests. Perfect. Straight to the phone to record a video of them standing there, explaining what they'd just tried to do, showing the screen of the kiosk. "HUMANS FIRST UK *DENIED* RIGHT TO PROTEST CONCENTRA PUBLICITY STUNT!" Their plan was only a few hours old, but it was already paying dividends, the views and re-posts ticking up fast, amplified by Siobhan's mastery of that particular craft.

At her suggestion Elizabeth grudgingly agreed to ambush a Met Police official on the way out of her office, asking why nobody would even agree to meet with them about their request. Siobhan had tweaked the language, making it slightly untrue, as they'd not even asked for such a meeting. But in their defence, she'd argued, there was no mechanism for doing so. Besides, it would make for a much more viral clip. "MET POLICE IGNORE ELIZABETH MARSH DEMAND FOR HEARING!" Comments rolled in faster than they could read them. Siobhan had encouraged everyone to tag the Police in their replies, leading them to disable the ability to be tagged, which spiralled into even more outrage. "POLICE REFUSE TO HEAR PUBLIC COMMENT ON FREEZING OUT OF ELIZABETH MARSH FROM CONCENTRA EVENT!"

Within a week of starting, they'd already secured a live interview on UK News to discuss it. The BBC had so far not gotten back to Elizabeth, with Siobhan wildly speculating they'd been ordered to ignore them. She pushed hard to convince Elizabeth to mention this during the UK News interview, something Elizabeth struggled with. The BBC had always been fair to her, even while holding her to account. But she could see the disappointment in Siobhan's face, which killed her. So she agreed to drop it in if the presenter asked about it.

"So, Ms. Marsh," asked the virtual presenter. "We're happy to help you get the word out about this shocking infringement of your right to protest. We are curious, have the other news networks been so forthcoming?" Like clock-work, Elizabeth thought, a grimace briefly crossing her face. Siobhan squinted at her and nodded from the other side of the phone, as if to say "go on then."

But in spite of all her various misgivings and hesitation along the way, Siobhan's push for these more aggressive gambits finally paid off. They found themselves sat in a small office at Met Police HQ, meeting with their head of Political Affairs.

"We're happy to offer you and your team credentials to be inside the exclusion zone for a modest press conference, Ms. Marsh. And I do apologise for the tremendous amount of effort you've had to undertake to get here."

"That's fantastic, thank you so much, Jeffrey," Elizabeth said, a tremendous relief in her voice. Siobhan would ease up now, she hoped. "My colleague here will get you the list as soon as she can."

They strode out of the office and onto the street with quite the confidence boost. They'd done it. They'd won. It was a very compromised result, of course—the original goal was a massive protest, drowning out the event, making everyone uncomfortable—but it was a result nonetheless. Honestly, it was more recognisable to Elizabeth this way. And now Siobhan was shifting back into her proper gear. Less whining, less pleading for adult help, more action. She'd get the right people together for the press conference, she'd write the release, she'd alert the media, everything. "Just rest now, dude, you look like you're about to fall over dead."

Back at the hotel, Elizabeth lay with a cool rag on her forehead, listening to Siobhan make endless phone calls in the other room. Her migraine, which she'd naively assumed was a tension headache, had taken control of her day. It would be fine, though. Siobhan would sort them out. They had a week left to prepare.

Preparations rolled on brilliantly, and before long the day had arrived. Elizabeth paced around and rehearsed her speech in her head, though from the outside it just looked like she was muttering nonsense in a dressing gown. Siobhan donned the requisite green hoodie, her hair in a messy bun, and blared music Elizabeth had no hope of recognising, shadow-boxing around the suite. This was a huge day from them, with a chance at catching the gaze of the nation, breaking out of their bubble. They loved their passionate supporters, but it would take more than 6% in the polls to win a seat in Parliament, or to have any hope of moving the conversation.

The black cab rolled to a stop in front of their hotel. Elizabeth smoothed her blazer and closed her eyes, the pain behind them dulled from half a dozen Paracetamol. Siobhan bundled a huge crate of flyers and sign-making kit in ahead of them. She took Elizabeth's hand and looked up at her. "Let's make history."

The ride to the hospital was short, but felt like an eternity. Elizabeth's migraine had only persisted over the course of the week, if not longer. It was all she could do to not break down in tears, or worse, from the pain. She leaned her head against the cold window of the cab, eyes shut, feeling the vibration, focusing on the motion. In her mind she pictured herself vomiting from the pain, passing out. Siobhan was mostly quiet, her fingers tapping wildly away on a phone.

Arriving at the site was a whirlwind. The cab panicked as Siobhan shouted at it to proceed while it received contrary instructions to turn around from the Met Police computer. It eventually compromised by flashing an anxious emoji on the screen and shutting down. Security kicked off a massive row, insisting they were meant to go to some other entrance, get scanned, that nobody was allowed to drive on, that they must be dreaming to think they could simply bring crates of protest signs into such a high-security zone.

Finally, Elizabeth was allowed to get out and explain the situation. The cab calmed down, downgrading from anxious to a smile with a sweat drop next to it, and she was able to pick up their credentials and get it cleared to drive to their designated spot within view of the main ceremony. She had stressed that if the hospital, and the ribbon-cutting itself, weren't visible behind them, then well, what were they even doing? It was a good point well made, or so felt Jeffrey at the Met Police. She'd be proud of her work there if she could even think. Sweat had started to drip down her forehead even as the freezing air nipped at them.

"Dude, we're here. Are you going to survive?"

"Yes, oh Christ, yes, yes I'm fine. Sorry, this bloody headache, I can barely see."

"Do we need to get you to hospital?" She tossed in a wry chuckle.

"Very funny. Come on then."

The familiar sight of a dozen or so volunteers, replete in their bright green hoodies, did make her smile. All the effort and stress had paid off. Although they'd put in plenty of work, with decent results, this felt like their real coming out party. Media were everywhere, an absolute circus of cameras. And real, honest-to-god human reporters dotted around. A decadence they couldn't afford to waste.

Security ushered them both to the stage, Siobhan kicking up a fuss about not wanting any help with her boxes, her independent streak surfacing at the worst time. Finally, they'd gotten in position. Elizabeth legitimately couldn't see. Huge, blurry shapes danced and twinkled across her entire field of vision, throbbing and pulsing in time with the pain. Siobhan took her hand and pulled her through the crowd of crew, press and supporters, toward their small stage. A camera spun round to catch her as she crossed, the light striking her eyes. A wave of nausea hit her as her eyes closed involuntarily.

"Siobhan, I don't know if I can do this." She leaned down on her shoulder, her eyes still closed.

"Elizabeth. Listen to my voice, yeah? They're giving us maybe two minutes, five at the most. And then it's over. Okay? Are you with me?"

She nodded.

"No regrets, no apologies, okay? This is why we do it, yeah? Bigger than us."

She nodded again, not quite sure what was happening. She knew what she wanted to say, she could muddle through. Just five minutes. Five minutes.

A hand patted her on the back, two more on her shoulders. She opened her eyes, on the stage, looking out at the cameras, the lights. Behind her, chanting had started.

'CONSCRIPTION! IS! SLAVERY!'

'NHS NOT FOR SALE!'

'PEOPLE NOT PROFITS!'

In the distance, she could hear the echo of a loudspeaker, a voice she recognised, followed by thunderous applause. She turned, looking past the volunteers, squinting to see the ribbon-cutting stage a short distance away. It was her first look at the hospital, transformed from the renovation, smooth concrete and glass. A massive Concentra logo etched into the side, alongside an impressed NHS logo. At the entrance, atop the stairs, stood an elegant wooden lectern. There they were: Alex Singh, the local Tory MP, his usual off-the-rack M&S suit. And his arm was firmly around Concentra's European leader, David Ryan, with a sharkskin suit worth more than Elizabeth's car. The crowd of sycophants cheered and clapped as they waved.

She took a deep breath, finding her camera-ready smile. Another breath, and another. She could power through this, she knew it. Where was Siobhan? She looked around quickly, only seeing other volunteers.

"Ms. Marsh!" A voice from behind the lights. "Ms. Marsh, can we take you live?"

She swung her head back and forth, squinting again, seeing only shapes and streaks.

"Ms. Marsh!" She felt a light tap and turned. An older man, someone she recognised, in his bright green. He held his hand up then pointed slowly out, extending his arm. She followed, eventually seeing someone waving, a BBC lanyard around their neck.

"Yes! Sorry, quite bright up here!"

"Ms. Marsh, we're coming to you live right now." A young man leapt the short distance from behind the camera to the stage, a microphone in hand, kneeling down just below her, holding it up for her.

"Ms. Marsh, we've just seen Alex Singh and David Ryan dedicate this new facility to the people of Britain, saying it's a concrete step toward eliminating patient backlogs forever. Why are you protesting tonight?" She desperately wished she could roll her eyes at the question, but she smiled instead.

"We're protesting tonight because this monstrosity is a wolf in sheep's clothing. Not only has it already cost hundreds of high-skill jobs, but it's—"

Loud screaming from just behind her startled her silent and made her flinch. She spun round to see a blinding bright light and screamed as the pain hit her, an unbearable, sickening onslaught. A wave of intense heat blasted her face. She ducked backwards and threw her arms in front of her, trying to shield herself from whatever it was. Suddenly she had fallen backwards off the stage and tumbled into a pile of people and equipment, screams all around her. Ash and debris soon followed. She was tangled up in a squirming pile of reporters and crew, coughing and moaning, both her and them. She could feel the heat from a fire as she tried to work her way up. Footsteps, a stampede. The ground vibrated as she fell back down, and a shoe stomped her hand.

Finally, she managed to get to her feet. It was impossible to see more than a few feet in front of her, a cloud of smoke where the hospital should be. Just ahead of her, a few of the volunteers in green hoodies, covered in soot, also stood. Some stunned, some chattering. Nobody seemed too hurt, but Elizabeth's ears rang so loudly she couldn't make out anything anyone was saying. She shook her head a few times and blinked. Her eyes watered uncontrollably, filled with ash.

"SIOBHAN!" She screamed, a guttural panicked scream. "SIOBHAN!"

No answer. She looked around, stepped forward a couple steps and nearly tripped as her foot got caught on a stray cable. The ringing was unbelievably loud. She rubbed her ear. Several hands patted her shoulders, her back. A low muffled voice said something she couldn't make out, and she nodded, reaching out, trying to pat them back.

"SIOBHAN!"

She kept inching forward, avoiding the stage, going round the side. Her foot got caught up in something else and she looked down. A green hoodie, laying crumpled on the ground next to the stage stair. She spun round in a panic.

Vibrations came from her pocket. Her phone. She thrust her hand in and took it out. Oh thank Christ. She answered.

"Siobhan."

"Elizabeth. You're alive."

"You are."

"I am, I am."

"Oh my god, oh my god. Thank god."

"Where are you?"

"I got out, security led us out. They won't let us back in, the whole area is locked down."

"I'll come to you. Are you safe?"

"I'm safe, Elizabeth. I'm safe."

Her legs gave out, her hands shook. She went straight down and landed hard on the edge of the stage. She sat there, the phone pressed to her ear. Her lip quivered, her whole body trembled. She stared at the green hoodie on the ground.

It was hours before they were reunited, in the waiting area of a different hospital, a few miles away. Siobhan sat in a chair, her fingers tented, staring at the doorway. As Elizabeth stepped through, blanket around her, she jumped to her feet.

"Shit!" She ran over and jumped on Elizabeth, giving her a huge hug. "Dude, I was terrified something had happened."

Elizabeth laughed. "We spoke on the phone!"

"I know!" Siobhan let go, then hugged her again. "I know. They wouldn't let me see you. Thought you lost a limb or something."

"Oh, you know how it is. They were worried I was in shock, or might have a concussion. Overly cautious. I'm fine. Are you okay?" She looked Siobhan up and down. Mercifully, she seemed no worse for wear, aside from a load of ash and dirt staining her white T-shirt. The experience certainly hadn't sapped her energy.

"I'm fine boss, I'm totally fine. I was off looking for the loo when the bomb went off."

Elizabeth shook her head. "A bomb? My God, is that what they're saying?"

"It is." A voice from the side. Elizabeth looked over, and there stood Cassandra Cooper. No makeup, hair a fright, baggy Oxford jumper with track bottoms and, heaven help, flat slippers. Her eyes looked red and tired. "You're lucky to be alive."

They sized each other up. Siobhan dropped back a bit, cautiously observing. The sheer exhaustion, the medicinally-suppressed pain in her head, the intrusive reminder that life was short and fragile. Something helped her get over whatever hang-up she had. Whatever it was, she tipped herself forward, arms out, falling onto Cass. They embraced, Cass's arms coming up around her. They pulled each other close. Elizabeth clutched her tight. She wanted to say hi, or thank her for being there, or ask her why she was there, or what she knew, or any number of colliding responses, all stuck in a huge tailback in her brain. Instead, she just closed her eyes and sighed.

"Sorry," Cass added. "Don't mean to wind you up. I'm happy you're alive. I did warn you."

Elizabeth squeezed her again, not wanting to process the idea of anyone thinking she might be anything other than alive. Or why. She exhaled again, her body relaxing. She wanted to just collapse. She was so tired.

Siobhan coughed. Elizabeth let go of Cass, stepping back. "It's good of you to come," Elizabeth directed at Cass, nodding. Cass looked down.

"Of course."

"I know it's, dude, I know this is going to sound, uh. I don't want to, I mean, I know we both went through it." Siobhan stuttered and stammered impatiently.

"What is it, Siobhan?" Elizabeth pivoted toward her, the

blanket still wrapped tightly around her, Cass just to one side. Cass suddenly looked a bit out of place.

"There's just a lot of talk. About who did this. Look." Siobhan pointed up at the corner of the room, where a TV hung. It was the same old virtual presenter, she noted, but the story had moved on. Though the sound was off, they could see the text on the screen. "GOVERNMENT VOWS PUNISHMENT AS TERRORISTS STRIKE HOSPITAL IN LONDON."

"I'm not sure what the concern is," Cass quipped. "Would you prefer the government not punish them?"

"I think there's a vacuum right now that the government is rushing to fill." Siobhan aggressively fired back, surprising both of them. "David Ryan, Alex Singh, we don't know what happened to either of them. Nobody's saying. Nobody's seen them. Are they okay? Are they dead? Are they—"

"Siobhan," Elizabeth interrupted, her voice soft, measured. She pulled the blanket more tightly around her shoulders. "Stop. If this was an accident, it was a tragedy. If this was... christ, heaven forbid. If this was a terrorist bombing. *If.* In the middle of central London. At a hospital. We can only denounce it."

"It's been denounced," Cass added flatly. "Focus on rest. Both of you." Her words were supportive, but her tone of voice suggested something else. An edginess. She was keeping her distance. She'd drifted further away, moving toward the back of the room, leaving Elizabeth and Siobhan alone in the centre of the sterile lobby, bathed in fluorescent light.

"Things will happen fast now." Siobhan stepped closer, closing the gap between herself and Elizabeth. "Every party is going to issue a statement. We were right there. Right there where it happened. It'll look weird if we don't say anything, dude. It'll look suspicious. Everyone saw us."

"I only saw Elizabeth." Cass, her back against the wall, fired a shot across the room. Elizabeth forced herself not to turn around and look.

"It's late." She felt this was a safe enough concession. "Surely we have until morning to think through what we want to say, officially. Up until a few minutes ago, they thought I might have a concussion." Nobody spoke. Siobhan looked past Elizabeth, dodging eye contact. "I really do just think it's best to head to the hotel, get some rest."

Siobhan nodded. "Yeah, yeah. No, you're right. Dude, you're right. I'm just amped up. Wild night." She made eye contact with Elizabeth, a smile on her face, her cheeks still smeared with soot. "Wild night."

TWENTY-THREE

BLACKOUT

"Some of my fondest family memories are from the 2028 Power Crisis. I found an ancient copy of Monopoly in an upstairs closet and made everyone play. My father landed in jail, waved his arms angrily, knocked over a candle, and nearly burned up all the Chance cards."
— Elizabeth Marsh, "What We've Lost"

February 2044.
Trawsfynydd, Wales.

GEMMA STOOD outside the door to the toilet, having left Cian behind at the bar. She'd given him permission to just head back without her, but she wasn't sure if he'd actually go. She rapped her knuckles on the back of the door again.

"Mike?" She figured she'd try again. "I'm not saying you need to come out. I can come in." Silence. She knew he had gone into this one. "Mike, I'm going to be right out here, okay?" She leaned against the door, wishing she at least had her phone to fiddle with while she waited.

In the moments after they saw the explosion, a lot had happened. The presenter let them know, in broad strokes, there had indeed been an explosion. Police weren't taking questions. They said they'd go live now to the scene, and then didn't cut away, instead leaving another awkward shot of the virtual character, staring ahead silently, with their virtual breathing. And then? Nothing. The screen had gone completely dead. One by one everyone went into a bit of a panic, and had pulled their phones out, desperate for more news, some kind of information. Except none of their phones had service either.

Mike had flown into a rage, rambling, shouting. He had to get to her, he'd said. He had to get to London. But first, he told them, he had to use the toilet. That was 45 minutes ago. And so Gemma had waited. And waited. And waited. Waited through the speculation that some sort of coordinated attack was ongoing. Waited through further speculation that it was some sort of "Skynet type situation," and soon all the humans would be dead. And finally, watched everyone filter out, alternatively wanting to just go home, wanting to go see if their phones worked elsewhere, or wanting to get off the grid before the robots descended and killed them all.

The bartender didn't seem to care. Good for them. Keeping calm in the face of madness was an important bartender skill. But Cian couldn't cope. And Gemma was worried. So she bid him goodnight and took up her post by the door to the disabled toilet.

"I need to close up soon," the bartender said, poking their

head round the corner. "You need me to get you through that door?"

"I know how to do it," Gemma replied. The bartender nodded. She rapped on the door one last time. "Mike. I'm going to come in, okay? I hope you're decent."

"It's locked," said Mike. Finally, contact.

"Love, this is a bar," she said. "You think there's no way to get the bathroom door open when it's locked? They probably have to do it multiple times a night."

After a moment, the handle turned and the door popped open a crack. She pushed on it gently and it creaked open a bit further. She slipped inside, shutting it behind her again. Mike sat on the toilet lid looking frazzled. "Have they said what happened?"

Gemma shook her head. "No, love."

"I'm sorry. I know they're kicking us out. I just needed some space."

"I know, love."

"You don't have to be like this, you know. I know what you really think of me. You don't need to pretend to be nice just because I had a panic attack." He wouldn't look at her, instead staring down at his shoes.

She kneeled down in front of him. "Hey. Listen." She tried to strike a warm, playful tone. "A guy out there? Older guy? He looked *pretty* wise. He said, and remember, he looked quite wise, he said if we're not out of here in the next ten minutes, a load of Terminators are going to burst in and gun us all down."

She could see him fighting a smile, which made her smile. "We'd never get that lucky," he said.

"No, I know. You're right. The bartender will actually

kick the door in and murder us though, honestly, if we don't get out of here."

Mike sighed heavily and looked up at her. "You can go. I'll be fine."

"Nope," she said. "Can't do it. It's taken me a few years but I'm finally paying it forward. Okay? Come on, up you get." She put her arms around him and started trying to stand him up, and he quickly relented.

They'd stood at the shuttle call point for a while, pushing the button at varying frequencies and with varying degrees of desperation. But it never came, and indeed, the ring around the button never even lit up. "Whatever knocked out the TV must have also knocked out the bus," Gemma said.

"Famously on the same system, buses and tellys," Mike said.

And for that glib remark, she declared they had to walk back. "Just be happy it's not raining," she added. "Come on."

The road seemed to stretch on infinitely, the blackness complete, total, except for the stars in the sky, and a thin strip of slightly lighter dark at the edge of the horizon. Their phone torches could barely show them the road under their feet, but with them off, their eyes adjusted just enough to be able to stay on the road. A few tiny specks of light danced in the far distance, guiding them to the facility.

"What do you think's going on?" Mike asked. "Do you really think it's a coordinated attack or something?"

"Well, the lights are clearly on out there," Gemma said. "And they were on where we came from. And there's no sign of a fire, smoke, anything. So no, I'm going to say no, I don't think that."

"This walk is going to take an hour, at least."

"But hey," she said, "we get to walk for an hour. So swings and roundabouts, really."

He tried to laugh, but it just came out as panting. They were both perpetually out of breath: they rarely visited the gym, left the facility or did anything resembling a cardio workout. "Your set was amazing, by the way, Gemma. I still want to know about the Walsall song."

"You know," she said, "you can talk about her. We've got nothing but time."

"It's fine. I was just, I think I was in shock. I'm okay now."

"Bollocks."

"I'd obviously like to know she's okay."

"Will you go?"

"I don't know," he said. "I suppose I should."

"Should you? She's your ex-wife. It's been what, a decade you said? Why haven't you both moved on? Has she?" Her words were unexpectedly acidic.

"I still care about her, Gemma. We were married for—"

"—for what, four years? Barely?" He stopped walking, causing Gemma to stop as well. She looked at him as best she could in the moonlight, but couldn't quite make out his face. Just that he was staring at her. "Mike, I'm sorry. I'm just tired."

"It's been more like... fifteen years. Since we divorced, I mean." He sounded a bit ashamed. "I just say a decade. At some point I stopped counting up."

"After about ten years?"

"Yeah," he chuckled. "I guess so."

"You can't get hung up on people like this, Mike!" She hammered him, her voice quite forceful. "You can't get stuck like this. Look at you, you're a fucking old man. You've let her take the best years of your life and she wasn't even around."

"Old man!" Mike was indignant. "I'm not even 50! And it's not exactly like I wasn't dating, working, living my life."

"All while Elizabeth Marsh lived rent-free in your head, her memory stalking around in there, making you self-sabotage."

"Why are you acting like you know me? Gemma, you don't know me at all."

"Mike! We talked on Linkup every night for months! Months and months! Do you know how often you brought up Elizabeth? It was a fucking lot! I never wanted to talk on the phone, or see you, because I didn't want to come in second place behind a ghost."

"That's ridiculous," Mike shouted back. "You never even gave me a chance. You could've at least told me hey, you talk about your ex too much."

"How does she even still qualify as an ex! It was so long ago! If you'd had a child together, they'd legally be able to drink if they got it with a meal!"

Mike paced back and forth in the dark. They had to go far enough as it was without all the extra time they were wasting on his endless tantrums.

"You know me so well from all our months and months of talking, you say. You know how much I know about you, Gemma? I didn't even know your goddamn surname until I saw it on your ID badge. What are your hobbies? Where are you from? What did you do before all this? How did you wind up in Wales?"

"Why would I share any of that with you?" Gemma rolled her shoulders, the weight of the guitar on her back starting to become unbearable. She lifted the straps up and slid it down, letting it dangle in her hand just above the ground. Her back and shoulders both gave one final cry of pain before settling into a soreness.

"I don't know," Mike said. "Why wouldn't you?"

Gemma turned and wandered a few steps away, off into the grass on the side of the road. It was thick, soft, clearly not having been mowed in a while. She slowly lowered herself and the guitar down into it. "Mike, I don't owe you my life's story. I don't owe you anything. I waited for you, can you not punish me for it by berating me?"

"Are you serious? You—"

"—can we please, I can't," she interrupted. "Please. I'm so tired, Mike. This night has obviously not gone to plan. I'm fucking knackered, I just want to sleep. I'm not walking all the way the fuck back at this point." She slid her shoes off one at a time, putting her socked feet into the grass. "You can keep going if you like."

"Fine."

She pushed her lower body out, slowly, taking care not to damage it further. She was feeling extremely fragile. Finally, ensconced in the long grass, she lay her head down on the padded guitar case. It sank down into the grass as well, leaving it at a decent height to serve as her makeshift pillow. She looked up into the sky, at all of the stars. The night air was brisk, and made her shiver a bit when the wind blew. But it was dark. Finally.

She heard shoes scraping aimlessly on the road a few feet away. Closing her eyes, she let out a light sigh. "Come on, then."

"Are you—"

"Hush now."

Mike laid down in the grass next to her, putting his head

on the other side of the guitar case. She didn't look over at him, instead looking again at the stars.

"I was in a band," Gemma whispered.

"What?"

"You asked what I did, before all this. I was in a band."

TWENTY-FOUR
LOCKDOWN

The next morning.
Trawsfynydd, Wales.

THE SUN ROSE, and it was surprisingly quiet outside. Mike woke first, as he was freezing and badly needed the toilet. He was shy, and the ground was generally quite flat in all directions around them, so he wound up going an unreasonable distance away. By the time he found his way back, Gemma was up too.

"I thought you'd ditched me, you bastard."

"Had to wee."

Gemma cracked up. "I used to go to Glasto every year. You don't need to run off and hide every time you need a wee. I've literally seen it all."

"Right, okay then," Mike said. "I'm sort of surprised nobody's come to find us."

"They might've done if we were meant to have worked last night," she said. "But since we're just missing presumed dead on our own time, that's completely fine."

The facility looked attainably close in the light of day, its cooling towers looming large where only a couple of tiny lights had been overnight. It still took them over an hour to reach it, which would've probably been a bit less had Gemma not stopped to also wee. "Come on," he'd pleaded, before quickly moving to a safe distance and turning his back.

As they approached it became clear something was amiss. Temporary barriers were being dragged out, and in the meantime, a couple of trucks blocked the entrance into the facility proper, with a couple of blue badges stood guard.

"Heya," Gemma said, waving. "We uh, work here." She threw air quotes around 'work'.

"The facility is in lockdown I'm afraid," said the blue badge on the left. Gemma and Mike looked at each other, confusion on their faces.

"We live here," added Mike. "We were out in the village last night and the shuttle never turned up. We ended up just—"

"—I'm sorry to hear that," said the same blue badge. The one on the right kept their stoic vigil.

"We're prisoners, man." Gemma sounded supremely irritated. "I'm not sure what exactly to do next. We can't turn round and go home."

"Why is it in lockdown, anyway?" Mike asked. "Is it because of what happened in London?"

They both stared, unflinching. After a moment Gemma rolled her eyes and threw her hands in the air. "Fucking great! Once again, for my sins, I am somehow denied entry to a place I'm also not allowed to leave." She leaned over to Mike and whispered. "This happens to me sometimes. Like two times, but still, you'd expect no times, right?"

Mike looked between the two blue badges as Gemma wandered aimlessly away, her guitar sticking up off her back. He squinted and leaned his head out, staring at the one on the right.

"You're Bertie's friend, yeah?"

Silence. Mike took a half-step closer. "Yeah, I've seen you and Bertie talking sometimes between shifts. In the hallway. Surely you've seen us, too. You know we live here."

"Course we fuckin' live here!" Gemma shouted up into the sky. "Where else would we be from? There's a fence around this place the length of the goddamn Thames! And who would—"

"Fine, fine." The blue badge on the right broke his silence. "Just go in, go quickly." He nodded them in a few times, then looked at his companion. They both just went back to looking straight ahead.

The vibe inside wasn't much better. The few people they saw shuffled around quietly, and all the doors to the bunks were closed. The bar in their block was shut and locked, which Gemma had never seen before. And nobody seemed to be working. As they turned the corner to Hall R, another goddamn blue badge was in their path. Not some security guard, but a fairly mundane looking man in an orange chunky-knit jumper and sensible slacks, his badge on a colourful lanyard round his neck.

"What room?" He was trying to make himself sound tougher than he was. Gemma felt a pang of guilt and decided she had no quarrel with this man.

"Room 62."

He nodded and escorted them accordingly. As Gemma put her hand on the knob, he reached out and grabbed her wrist. "You're really not supposed to be out. Where were you just now?"

She immediately and instinctively smacked his hand away. "None of your fucking business. What are you, the fucking bouncer, mate? This isn't the Electric."

Mike froze, his eyes wide, as the blue badge stood between him and Gemma. He braced himself for an unspeakably bad time. Instead, the man's shoulders slumped. He shook his head, turned and brushed past Mike as he headed back down the corridor. As he went past, Mike noticed the lanyard was definitely Garfield & Friends — little cartoon Garfields and Odies all over it. Gemma shook her head and rolled her eyes, then turned the knob and shoved the door open.

Bump. "Augh!" The distinctive cry of Cian as the door slammed into their back. They slid out of the way and let everyone in. "Christ almighty, look who it is." Bertie and Cian both shuffled toward the back of the room to make space. With the four of them in, it was supremely crowded.

"How did you get back in," asked Bertie. "We assumed you were just stuck in the village or something. They've got the whole facility on lockdown."

"Your mate, actually," Mike said. "Your secret blue badge mate."

Bertie's eyes darted around, but he said nothing. Gemma had been jostling around in what tiny space she had, trying to get her guitar off her back. Now that it was sorted, she went straight up to her top bunk.

"Aye, yer man's been of tremendous use today then," Cian said. "We got the craic from him round 6 a.m."

"There's some sort of protocol they've enacted," Bertie

admitted. "Something to do with some sort of terrorist attack. It's not just our facility that's locked down."

"Every connie in Britain. No phones, no Rings, no walkin' around," Cian said. "No work either, so, not raging about that."

Gemma's head thudded loudly into the ceiling above the bed. "Damnit! Fucking shite!" She let out a long, anguished groan. "No, I can't. I can't. Nope." She wriggled back and climbed out of the bunk.

"Apparently they think the attack was planned by connies," Bertie continued, "possibly even carried out by them. But they don't know who yet, or where, or how many were involved. So, we've all lost our privileges until they can sort it out."

"Comforting that they've had the ability to just cut off our phones and our freedom at the push of a button all this time," Cian said. "Can't feckin' take us anywhere, yeah? Little miscreants we are."

Gemma stared up at the ceiling. One of the light tubes was flickering. It hadn't always done that. Just one more thing.

"Did they say how long we were going to be stuck in here," Mike asked. But Gemma was already putting her guitar case back on her shoulders.

"I'm not stuck. I'm not their fucking property." She sidled past everyone and put her hand on the doorknob. "I'm going back out." Mike quickly put himself in between her and the door.

"You can't," he shouted in a panic.

"Mike, you don't know me well enough to know not to do this. But I'm asking you. Get out of my way."

He looked her in the eyes. She was not joking. He nodded. "I'll come with you."

"Great," she immediately replied. "We'll both get gunned down." She pulled the door open and strode out into the hallway, Mike sheepishly in tow.

TWENTY-FIVE

CHUNKY-KNIT JUMPER

Later that day.
Trawsfynydd, Wales.

"I REMEMBER... not remembering why we had even been fighting," Gemma said, playing with the rings on the chain around her neck. "But it was horrific."

"You don't remember now? Or you didn't remember then," Mike asked.

"Neither. Both. I think 23 was...not quite the height of my love of drink, but I was well into the ascent by then. Not a great year for me. Broke up a marriage *and* a band."

"Your band! It was you and your husband?"

"Oh, yes. King Charles Xavier, the worst two-piece rock you've ever heard. His drums, my guitar. We played basement gigs in Leytonstone. Bloody terrible. I loved it."

"And you were 23? What year was that? Twenty..."

"Christ, that would've been... 2018."

"Pre-COVID!"

"Ha," Gemma shook her head. "Old man Mike, still saying 'pre-COVID.'"

"COVID was my 9/11," he said.

Gemma rolled her eyes. "9/11 was your 9/11, Methuselah."

"I was five! You were, what, six?"

She rubbed her fist over her heart and nodded. "Too young to bear such a burden."

Mike slid up and down, and generally fidgeted, trying to find a slightly different position. They'd been crammed into this storage shed for a couple hours now, situated outside near the facility's motor pool, waiting for nightfall. Gemma's wild idea was that even though the shuttles were all automated, they didn't used to be, as evidenced by the fact that a driver had to pick her up her first day. She wanted to gamble that the old, manual-drive vehicles were still in a garage somewhere, and maybe they could use one to get out. And after watching her get them out of the bunks in the first place, Mike wanted to let her do whatever she wanted.

"We've got at least another few hours until the sun goes down," Gemma said, similarly fidgeting. "I'm not going to be able to fucking stand at the end of this."

"And we'll be caught immediately—"

"And we'll be caught immediately, yes."

"I'm glad we agree on the hopelessness of this plan," Mike said.

"Hopeless is where I thrive."

"So," Mike said, straightening up. "You're rough with me about being hung up on my divorce from fifteen years ago, and you wear a wedding band from a divorce that was, what, a quarter-century ago."

"Yeah," Gemma scoffed, "but I don't go round moaning about it now do I?"

"Do you ever hear from him?"

"I did, once or twice, not long after, just for admin-y type things. And his new wife reached out a few years later to invite me to his funeral." She was staring at the ring, slowly rotating it back and forth, passing it between her fingers.

"Shit. I'm sorry."

"It's fine. I'm the one who murdered him." Mike squinted. Gemma chuckled. "No. But see, I've cultivated a reputation such that you genuinely considered it." She sighed, still looking down. "Car accident. In Cozumel, actually, on their honeymoon."

"Jesus."

"So cliché, really." She pursed her lips and shook her head. "Dying on your honeymoon. But in such a mundane way. Not quite poetry, that. I didn't go, though. To the funeral. I couldn't face him. I *really* couldn't face her."

"Why?"

"Too embarrassed? It's a regret. I should've been there. I owed him that, at least. And her, because I don't know. Because I was still jealous and angry." She shook her head again, much bigger this time. "Ancient history."

"Did you ever re-marry?"

Gemma started to crack up, then put her hand over her mouth to stifle it. "No, no, no," she waved dismissively. "No. A lot of bad dates, a *lot* of bad sex. But nothing ever serious, except work. I got mad serious about work. I guess I wanted to prove to myself I wasn't the fuck-up he died thinking I was."

"That's... heavy." Mike nodded, trying to come off a bit sage-like.

"There's that word again!" Gemma said in a low, manic whisper. "Is there something wrong with the Earth's—"

"—with the Earth's gravitational field—"

"—in your time?"

They both laughed as silently as they could. "Hey, though," Mike added. "I'm impressed you found sex, even if it was bad. I think London's slowly going celibate."

"I KNOW!" Gemma whisper-shouted. "When did that start? This bloody generation. They refuse to touch for any reason." She looked at Mike and smirked. "I should, before you uh, start tomcatting around our little slice of paradise here. I'm good on that."

He nodded. "No, of course. I mean, you are my boss."

"And yet," she said, "you're still trying to turn me on."

A few more hours, and a few more stories later, they felt like it was almost certainly night. The sounds of random passers-by had also subsided, and they didn't hear many doors closing, cars driving, or anything really. It was as good a time as any to burst out and be immediately caught on CCTV, they agreed.

Mike pushed the door to their hideaway open a bit and peered through the crack. It was what they'd been hoping to see: a car park, dimly lit by a smattering of halogen street lamps, with no people around at all. He looked over at Gemma and gave a cheesy thumbs-up. She bugged her eyes out and nodded a little. "What does that mean," she whispered.

"Right," he whispered, and slid it open a bit more to have a better look. A few metres away there were a handful of boxy white-and-blue shuttle buses, the kind with no manual controls whatsoever. Not useful. A slightly sleeker navy blue car with a prominent Concentra logo on the door, and also, no manual controls. Great. He turned back to Gemma and shrugged. She put her hand gently on his shoulder and pulled him away from the door, then just crawled through it herself and stood outside the shed. After a quick irritated glance, Mike also stood right next to her.

"It's gotta be here," she said. "Why would they have gotten rid of it?"

"A whole host of reasons? Money? Space? It broke down?" Mike could think of more, but she'd already walked off, wandering between two of the shuttles.

"Come on," she whispered loudly. "They can certainly see us on cameras if they're watching."

It didn't take long to check every vehicle parked there and come up empty. Gemma looked around flabbergasted, seemingly at the end of her plan as it stood. Mike rubbed his eyes. "We can't even go back," he said, deflated. "They'd arrest us."

"Mike, we're already prisoners. How many layers of arrest do you think there are?"

"They could put us in an actual prison?"

"That's...yes, no you're right."

"I wouldn't count on it." They both heard the voice from off to one side. A door was open on a small service building on the far side of the car park, a man standing in the doorway. "The real prisons are full." He was walking slowly toward them, a high-powered torch in his hand, shining brightly on them both. "They might deport you. To where I'm not sure. They don't tell us stuff like that, innit."

Mike and Gemma both tried to shield their eyes, the man only visible as a silhouette to them behind the blinding light. It was no use. "We can go back inside," Mike finally shouted over to the man. "Well, I can go back inside. I can't speak for her."

"I'd just as soon walk," Gemma added. "I can just walk, if you let me."

"Just come in here, please." He gestured with his torch back to the building he'd just exited, then turned and went back toward it. Mike looked at Gemma, her face one of desperation, but not defeat. He pat her shoulder and started to follow the man. Might as well. There was nothing to lose at this point. She already lacked her freedom.

They both followed the man into the building. A single, windowless room, filled with old steel file cabinets, empty peg boards, a stainless steel desk and the most uncomfortable metal stool Mike thought he'd ever seen. A warm glow came from a domed lamp on the desk. The man turned off his torch and spun round. They both instantly recognised him. The smile grew so wide on Gemma's face.

"Chunky-knit jumper!" There he was, Garfield lanyard still around his neck. She threw her arms wide open. "Come here!"

He actually laughed, seemingly in better spirits than their last encounter. "Look, I'm not a—" he started, but was interrupted by Gemma diving in for a massive hug. She threw her arms around him and squeezed. He was about a head shorter than Gemma, plus a lot scrawnier, so was absolutely enveloped by her for a moment. Mike chuckled, but stood back away from them near the doorway.

"Don't worry," Mike said. "I won't hug you."

"Right, okay, look," the man started again, trying to compose himself. "I'm not a monster. I didn't take this job to be a prison guard. You know? I'm a technician. This is just something they asked me to help with."

"That's a pretty shit thing to be asked to do," said Gemma. "Guard convicts, get pushed around by them. You don't even have a weapon. What if we were violent?"

"Are you?" He sounded a bit sheepish.

"We are not," Mike replied. "Well, I'm not, but her—"

"Enough with the good cop, bad cop," Gemma barked at Mike. "Listen," she turned back to the man, "we're just trying to get out of here. He's putting on an uncharacteristic front because his wife might have been in the London bombing last night."

Mike looked at Gemma sternly. We're going to do this now apparently. Speaking of being asked to do things one didn't agree to do.

"I'm... shit, I'm sorry," the man said, and he did seem like he was trying to mean it. "Look, I'm Romesh by the way," and Gemma and Mike both introduced themselves. Nobody attempted a handshake. "I know why you're out here. I saw you on the monitors earlier, walking all the way here, climbing in that shed." Gemma elbowed Mike hard and nodded toward Romesh. Mike leaned his head back and sighed. "You're looking for a car, yeah?"

"We know," Mike said. "There aren't any manual-drive cars anymore."

"Ah, no," Romesh quickly replied. "Well, I was going to say, here." He tapped the cold steel desk against the wall. Sitting on top of it was a long, skinny key. "This is for the old passenger van. You can take it if you want. I moved it into the garage hours ago, put on fast charge. I had a feeling you might be looking for it."

They both stared down at the key. Mike started to talk but was quickly interrupted by Gemma. "What? What the fuck?" Mike pointed at her and nodded.

"I don't know. Fuck it, man, I'm from South London, man." Romesh said with a wild cackle. They both looked at him. Gemma squinted. "The Electric," Romesh continued. "I never bounced there. Like I said, I'm a technician. City College! I've been to gigs there though, back in the day. Waaaay back in the day. Back when there were gigs!"

Gemma started breathing normally again. She got a nice tingle in her brain thinking of The Electric, an old venue in Brixton where she'd seen loads of shows. "Did say that, didn't I. Sorry, I don't react well to being grabbed."

"I was out of line. This whole place is out of line," Romesh said. "It's messed up, what they put you guys through. Making you do all this work for free, barely letting you leave. And now they're taking away your phones? Blowing up their political enemies?"

"Blowing up... what?" Mike stepped forward. "Who blew up who?"

"I don't know, man, it's a bit suspicious, yeah?" Romesh lowered his head and spoke in a more hushed tone. "That old book by that woman politician starts going viral on Telly and Understairs, and she's running for election down in London, and starting to do well, and suddenly she gets blown up? On a live stream? Pretty suspicious innit. The feds weren't gonna let her be at the protest at all. And suddenly they did? And then there's a bomb? It's pretty suspicious. Everyone's talking about *that* now. It's crazy, bruv."

Mike started shaking his head, and steadied himself on the desk. "Mike? Mike." Gemma grabbed his shoulder as his knees buckled a bit. Romesh backed up and Gemma pulled the stool out, guiding Mike down onto it. "That's his wife," she told Romesh as Mike breathed heavily.

"Ex-wife," he said as he closed his eyes.

"What! Linking with Elizabeth Marsh! Bruv listen, I wish I could tell you she was okay. But they aren't saying anything. And she hasn't posted in a day, none of them has."

"Your phones all still work?" Gemma knew the answer, but fished for something to be freshly irritated about. Mike quietly counted backwards from five, breathing slowly and deeply. Gemma squeezed his shoulder and dug her thumb in, massaging it.

"Bet, and it's fucked up, innit." Romesh shook his head. "Listen though, you should go, if you're gonna go. I said I'd handle this and nobody really checked back up on it, but eventually they will."

Gemma nodded, blinking a few times. "Romesh, I love you. Thank you." She was choking up a bit.

"Londoners have to stick together, right?" Romesh said, cackling again. "Or not really, I don't know, it's good to be unpredictable, yeah? Once in a while. We lost that, you know. Unpredictability."

"There's still gigs, you know." Mike looked up at Romesh, then gestured at the guitar case on Gemma's back. "She played The Harp last night. She's great."

"Ah, bet, I don't know if harp music is for me, mate." He nodded keenly at both of them. "But keep the dream alive."

TWENTY-SIX

FALSE FLAG

Late February 2044.
Westminster, Central London.

"THIS IS INCREDIBLE, OH MY GOD!" Siobhan shouted,
having been so blown away by what she'd just seen that she
had flung her phone onto the hotel bed and jumped backwards from it. Elizabeth laid on the bed with a pillow over
her head, trying desperately to block out the light from the
window, and incidentally, trying to block out Siobhan. "Ms.
Marsh, have you listened to any of this? They think it was the
government."

"What?" Elizabeth was weary, but too curious to keep
ignoring it. "Who?"

"Everybody! Dozens of vids on Telly, a hundred
comments on Under, so far," she exclaimed, running back
and forth past the end of the bed, unable to sit still. "Listen.
Listen." She grabbed her phone back from the bed and
flicked through it. "'So sus that Elizabeth Marsh was
approved to protest event and then suddenly there's a bomb.',

and this, 'Anyone else find it weird that we know how everyone who was hurt is doing *except* for Liz Marsh and Siobhan Campbell?'"

Elizabeth sat up, the pillow falling to one side. She rubbed her temples, her face pale with red blotches and creases around her eyes. "What are you saying, Siobhan? Forgive me, I don't fully understand."

"They think it was a false flag! This is incredible! You were absolutely right, not saying anything was bloody brilliant." Absolute giddiness as she twirled around and flung herself into the bed, landing next to Elizabeth. "They honestly think the government blew up their own event. This could not have gone better, Ms. Marsh." She put her arms around Elizabeth's shoulders and hugged her from the side. Elizabeth winced and closed her eyes, inhaling sharply.

"Okay," she said, patting Siobhan's back. "I do think it's time we let people know we're safe. It's not right for people to be left speculating about it."

"Well," Siobhan said, "let's not get ahead of ourselves, dude. I think part of the reason this is going so viral is because people assume we're dead. Saying something now would be a huge mistake. We have to find a way to make it super impactful when you re-appear. If we do it right? I think we can actually win." She hopped away, into the adjoining room.

Elizabeth was silent. Even without the migraine, she might still choose this moment to be silent. But any chance of a quick rational response to this was off the table right now. She instead chose to lay back down and close her eyes. Siobhan was looking after their communications, after all.

"Siobhan?" Something was bothering her, though. "Are they any closer to figuring out who *was* responsible?"

"Who says it wasn't the government," she shouted from the other room. "If this many people are saying it, maybe it's true?"

"Right, but have we heard from the authorities?" Elizabeth heard Siobhan come back in, felt her sit down on the edge of the bed.

"Dude, I think we should leave it alone," Siobhan said. "We were victims of this. We're not involved with it." Elizabeth felt a cold, damp cloth lay across her eyes, and let out an involuntary moan. The headache had gotten so bad she could scarcely stop herself from crying any given moment.

"Thank you, Siobhan."

"Of course, Ms. Marsh."

"I do think I should get back to work, however." She'd been in bed practically since they'd returned from the hospital, the migraine persisting, worsening. They usually went away after a few hours, but they'd gotten more frequent, more intense. This close to the election she couldn't let it beat her. There would be time to rest after.

"Ms. Marsh, there's nothing for you to do, dude. I don't want your head to explode or somethin'. Besides, you're dead, remember?" Siobhan kissed her cheek. "Please rest, you've done so much for us already."

She awoke suddenly and it was night. She'd slept the entire day. But her headache had subsided. Sweet, merciful relief. The room was pitch black aside from the light on the clock, showing 22:07.

"Siobhan?" No answer. She must be out. Elizabeth could only hope Siobhan had relented and put out some sort of note saying they were okay. If not, she'd have to simply break the silence herself. Not to interfere with the campaign's messaging, or any carefully-plotted rollouts, but just to show a modicum of human decency. You can't let people just believe you're dead. It's not done. No matter how appealing it might seem, or how much you'd wished you were just a few short hours ago.

Elizabeth struggled to her feet and found the light switch, then made her way to the dresser to change into a tracksuit. As her hand went for the ornate knob she glanced at the top, where her phone had been sat on the pad charging. It was empty.

She glanced quickly around the room, assuming she'd just mislaid it while she was poorly. But a cursory search turned up nothing. Huh. It was a fairly large room, owing to the need to share with Siobhan while they were in town, and also to Elizabeth's ability to easily pay for such a thing. But it was still just the two bedrooms and a living room. It wouldn't take long to find.

Inside every dresser, under every table, under both beds and all the pillows, even a quick rummage through the bathroom, all turned up nothing. Elizabeth's phone was gone. Extremely odd.

She turned on the news to distract herself while she continued looking. That at least couldn't be taken, she thought as she tapped the mirror above the fireplace, the controls appearing. She tapped again on the small BBC logo and the virtual presenter appeared, floating in their red-and-white void. Upsetting as always. She truly hoped they'd get rid of this. The savings made from letting go of all the human presenters could not possibly be worth it.

"While police continue to search for the five unidentified suspects, David Ryan, the head of Concentra UK and one of the victims of this week's tragic attack, remains in critical condition. For more on this," the presenter droned on neutrally, "we spoke earlier with Concentra CEO Rebecca Prue, from her home in the Hollywood Hills in Los Angeles, California."

Elizabeth stopped her search and stared at the screen. Rebecca Prue appeared, looking almost as stunning as she had back in '28. That too had been on a screen, albeit a smaller one, in the cabinet room at Number 10. And at the time Rebecca had been in a rather plain glass office, a small white conference table in front of her, the camera at an odd downward-facing angle, her skin made unnaturally pale by the fluorescent lighting. Her cerulean hoodie had fit her perfectly, her red hair up in a tight pony tail, her mannerisms almost robotic as she explained to them in detail the 'awesome' new idea her public policy team had come up with for the UK Works Programme. The Prime Minister was so taken in, so emboldened. So convinced this was what would save Britain. This deal with Rebecca Prue and her miraculous company would be his legacy.

And now here she was in the present, her voice expressing the appropriate level of dismay at the events unfolding in London. They showed her at her screen-less desk, in an office reminiscent of a 60s-era James Bond villain. They alternated between that and some B-roll of her walking down a long, perfectly-lit hallway, brass fixtures holding electric candles, various works of art hanging on each wall. She looked remarkable in both, having aged impossibly well, as a person of her means tended to do, wearing a well-tailored charcoal suit, her hair down past her shoulders, her makeup calculated to give the impression that she's losing sleep over the disaster.

'I'm Rebecca Prue', Elizabeth mocked. 'I'm the richest

woman in history, and I care the right amount about all the things you'd expect.'

She shouted for the screen to turn off, and it dutifully obeyed. She bloody hated using voice controls for anything, but she couldn't look at that face one more second than necessary. It did give her an idea, though. She closed her eyes and grimaced.

"Phone? Where are you?" Like clockwork, she heard some pleasant chimes and vibrations. Bloody voice controls. The vibrations sounded like they were against wood, rattling away in a drawer perhaps. She gave the room yet another sweep, this time focusing on the drawers and cabinets, occasionally asking the phone where it was again, waiting for the chimes to start anew.

She finally opened the one drawer she'd subconsciously skipped the last time — Siobhan's underwear drawer. It felt extremely invasive, and somehow more-so of a violation given their age difference. But we must do what we must, and she opened the drawer. The sound doubled in volume as she did.

"A-ha," Elizabeth announced to no-one as she fished the phone out past Siobhan's garish underthings. Except, it wasn't hers. Oh, bloody hell. She's gone through Siobhan's private things so she could steal some of Siobhan's private things.

It didn't look like Siobhan's phone, though, which she'd seen recently, and quite often, and moreover knew she'd never be without. Especially now with everything going on. Hers was definitely an old Samsung which she prided herself on keeping running, a large crack running straight down the middle. "You can't get these anymore you know," she'd find some way to point out. But this was a sleek, ultra-thin Concentra Portal, and it looked box fresh.

It had taken one look at her and politely but firmly declined to unlock, the screen having gone a tinted red, a frowning face taking up most of it.

Elizabeth once again felt a roiling in the pit of her stomach. Something was very wrong about this. Siobhan having a Concentra phone at all seemed uncharacteristic. Her having a second phone of any kind seemed even less likely.

She lamented the death of passwords, of PIN codes, either of which would've given her the false hope of somehow getting into the phone, seeing what's on it, putting her mind at ease. As it stood, she was left unsettled. Was it a second phone? Could she perhaps have a job, was it a work phone? Maybe it would ring, and she could answer it? But alas it did not, so she simply placed it on the top of the dresser. Putting it back seemed like even more of a betrayal. This way Siobhan would see it out, know it had been found, and they could discuss.

None of this got her any closer to knowing where her own phone was, unfortunately. And the extra, the superfluous one, had started to feel like a larger and larger presence. Her eyes kept drifting back to it, her guilt immeasurable, or perhaps it was embarrassment, as she did her third sweep of every nook and cranny of the room, desperation about to give way to panic. Elizabeth was out of sorts.

"Fine," she yelled to the phone. "I'll put you back." The idea of explaining any of this was far too much to bear. She had to undo it all. Undo, undo. Proper tradecraft. Like it never happened.

The subterfuge wouldn't be complete without re-burying it beneath the unmentionables. She tried to slide it around the edge of the drawer and under, roughly into the same spot, without having to empty out the whole thing, and also without having to look, because she'd violated enough privacy for one evening, and because it made her uncomfortable for some reason.

Her knuckles hit the bottom of the drawer. That was odd. Was that plastic? She let go of the phone but left the drawer open, staring at it. Hmm. Unwilling to investigate, but she could perhaps check a different one. She opened one of her own drawers so she could really cut loose. Under a stack of her sensible slacks she confirmed the bottom was, in fact, wood. Hmm. Back to the first drawer. She'd have to just take a look. Surely Siobhan would indulge her this. She pushed everything aside and peeked. What a fun story it would be.

Once she saw inside, she regretted having looked.

TWENTY-SEVEN

WHEN WE WERE YOUNG

Moments later.
Westminster, Central London.

THE GATES to Westminster Station opened as Elizabeth got close, responding to the phone in her bag. She dashed through them out of the pouring rain, but was already soaking wet. Her heart had started beating a lot faster. She couldn't go back now — not only had she taken Siobhan's secret phone, but she'd just paid a tube fare with it.

The Jubilee line would take her straight there. She had no way to arrange anything in advance, no way to reach out, no way to even use the phone she was carrying aside from paying for transit, checking the time or looking at a red frowning face. But it was all she could think to do. It wasn't an option anymore to simply wait for Siobhan to return, to ask for an explanation.

"This is a Jubilee Line service to Stratford," said the recorded announcement. It soothed her a bit, this relic of the past, this artefact that society absolutely refused to let go of, recorded tube announcements. Where everything else had long since switched to synthesised voice, this stalwart recording remained. It wouldn't surprise her if it was on a magnetic tape.

Her arm looped around a pole in the narrow steel carriage, her bag clutched tight against her, what she'd found in the drawer tucked into the bottom. She had no plan. But the clock was running now.

"The next station is, Bermondsey." It was a short journey, in theory, but in practice at this moment, it felt like an eternity. Elizabeth was jumpy, unnerved. She tried to be aware of everyone's place on the tube, never letting anyone behind her, rotating around as people moved about. Her hands were sore from tightly clutching the strap of her handbag, her leather gloves creaking and stretching.

"The next station is, Canada Water." Just a couple more stops, she told herself. Her eyes darted around again. Everyone here was catching one of the last trains of the night. They were mostly young, she noticed. Young and well-heeled looking, in pairs or groups. Some laughing, some silent, most looking at their Rings. Nobody else who looked even close to her age. At the far end of the cab, a couple sat in the corner, both dressed much more simply, in polo shirts and matching slacks, likely a work uniform. He had his arm around him, their heads together, engrossed in a paper book. Elizabeth's mouth curled into a slight smile when she saw what it was: a tattered old copy of What We've Lost. But she quickly let it agitate her, worried they might see her. She spun round again, putting her back to them.

"The next station is, Canary Wharf." Most everyone onboard gathered their things and queued up at the doors. Elizabeth continued to clutch the centre pole. Was this a terrible idea? Yes, of course. But she watched herself step off the train and onto the platform, the cavernous steel tunnel of Canary Wharf Station ahead of her, the two massive escalators up. She observed as she stepped into the queue, stood on the right and was carried to the top. She nearly asked herself to stop as the moving walkway took her past the shops and crowds, as the glass elevator brought her to the surface, into the freezing, torrential downpour. As her legs took her around and through the glittering corporate high-rises, dystopic megastructures, automated Scottish chain pubs and luxury tower blocks.

And then, there it was, right where it had always been, looking no worse for wear. The heavy glass door to what had been, and what may still be, the building where Cassandra lived. All those years ago she'd been able to simply let herself in with a guest pass. This time she'd have to commit an unthinkable crime in modern society: drop in unannounced.

She crowded in under the narrow overhang, getting a bit of reprieve from the rain, having already been fully drenched. She adjusted the bag on her shoulder, making sure it was still closed, and reached her finger toward the pad. It lit up when she got close. There was no camera, the QR reader and the buttons were gone, all replaced with a small screen and blocky, grinning face with some text underneath: "WHO ARE YOU HERE TO SEE?"

She leaned forward and shouted over the sound of the rain: "Cassandra Cooper."

The face animated and the text changed. "CALLING."

There was no speaker visible, and indeed no sound was audible. Even this primitive form of a door agent would still handle that side of it, making sure the person in the flat didn't have to speak directly to whomever was outside. "WHO MAY I SAY IS CALLING?"

Elizabeth closed her eyes and cleared her throat. "Elizabeth Marsh."

She stood waiting, and waiting, and waiting. The face had gone, as it was wont to do when it was technically "upstairs." And finally, it reappeared.

"PLEASE DO COME IN, ELIZABETH MARCH."

The face beamed, unaware of its mistake, followed by a loud clonking sound. She pushed the door open and stepped inside.

"Aren't you dead?" Cass was waiting in the hallway wearing plaid pyjamas and a worried face, her grey hair in a messy bun. "And don't you own an umbrella?"

Cass set down two mugs of tea on saucers just as Elizabeth emerged from the bathroom. She was a bit more dry but still quite disheveled. The flat was startlingly similar to her memory, though looked to have been recently modernised, with far fewer plants and the addition of a small dining table. Elizabeth sat down at the table and put her hands around the mug to warm herself. She watched the steam curling up from the tea.

"Liz, I've got an extra set of pyjamas if you want to change. The bottoms might be more like shorts on you, but you're welcome to them."

She shook her head and stared down into her tea, fidgeting a bit with the tag on the string. "Cass, thanks for seeing me."

Cass sat down at the table across from her, accompanied by a small pot of milk. "Of course. It's been a while since you've been here."

It would be overwhelming, if she hadn't already maxed

out her capacity to be overwhelmed earlier that night. She had no idea how to even begin to broach it. Maybe Cass would ask. Maybe it would never come up at all, which might also be fine. She picked up the teaspoon resting on the saucer and dipped it into the mug. She watched it briefly fog up before it went in.

"I was surprised you didn't reach out first," Cass said. "I can't even begin to think of the last time someone just called on me unannounced. Not that it's a problem. Just a bit retro, yeah?"

Liz smiled. "I suppose."

"Unannounced drop-ins." Cass's mouth curled into a grin. "What we've lost." Her voice was low and goofy, imitating Liz. "I'll miss those most of all."

"Oh, don't you start," Liz scoffed. She lifted the bag out of the tea and pressed her spoon against it, squeezing the last bits of liquid out. "I read once that this makes it more bitter, that you're not meant to do it. But I've never been able to help myself."

Cass smiled and poured a bit of milk into Liz's tea. Liz watched the tea get a bit lighter, and a bit more, stopping at just about the perfect colour. Liz smiled back, giving it a light stir with the spoon.

"Good?" Cass asked.

"Yes that's perfect," Liz replied. She laid the spoon aside, picked up the mug and took a sip. "Absolutely perfect."

"Good." She inhaled deeply after her sip and closed her eyes, listening to the sound of Cass stirring her tea, the spoon clinking a few times on the side of the mug.

"Thank you. God, I needed that." They both sat, sipping from their mugs, otherwise in silence. Elizabeth felt herself actually relax. The light in Cass's flat was quite soft, a few orange glows coming from a few dim lamps scattered about, the city light out the window providing the rest.

Cass seemed content to just let her sit with no questions asked. She wanted to embrace it, take it at face value. But the longer they sat, the more she could feel a different tension start to build. She had to tell Cass why she was there.

"Cass, have you been watching the news?"

"I have," said Cass, "as much as I try to avoid it. Morbid curiosity I suppose. I notice they still haven't caught anyone from the other night. Have you heard anything?"

Liz held the mug in front of her face, both hands wrapped tightly around it. She shook her head.

"That seems unusual. I'd expect they'd want to interview everyone who was nearby at the time."

"Cass." Liz set the mug down and stared down into it. "They're looking for five people."

"Yeah?"

Liz leaned down and reached into her bag, which was slung at the foot of her chair. She fished something out from the bottom, lifted it up and slung it down onto the table. Cass set her mug down and leaned forward. "What is..."

"It's five of them, Cass." She spread out the tangled pile as best she could, her movements frantic. Her hands shook as she tried to lay them out next to each other in a panic, arranging and re-arranging and nudging and straightening and re-straightening them.

"I don't..." Cass leaned down and studied them, squinting to better see. She gasped a bit. "Oh, my." It was five sets of credentials for the Concentra Hospital ribbon cutting ceremony. "Where did you—"

"They were in a drawer." Elizabeth was breathing heavily, trying to catch her breath. "They were in a drawer, hidden under some clothes, in a drawer. In the room, in our room."

"Slow down, slow down," Cass said. Elizabeth was still fidgeting with the passes on the table. She took Elizabeth's hands, steadying them. She squeezed, and Elizabeth squeezed back. "What drawer?"

"One of the drawers in our hotel room. A chest of drawers that Siobhan has her things in. I was looking for something and I found these."

"Okay. Could they just be extras?" Cass was cool and measured. "Did you get more passes than you ended up using?"

Elizabeth shook her head vigorously. "No, no no, they would not have done that. They were very strict. One pass, one person. They told me they'd reclaim any unused passes on the spot."

"Okay, but is it possible they simply didn't? Or they just handed them back to—"

"No, Cass. No. I don't think so, it's not possible." Elizabeth was riding the line between panicked and frightened. "They're biometric, they are coded to the person that they're issued to, that's how it always works." She kept squeezing Cass's hands, staring down at the passes underneath. "If you're the wrong person wearing it, they know immediately. And you have to give it back when you leave, Cass. Why do we have these?"

Cass nodded. "I know, right, of course. That's how passes for the Commons work now, as well. But of course, the bombing, all the confusion."

"No, no, they collected them, I promise you. I watched them do it."

"Okay, Liz, I believe you." Cass gave Elizabeth's hands

one more squeeze, then let go. She picked up one of the passes. "So they'll know immediately who these were issued to, then?" She turned it in her hand. "There's no name."

"They'd be able to scan it, I suppose, yes."

Cass nodded. "That's it, then." She slid her chair back and stood up, then nodded down at the credentials on the table below. "We take these and we go turn them over to the police. First thing in the morning."

"I... I don't..." Elizabeth stared at them.

"You did the right thing, they'll see that," Cass insisted. "You found them and you brought them in."

Elizabeth had fought so hard to get them. Made so many promises, talked her way past and around so many bureaucratic obstacles. Staked her reputation on this. Publicly and privately. "It can't be. It has to be a coincidence. It can't be."

"It either is or it isn't, Liz. But they can at least tell us who these belong to, yeah? They can get to the bottom of it." Cass reached down to gather them up. Elizabeth's hand came swiftly down onto hers, stopping her.

"Wait. This isn't..."

"Isn't what?"

"I just need a minute."

Cass pulled her hand out, then crossed her arms in a huff. "Where is your shadow, anyway? Siobhan?"

Elizabeth shook her head as she gathered up the credentials back into a neat pile.

"You don't know? You won't say?"

"I shouldn't have come." She pushed up off the table and got to her feet quickly, her knees popping, her back cracking.

"Liz. Please. What is going on? You can't just run from this! Talk to me." Liz stuffed the passes back into her purse, her back to Cass. This was entirely predictable. Of course

Cassandra Cooper was going to make this about her, to seize an opportunity, as ever, to make her feel foolish. She felt Cass's hand on her back. "Elizabeth."

"What?"

"Please." They made eye contact. Cass's face was pleading, desperate. She was instantly back in that moment, the last time she'd seen that face, intrusive memories pushing their way to the surface. "Please, just sit." Elizabeth wrenched herself away from Cass, putting a foot of space between them.

"Cass," Elizabeth started. But there was nothing else.

"Take the time you need."

Elizabeth sat on the stool in front of Cass's writing desk, on the far end of the flat. She'd been so stupid to come here. Fragments of that night came at her thick and fast, making her want to flinch, close her eyes, look away. She was so prone to meticulously recounting her mistakes to herself in the dark hours. Every awkward thing she'd said, every foot she'd put wrong, every name she'd mixed up, every mansplanation she'd ever quietly put up with, every social media post she'd quickly deleted. But she never dared think back to this.

"Cass, I'm sorry." Tears streamed down her face. "I'm so sorry. I should've apologised so long ago."

Cass was stood by the window near the sofa, staring. Her lip quivered. "It's okay." Her voice cracked. "Elizabeth, it's okay." She crossed the room, approaching cautiously as Elizabeth put her head in her hands, her elbows on her knees, and started sobbing. She felt so incredibly tired. She hadn't slept right in a week. Siobhan had kept her on a diet of biscuits, Paracetamol and adrenaline. And she was ready to simply disappear. "Liz, can I..."

"Yes you can bloody hug me you elf," Elizabeth sputtered as she threw her arms around Cass's waist.

"I'm an elf, now," Cass laughed even as she started to cry.

"The short kind," she clarified, "not the tall kind."

"Oh Christ, Elizabeth Marsh," Cass said. "We're too old for this."

Cass poured two glasses of merlot as they migrated to the sofa, the city lights spread out before them. Liz was almost certain the skyline was different now, but she couldn't pick out what had changed. Life was funny like that. She could spot when things went suddenly missing, but if you slowly added things over time, it just felt like it'd always been that way.

"Back here again, are we, Ms. Marsh?" Cass sipped her wine.

"It would appear so, Ms. Cooper. It's bizarre, after all this time. How have you never moved? I just assumed you'd be partnered up and off somewhere like Hemel Hampstead by now."

"Hartfordshire, are you mad? Here I thought you knew me. No, no. And you? Is there a *Mister or Missus* Elizabeth Marsh?"

"Heavens."

Cass put her head on Elizabeth's shoulder and sighed. "Liz, I'm old, I'm retiring. Soon I'll vanish from this world like a dead Jedi, just some robes and a broken wine glass."

"You're not old, you're 52. You're still fit."

"I've got to tie up my loose ends before I go."

"Mmmhmmm." Liz sipped her wine and smiled.

"I just want you to know that I love you."

"Mm, I, oh, goodness." Elizabeth's eyes went wide. She looked out at the city, floated out through the window, looked back at herself sat on the couch next to Cassandra Cooper, a woman unafraid to admit she loves someone who, perhaps... "I don't deserve that."

"It can't be helped, Marsh. We can't choose these things. I've loved you since the moment we met, since the moment I laid eyes on you. And selfishly, I want you to know that."

Elizabeth felt her face go flush. She set down the wine glass delicately on the floor. Cassandra was a woman unafraid to hand you red wine and give you nowhere to place it. That's trust.

"Gosh, Cassandra." Elizabeth's voice fluttered to the rapid beating of her heart. "I... when we met..."

"You don't have to say it back. Like I said. I'm being selfish."

"No, no, it's not that. You were there for me. It was, from the first moment, such an intense friendship. You were a very intense person. And so private."

"I was shy, Marsh. I didn't want you to know I was crushing on you so hard."

"You hid it well!"

"I absolutely did not!" Cass played offended. "I couldn't keep my hands off of you that night at the hotel. And when you smiled at me, I was yours forever. If you wanted me."

"Oh." Elizabeth rubbed her neck, managing to find her way to these memories. To see them through fresh eyes.

"I was happy to be your friend, Liz. But it hurt. But I preferred the hurt to not having you at all."

"And then I buggered it up." She couldn't look at Cass now. She felt so small, so childish in how she'd handled everything. She'd done well to protect herself from remembering any of this until tonight.

"Hey." Cass gently touched her arm. "Hey. No regrets. I

knew it was a risk. You were a risk I was willing to take." Liz said nothing, instead leaning her head down on top of Cass's. They sat together, relaxed against the back of the sofa, against each other, in silence.

"Liz, there's something else I want, selfishly," Cassandra said.

"What's that?"

"I want you to not go to prison for terrorism."

"Oh, Cassandra, really." Elizabeth rolled her eyes dramatically, then fidgeted as she was forced to remember why she was here in the first place. Why she hadn't been comfortable staying in the hotel room. "I was a wreck, I'm sorry."

"It's justifiable."

"I'm calm, now. I appreciate you riding it out with me. I think I've decided to just confront Siobhan about it tomorrow."

"I don't like that idea for you. I'm worried what you're getting yourself into. I saw how angry she got, the other day at the cafe."

"She's passionate."

"Liz! She set off a bomb at a hospital! People were hurt!"

"We don't know that, that is a *massive* leap."

"Fine, you're right. We don't know that."

"Thank you."

"Liz, you're not... are you two...?"

"What?" She wrung her hands and furrowed her brow. "No, Cass you've already asked this."

"Well, I wanted to ask again. Selfishly. I'm sorry, that was crass. Again."

"I've spent a lot of time with her though. She's passionate but she wouldn't hurt a fly. I promise you."

Cass turned to face her. "Can't stop me worrying, bab. I've been worrying about you for years. You seemed so distraught in your book. So lost."

Elizabeth wasn't sure how to take that. She pushed her hands across the sofa, feeling the velvety texture. Listening to the sound it made. She tried to appreciate someone expressing so much concern for her, especially Cass of all people. Cass was someone she had such a history with, who she'd slipped right back into feeling comfortable around. But something about it felt off.

Cass chuckled, as if she'd suddenly remembered something. "Oh! I got one more tattoo." She looked over as Cass slid her pyjama sleeve up, turning her wrist. Written in beautiful calligraphy on the inside of her forearm was the phrase "She Never Married."

Elizabeth burst out laughing. "Cassandra, my god."

Cass giggled. "My fiftieth birthday present to myself."

"It's strange," Liz said, "being here tonight. Nobody knows I'm here. Nobody has a way to reach me." She looked at Cass as if she'd just surprised herself. "I don't have a phone!"

"No?"

"No, it seems to have gone missing."

Cass let out a heavy sigh, recognising the weight of what Elizabeth had just said, piling it on top of the weight of everything else they had with them tonight. "Oh, Elizabeth. It's so late." She got up and went to a small switch on the wall, flicking it down. The windows instantly went black, the room now almost dark, bathed in a muted orange. "Stay with me?"

It was after midnight, and though she hadn't seen clear to admit it, she didn't even have a way back into the hotel unless

Siobhan was there to let her in. That, too was on her missing phone.

Liz nodded. "I had better do. I appreciate it, I really do." Cass stood up, leaving Elizabeth sat on the sofa. She reached to the far end and picked up one of the throw pillows, a cartoon squid against a rainbow background. Bit garish, but at least Cass had finally started to add pops of personality to her flat.

"What are you doing?" Cass had stopped at the edge of the hallway. "On you come. Come on, bab, don't be silly. It'll be freezing out here by the window and I've passed out on the sofa reading enough times to know it's not comfortable."

"Are you sure? I don't want to impose."

Cass sighed. "In spite of your efforts, you are not an imposition."

Elizabeth picked up her bag from the floor by the chair then joined her. Cass gently took her by the hand, and they slipped down the hallway and into the bedroom.

It was around 4 a.m. when they were startled awake by Elizabeth's bag loudly ringing.

TWENTY-EIGHT

FORK IN THE ROAD

Early March 2044.
East of Trawsfynydd, Wales.

THE AGREEMENT WAS to get as far as they could on the charge that they had, without committing to a single direction.

"We'll just get out of Wales at least," was Mike's pragmatic idea, and the city snob in Gemma had a hard time arguing with it. As they bopped down the road in pitch darkness, Mike in the driver's seat and Gemma with her feet on the dashboard to his left, it had gotten oddly quiet. Neither wanted to bring up how they'd simply driven away, abandoned Cian and Bertie, even Shruti, and the countless others Gemma had met and worked with over the past few years. Compounded by the fact that their escape vehicle was literally a passenger van, it felt terrible.

They'd very briefly discussed it, but Mike had pointed out how urgent their benefactor had made things sound, and how unlikely it would be for them to make it back to the bunks, convince everyone to follow them, then make it all the way back to the vehicle. So that was that. They were on their own now — Gemma, Mike, a guitar, no food or water, and maybe 100 miles of charge.

The thought of Bertie being with them as they crashed the van through the gate amused them both tremendously, though neither had said it to the other. He would've insisted they pay Concentra for the damages.

Gemma also decided to just "forget" that there was, in fact, a series of automated defence turrets just outside the gate, being as it was to one of the country's highly-secure nuclear facilities. She assumed Mike hadn't gotten the luxury of experiencing this, as he'd come in on the staff train. Why trouble his mind with such thoughts? Gemma had looked out the window as they broke through, and there it was, same as it had been several years ago. The red light, however, wasn't lit. Likewise, the screens on the gate were off. She'd smiled and yelled "Hey, the gun wasn't on!," and then spent the next fifteen minutes calming Mike down.

Now though, they'd managed to get out of Snowdonia. The weather had eased up a bit, and the sun was starting to come up. The road was narrow, boxed in on both sides by hedge rows, with huge swathes of grazing land just on the other side. Gemma watched with measured curiosity as a horse stood alone in the middle of a field, nibbling on some grass.

"This isn't the first time I've done this drive in this hood-ie," she offered up in hopes of not riding in complete silence forever. "I was wearing it when I first got there."

"You don't have the most diverse wardrobe, to be fair."

"Oi fucker, it's a special memory."

"You drove? Not the train?"

"It's a long story. I might tell you someday."

"Hey, look." Mike pointed out the windscreen and gestured to Gemma. She took her feet down and leaned forward. Sticking out of the bushes, overgrown and barely visible, was a small white sign that read "Welcome to England."

"Great," Gemma said. "We're in Shropshire. Shropshire is where we make our stand."

"I honestly could not name more than maybe four counties."

"London isn't a county."

"So, three maybe."

She peered over the centre console and saw they had about 50 miles of charge left. That meant they were gonna need to find somewhere to top up in the next town. Even though they still appeared to be in the middle of nowhere.

"We're going to need to charge up soon," added Mike, uselessly.

"I'm aware."

"Not much out here."

"Can you at least slow the fuck down? It uses more battery to go this fast. Use your head, mate." She'd never driven in her life, but was almost positive that was true.

She stared out the window, feeling her blood sugar crashing and her irritation levels spiking. Mike had slowed the van to a sarcastic crawl, which would've set her off, had she not been able to spot a crumbling wooden sign just off the side of the road.

"Hell, there's a castle here." The sign was badly faded, but she could barely make out "Something, something castle, your dream wedding awaits." "A mate from work got married in this bloody thing. Felt cursed. They divorced two years later, so, you know. Think about that."

"Should we stop?"

"God no, Victorian ghosts will kill us. But there's a town nearby. Yeah, the bride had us all staying at some bloody Holiday Inn Express on the other side of Shrewsbury. All us commoners, while her and the bridal party were in the bloody castle."

"Unbelievable." Mike courteously indulged her.

"Right?! It was unbelievable. But right, yes, just keep driving. Go on, step on it then."

Though Mike had never been there at all, and Gemma claimed to have never been there sober, it was clear as they entered town that Shrewsbury had seen better days. As they approached the land around the town was mostly massive wind turbines, the bases of some uncomfortably close to the road. A collection of empty lots, rubble piles and half-ruined walls seemed to show an area where housing used to be, which they'd started to raze at some point, then gave up. Construction signs and orange netting were everywhere, along with a few abandoned work sites. Gemma pressed her face against the window, a feeling of dread setting in.

Mike tried to head toward something he recognised. They went round a small roundabout and came upon a massive multi-story grey-brick building which loomed over the area, the Concentra logo emblazoned on one side. An enormous car park surrounding it, filled with low-end vehicles.

"Surely we can find a spare charger here," he said.

"We're in a stolen Concentra van, so yes, let's drive on in."

"It might be our best shot. At a glance we look legitimate."

"Fine."

Mike pulled into the car park and circled round, looking for a free spot with a charger, and finally finding one in a less conspicuous location a decent distance away from the building. Gemma jumped out as they came to a stop and ran around to the side, keen to get it on charge immediately. As soon as she tried to pick up the charge socket, she frowned. It didn't budge. The screen displayed a frowning face.

"What the fuck does that mean," she yelled. "Why are you sad?!"

Mike circled from the other side and laughed. "You have to pay. Oh." He had quickly stopped laughing. "It probably needs a Concentra employee to tap."

"Great."

"Work your magic, I suppose."

She stared at him and tried to remind herself that her extremely low mood was because she was starving. "My magic?"

"You know, like with Romesh."

"Romesh is just a chill fucking dude from Brixton. I didn't work any magic on him."

"Well and, you know, everyone. You have a whole cult of personality thing going on for you."

Gemma took a deep breath. "What are you asking for, Mike?"

"Just talk someone into helping us?"

Mike gestured toward the building, which was the standard windowless variant of Concentra facilities. Next to an unassuming steel door, a couple of people stood smoking. Both looked older, which made sense given the laws around it. Both had the tell-tale bright blue badges dangling from lanyards around their necks.

"We just need one of their badges," Mike said.

"Oh! Okay! Thanks for clarifying!"

"Look, we can try elsewhere in town."

"No, no, I'm going." She shook her head, her stomach continuing to eat itself, every little thing irritating her. She'd talked her way into probably a hundred gigs for free back in her prime, so this should be pretty straightforward.

It was all about charm, she thought, as she covered the length of the car park toward the unsuspecting pair. Charm and nonchalance. And confidence. You had to be confident. You had to believe you were meant to be there, and then they, too would believe it. And you had to be someone they'd want to help, shortly before you presented them with your problem, a problem they were uniquely suited to help with. And their help would be easy for them to provide, but a real lifesaver for you. Yeah. She cranked up her smile and gave her hair a toss.

"Hello! Quick question, my—"

"Aren't you one of the escaped connies from Wales F?"

"Fuck."

One of the blue badges held up their Ring, revealing Gemma and Mike's faces. "Gemma Thomson? Wow, and you've just come walking straight up." They smiled and waved, looking past Gemma to Mike, who also smiled and waved back from next to the van. "And that's the van. You two aren't exactly master criminals here."

Gemma sputtered out a weird laugh. "Right, no, but listen."

"Surprised you stopped," interrupted the other blue badge. "You're over half way there. Run out of battery?"

"Not quite, but sorry? Half way where?" The two of them looked at each other, one flicking her spent cigarette away. Gemma made eyes at it as it flew past, then smiled. "Bum a fag?" One nodded and produced a pack of pre-rolled from their pocket, and helped Gemma light up. Gemma took a slow drag and smiled. "Christ, that's good," she said.

"So you're not on your way to the usual spot? Everyone's talking about it internally. Connies all around here just bailing on work and heading there, like word is spreading virally or something."

"It was, briefly," said the other. "On Understairs, but I know they're quick to delete those posts now."

"What are you talking about," Gemma butted in, the cigarette barely tamping down her irritation. "We're trying to get to London. I think. We're trying to have the option. Mike's wife is down there. He's like a dog with a bone, that one."

"London? Oh. Bit far. Good luck with that."

"Where did you *think* we were trying to get?"

They looked at each other again, and the one who loaned Gemma the cigarette shrugged. The other shrugged back.

"Walsall."

TWENTY-NINE
GO

29 February 2044.
Canary Wharf, East London.

IN THE DARK, under the warmth of the duvet, in her ill-fitting borrowed pyjamas, Elizabeth waited. A bit of light came through the crack where Cass had left the bedroom door ajar, and a bit more came from the clock, which read "04:21."

They had laid there, motionless, surprised, staring at each other, until the phone in Elizabeth's bag stopped ringing. Elizabeth, frozen in fear, at the thought of who might be calling it. And Cass, staring at her, wondering why she'd lied about not having her phone.

Cass sidled into the room holding a glass of water. She climbed back into the bed, manoeuvring under the duvet, sitting up and holding the glass. They both shared a sip.

"I can explain," Elizabeth finally said as she put the glass on the bedside table.

"I think you better."

She talked through everything. How she'd slept all day. How Siobhan had been gone when she woke up, and her phone gone as well. Her search through the room. How she'd found the phone in the drawer with the passes. And how she knew it wasn't Siobhan's actual phone. When she finally finished, Cass put her hand on Elizabeth's shoulder and stroked it a few times.

"How's your head?"

"It's okay today," Liz said. "Well, last night. And now, today, I suppose." She choked up a bit. "It's been bad lately. It's been—"

Cass leaned over and slid her arms around Elizabeth, nestling her head in the nape of her neck. "I remember you'd get them sometimes."

"Never this bad. It's nearly every day."

"Have you been to your GP? To a specialist?"

Elizabeth nodded.

"And?"

A tear rolled down her cheek as she shook her head. She squeezed Cass back. "It's not good."

Cass nodded and kept hugging her, giving her a small kiss on the neck. "I'm sorry."

It wasn't anything Elizabeth could even focus on, the tension now oozing from her every pore, her mind fixated on Siobhan. On the explosion. Seeing it again and again in her mind, even though she hadn't even seen it at all. Wondering if that was Siobhan just then, calling her own phone. Wondering if she was out looking. Wondering if she'd even gotten back to the hotel yet. Or if this was all a misunderstanding.

"I don't know what to do," Elizabeth said. "The election is next week, there's so much planned already, and now, with all this." She gestured toward her bag, now sat on top of the chest of drawers, the phone still inside it. It was barely visible in the darkness, a bit of stray light coming in through the door giving everything a yellow pallor. "What have I done?"

Cass slid down the bed, laying her head on the pillow. Elizabeth joined her. Their faces were an inch apart. "We could just go, Liz."

"Go? To the hotel? Or the police?"

"Lizzie, we could go. Away from here. I'm already done. You could withdraw. We never have to think about any of this again."

Elizabeth cracked a smile. "You called me Lizzie."

Cass put her hand on Liz's cheek, looking her in the eyes, glints of colour amongst the greyish-blue shapes in the dark. She touched the tip of her nose to the tip of Liz's. "I'm not joking."

"Cass, it would be easier if you were." She reciprocated, putting her hand on Cass's cheek. They shared a brief, tender kiss. "I can't just go. This is what I've been working towards."

"I don't understand," Cass whispered. "I don't understand what it is. One seat in Parliament, from a fringe party? Even if you won, you'd have no power whatsoever. You have more now, writing books. I see someone with your book every day it seems. A year ago I'd only ever seen it on my bookshelf, Liz."

Liz kissed her again, stroking her cheek, sliding her hand on her neck. "It's sweet that you read my book. I think maybe you were the only one until recently."

"Me and the little terrorist you've got back in your room," Cass said a bit playfully as she kissed Liz's nose.

"Don't," Liz said. "We don't know. If the phone rings again, we should answer it."

"If the phone rings again," Cass replied, "we should bin it. After all, I heard on Telly that you're dead."

They fell asleep without meaning to, their hands still on each other's cheeks, their noses still touching, their heads on one pillow. The blackout windows, combined with it being Saturday, meant they overslept. Liz woke first and immediately chuckled. She could hear Cass's snoring had gotten louder over the years. A puddle of drool was on the pillow, but that really could've been either of them. She pawed at the bedside table until her hands found the controls, again unwilling to even entertain using the voice controls, if Cass even had them. What she'd hoped was the lamp was actually the window control, and the sun flooded in.

Cass jumped, a full-body jolt.

"Sorry," Liz whispered, then collapsed back down onto her side of the bed.

"It's fine, oh dear, what time is it?"

Liz squinted at the clock. "9:57."

Cass snickered, a huge smile on her face. "I've not slept this late in years, years and years. You wore me out, Marsh."

"We just laid here!"

"It's exhausting to be around you, I suppose."

They worked their way to Cass's cosy lime-green bathroom, still half-asleep, still wiping the crust from the corners of their eyes. They could fit, only just, side-by-side in front of the mirror. Cass handed her a spare toothbrush from the drawer and they brushed together without saying a word. Elizabeth precariously balanced her new toothbrush on the side of the sink when she was done, but Cass picked it up and dropped it into the little pink-and-blue holder next to her own.

The smell of coffee had already started to work wonders before Cass even poured it. Liz felt a bit exposed, sat at the two-seater table in a pyjama top that barely closed and bottoms that were just about wide enough and not nearly long enough. But she appreciated the loan nevertheless, preferring it to the other offer of a dressing gown that she figured would come down to just below her waist.

Cass joined her at the table with a mug of tea. "Now I don't have loads of storage here," she said with a goofy grin, "but this is our pied-à-terre, obviously. We'll mostly live at yours up in Cambridge."

"You're ridiculous," Liz said with a shake of her head. "I obviously have to live in my constituency."

"Going to win that election, are you? That would really set us back a few years. I'll be so lonely in that big draughty house up there all alone with my knitting." She took a sip, smiling at Liz over the top of the mug.

Elizabeth felt it again. Something was off. It was distracting her, leaving her unable to focus. Cass was making this so easy. And she could take one look at her, sat there in her oversized plaid pyjamas, her hands wrapped around a Christmas mug even though it was February, and know that it would stay this easy. They'd live together in a bubble made of Cass's love and shut the world out forever.

"Cass," she said with a note of severity. "I still thought about you, I still think about you, all the time."

"We don't need to look back."

"I'm not looking back. That's the point." She set the mug down and pushed back from the table, standing up. "Have you seen it out there? Cassandra, it's so grim. It's so, so grim.

The way people are living. Half of Central is a tent city." There was a growing passion in her voice, her volume rising. "I was in this cab the other day," she continued, "going down Oxford Street. I saw the old Apple Store, which is a bloody tip now of course, vandalised beyond recognition, people living inside it. I had such a strong memory, which is ridiculous I know, of queueing in front of that shop with an old boyfriend to buy a damn iPhone."

Cass was smiling, clearly not sure where Liz was going with this, but captivated nevertheless. "That must've felt like a lifetime ago."

"It did, it really did." She was nodding, looking off to one side at the window, which was still fully blacked out. "And I tried to speak with Siobhan about it."

"I can't imagine she had any frame of reference for that."

"No, no, she didn't, you're right," Liz said. "She was focused on the human element. The people. Penniless, unhoused, hungry. And all I could do was think of how I used to buy my luxury phones there, and wished I still could."

"You care about people, Lizzie. Remembering that one day doesn't mean you *only* care about that."

"It's painful to think about. It was a painful memory. Seeing it all." She threw her arms up in the air, exasperated, shouting. "We just let it all slip away, Cassie! We were the ones they fucking put there! To look after them, to stop this sort of thing from happening. They looked to us for answers!"

"'And we had none.'" Cass nodded and looked down at her half-empty tea. "No need to quote yourself, I read your book. But you mustn't blame yourself. You have to stop blaming yourself. There was nothing you could do. Nothing any of us could do. It was a sea change for society. And society is adapting."

Elizabeth let out a deep sigh. She marched over to the window and pushed the button, letting the light come in. Outside in the morning fog you could only just make out the neighbouring tower, and nothing of the ground below.

"Ridiculous. We're just hiding up here, Cassie," she said, her voice calmer now, a finality to it. "Hiding inside our little lives. I can't let this all get in the way again."

Cass was still sat with her tea. "Elizabeth." She cleared her throat. "It was me."

"It was, what? You did what?"

"I don't want you to keep blaming yourself. It was bigger than you, than me, than all of us. It was a sea change for society."

"Cass, what did you do?"

"I'm the leaker. I leaked."

Elizabeth leaned against the wall by the window, staring across the flat at Cass. It seemed like such a massive distance now.

"You what? I don't understand." Elizabeth was clutching her arm with the opposite hand, hugging herself anxiously.

"I'm the one who told The Guardian about your Concentra connection. I knew a reporter I trusted, through my...through an old friend. And I was angry at you, I was so angry. And I wasn't certain you'd see it through. So I called her and I just told her."

Elizabeth paced back and forth, staring down at her feet, her head shaking almost imperceptibly. Her arms were crossed so hard over her chest she thought she might break herself in half.

"And then," Cass continued, "the party decided to put in

for the urgent question, for the debate in the Commons. And I got blackmailed, Elizabeth. I got sent photos. Of us. They told me to put a stop to everything, or they'd release them." Cass took a deep breath. "And I didn't tell anybody."

Elizabeth had stopped pacing, and now stood staring. "I don't understand."

"I'm not sure I do either. I needed you to go through with it. Even if it meant everything else exploding around me."

Cass put her head in her hands. Elizabeth turned her back to the room and stared out the window. She put her hand on it, feeling the ice cold glass under her palm. "Cassandra, that was nearly sixteen years ago. How have you never told me?"

"It never came up."

"Cass!"

"I was ashamed. And I was morbidly fascinated by what might happen if the photos came out. But that's not why I did it. I really did want you to just get on with it. I wanted you to just bloody do what you went there to do."

"It's just."

"And then the photos of us never came out. But those others, of me...with your ex-husband. I was completely blindsided, Liz. And I thought for sure you would've found out, that they would've gone through with it. And I made him, Liz. I made Mike promise to—"

"—I need to go." Elizabeth took her hand off the window and spun round, crossing her arms again. Her fingerprints were still visible as oily residue on the glass behind her. "I'm sorry, no. This is too much. I have to go. I've got to speak with Siobhan."

She stepped quickly through the flat, disappearing down the hall toward the bedroom.

"Elizabeth, please!" Cass got to her feet just as the bedroom door slammed. Elizabeth hurriedly changed back into her clothes from the night before, which she'd hung to dry on the radiator. With any luck she'd catch Siobhan at the hotel, or if not, well then...she'd simply wait in the lobby.

Cass was waiting by the front door when Elizabeth came into the room. She had Liz's bag, ready to hand her. Elizabeth reached out with a gloved hand and took it from her gingerly, peeked inside, then snapped it shut. It was all still there.

"I wish you'd stay. I'm sorry. I'm so sorry. I wish it hadn't happened the way it happened. I wish I'd told you sooner. But we're here now. We have this, right now."

Liz shook her head. "It doesn't matter. We're both just doing whatever we feel we have to do."

Cass nodded. "It's not...I just, I...okay. I hope you believe everything you're saying."

"Oh, Cassie." She frowned and put her arms around Cass, pulling her close. They stood there, embracing in silence.

"Do you love me?"

Elizabeth smiled and hugged Cass even tighter, her head resting on top of Cass's. "O heaven, O earth, bear witness to this sound."

Cass started to giggle. "What?"

"I, beyond all limit of what else in the world, do love, prize and honour you."

Cass was laughing with her whole body, her eyes welling up, her smile shining brightly, though Elizabeth couldn't see it. "I'm a fool to weep at what I'm glad of." She pushed Elizabeth away and looked up at her, then nodded. "Go."

The world beyond the huge glass doors on the bottom

floor of Cass's building looked to be solid grey, the fog was so thick. Elizabeth rested her hand on the handle, about to push her way out into morning, to head back to the tube station, back to reality. To her right she noticed a small steel bin, which gave her pause. She glanced around, noting that while the lobby had been designed to look sleek and modern, it was getting old. In need of a refit. The doorbell didn't have a camera, and even more so, the lobby itself seemed to have no cameras in it either. A rarity.

Elizabeth reached into her purse and took the five credentials into her hand. She pulled them out, again looking around, cradling them protectively, brushing them clean with her leather gloves. In a swift motion she thrust her hand through the front of the bin, letting the credentials go, hearing them hit the bottom.

She pushed on the long steel bar, opened the door, and walked out into the fog.

THIRTY
STAY

29 February 2044.
London Bridge Station, Central London.

IT DIDN'T TAKE LONG for Elizabeth to find Siobhan. Not that she was looking. But nevertheless, there she stood in the ticket hall, between Elizabeth and the door to the train platform. She was a formidable presence even as Elizabeth towered above her.

"Miss Marsh." Siobhan's voice was calm, if a bit sleepy. It was nearly noon, and judging from her looks, she'd been up all night and all morning.

"Are you tracking me?"

"What?" She chuckled. "Tracking you?"

"How did you know I'd be here?"

Siobhan nodded over her shoulder. "The 12:30 to Cambridge. I took a guess."

"Right."

"Dude. We need to talk."

"Siobhan, I need to know we didn't do this."

"I think we should go somewhere to talk." Siobhan smiled and took a step forward, her hand reaching out towards Elizabeth's.

"No. I need you to say it." She pulled sharply back. They stood a foot apart in the empty hall, boxed in by glass, the sun warming Elizabeth's back, her long shadow stretching across the space between them. "Tell me we didn't do this."

"I can't."

"Why?"

"You know why."

Elizabeth's breathing was shallow. Her throat tightened, her face an involuntary grimace. "I can't believe it." She pulled her arms tight across herself, rubbing her hands up and down her biceps. She felt the colour leaving her face.

"Miss Marsh."

"Cassandra was right. She was right. About you, about everything. I can't."

"Miss Marsh," Siobhan's tone was of measured concern. She squinted in the sunlight. "I think you'd better sit. You're looking faint. You've not been well."

Elizabeth shook her head. "No. No! I'm sorry, but no."

It was quiet for a time, the two of them standing opposite each other. Elizabeth could see a few strangers milling about on the platform just a dozen or so feet away. She nodded imperceptibly, following a couple with her eyes as they meandered down the length of it. Part of her, a tiny fraction, wished it had somehow been Cass standing there, waiting to ambush her. So she could've apologised. The apology that had been rolling around in her head the entire tube journey back from Canary Wharf. To explain what really happened that day at The Grand Hotel. She owed that, at least.

"Elizabeth," Siobhan finally broke in, "where are they?"

"What?"

"Where are they?" There was an edge to her now, her ferocity that was always just below the surface.

"Oh, you mean your bloody passes. The passes I got for you. The passes you duped me into getting for you." Her voice got louder with every word. "The passes you used to bloody kill—"

"—Whoa, dude, no," Siobhan hissed through gritted teeth. "Nobody focking died. Okay? Lower your voice."

"People were hurt!" She didn't lower her voice.

"What, some corrupt politicians? Some Concentra middle management? The hospital was empty! That was the whole focking point, Miss Marsh! No patients, no staff, no focking humanity. Yeah?"

Elizabeth closed her eyes, rubbing the bridge of her nose. "Siobhan. I'm at a loss. I can't even begin." She lowered to a hushed whisper. "You've...you've made us terrorists. You've made me complicit in terrorism. Do you have any idea?"

"Miss Marsh, I absolutely do."

"Okay, fine. You know what? I can see that. The manipulation. The exaggeration. The lies. And now violence! Nothing's beneath you, nothing's stopping you from getting what you want. Is that it? I didn't want this, Siobhan. I wanted to do it right."

Siobhan stepped to one side, out of the sun, and a bit closer to Elizabeth. "I never lied to you, Miss Marsh. Maybe I wasn't offering it up, but you didn't want to hear it anyway. You've barely wanted to hear anything."

"You were managing me." Elizabeth turned to face her. "You were just managing me and using me. I never would've possibly even *considered* going along with—"

"—exactly, dude." She clapped her hands and smiled.

"You never would've considered it. But you didn't have to. I took care of it. And please, we're using each other. Your book is everywhere now, you're everywhere now."

Elizabeth scoffed and spun on the spot, then began pacing around the hall. She wrung her hands together repeatedly, the leather of her gloves creaking, her hands sweating as the winter sun baked them.

"Miss Marsh. You want back into Parliament. You want to try to put things right. I respect that. And I want to help you." Siobhan threw her hands up, exasperated. "I *have* helped you! Have you seen our poll numbers today?"

"Not like this."

Siobhan groaned and shook her head. "Change is messy! Look around us! Look around this city, this country! The mess created by the last change is piled up around us. But we're waking people up to it! Your words inspire them, and I show them they can actually stand up and do something! We're focking brilliant at it, yeah?"

Elizabeth felt her purse vibrating, and looked up instinctively. The 12:30 to Cambridge was gliding into the platform. People started gathering their things, queuing near the doors. Siobhan looked over at the train, then at Elizabeth.

"Miss Marsh."

"I never meant for it to get to this point, Siobhan. I'm sorry. I'm sorry for everything. I never should've come back to London in the first place. It's just gotten so goddamned messy." She opened her purse and took the phone out. "I bloody tapped in with this, the train guard is going to be in a tizzy," she muttered to herself as she dropped it into Siobhan's waiting hand.

"The passes," Siobhan said curtly.

"Right. It's fine. They're gone."

"Gone?"

"I took care of them."

The tannoy rang out a chime, and a pleasing synthetic voice followed. "Please board now for your twelve-thirty British Rail service to Cambridge." Elizabeth looked over her shoulder as the few stragglers left on the platform climbed aboard the train.

"Christ. That's me, then."

"Miss Marsh?" Telltale beeps filled the air as the doors prepared to shut. The tannoy made one final plea to finish boarding.

"What is it, Siobhan?"

"Stay."

THIRTY-ONE

MORE LIKE WALL-SALL

Early March 2044.
Walsall, West Midlands, England.

"IT'S CLOSE, we can make that," Mike said as they both climbed back into the van. "We can't make it past that, but we can make that. And presumably there we can find a charge?"

"I don't know, Mike," Gemma said. "I didn't exactly want to push our luck. We're lucky they're just lazy fucks on a smoke break. When it ended they might've turned us in."

They sped quickly out of the car park and back onto the road, finding their way to the M54. There were so few cars on the road between cities these days. You really could just get on the road and go.

Anxiety ran high as they watched both the remaining charge tick down and the road behind them to see if anyone was giving chase. It seemed like a poor use of police resources to track them down, Mike had said, to which Gemma responded with quite a few unsavoury slogans relating to her feelings about the police.

They were nearing the final few miles when they saw the first sign: quite literally a sign, hanging across the motorway, calling out Walsall and Birmingham. Underneath Walsall, covering Birmingham, read some graffiti: "MORE LIKE WALL-SALL."

Gemma and Mike looked at each other, and Mike nodded. He followed the sign, the arrows leading them toward this place that was apparently a magnet for AWOL connies. "Is this a trap," Mike posited. "It seems odd."

"You have no idea how odd this is, Mike." Gemma stared out the window at the motorway.

Mike rolled the van to a stop as they approached what seemed to be a massive tailback. Except the cars all seemed to be off. Stopped, parked, just clogging up the road as if they'd been abandoned. Especially with the size of their van, they could make no further progress, so they, too climbed out of the van.

"This is all feeling a bit World War Z," Gemma said. "Maybe more I Am Legend. Or 28 Days Later."

"None of those are good things for this to feel like."

They worked their way up past the cars, Gemma's guitar slung over Mike's shoulder. As they approached they could finally see it: the cars were all essentially parked in front of a massive, makeshift wall blocking the motorway.

Gemma stared up at it. "This was definitely not here the last time I was in Walsall."

It was almost as impressive as it was clearly unofficial. The bottom made of concrete road barriers, with various sheets of metal and wood of differing heights forming the wall itself. Mike noticed some street signs mixed in which he found charming, but not enough to offset how incredibly distressing it was.

"I don't think whoever's in there wants anyone else in there."

"It just covers the road. They just don't want us driving in there, that's all."

"How are we going to get the car in to charge, then?"

Gemma had already climbed over the guardrails along the side of the road. "We'll ask. Come on." She turned back to face him, still standing alone in front of the wall. "Come on. It'll be fine." She smiled and extended her hand, and he stepped forward to take it.

It didn't take long to realise why they'd blocked the road, as the roads were well in use, all filled with tents, makeshift structures, camper vans, old festival kiosks and loads of outdoor furniture. Gemma spotted a group of people at a wooden picnic table not far from the other side of the wall, sat round playing cards.

"Hiya," she shouted with a quick wave, causing them all to look over—two men and two women, all looking rather middle aged, in black down jackets with differently-coloured beanies on.

"Hello," said one of the women. "You just arriving?"

Mike had tucked himself behind Gemma as they slowly approached the table. He tried to make himself as small as possible, if only he could disappear entirely.

"We are," Gemma replied. "We drove in from Wales. Our van is out of charge. On our way to London."

"Us too," she said with a smile.

Gemma gave a confused smirk and glanced around. It was unreal how many more tents there were now.

"If you don't mind me asking, what the fuck's going on

here? What is all this?"

"This is the Walsall Collective," said one of the men, in a way that betrayed how much he enjoyed being asked that question.

"Walsall Collective?" Mike had decided to step slightly out from Gemma's shadow.

"We live for ourselves here," continued the boastful man. "No conscription. We try to be self-sufficient."

"It's bloody Burning Man," Gemma said under her breath.

The other woman laughed and rolled her eyes. "Forgive Richard, he's so dramatic." She was older, with a deep tan, her skin seeming like it made her look even older than she was. A large-brimmed straw hat kept the mid-day sun from her eyes, which was finally breaking through the clouds. "I'm Claire."

"Gemma. That's Mike. He's shy." Mike flattened out his face and looked around awkwardly.

"Nice to meet you Gemma," Claire said, and put out her hand.

She walked them around the immediate area, what must've been hundreds of tents, many pushed straight up onto the front gardens of terraced houses much like Gemma had seen last time she was here. It was a gloriously chaotic mix of styles—some basic pop-up tents, some nicer, larger ones and even some full-on glamps. It certainly wasn't egalitarian. Which suited her just fine.

"Do people live in the houses too?" asked Mike.

"They do," Claire said. "And I suppose it was a bit first-come, first-serve on those. We've only been here a few months. We brought a tent with us because we'd decided to make the move, so we had a bit of time to prepare."

"You, uh, wanted this?" Gemma asked with more than a little derision. "Why on earth?"

"Richard had lost his job when the Jaguar plant closed. He was our provider. We were just down in Birmingham and we'd lived there our whole lives, both of us. And we knew we'd be sent to the coast, or out to Wales. So, we used the rest of our savings to buy our tent and supplies, and up we came."

"Wow."

"But," said Mike, "what do you do for food? Water?"

"We grow some, we trade for some, people bring some. We're not cut off love, the world's still out there, you know? It's not the apocalypse."

"Oh, right."

Gemma chuckled. "Having just come from two years of conscription, I fucking beg to differ."

"Conscription," Claire said with a glower. "Bloody dark times for this country. Your husband as well then?"

Gemma and Mike both laughed, though Mike sold it a bit less.

"He's married to his ex," Gemma said with a flippant hand wave. "Whatever that means. That's why he wants to go to London."

"London, never had much time for it. But please, join us for lunch. you can tell us all about it."

She led them down and through rows and rows of tents, and it made Gemma nostalgic for camping festivals in her 20s. Though from afar it looked chaotic, given time to look she could see a lot of care had gone into the layout. Each person keeping theirs a respectful distance from those around them, some people clearly asking for a bit more room than others, some people with a sort of shared outdoor "living room" under a canopy between two smaller "bedroom" tents.

Random tacky garden furniture was sprinkled liberally around — ceramic gnomes, plastic flamingoes, and surprisingly, even the occasional Union Jack bunting (Gemma truly wanted an explanation for *that*, but nobody was around when they walked by.) Finally, they came to a road with nothing in it, and on the other side was a wide open green space.

Gemma stared at it, feeling a passing familiarity. She turned to Claire. "Why are there no tents on the green?"

Claire smiled. "Isn't it lovely? They've only just recently finished clearing them. With the roads blocked we were able to free up the space."

The green looked beautifully wide-open, though with clear damage from where it had been under tents for so long. The Ash tree still stood proudly in the centre, along with the old Council barbecues and some free-standing exercise equipment. At one of the barbecues stood Richard, who gave a nod as he saw them.

Soon they were spreading a blanket, Mike having been instantly put to work helping with the grill by Richard. Forming patties from mince, fumbling about with a spatula, nearly killing them all trying to re-light it—he looked so wildly out of his element, which seemed to bring out some sort of fatherly instinct in turn as Richard insisted he learn to do this properly. Gemma would find something worth shaking her head at every time she looked over.

"So where does this all come from? The meat? The bread?"

"There's a livestock farm not far from here," Claire said with a matter-of-factness. "And we bake the bread!"

"Fuck," Gemma said under her breath.

"It's not an easy adjustment," Claire admitted. "Not

being able to just tap the Saino's app for whatever you need. But we're getting the hang of it."

"You could do that though," Mike said. "I mean, maybe not here. But down in Birmingham. Or anywhere, really."

"We don't have any money. We haven't, for some time. We try to help out wherever we can. Richard does handy work over at the farm. And they help us out in return."

"It's not just us." Richard's voice boomed, everything he said sounding like it was out of annoyance. "I've heard Liverpool's fightin' back, too."

"We're not fighting," Claire insisted. "It's just a calmer way of life."

They all settled cross-legged on the blanket as Mike brought over the food and Claire handed out small plates from a little picnic hamper. Mike seemed rather unsettled, not able to sit still.

"But, really, none of this is legal." Everyone looked at Mike and said nothing. He burned under their collective glare.

"Fuck, he's not wrong." Gemma decided to bail him out.

"No, you're right," Richard said with a grunt. "And there used to be a fence around all these bits of the city. They'd wall everyone in, signs up, warning everyone about the laws they were breaking. I'd seen it when I came up through here. They were desperate to keep things 'normal,' all the roads open, pretending everything was fine, even as entire streets were closed, parks were all full. Just fence it all off. But they gave up. For now, anyway."

"There's still fences up here and there," Claire said. "We're slowly taking it all down. Just need to block the roads in so nobody accidentally drives through. That's all."

The burgers were absolutely delicious, even as Gemma

tended to not eat beef. It made her realise how atrocious and shite the food was at the plant. She'd adjusted so readily, even as the portions had gotten smaller and smaller.

"About that," Mike said. "We do need to figure out how to charge our van. I have to carry on to London I'm afraid."

"Mmmphh." Gemma tried to get words out with a mouth full of burger. "Ex-wife." She gestured at Mike. "Famous."

"Oh?" Claire perked up as Mike faked a frown.

"She's not famous. She used to be an MP."

"Rebecca Marsh," Gemma finally was able to blurt out.

"Used to be, sure," Richard said with a nod. "And she is again, heaven forfend. Can't believe she won. Sympathy votes, I say, after the bombing."

"You have the news here?" Gemma asked.

"It's not the bloody dark ages, we have phones—"

"She's alive?! She's okay?!" Mike looked stunned. "That's..."

Gemma made a sympathetic little whimper and put her hand on his shoulder. "That's good, love. We like that." He nodded, looking down.

They helped Claire and Richard pack up their picnic, and Mike stood up to follow Gemma. Richard coughed and looked at Mike, who nodded and picked up the hamper, knowing what he must do. Their tent was a short walk from the green and was a simple little affair, a little red two-person dome tent like you'd pick up from Argos. Gemma figured that's exactly what they did. It was incredibly sweet.

She pictured them carefully picking it out. Scrolling up and down, looking at star ratings, little tiny pictures of tents from two or three angles. Seeing what Jenny, 45, Essex thought of hers. One final use of all the modern conveniences before they drove a half-hour north to start their new bohemian lifestyle, in a tent on a street in front of an abandoned JobCentre.

It's the kind of thing that used to inspire her to write songs. Maybe it would inspire her to write one again.

Richard and Claire retired for a post-lunch nap, leaving Gemma and Mike to their own devices. Gemma started ambling up the road, her guitar still on her back.

"So, off to London then are we?" She looked over at Mike.

"I feel I may be a bit of a third wheel if I go," he said with a hint of resignation. Gemma gave him a nice collegiate pat on the back.

"But I'm not sure I get it," he added. "This all seems so temporary and unsustainable. What if they run out of food? What if they get arrested? What is their plan?"

Gemma laughed, looking up at the sky. "I don't think they have one. I think they just wanted so badly to stop that they came here."

"To stop?"

"Yeah. To just...stop."

"You know," Mike said. "You're being awfully nice to me. You haven't sworn at me in at least an hour."

"Oi, fuck off. Absolute melt." She turned and smiled at him as they kept slowly walking. They reached the end of a cluster of tents and across the road was a makeshift football pitch, with a handful of people kicking a ball around.

With a gentle breeze cooling her face and the sound of friendly competition in the air, Gemma took a deep breath and closed her eyes. She didn't know how long this would last. But for now, she was free.

ACKNOWLEDGMENTS

Frances, for being endlessly supportive, and for suffering my near-constant WhatsApps while I worked on this.

My mother, for everything.

My developmental editor Melinda Crouchley, for the kind words and the brilliant advice expertly delivered.

And a special thanks to the staff of the various pubs and cafes I wrote this in around London and Edinburgh, for tolerating my being sat there hunched over a tiny laptop driving away all the customers.

Printed in Great Britain
by Amazon